Ilana Fox has worked for a variety of national newspapers and websites, including the *Daily Mail*, the *Sun*, ASOS.com and Shopcade. She lives in East Dulwich but can mostly be found causing trouble in Shoreditch.

Find out more about Ilana online at www.ilanafox.com or follow her on Twitter @Ilana.

Also by Ilana Fox

*Spotlight*
*The Making of Mia*
*All That Glitters*

# All That Glitters

## ILANA FOX

First published in Great Britain in 2012 by Orion Books,
an imprint of The Orion Publishing Group Ltd
Orion House, 5 Upper Saint Martin's Lane
London WC2H 9EA

An Hachette Livre UK Company

1 3 5 7 9 10 8 6 4 2

A CIP catalogue record for this book is
available from the British Library.

ISBN (Mass Market Paperback) 978 1 4091 2080 3
ISBN (Ebook) 978 1 4091 2286 9

Typeset at The Spartan Press Ltd,
Lymington, Hants

Printed in Great Britain by Clays Ltd, St Ives plc

The Orion Publishing Group's policy is to use papers that
are natural, renewable and recyclable products and made
from wood grown in sustainable forests. The logging and
manufacturing processes are expected to conform to the
environmental regulations of the country of origin.

www.orionbooks.co.uk

For my father, Peter,
with all my love.

# Acknowledgements

As ever, enormous love and thanks to Michael Sissons and Fiona Petheram at PFD — I am very grateful that you represent me and I hope my entertainment value makes up for my laziness. Also thank you to Jemma Pascoe.

At Orion Books, thank you ever so much to Kate Mills for being such a sensational editor. I don't say how grateful I am often enough. But I am. Also thank you to Lisa Milton, Gaby Young and Jemima Forrester.

My family is amazing; Harry and Nan, Peter and Magda, Naomi and Christian, Abi and Ben, Sue and Craig, George and Isabella, and Goldie, Marla and the rest of my family in the States. Thank you for being the best.

I literally couldn't have written this book as factually as I have (and I have! I did loads of research!) without the help of two former colleagues: Jim Munro at the *Sun* and Adam Cannon at the *Telegraph*. Thank you. I'm also grateful to the football players and girlfriends who shared their stories with me, and for those who put me in touch with them. You know who you are.

Additionally, lots of my newspaper mates helped with my *Sun*-pun headlines and assisted in naming characters when my brain got stuck. Thank you: Nadia Mendoza, Karen Brown, Marc Webber, Marcus Barnes, Luke Bishop, Kevin O'Conner, Seamus McCauley, and Ian Strachan. I promised I'd thank you at the front and I have.

And finally, my friends — it sounds ridiculous to say there are too many to name, but it's true. I'm very lucky. Thank you to Hannah Weimers and Andre Litwin for painstakingly reading every first draft I ever write, and Justin Myers, Jenna Good, Lindsey Kelk, Ronnie Henry and Natalie Wall for the hand-holding. And because they've entertained me so much during the last year (and because having cameos in Paul Carr books is old news), thanks to Julie Allen, Robert Loch, Jamie Klingler, Tom Boardman, Simon Prockter, and Milo Yiannopoulos. All roads to ruin begin with you.

'Fairy tales are more than true; not because they tell us that dragons exist, but because they tell us that dragons can be beaten'

G. K. CHESTERSON

## Chapter One

Ella Aldridge hadn't known happiness like it – she felt like she was going to burst. Finally, after years of kissing frogs, she'd met the most perfect man in the world, and she was about to have her happy ever after.

'You look beautiful,' Stacey remarked wistfully as she gazed at her step-sister in her wedding dress, and Ella caught her eye. She knew what she was thinking: when they'd been growing up Stacey had always been the pretty one, the one the boys asked out first. But in the last year or so, something had changed. Ella had blossomed – become popular and beautiful and fashionable and sexy – and no matter how much Stacey wanted to hang out with her step-sister, or how much Ella tried to include her, Stacey had got left behind.

Even in her wildest dreams, Ella never could have imagined this whirlwind transformation of her life was possible. Her life had flowered into a glamorous, busy, fun wonderland, and it was all because of Danny. Okay, she'd hit rock bottom when she'd found out Fin had cheated on her, but what nobody had expected – least of all Ella, as she used to be so cynical about happy endings – was that in taking herself off to Thailand, Ella would meet Danny

Riding on a beach, and he'd slowly mend her broken heart. In that one moment, everything changed . . . and it kept on changing, right up to when Danny got down on one knee and presented her with a pink diamond solitaire from De Beers. It didn't matter that Ella hadn't known Danny for that long. She knew he was the one; he was her Prince Charming.

'Do you remember when we went to that bridal shop last year, when we thought Jay was going to propose to you?' Ella asked Stacey as she lightly sprayed her wrists with a custom blend of rose, iris and orange blossom. Danny had insisted she create her own signature scent, and if things went to plan – which they would; why wouldn't they? – a less expensive, more synthetic version of it would appear up and down the high street the following year. It would still be classy, still be perfect, but it would be obtainable. People could buy a tiny slice of Ella's lucky magic.

'Yeah. We tried on those dresses that cost over a grand,' Stacey said as she pushed her flaming red hair behind her ears and struggled not to sound jealous. 'Who'd have thought that you'd be the one getting married first? And that you'd be doing it in couture Vivienne Westwood?'

Ella stood before Stacey in a dress so exquisite, so perfect, that she looked like a princess in a fairytale. The bodice was made from antique Chantilly lace speckled with hand-sewn pearls, and it glimmered over the swell of Ella's small breasts and hugged her lithe, perfect body like a second skin. The boning of the bodice made her waist appear tiny as it clung and dipped in all the right places, and layer upon layer of creamy satin and lace fluted from her hip. Ella couldn't help spinning around again and again, and when she did the crystals and semi-precious stones glittered as they cascaded down the chapel train.

Neither Ella nor Stacey could ever have imagined wearing a dress like this. Being Danny Riding's fiancée definitely had perks.

'And who'd have thought that I wouldn't be a bridesmaid at your wedding,' Stacey continued, now unable to keep the bitterness from her voice.

Ella swallowed hard. She'd known this was coming – God, she'd feel the same way if Stacey and Jay were getting married and they excluded her from the ceremony – but she'd hoped Stacey wouldn't make a big deal about it. She'd campaigned relentlessly for Stacey to be her bridesmaid, but in the end Danny's manager and agent was having none of it. What Aaron Kohle wanted – and he wanted the bridesmaids to be celebrities, C-list and up – Aaron Kohle got. It was why he was the most powerful football manager in the country . . . and partly why Danny was doing so well. She couldn't go against his wishes; she just couldn't. Not when he'd been so good to her.

Ella reached for her step-sister's hand.

'Look, you know that you'd be my first choice of bridesmaid if it were down to me,' Ella said softly, hoping that her eyes wouldn't fill with tears. She hated letting people down – especially Stacey. 'But it wasn't my decision to make. You *know* it wasn't.'

Her violet, mesmerising eyes pleaded with Stacey's, and Stacey knew she had two choices. She could tell Ella exactly what she thought of *that* – who agreed to a wedding where she couldn't choose her own bridesmaids? – or she could accept it for what it was. Ella was teetering on the brink of becoming one of the biggest footballers' wives going – up there with Victoria, Alex and Coleen – and Stacey knew she had to let her step-sister go.

'I know,' Stacey said eventually. She caught sight of herself in the mirror and had to look away. She'd got a multi-coloured dress from a department store that had looked amazing in the shop, but next to Ella she looked cheap and tired. It just wasn't fair. 'Look,' Stacey continued, 'are you sure you want to go through with this?' Her voice was light, but Ella heard steel behind it, and she felt her good mood start to deflate. 'This is going to change your life for ever, and, well, you don't seem like the right sort of person to marry Danny.'

Ella frowned. 'What do you mean?' she asked.

'Well, it's normally pretty girls who don't have much in the way of brain power who end up marrying footballers.'

Ella concentrated on her dress again. 'That's a stereotype, and you know it,' she said dismissively.

'Okay, but have you really thought this through? Ever since I've known you you've wanted to run your own business, to take the world by storm . . . and you've given it all up to be with this man.'

Ella shrugged. 'People change,' she said lightly, and she tried not to think about how her cupcake company had gone under. Everything had started so well – she'd hired the perfect kitchen premises, got her health and safety organised, hired an accountant and had ensured her cakes were divine – but something went wrong. Demand for her cakes wasn't there, the profit margins were too small, and after two years of working her ass off her business went under. Less than a month later Fin broke her heart. It hadn't been the best time of her life.

'Running Sweet Dreams took up all my time, and I'm still exhausted just thinking about it. Danny says I don't have to work if I don't want to, and at the moment I don't; I just want to take a break and be the best wife I can be.'

Stacey bit her lip. 'But you're not being true to your-self—'

Ella cut her off. 'Danny loves me for who I am, not for what I can achieve,' she said simply, and as she said it her eyes shone. 'And I love him. Okay, so Danny's a famous footballer. But that doesn't mean he wants some bimbo, or someone who pretends to be dumb when she's not. He wants *me* – he wants me to be his wife – and that's what I'm going to become.'

Ella's voice was calm but Stacey knew her well enough to know when she was getting angry. She knew it was inappropriate to bring up her concerns on a day like this, but she felt like she'd hardly seen Ella since she'd met Danny, and she couldn't *not* say how she felt. She just couldn't.

'I'm sure you've thought about this, and that you're making the right decision,' Stacey said eventually, and she forced a bright, fake smile that Ella returned with equal sincerity. 'I'm sure you're going to be happy, but don't forget me when you're rich and famous, okay? You're my best friend. And you always will be.'


'We're best friends now, you know,' Chastity smiled delightedly, as they waited outside the Baron's Hall for the signal that it was time for the ceremony to start. She was talking, chewing gum, and applying an orangey-pink lip-stick all at the same time, and Ella wondered how she did it. Even though she was standing still, energy radiated off her. She hoped Chastity wasn't on drugs.

'I'm really glad you could be one of my bridesmaids,' Ella said politely, as she took in Chastity's dress. The cocktail-length nu-georgette strapless dress was demure enough, but somehow Chastity managed to make it look, well, slutty. Her large breasts strained against the empire-line bodice, and the colour – a firecracker pinky-orange that everyone had insisted she choose because it was apparently 'the bridesmaid colour of next season' – clashed terribly with her deep tan. 'You look great,' she lied.

'Yeah, you know, this really isn't my colour, and normally I wouldn't be seen dead looking less than a hundred per cent beautiful, but I've been told it's my job not to steal the limelight from you, so for once – and just this once! – I'm going to take a backseat and let you be the star of the show,' she said seriously. 'Not that you need any help in that department. You look stunning.'

Ella beamed – she didn't think she'd ever get bored of being told she looked wonderful – but a tiny part of her wondered if she wanted Chastity Taylor (wife of Freddie Taylor, captain of Kingston United and defender for England) to think she looked good. Chastity was known for her hundreds of fashion faux pas, and regularly topped the 'worst dressed' lists in magazines. She told everyone it was because the journalists were jealous that she was married to Freddie. Ella wasn't so sure.

'I mean, *look* at you, you look like something out of a Disney cartoon,' Chastity continued, oblivious to the huge security guards pacing the corridor. Even though they'd hired the whole of St Immaculata's Castle deep in the Surrey hills, and there was no way paparazzi could get over the moat – let alone infiltrate the castle walls – Danny and Ella weren't taking any chances. There was no point trying to be modest. This was one of the most talked-about weddings in ages.

'You do!' piped in Krissy, fresh from the set of

*EastEnders*, where she played the part of a teenage single mother. 'You look gorgeous! I wish I had your skin. How do you get it all dewy and fresh looking?'

Ella couldn't work out what she should say. Should she admit to a facial peel, or should she just smile and act all coy? She didn't really know these girls. God, she still couldn't quite believe that Chastity Taylor and Krissy Hawkes were her bridesmaids. Did that mean that they really were friends, just like Chastity had said? Before she could really consider it, Krissy's perfect RADA voice – so different from the cockney she'd perfected for the TV – cut through her thoughts.

'Now, before we go in and make you Mrs Riding, I need to be told my lines.'

Ella looked at Krissy in confusion. 'Your lines? What do you mean?'

'Um, yes, my *lines*,' Krissy said slowly, as if Ella was stupid. Perhaps she was. Nobody could look that good and be clever, too. 'You know – what I need to say at the altar. My agent said this was a speaking part.'

Ella was about to smile, to catch Chastity's eye about how ridiculous Krissy was, when she froze. The excited chattering from inside the Baron's Hall began to quiet, and trumpets signalled the start of the ceremony. Here she was, standing with a soap star she'd never met before and a WAG she'd really only known for a couple of weeks, and she was about to play centre stage in what *Hello!* was calling the Wedding Of The Year. Could she do this, really? Everyone always assumed Danny would marry someone as famous as he was – especially as he'd dated so many actresses and pop stars. Instead, she was standing here feeling a bit like Cinderella. She was a wannabe who'd got lucky with a footballer on a beach, for God's sake, and she wasn't anyone special.

The heavy oak doors opened, the pianist began to play 'Clair de Lune' – which was one of Danny's favourite pieces of classical music, mainly as it had been in *Twilight* and he was addicted to vampire shows – and all eyes were on her. Ella knew this was it.

This was her destiny. She was not only about to become a footballer's wife, but she was going to live happily ever after.

Ella stretched luxuriously in the golden light of the sun. She was lying on a sun-lounger on the upper deck of the biggest yacht she'd ever seen, and as the sunshine beat down on her already bronzed body, she felt herself relax even more. Things couldn't be more perfect: she was married to a lovely man, she had a glass of freshly pressed raspberry juice, and she wanted for nothing. She was in heaven.

'You look like a model in that Gucci bikini.' Danny grinned, as he pulled himself out of the infinity pool and walked towards her. Ella shielded her eyes and watched him approach. He was so sexy. Danny's body was tanned and ripped, with every muscle clearly defined, and his piercing green eyes, reddish-brown hair and full lips made thousands of girls weak at the knees. He was gorgeous, so absolutely perfect in every way. And he was her husband. Wow!

Ella looked down at herself. Even though people kept telling her just how hot she was, she was only just starting to come to terms with it, because it hadn't always been that way. When Danny and Ella had first met, Ella fully admitted she looked like shit. She'd been desperately in love with Fin, so when she found out he'd been cheating on her the whole time they were together, she was devastated. She'd comfort eaten, got bloated, and stopped looking after herself. It was only when she met Danny that she started to gain a bit of self-respect again, and with it came healthy eating, working out, and taking care of herself. Now her long light brown hair had subtle strands of honey running through it, her body was curvy and firm, and her skin was sparkling. She didn't quite think she was as attractive as Danny was, but she knew they looked good together. The wedding photos that had appeared in *Hello!* the week before had proved it.

'I'm all right.' Ella smiled, as she looked down at her body. She looked so much better with a tan. 'It's a great bikini though, isn't it?'

'It certainly is,' came a voice, and both Ella and Danny turned. Aaron.

'All right, darling? How are my little lovebirds doing today?' Aaron Kohle said, as he pulled a sun-lounger over and sat between them. Ella felt her heart sink a tiny bit, but she told herself to stop acting so spoilt. They were on Aaron's yacht, after all, and it had been so good of him to let them use it for their honeymoon. And it wasn't like they saw him that much – only once every couple of days.

'We're great!' Ella said happily, glancing at Danny as if to check she could speak for both of them. 'We're having the best time.'

Aaron smiled, and while Ella was locking eyes with Danny, he let his gaze wander up and down Ella's body. He'd always taken a very keen interest in everything Danny did – both professionally and personally – and now he had Ella to look after too. Making sure she was in great shape was just part of it.

'I just wanted to let you both know that the wedding issue of *Hello!* had record circulation figures,' Aaron continued, as he ran his hands through his slightly greasy, greying hair. 'I know you don't want to think about work stuff on your honeymoon, but I thought you'd like to know. You're the hottest couple in the UK as of right now, and you're all anyone can talk about – the normal girl who married the Kingston United footballer is the story of the year. You're like Kate Middleton marrying Prince William. You, my girl, are *it*.'

Danny put his arm around his wife and gave her a little squeeze. 'That's brilliant,' he said, his green eyes shining. 'Absolutely brilliant. Aaron, you're amazing.'

'I aim to please,' Aaron said wryly. 'Now, the captain tells me we're on course to Nassau and we should be there in a couple of hours. I'm going to be hitting the casinos, knocking back some drinks and surrounding myself with hot birds. You're welcome to join me.'

Ella smiled. She wasn't keen on how Aaron controlled so much of Danny's life – or hers – but she couldn't help but like him. He was larger than life, knew everyone in football, and even though he was a little smarmy and sexist, he could still be good fun.

'We're having a low-key supper on the beach,' Ella said, almost shyly. Sometimes she felt a little intimidated by Aaron. He was so powerful. 'One of the stewards has organised it all for us. We've got a spot on the west of the island so we can watch the sunset.'

'It will be exactly two years since we met on the beach in Thailand, you see,' Danny added. 'We wanted to celebrate it by doing something special and private. Just us.'

Aaron rolled his eyes. 'Are you sure you wouldn't rather

join me in the casinos, Danny-boy? Be in it to win it? Unless . . .' His voice trailed off, and Ella could see his brain was whirring. 'I could probably get some paparazzi to record the special moment for you, you know. Sell it to the *Daily Mail* or *Daily World* or some rag. Make a bit of money and show everyone how in love you are?'

Danny shook his head. 'No, tonight's just for us,' he said, and Ella smiled. She really did have the best husband.

'Here's to us,' Danny said, raising his glass of champagne as they watched the sun set from Cable Beach. They were sitting on multi-coloured batik cushions behind a low-slung rosewood table, and tiny lanterns surrounded them. It was incredibly romantic.

'I know that a wedding day is meant to be the best day of your life, but the day I met you on Ko Phangan was mine,' Danny continued. 'There you were, looking absolutely miserable, and rather than being polite to me you were absolutely horrible. In that one moment I knew you were special.' He laughed. 'You were the first person in years who hadn't fawned all over me.'

'That's partly because I didn't recognise you,' Ella explained, 'but also because I was having a terrible time. I know you're one of the most famous men in the whole wide world,' she teased, 'but I don't really care about football, or football players. I just thought you were pretending to be concerned about my tears because you were hoping to hit on me. Little did I know how you were about to change my life.'

Ella and Danny stared at each other for a moment, and then they both smiled.

'Ella, I wasn't looking for a girlfriend or a wife, but after we spent that time together I knew that we were made for each other. We like the same things, have the same sense of humour, and I'd never had a female friend like you. I just love spending time with you.'

'I do too,' Ella said softly. And it was true, she did. Whenever she was with Danny they had so much fun. After they'd got bored of the beach they'd gone trekking in the Thai jungle, watched a ladyboy performance in Chiang Mai, and eaten candied insects on the Koh San Road in Bangkok. And after the trip – which Danny had insisted on paying for, as Ella had only left England with enough money to stay in a beach hut – they'd hung out in Ella's grotty London flat until Danny had to start training again. They watched movies, played games, and never left each other's side. They had everything in common, and they never got tired of each other. They were best friends.

'You're everything I want in a husband, and perhaps most of all,' Ella said seriously, 'I know you'd never hurt me, not like Fin did. I know where I am with you, and I'm grateful for that.'

Danny smiled, and he pulled Ella closer towards him. In his arms, Ella felt safe, happy, and secure.

'We're going to have a hell of a life, you know,' Danny whispered, and he gently stroked Ella's arms as goose bumps appeared. 'We're going to have the life that every-one dreams of. And we're going to make it so, so special. It's you and me all the way – and we're going to go further than anyone else ever has. We're going to be constantly, deliriously happy. It's going to be perfect.'

Ella sighed contentedly. This was her life now. This was what had been given to her when she'd been down on her luck and down on herself. Danny. He was everything. He was hers.

The sun started to reach the horizon, and both Danny and Ella watched as it hit the dark-blue ocean and then disappeared. It left ghostly whispers of pinks and reds across the sky.

*Chapter Two*

'So what do you reckon?' Danny asked Ella, with one of the trademark cheeky grins that he normally reserved for when he scored a goal with Kingston United. 'Think this – Castle House – can be our home sweet home?'

It was a bit of a non-question, as Aaron had already bought the mansion for them to stay in, but Ella didn't really mind not having a say in where they lived. Whatever sort of house they had, she knew she'd love it. It was the start of her brand new life with Danny, and regardless of what the house looked like she knew she could make it a home.

She opened the limo door, and with a final smile at Danny, looked towards Castle House. Only . . . it wasn't really a house. It was a mansion. And it was absolutely massive. The perfectly symmetrical mock-Georgian manor house gleamed in the sunshine, and Ella could practically smell how new it was. But even though it had clearly just been built, care had been taken to make it look like it was hundreds of years old.

Fragrant honeysuckle crept over the classical columns on either side of the heavy dark grey front door, and Ella's eyes followed the pale-pink flowers up to the fourth floor of the house and back down again. God, it was stunning. Perhaps not exactly to her taste – she'd always fantasised about living in a little thatched cottage somewhere – but there was no denying that this house, this *mansion*, was spectacular.

Ella quickly took a look at the long, circular driveway in front of the house – complete with an Italian-style fountain in the middle of it – and then let her eyes trail over to the perfectly manicured grass on either side. Well-tended beds of roses and azaleas bordered the sweeping lawns, and, *God*, was that a peacock? Ella focused her eyes on a movement behind some pinky-purple rhododendrons, and yes! There they were, two peacocks, displaying their iridescent blue-green plumage as they strutted around. Peacocks. She was about to live in a home that had peacocks in the driveway. It was absolutely mental. It was a palace in the Surrey countryside. She loved it.

'It's more than I ever thought we'd have,' Ella whispered, as she squeezed Danny's hand. She was utterly awestruck. Was this house really where they were going to live? Really?

'Me too,' Danny remarked, as he led her out of the limo that had picked them up at the airport. A valet – where had he come from? – was taking their Louis Vuitton cases up to Castle House, but Danny hadn't taken any notice of him. Ella, however, was trying not to gawp. Did they have *staff*?

'Apparently Aaron had to pay over the odds to get us this place,' Danny continued, amused at how mesmerised Ella was by their new home. 'This house is scandalously close to the Chelsea training ground, you see, so Chelsea players normally snap these mansions up. John Terry's place is just around the corner . . .'

But Ella was barely listening to him. She'd walked up the

path to the house, and had gently pushed the front door open.

'Hey! Wait!' Danny yelled, jogging over, and it snapped Ella out of her reverie. 'Don't go in there!'

Ella turned and stared at her husband.

'Don't you know it's bad luck not to let me carry you over the threshold?'

He effortlessly scooped Ella up in his arms, and carried her into their new home.

Castle House was divine. Everyone said so. Once they'd got settled they had Freddie and Chastity Taylor over for dinner, and Ella took great pride in showing Chastity around.

'I know it looks Georgian from the outside,' Ella explained to her new friend, as she started the tour of the house, 'but it's actually really modern. Come and take a look at this – it's amazing. I've never seen *anything* like it.'

Ella had led Chastity through the house to the back garden, and in contrast to the front of the house – which was built from honey-hued brick – the back was a wall of glass and industrial steel joists, overlooking a twinkling swimming pool that was lit by ever-changing rainbow colours. Ella pulled a tiny remote control from her pocket, and with the slightest touch of a button the glass wall instantly turned black. Nobody could see into the house, but whoever was inside could still see out. It was perfect for foiling any paparazzi who managed to get through their top-of-the-range security system.

'It's all right,' Chastity sniffed, and she glanced at her Chopard diamond cube watch. 'It's kind of standard, you know. Everyone has that.'

Ella's face dropped. 'What do you mean? Everyone has a pool, or . . . ?'

'I mean, everyone has that black-out-the-windows thing. It's been out for a couple of years. Don't tell me you've not seen it before.'

Ella bit her lip. Since she'd got back from her honeymoon she'd barely heard from any of her friends, and had only spoken to Stacey once. She knew she had to integrate herself with the partners of Danny's teammates – who better to understand her new life than people who were already living it? – but she wasn't sure how to do it. They seemed impenetrable. Normally she'd talk about her job, but since Danny had insisted she didn't need one, she didn't feel like she had much to talk about. And her first approach, to share the excitement she had about her new home, didn't seem to be working.

She tried again.

'And, guess what! Our swimming pool turns into a dance-floor! You touch this button here, on the remote control, and the pool drains and converts itself in ten minutes. It's amazing. I can't even begin to imagine what our summer parties are going to be like.'

Chastity eyed Ella and sighed. She looked bored. 'That's great babes, really cool. Shall we go and rejoin the boys again?'

Ella tried not to feel disappointed. Just because Chastity took luxury for granted, it didn't mean she ever would.

'Do you know what Danny's got you for a wedding present yet?' Chastity asked conversationally, as Ella led the way back to the dining room. 'In our circle, wives normally get gifts a month after the ceremony, depending on how the day went, what sort of press coverage it got, etc. Freddie got me my darling Gus, who I keep in our stables. But I expect Danny won't have got you a horse. You don't really have anywhere to keep it and your grounds aren't *quite* big enough.'

'I don't think we're doing wedding presents,' Ella began, but Chastity cut her off.

'Of course you're doing wedding presents. Oh darling, I know you're *very* new to this still, but you must remember that we have our own way of doing things, and players for Kingston United have their own ideas about stuff, too. I can guarantee that whatever you get it will be big, and Aaron Kohle will have been involved in the gift-advising stage, too.'

Ella was silent for a moment. 'Am I meant to get Danny a gift? Because I haven't . . . I didn't really know I had to.'

Chastity snorted with laugher. 'Don't be silly. You don't need to get Danny anything at all. You're the *wife*. It's not like you have a job, and spending all your time shopping and going to the gym doesn't exactly pay, does it?'

They walked back into the dining room, where Danny and Freddie were talking about another player's latest sponsorship deal.

'Danny,' Chastity said, rolling her eyes. 'Why haven't you given Ella her wedding present yet? She was asking me all about it in the garden.'

'Um, well, I wasn't exactly asking about it,' Ella began. 'I didn't know we were doing wedding presents, you see, and . . .' She trailed off. She felt desperately awkward. She didn't need anything at all. She had Danny, she was living in this amazing house, and she was blessed. She hated the thought of anyone thinking she 'deserved' a present when she was so lucky already.

Danny chuckled. 'I was planning on giving it to her tonight, just after you both left, but I can see you're desperate to know what it is, Chas.'

'It's *Chastity*, and I'm not desperate at all. Just looking out for my new friend here.' Chastity hated anyone shortening her name, and hated the insinuation that she was being nosey. Whatever Danny gave her it wouldn't be as good as her beautiful thoroughbred colt.

'Well, it's outside. Ella, would you like your wedding present now?'

Ella blushed, and took Danny's outstretched hand. He led her to the front door, and put a blindfold on her. She could feel Chastity and Freddie standing behind them, and then the sweet smell of the evening air as Danny opened the door.

'Easy now, just a few steps; that's right.' Danny led Ella down the gravel path, and she laughed nervously. Where were they going? But as quickly as she wondered how far they were going to walk, they stopped. And Danny whisked off the blindfold.

Ella blinked. She couldn't quite believe it. Was this for her?

'What do you think?' Danny asked easily, as though he was asking how Ella's supper was. 'Do you like it?'

'Oh my God, oh my God, oh my God!' Ella screamed, and she jumped up and down in excitement.

In front of them was a gleaming, bright-red retro Ferrari, with a large white bow around it. It was beautiful.

'Thank you for being my wife,' Danny said, as Ella jumped into his arms and smothered him in kisses.

'I can't believe you bought this for me! I can't believe it!'

'It's a recreation of a 1961 convertible Ferrari, no expense spared,' Danny explained, as Ella began walking around it in exhilaration. It had gorgeous brown leather bucket seats, a silver interior, and was absolutely perfect.

'Wow,' Freddie said, as he stared at the car. 'Those are some wheels.'

'Yes,' Chastity agreed, trying to keep the jealousy out of her voice. She only had a Mercedes, and she couldn't quite believe that little Ella had a better car than she did. She'd have to upgrade, and fast.

'My wife deserves a carriage good enough for a princess,' Danny smiled, and Ella's eyes shone.

'Danny, I don't know what to say,' Ella began, but Danny put a finger to her lips.

'You don't need to say anything at all,' he said. 'You deserve this, and so much more. And I hope this car makes you as happy as you make me.'

'I'm glad you're home and not out shopping,' Aaron said insultingly, his eyes fixed to Ella's breasts as she poured him a cup of tea. 'One of my meetings fell through at the last minute – stupid fools, I won't agree to see them again – and as I was in the area it seemed like the perfect time to drop in.'

Ella smiled as brightly as she could. Okay, so she *had* been thinking about going to the shops to kill some time, but just because she didn't have a job it didn't mean she was some vacuous bimbo obsessed with clothes. Yes, she liked clothes, but she thought she had a bit more depth than that.

'I'm pleased to see you,' Ella said charmingly, hoping her murderous thoughts weren't reflected in her expression. 'It's been ages since I saw you last.'

'Quite,' Aaron said, and he stretched out on the sofa as if

he owned the place. In a way, Ella thought, he did. 'I hope you're settling in okay in this house? And I heard you loved your wedding present.'

'Oh God, that was such a surprise!' Ella exclaimed, and this time her smile was genuine. 'It was so generous of Danny. I drove it over to my step-sister's house, and her eyes nearly popped out of her head. She couldn't believe it!' Which was true, she supposed. As Stacey stood next to her beat-up VW Polo and checked out Ella's Ferrari she had struggled, hard, not to appear sick with jealousy.

Aaron smiled. 'Danny wanted to get you a car, and I suggested something a little different. So many footballers' wives drive around in Mercedes, Porsches or four by fours, and I think it's important that you stand out from the crowd, don't you? I thought it was important to get you a classy little number.'

Ella beamed. She wasn't quite sure what to say. She knew her car made a statement – she just wasn't sure *what* statement Aaron thought it conveyed. Could a car that ostentatious be classy? Really?

'Which brings me to what I want to talk to you about. When Danny first introduced you to me, I thought you were perfect for my plans, and since you've been back from your honeymoon, I can see that I was right.'

'Your plans?' Ella asked with interest. 'How am I involved in them?' Aaron was Danny's agent – or manager, as he liked to call himself – and while he mainly brokered marketing and sponsorship deals, Ella knew that Aaron took more of an interest in Danny than other agents did with their clients. He controlled his image – his brand.

'Quite simply, darling, I'm going to make Danny Riding

a superstar – bigger than Rooney, Gerrard and even Beckham – and you're going to help me do it.'

Ella took a deep breath. She knew Aaron was ambitious, but it was the first time she'd seen him in action. When he talked about Danny, his whole demeanour changed. His brown eyes narrowed, his facial expressions became more intense, and even his body language became more overt. He became the man that intimidated the fuck out of Ella – but she was determined not to let him see it.

'Aaron, when I first met you – after Danny and I got engaged – you talked a bit about the obvious *benefits* of Danny having a wife. I married Danny because I love him, and I don't mind doing the media things, like having our wedding in magazines and doing interviews sometimes, because I know it goes with the territory . . . but I don't know what else I can do to make Danny even more famous.'

Aaron smirked knowingly, sat back on the sofa, and let his eyes slowly wander over the girl in front of him. Ella looked sensationally sexy. She was wearing a gaudy, floral fitted Dolce and Gabbana dress with cap sleeves, and it fitted her so closely that it looked as though it had been made just for her.

'I don't want you to be just another footballer's wife.' Aaron remarked matter-of-factly, and Ella took a sip of her tea to steady herself. What was he saying, exactly?

'I want you to be *the* footballer's wife. I want you to be better than all the others, and I want you to be something different. Something amazing.'

Ella bit her lip uncertainly. 'What do you mean?' she asked.

'Well, look at what you're wearing, to start with. Where did you get that dress?'

'Chastity and I went shopping in town last week,' Ella began, and Aaron jumped to his feet.

'Exactly! You went shopping with Chastity and bought this dress because it's what footballers' wives are supposed to wear. Everyone's the same. They want to look as sexy as possible to try to keep their man, but as a result they go overboard and end up looking trashy.'

'I don't understand.'

'Think about it. You're married to a footballer who has girls throwing themselves at him all the time, so when you're a wife you make more of an effort to keep your husband interested. You wear revealing designer clothes and get manicures and pedicures and funny face treatments that freeze your face. You get your eyebrows over-plucked, your eyelashes tinted, and you always wear full make-up, even when you go to bed, because you can't stand the thought of your husband seeing the "unpolished" you,' Aaron exclaimed. God, Ella thought. He was intense.

'You go to the gym five times a week and lose your curves in an effort to stay thin, you get your pussy waxed to nothing, and you get boob jobs, your bum bleached, and shiny white veneers.' Aaron's eyes flashed angrily, and Ella tried not to flinch at his language. Truly, he could be disgusting.

'But Aaron, I hardly do any of those things, and I'm not about to start,' Ella said, hoping she sounded stronger than she felt. Nobody dared talk back to Aaron Kohle, ever. He was a former boxer and he looked like it. 'I know that Danny won't leave me or stray – we both know he wouldn't – so why *would* I do any of those things?'

'Exactly!' Aaron practically yelled. 'Why would you? So

why are you dressing like Chastity? Why are you already conforming to type?'

Ella looked down at her outfit. Okay, so the dress was slightly revealing, and her Louboutins were quite high for an afternoon of doing practically nothing, but so what? She wanted to look nice for her husband, and prove she was a good enough wife for him. She wasn't going to extremes.

'I didn't think I was,' Ella said eventually. 'I just thought it was a nice dress.'

'Ella, think about it. If you're married to a footballer, if you're a WAG, people don't take you seriously. You're seen as a shopaholic who doesn't have a proper career and whiles away her days spending ridiculous amounts of money and getting beauty treatments. People think WAGs are a joke, and to a point, they're right. Why should women who are married to footballers be famous? What have they ever done to get that sort of attention?'

Ella frowned. She didn't know what to say. She'd never thought badly of WAGs – in fact, when she was going out with Fin she used to love reading about them in trashy magazines – but she also knew he had a point. WAGs *were* thought of quite badly. He was right.

'Sweetheart, I don't want people to *ever* think badly of you – not when you and Danny make such a good couple, and, more importantly, when Danny is teetering on the edge of being one of the all-time greats.'

'So what are you suggesting?'

'I want to make you the anti-WAG,' Aaron said triumphantly, and Ella could have laughed out loud. What was he on about?

'I want you to lose the bimbo image you're starting to unconsciously adopt. You're not stupid – I heard you ran your own little cake business a while ago – and I want to make you classy, respected, and someone who has every right to be famous . . . and not just famous because they're married to a footballer. I'm thinking Princess Diana meets Carla Bruni-Sarkozy meets Michelle Obama. I want to make you a role model.'

Ella's eyes widened. 'You sound like a fairy godmother,' she said, and as Aaron sat down she relaxed. She could handle the calm version of Aaron, coarse and crude as he was, but she felt a little freaked out by the manic side of him. 'But why would you do this for me? I don't understand.'

Aaron shot her a big, wolfish grin – one that showed off his perfect teeth. 'I'm doing this for my career, and for Danny's. Like I said earlier, I want Danny to be bigger than David Beckham, and everything needs to be in place to do that. He has the dream house, and a gorgeous wife, but darling – and excuse me for saying this – you're lacking ever so slightly. You're a beautiful girl with a great body, but that's all people know about you. I want to make you so dazzling, so incredible, that it will reflect well on Danny. It's my job to make him the best, and that means I need to make you the best, too.'

Ella was sitting by the pool when Danny came home, and he was buoyed up with energy from a training practice. Kingston United were playing Arsenal that weekend, and Danny wanted to get a hat-trick against them. He loved being a footballer, and genuinely believed that if he worked hard enough, he could achieve anything. It was one of the things Ella loved about him. He was so determined.

'Hi honey, I'm home,' he called, in a camp impression of a 1950s husband. 'Did you miss me?'

Ella grinned. She always did. And now that her real friends – the ones she'd grown up with, like Stacey – were melting away, he was the person closest to her. 'Of course I did. But guess what: Aaron came to see me today. Did you know?'

Danny looked slightly uncomfortable, but only for a moment. 'He did mention it, yes. What do you think of his plans?'

Ella shrugged. 'I'm not really sure. He was going on about making me into a role model, but he didn't say exactly how he was going to do it. Do you have any ideas about what he's thinking of?'

Danny shook his head. 'No, not really. But you don't mind, do you?' he asked gently. 'I'm so used to Aaron controlling my image – right down to what suits I wear – that I forget what he can be like sometimes. It's natural that he's taking an interest in you, too. I'm Danny Riding, striker for Kingston United, but together we can be The Ridings. We could be a brand.'

'I know,' Ella said. 'That's what Aaron said. But can we be, really? I mean, you're an amazing footballer, but I'm nothing special. Maybe you should be married to an Oscar-wining actress or something.'

Danny sighed, and took Ella's hands in his. 'Ella, you *are* special. You agreed to be my wife, for one thing – and I know that can't have been easy for you.'

Ella laughed. 'Are you kidding me? You have thousands of girls after you who'd kill to be in my position.'

'Well, yes.' Danny raised an eyebrow. 'But the point is, I wanted to marry you, and being married to a footballer isn't exactly plain-sailing. My schedule isn't like other people's, and I appreciate that you've given up on your career dreams so that you're at home more.'

'But it was my choice to do that, and I'm happy with it,' Ella said firmly. 'Working all hours and trying to get a business off the ground really affected my relationship with Fin, and I'm choosing not to do that to us, to you. Getting ahead used to be so important to me, but . . . I don't know. I just don't feel that drive any more. I want to support you. I don't care that you're a footballer, or that your agent wants to turn me into some modern-day saint. I just want us to keep being happy, and if doing things like "being a brand" makes our relationship stronger, then I'll do it.'

Danny raised Ella's hands to his lips and kissed them. 'You're an angel, you know. I don't know what I did to deserve you.'

'What, apart from helping me get my self-respect back after being dumped, taking me on trips in an exotic country, and then making me the happiest girl in the world? No, I can't possibly think what you've done,' she teased.

Danny smiled. 'So you're cool with Aaron's plans, really?'

Ella nodded. 'I'm your wife, and if it helps with your career, you know I'll do it. We're in this together, you and I, and don't you forget it.'

'Ella, I never will.'

*Chapter Three*

Ella stood in the doorway of her huge, mirrored, walk-in wardrobe, and stared in astonishment. True to his word, Aaron had started his 'Ella Riding Makeover' project, and the first thing he'd done was get rid of all her clothes. Gone were her cute summer dresses from Topshop, her perfectly fitting jeans from Wrangler, and comfortable jogging bottoms and hoodies from Hollister. And in their place were . . . well, Ella wasn't really sure. All she could see were boxes and boxes of new clothes, from stores like Pringle, Hermès, Nicole Farhi and Michael Kors.

'Aren't you going to open them?' a voice said from behind her, and Ella turned to see Danny leaning against the wall in the hall. He'd been working out in their gym, had his top off, and was glistening with sweat. He looked so hot; Ella knew that a million girls would have killed then and there to take her place.

'Aaron made sure that everything is in your size. All you need to do is work out which pieces you want, and someone will come to collect the rest. You can keep whatever you like, and send back what you don't.'

Ella spun around again and stared at all the boxes. She wasn't sure where to begin, as there were so many. She tentatively opened up one from Lanvin, not knowing what to expect, but when a flash of ivory silk peeped through the tissue paper her heart raced. She pulled out a beautifully demure shift dress, with a high neck and a sweet bow around the waist, and when Ella turned it around, she saw the back had draped panels that would swing seductively when she walked. It was sophisticated, elegant, but also very sexy. If this was Aaron's idea of classy, she was excited. Very excited.

She opened the next one. Fendi: a draped, v-front dress in a juicy papaya crepe. And then there was a package from Marc Jacobs containing an opulent antique rose and gold embroidered jacquard dress that would fall just to the knee. Next was a canary silk cocktail dress from Alberta Ferretti. Cream silk-blend wide-leg trousers from Chloé. A belted navy origami dress by Roland Mouret. Black crepe, slim-leg trousers by Vanessa Bruno. And a stunning, floor-length Zac Posen gown in a deep indigo. The clothes were so beautiful, so classic and so stylish that Ella couldn't quite believe they were for her. They were so *grown up*.

'Or, you can keep everything and not send back a single piece,' Danny remarked in amusement, as he caught sight of Ella's expression. She looked like she was in heaven.

'It's too much,' she whispered. 'It's just all too much.'

Just when she thought her life was utterly perfect, it got better and better and better.


'The next stage of your anti-WAG makeover is to sort your hair out,' Aaron said to Ella distractedly as he played with his Blackberry. 'You look great, darling, but we really need to sort out your barnet.'

Ella fingered a strand of her light-brown hair. She'd got it highlighted at Michaeljohn just before the wedding, and she thought it looked pretty perfect. What was wrong with it?

'WAGs all have that hair-extension, Barbie-doll thing going on again,' Aaron explained, as if he were reading Ella's mind. 'Apart from Victoria Beckham. This week. She's probably the only one to have something a bit more avant-garde, but then, she's really old so she can get away with it.'

Ella opened her mouth to speak, but nothing came out.

'We're positioning you as a self-assured, self-confident young lady, so we need to chop your hair off,' Aaron said, and he looked up from his hundreds of emails. He stared at Ella as if challenging her.

'So I don't look like the other wives?' Ella guessed, and Aaron nodded.

'Partly. But have you ever thought about *why* all those girls have such long, porn-star hair? It's to keep their man. They think their husbands won't cheat if they look as perfect as possible, and they think having long hair's sexy.'

Ella bit her lip. She was confused. 'But long hair is sexy, isn't it?'

Aaron let out a little snort of laughter. 'On a normal girl it is. On a WAG it just looks desperate. Don't worry, we're not going to get all your hair chopped off – I want it just off the shoulders. I want you to look fresh. Modern. Smart. And not at all desperate to keep your man. You'll see what I mean.'

After Ella had her haircut, she did. Her gorgeous long hair was now cut to just above her shoulders, in a sexy, messy bob. Her heart-shaped face looked slimmer, her violet eyes sparkled, and she looked cool and chic. She loved it . . . and when she popped into Aaron's office just around the corner from the exclusive salon she'd visited in Mayfair, Aaron did, too.

'Wow,' he said, as he looked her up and down approvingly. She was wearing an olive-green Stella McCartney chiffon dress, Yves Saint Laurent braided sandals, and was carrying a suede and crystal Marni clutch. With her choppy new haircut, she looked like someone special – like someone who led the fashion pack, and didn't care what anyone thought of her. She appeared effortlessly sexy, unfussy, and if you saw her on the street you'd think she was a magazine editor or someone important in her own right. Not a footballer's wife. 'You look sensational.'

Ella blushed under her new fringe. She knew she looked good, but she couldn't quite come to terms with her appearance. Where was the girl who'd sat at Heathrow airport when Fin had broken her heart? Back then she'd worn jogging bottoms and a ratty old vest top, and she'd not cared about split ends, her spare tyre, or what she looked like. How had that girl transformed into the woman she was now? She couldn't quite believe how Aaron had worked his magic on her.

'Thank you so much,' Ella said simply, as her eyes shone with happiness. Words couldn't really describe just how grateful she was to Aaron for everything he'd done for her. She knew, deep down, that he was only doing his job, and that he'd be this generous with whoever Danny Riding had chosen to settle down with, but it didn't make any difference to her. She was so blissfully happy with Danny and her new life, and a lot of that was due to Aaron's relentless organisation and care.

Aaron smiled, and ignored a ringing phone. 'It's my pleasure, sweetheart,' he said softly. 'With your new look we're going to make a lot more money. You and Danny can now really be a brand. You're fresh, you're different, and you definitely stand out from all the other couples. Forget the Beckhams and the Rooneys. The Ridings have got it all.'

Ella laughed in delight. This was ridiculous, so ridiculous. No way would people think she and Danny were like the Beckhams. It was just impossible!

'And now the next thing for you to do is get a "career" going.' Aaron leant back on his desk and waited for Ella's reaction. He wasn't disappointed.

'But . . . Danny's always said being his wife was my job,' Ella said. 'We made the decision together that I wouldn't work – that I wouldn't pursue a career because it would mean that Danny and I hardly saw each other.'

'I'm not talking about a real career,' Aaron said simply. 'I'm talking about magazine work.'

'You mean you want me to pose for *Loaded*?' Ella felt sick.

Aaron rolled his eyes. 'Ella, haven't you been listening to a word I've said? No, I don't want you to get your tits out for the lad mags. The last thing I want is for you to come across as the type of girl that needs that sort of validation. I was thinking more along the lines of you being a high-end fashion model who can talk about the clothes she wears. Didn't you once tell Danny that you love clothes?'

'I did. I do,' Ella said slowly. 'But not in an obsessive, brain-dead way. And I haven't got any experience, and I'm not built like a model. I'm too short, have curves, and I don't have the greatest bone structure.'

'Oh, anyone can look good on camera so long as they're wearing the right make-up,' Aaron said dismissively.

32

'Besides, that's not the point. Your favourite Uncle Aaron has landed you a job at *Cerise* magazine. And unlike other magazine shoots, you get to put the outfits together and say why they're fashionable.'

'You're kidding,' Ella said slowly. She couldn't quite believe it. She was going to act as a stylist, model and fashion journalist all in one?

'When have I ever joked about your career as Mrs Riding?' Aaron said wryly. 'I'm all about making you and Danny superstars, aren't I?

Ella had to admit he had a point.

The moment Ella walked into *Cerise* magazine, she wondered if this was all going to be a terrible mistake. She'd been greeted warmly by Lucy, the editor, and had been shown a desk she could sit at while she looked over some clothes samples, but she felt really uncomfortable. Out of place. Everywhere she looked were well-dressed girls who were obviously super-clever and ambitious. In comparison Ella felt a bit dumb. Okay, so she wasn't stupid – she *had* run her own business for a while, and still tried to keep up to date with current affairs (so long as they weren't too boring) – but she was adamant that being a supportive wife to Danny was her new job. Her new career. She knew it sounded old-fashioned, but her relationship with Danny was important to her, and she'd made the decision to support him. It wasn't her being enslaved to him. It was about her making a choice, and she hoped other women – especially the ones in this office – could respect that.

'When Aaron Kohle set this up he told us you weren't into doing the usual footballer's wife thing of looking slutty . . . which is good, obviously, as we're not that sort of magazine,' Lucy began conversationally as she took a sip of her skinny latte. 'I take it you've read *Cerise*?'

Ella nodded. She had, but *Cerise* wasn't her first choice of reading matter – she preferred trashy magazines where she could secretly scour photos of celebrities' bodies for imperfections. And even though Ella knew most of the gossip in some magazines was embellished almost to the point of untruthfulness, she didn't care. Tacky magazines like *Heat* and *Now* were pure escapism, and didn't require much thought.

Magazines like *Cerise*, however, did.

It was high fashion, high intelligence, and one of those magazines that Ella never really bothered to look at because it didn't seem to have much of a sense of humour. Not that she'd dare tell anyone at the magazine that.

Lucy smiled briskly. 'Brilliant. Anyway, Tatiana's our fashion editor, and she'll be leading this column. She's out on a shoot right now, but she should be back in an hour or so.' Lucy looked at her vintage Cartier tank watch and frowned slightly.

'So what we want you to do is pick out six outfits from the rail – although we're only going to publish four – and when Tatiana gets here you'll get a car down to the studio. You need to make sure they're related to a something based in current affairs – and you can discuss that with Tatty later. There's a make-up and hair team all ready to go, and we'll shoot you in the outfits.'

'Okay, that sounds good,' Ella said in a small voice. Lucy was one of the best editors in the country, and even though she was being perfectly friendly, Ella was still intimidated. Lucy was a career woman who'd worked hard for everything she'd earned. In comparison Ella had just married Danny.

'Right, well, I'll see you later then. Have fun,' Lucy chirruped, and then Ella was left alone and in front of a rail filled with next season's clothes. Her hands trailed over a Burberry Prorsum tuxedo jacket, a silk-mousseline blouse from Fendi, a grey Stella McCartney cashmere sweater, white Helmut Lang skinny jeans, and a Matthew Williamson beaded chiffon gown. Ella sighed in pleasure. She may not be pursuing her dream of starting her own business any more, but there was definitely a buzz that only working provided, and it was coming back to her now, in droves.

She could do this.


'That's right, now tilt your head down slightly, a bit to your left . . . that's perfect. Hold it.'

Ella stood still in front of the muslin backdrop, and hoped that the hot lights wouldn't smudge her make-up. She'd had photographs taken before, of course, but nothing like this. She was being treated like a professional model, and it was just so much fun. There were two people there to do her make-up, one hairdresser, and the photographer himself had three assistants, who rushed around taking light measurements and calling out numbers from a computer. It was glamorous, exciting, and exactly how she imagined a photographer's studio to be like, right down to the tiny canapés and bottles of Evian laid out on a table to the side.

'Now swing your hip a little and look directly at me. Come on Ella, look like you want to fuck me but in an ice-cold model way,' the photographer said in a husky voice.

Ella pouted and then burst out laughing, and the photographer snapped away. She was wearing a ripped Wildfox tank vest, tight leather biker trousers from Alexander McQueen, super-high Giuseppe Zanotti ruched boots, and a Vivienne Westwood silver ring that had been sprayed with Swarovski crystals. Her hair had been tousled and backcombed, and lashings of smoky eyeliner made her violet eyes pop.

It was a sexy, aggressive rock-chick look, and something she'd never dare wear as Danny Riding's wife.

She loved it.

'Just a couple more frames to go,' the photographer announced, and Ella moved in time with the background music, letting the pink lights overhead shine through her glossy hair. She was having the time of her life.

'And that, my darling, is a wrap.'

Tatiana – the fashion editor for *Cerise* – put down her cup of coffee and walked from the back of the studio over to Ella. She was clapping.

'That was brilliant.' Tatiana smiled. 'You're a natural, and from the shots I saw on the computer, the camera loves you. And you really nailed that last outfit; you should wear pieces like that more often, and think about doing more modelling.'

Ella looked down at her ripped top and laughed. 'I'm not sure I could really get away with wearing this on the football terraces . . . although that dove Donna Karan dress would be perfect for a dinner party. I loved how the wisps of silk and chiffon softened the structure of it. It was beautiful.'

Tatiana nodded. She'd thought the same thing when Ella had been modelling it. The light grey of the dress had made her look sophisticated and classy. She really was a world away from the other footballers' wives.

'And before I collapse with exhaustion, I just wanted to say thank you for letting me do this. It's been so much fun to choose all these outfits and shoot them. It's been like a long day of dressing up.'

'A *really* long day,' Tatiana agreed. 'I know it's pressing ten p.m., but I'd really like to get some quotes from you on each of the outfits . . . you know, the inspiration behind them, where you'd wear them, and why you think they're revelant.'

'No problem!' Ella said happily. And it really wasn't. Because even though Ella was shattered, she was having the time of her life and she didn't want it to end. She loved fashion and had always been addicted to the high street, but since marrying Danny she'd really been able to indulge herself in it, and was starting to get to know and understand the designer pieces that inspired hundreds of high street copies.

'You know, I really liked how you put the Donna Karan with the Louboutin ankle boots,' Tatiana mused, as she concentrated on the photos. 'You must have picked up some tips from your stylist.'

'Oh, I don't have a stylist,' Ella said. 'I never have done.'

Tatiana looked up at Ella thoughtfully. 'But you always look so well put together when you get snapped by the paparazzi.'

Ella smiled and shrugged. 'I just like clothes, I suppose. For years I couldn't afford anything designer, and dressed quite scruffily. But I love fashion. Not the way-out, wearing-clashing-stuff kind of fashion, but I adore beautifully made clothes.'

'Well, if you ever decide to make a career for yourself, you could definitely work as a stylist,' Tatiana said. 'Or even a personal shopper.'

'Really?' Ella said in delight. Okay, so she'd always

dreamed of making it as an entrepreneur, but it was cool that a fashion editor thought she was good enough to make a career for herself in clothes.

Tatiana laughed. 'Well, if you weren't married to Danny Riding, you could. I can't imagine getting a job would ever be good for your reputation, or his. People would think Danny wasn't earning enough.'

Ella concentrated hard on ensuring her smile didn't fade away. Tatiana was right, of course. Who needed a job, or a business to call one's own, when you were married to one of the top footballers in the country? Working in fashion was just something Ella had to do for the Riding 'brand', and even though she'd enjoyed it, she knew she'd never be able make a career for herself out of fashion, or anything else. She'd promised Danny that she'd be there for him, that she'd play a supporting role in his career.

She tried not to wonder if in making that decision she'd also made a mistake.

## Chapter Four

'It was so brilliant!' Ella exclaimed happily, as she recounted the day before over dinner with her husband. 'I got to put together a couple of designer outfits, and then I spent the whole day modelling them. Tatiana, the fashion editor for the magazine, said if I wanted to, I could probably work as a stylist. She thinks I have a really good eye for it.'

Danny forked a piece of fresh pasta into his mouth and smiled. 'Babes, that's fantastic. I'm so pleased you loved it. Aaron wasn't sure if you were going to get on with it. He suggested you'd be more comfortable on a less highbrow magazine, but I knew you'd enjoy it. The feedback Aaron had was really good, too, and he's already had preliminary talks with the magazine about getting you to do it more often – when we need a bit of a PR boost.'

'That would be amazing.' Ella smiled. 'Putting together outfits and modelling just felt so natural. Deep down I know it's not something I could make a career out of, and because of that it felt so different to running Sweet Dreams – I didn't have to worry about profit margins, or food measurements, or distribution points . . . all I had to do was put some clothes together and model them. It didn't even feel like work because it was so much fun. Does that make sense?'

Danny nodded. 'It's how I feel when I'm on the pitch. When we're doing training sessions it can be bloody hard graft, but it's worth it when we're playing and thousands of people are chanting our names. When we win a game it's indescribable. It's that adrenaline – that addictive buzz of performing and being the best you can be – that keeps us hooked. I can't imagine doing anything else.'

Ella and Danny beamed at each other across the table. They didn't just understand each other, they *got* each other, and that was what marriage was all about.

'God, if I got to hang out at *Cerise* a bit more I'd be over the moon,' Ella continued. 'I know I don't want to start my own company again, but I want to use my brain a bit more. I want to *do* something.'

Danny took a sip of his orange juice and paused for a moment. 'I'm glad you feel that way, but remember, you're doing this stuff at *Cerise* for a reason – because it's "strategic positioning" of our brand, or something . . . not because we're pushing you to have a career on the side. And there's something else Aaron wants you to do too. It's kind of a big deal.'

Ella put her fork down as she swallowed the last of her supper. 'What is it?'

'Well . . . The *Sunday Times* wants to do a profile piece on you. Really high end. It's a great opportunity for you to talk about yourself and show how you're of a different mould to the other wives.'

'Wow,' Ella marvelled. All thoughts of working at *Cerise* were forgotten. 'That's amazing. I thought you were going to tell me I had to do something awful.'

'Would we ever ask you to do something awful?' Danny teased. 'The thing about this is, if you can win over the journalist and get them to write a really good profile of you, *Cerise* will probably want you even more. Or other magazines.'

Ella bit her lip. 'Really? How does that work if I'm not going to have a job?'

'Aaron said that if a quality newspaper does a piece on you, that it makes you look like quality. He says all the other WAGs just want bikini shots in the *Daily Mail* and the *Sun*, so this will make you stand out. Plus, the *Sunday Times* has a fashion magazine or something—'

'*Style?*' interrupted Ella.

'Yes, that's the one. Well, Aaron says if *Cerise* isn't interested in having you do stuff every so often, *Style* probably will be. So by agreeing to be in the newspaper it looks like you're talking to lots of publications. Apparently it will make *Cerise* – or any other magazine – quicker to say yes every time Aaron wants you to do stuff for them.'

Ella nodded thoughtfully. She could see how that would work.

'Aaron's PR offensive seems to be working with you, but now that he's looking after both of us, he's really busy. He's thinking about taking someone on to help out. What do you think? Do you think you could be comfortable with someone else handling you, so long as Aaron oversees whoever does it?'

'Of course I would,' Ella said, and it was true. Even though Aaron was a bully, she respected him, and they both had the same goal: to make sure Danny's career was as successful as it could be.

'Great, I'll tell Aaron you're cool with it, and he'll start looking for someone to hire. It will probably be a man; is that okay with you?'

Ella leant back in her chair. 'Sounds good to me,' she said honestly. If she could get some work at *Cerise* – even if it was on Aaron's terms and timings – she was going to be even busier, and having someone around to keep her organised and help would be brilliant.

God, she thought. She really was lucky. Now all she had to do was win over the journalist from the paper, and take it from there.

'Wow, this is some place,' Jim remarked as he looked around the Ridings' drawing room. The Palladian-style high ceilings showed off understated, decorative cornicing, and the room's perfect symmetry – along with the pale colour scheme of ivory and Wedgwood blue – made it feel effortlessly chic. Oriental rugs had been laid carefully on the oak floor, and pieces by Chippendale and Hepplewhite faced the marble fireplace. It was a ridiculously formal room, and Ella felt a little uncomfortable in it.

'Can I get you some tea? Some coffee?' Ella asked the journalist nervously, as Jim pulled his MP3 recorder and a notebook from his satchel. He was a big, burly man and he looked a little out of place on the delicate wooden chair he was sitting on.

'I'm fine,' he assured Ella. He'd interviewed all sorts of people – mainly footballers, sporting heroes, or movie stars – but he'd never come across anyone like Ella Riding before. He normally got the measure of people pretty quickly, but he couldn't quite work her out. She wasn't the sort of WAG he usually encountered. 'Tell me a bit about yourself, just to get you relaxed.'

Ella bit her lip thoughtfully. Where to begin? She nervously rattled off some bullet points about her childhood (born in Essex, grew up in Hertfordshire), and then let herself trail off. Jim saw she wasn't quite sure what to say and jumped in with a question.

'Rumour has it Danny's in line to be the new England captain next year – what's it like being married to him right now, while he's on the cusp of turning into a Three Lions legend?'

Ella smiled. 'It's a dream come true,' she said honestly. 'Danny's a great player, and I'm honoured to be his wife, and to stand by his side during his football journey. I'm lucky to be part of it.' So far, so bland: perfect understated-wife-of-a-football-player.

'And what about you? Will you use Danny's success as a platform for your own work?' Jim asked, looking at his notebook as though the question didn't really interest him. But Ella knew it did. This was the part that would prove to everyone she was more than a footballer's wife. It would show everyone she was *someone*.

'I'm really fortunate that doors open for me because I'm married to Danny,' Ella began smoothly. 'But I'm not sure you could say it's a platform for me. People who idolise Danny on the pitch aren't interested in what I do, especially not my fashion work.'

'You work in fashion?' Jim asked, as he raised an eyebrow. Was Ella going to be the new Victoria Beckham and launch a fashion label?

'I've just done some work with *Cerise* magazine. I do pieces where I create high-end fashion outfits with lifestyle and current affairs in mind. It's fashion with a twist,' Ella said, remembering that last sentence from the press release Aaron had insisted the magazine put out.

'I'm not the sort of girl who likes to sit around looking

pretty,' Ella continued, her wide violet eyes shining as she thought about *Cerise*. 'I like fashion, I like current affairs, and I like the fact that I'll be able to merge the two, and to bring about a more serious side to looking good.'

Jim stared at Ella for a moment. He'd interviewed WAGs before – vacuous types who doted on their husbands and didn't have a single original thought to their name – but this one was different. Jim had agreed to do the interview as a favour to Aaron Kohle as they went back years, but he could see now this wasn't going to be a puff piece. This could, potentially, be the newspaper profile that announced her to the world. Ella was a mixture of startling good looks and a decent brain. In a WAG, it was a dynamite combination.

'Tell me more,' Jim said with interest, and he leant forward as Ella began to speak. 'What gets you going, and what sort of current affairs will you feature in the magazine?' Ella smelt good – of orange blossom and roses – and she looked amazing. If he wasn't a married man, and she wasn't Danny Riding's wife, he would have been interested. Very interested.

Ella silently blessed the fact she'd watched *Newsnight* earlier in the week and began talking about how the recession had affected the British fashion industry. Her face was so serious, and she spoke with such feeling that Jim couldn't help but be surprised. Okay, so she wasn't exactly an economist, or the most intelligent woman he'd ever met, but she had something. A spark.

'So where do you see you and Danny in five years' time?' Jim asked, turning the conversation back to her. Whatever he'd thought of Ella Riding previously, he was practically in love with her now.

'Hopefully still being blissfully happy with our life to-gether,' Ella answered with a smile. It was all she wanted. She wanted Danny and herself to keep being exactly how they were, for ever and ever.

Jim reviewed his notes and thought about what Ella had been talking about, and how well she'd come across. England was desperate for a new sweetheart, and Jim knew that this profile piece would turn her from a moderately well-known WAG into a person in her own right. She was intelligent, self-assured, and the perfect role model for girls of all ages. Yes, she was married to a rich footballer and lived a life of luxury, but she was making the most of this opportunity to better herself, not to gain column inches or to show off. He'd never known anything like it.

'I think that's a wrap,' Jim said, as he turned his Dictaphone off and grinned at Ella. He felt honoured to be chosen as the first to interview her, and was certain that as soon as his piece was published, Ella would be a star. Move over Victoria, there was a new girl in town.

Ella sat back in her red leather seat and smiled contentedly. She'd just finished watching the first *Sex and the City* movie, and for the first time since she'd married Danny, she felt she identified with someone else. Her life was turning out to be just as impressive as Carrie Bradshaw's: she had the perfect man, the perfect new job, and a wardrobe that could rival Carrie's. Yes. Life was good.

She was just missing three equally glamorous friends to share it with.

Ella briefly thought about giving Stacey a ring to see what she was up to, but decided against it. What would she talk about if Stacey asked about her day? Saying she'd been interviewed for a profile piece in the *Sunday Times*, and that she'd watched a film in her home-cinema wouldn't really do her any favours. Ella thought hard. It was a Tuesday – Stacey would have gone to work in the day, and probably would have ordered a Chinese takeaway for her and Jay in the evening. In comparison she'd eaten scallops for a starter, and then guinea fowl with apple gravy for a main. No, she wouldn't phone Stacey. Ella still felt too awkward sharing her life with her, and Stacey still got jealous. God, it was hard.

Ella wandered from room to room, taking in the beauty of each. It was such a lovely house, and she knew she was very lucky. She just wished she had some friends that she could hang out with. The house screamed out for laughter and fun. Okay, so she had Danny, and that was great, but when he was busy with training or matches she had nobody at all. Stacey had been left behind in Ella's old life, and Aaron was against Ella spending too much time with Chastity because he thought she was a bad influence on her. So who did that leave her with?

Nobody, Ella thought. Nobody at all.

Ella sighed, and picked up the phone to give Chastity a ring. Okay, so Aaron might not like it, but what Aaron didn't know wouldn't hurt him . . . and Ella was sure that underneath her bitchy exterior, Chastity could become a true friend. She was sure of it.

'I don't know what to do,' Chastity sobbed, as she reached for another tissue. Her nose was red and her mascara was running down her face and dripping onto her pushed-up cleavage, but there was something in Chastity's eyes that made Ella wonder if she was enjoying the drama of it all.

'Freddie said he wouldn't cheat on me again, ever, but he got caught getting a blow job in a nightclub after the Liverpool match, and I can't trust him. I just can't.'

Ella sat on the sofa next to her and felt uncomfortable. When she'd phoned her earlier she hadn't expected Chastity to answer the phone in tears, and she had no idea how to help her. What could you say in a situation like this? Chastity would never leave Freddie – she loved her lifestyle too much – so Ella couldn't wheel out the 'all men are bastards' line, but at the same time, Ella wasn't sure what *would* comfort Chastity. Everyone in the industry knew Freddie played around. It was an open secret.

'Last time he did it he told me it was a mistake, and that he was so drunk he could barely remember doing it. He told me he loved me, and that he'd never do anything to hurt me again, but he has! He's gone and done it again.'

'How did you find out?' Ella asked softly. When Fin had been cheating on her, she'd had her suspicions: those nights when he came in at six in the morning saying he'd been drinking with the boys all night, the way he couldn't remember his lies, and how he got over-the-top angry and said she was mental, crazy, paranoid and insecure if she commented on it. But she never had any hard evidence to prove he'd been doing the dirty, so she chose to believe him when he said his flirtations with other girls were innocent. She'd been wrong, though. And by the time she found out just how wrong she'd been about Fin, it had been too late. She'd got burnt, and badly.

'His agent sat us down and told us the stupid little whore had gone to the *Sun*. We had to pay off the paper to get the photos from them.'

'The photos?'

Chastity laughed bitterly. 'They were in a corner of the club and the tart got a friend to take photos with her camera. She only did it for the money, of course, and the fame. I bet she thought this would make her a star . . . or get her a job on Babestation at the very least.'

'God, Chastity, I don't know what to say.'

Chastity wiped her eyes. Her face was blank and she looked a bit defeated and drawn.

'There's nothing you can say,' Chastity said softly. 'Freddie plays away, but I love him too much to leave him. I just have to put up with it.'

Ella bit her lip. 'You don't *have* to, you know. You could leave him, start again, meet someone who—'

'Oh don't be stupid,' Chastity interrupted. 'I can't leave him. I signed a pre-nup; I'll hardly get anything unless Freddie chooses to give me money, and I'll be for ever known as the girl who was once married to Freddie Taylor. I don't want to end up as a has-been.'

'But you don't want to end up sour and resentful, either,' Ella said boldly. 'Listen to me; I know what I'm talking about – I lived that life, I had a boyfriend who cheated on me, and when I confronted him about it he got, well, violent. It was horrible.'

Chastity rolled her eyes. 'Listen, honey, you're very sweet and all that, but this isn't the same kind of thing. We're talking about Freddie Taylor, you know. He's an English football legend. So what if your little boyfriend cheated on you and bashed you about? Of course you'd leave him. Why would you stay with him? There are hundreds of boys out there who are all in the same league, and they're all pretty interchangeable. But Freddie Taylor?

He's the top prize. And he knows that if he cheats he can get away with it.'

'You're better than that though,' Ella said softly, and Chastity sank back into the sofa.

'Am I? Am I really? If I was that good Freddie wouldn't give into temptation. Why would he? He wouldn't go abroad for matches and fuck foreign prostitutes afterwards. He wouldn't smile when girls elbow me out of the way to give him their phone number. And he wouldn't cheat on me. He'd *love* me. He'd *respect* me.'

'So why do you stay with him?' Ella wondered, and Chastity paused.

'Because despite everything I love him,' she replied solemnly as she hugged her knees to her chest. 'And I know he doesn't *mean* to cheat on me. There's temptation everywhere he goes, and sometimes he's weak and gives into it. He can't help himself.'

Ella shook her head. 'Can't he?' she asked, and Chastity's face turned hard.

'None of them can,' she spat. 'They're all the same. Don't tell me you think Danny's faithful to you. Because he's not, you know. He's definitely not. Since he married you he's had hundreds of girls throwing themselves at him, and he loves it. Freddie told me.'

Ella didn't quite know what to say.

'Danny doesn't cheat on me,' Ella said to Chastity as gently as she could.

Chastity laughed. 'Oh yeah? You sure about that?'

Ella stared at the girl opposite her. Despite the thousands she spent on her appearance – the Botox, the designer clothes, and the daily trips to the gym – she was desperately unhappy and insecure. Ella felt sorry for her.

'I'm one hundred per cent sure,' Ella said smoothly. 'Danny loves me, and he wouldn't ever hurt me.'

Chastity shook her head. 'You have a lot to learn about being married to a footballer,' she remarked knowingly, and she reached for her glass of wine. 'So much to learn.'

'I'm home!' Ella called out as she pushed open the front door, but Castle House was silent. Ella frowned and checked her phone again. Yes, Danny had definitely sent her a text saying he and Yves – Danny's best friend and French centre forward for Kingston United – were coming home to hang out after going for dinner, and as Ella thought of Yves she smiled. Danny was handsome and athletic, but Yves was on a whole different level – he was drop-dead gorgeous. Currently starring in a hair-gel advert, and with a legion of teenage girls plastering their bedroom walls with posters of his naked torso, Yves looked more like a boy-band member than a footballer. He was making a lot of money off the pitch because of it.

Ella walked through the house, picked up a nearly-empty bottle of wine that the boys had left on the kitchen counter, and then saw the swimming pool lights were on through the window. She grinned – going for a swim with Danny and Yves would be the perfect pick-me-up from having to handle Chastity's tears, and as she walked through the back door and ambled through the beautiful rose garden, she felt herself relax. Yet again, Ella thought how wonderful her life was. Aaron may be concerned that she'd get spoilt, and that she'd take it for granted, but Ella knew she never would. She was living the fairytale dream of millions of girls, and she knew it wasn't something to take lightly. She was grateful for everything she had. And she'd never, ever, think about throwing it away.

Ella turned the corner, and glanced at her swimming pool, lit up in ever-changing colours of the rainbow. It was gorgeous. And there, right in the middle of the pool, were Danny and Yves, chatting amicably in low voices. Ella began to walk towards them, but the men were so focused on their conversation that they didn't notice her coming, didn't hear her approach.

Just as she was about to speak to them, Ella froze. Her mouth hung slightly open in preparation for whatever she was about to say, and her eyes widened.

In one smooth movement Danny had grabbed Yves and kissed him on the mouth – passionately, desperately and fervently. Their chests touched, and as Danny let out a low moan, Yves ran his hands through Danny's reddish-brown hair before moving them down his back. Their bodies pressed closer together, and Danny clung to Yves in utter infatuation.

Ella stood still for a moment, and then silently crept away.

*Chapter Five*

When Ella first met Danny in Thailand, she hated him on sight.

'I've been watching you and you seem so incredibly fed up,' he said to Ella as he sat down, uninvited, in the sand next to her. Ella tried not to scowl. Yes, this stranger was really hot, but she wasn't in the mood to be hit on. She hadn't come to Thailand to find a rebound man – a one-night stand, a boyfriend, or anything in between – and she just wanted to watch the sea in peace.

'You're on a beautiful beach in paradise,' he continued, 'and you have the moodiest face I've ever seen.'

'Well, if your boyfriend had been cheating on you the whole time you were together, and at the same time your business went under, you'd be moody too,' Ella snapped, and she stood up. Tiny grains of sand fell from her bare legs, and she brushed the seat of her shorts to get rid of the rest. They were baggy with damp from being in the sea, but she didn't care. She wasn't out to impress this guy or anyone else.

'Sounds tough,' he said sympathetically, and Ella glared at him. How patronising!

'Yeah, it *is* tough,' Ella retorted. 'And if you'll excuse me,

I'm going to take my moody face somewhere else. Somewhere I can be alone.'

He sighed. 'Look, I'm sorry if I offended you. I just thought you looked a bit down and could do with some cheering up.'

Ella's laugh was hollow. 'I can guess how you were planning to cheer me up. Well, I'm not interested. Not in you, and not in anyone else. I'm off men for good.'

He reached his hand up to touch Ella's wrist. 'I'm not coming on to you,' he said softly, and as Ella watched him she could tell he meant it. 'Why not let me buy you a beer? We are on holiday, after all.'

After several bottles of Chang at a beach-side bar, Ella started to feel more relaxed. She didn't know why she'd thought going away by herself had been a good idea. On paper it had seemed perfect – get out of the country, get over Fin, recharge her batteries after being sucked dry by the downfall of Sweet Dreams – but Ella was lonely, and something had prevented her from saying more than two words to the other backpackers at her bungalow resort. This man was different, though.

'Fin – my ex – made me feel like I was going crazy,' Ella said eventually. The sun was burning the top of her head, but the beer had loosened her, soothed her. Up until then she'd not had a drink in case the alcohol brought on more tears, but that day it seemed okay. She felt okay. 'He convinced me he wasn't cheating on me, but it turned out he had been the whole time we were together.'

'Did you suspect?' The man took another swig of his beer, and Ella was struck by how dazzlingly good-looking he was.

'No. Yes. I don't know. I was suspicious, but Fin told me I was mad, that it was all in my head. But it wasn't.' Ella was so overcome with sadness for a moment that she hadn't been able to speak. How could her boyfriend – the man who said he loved her, and cared for her – have been so cruel? 'He made me feel really small . . . and when he got really angry, or felt like he wasn't controlling me properly with his words, he lashed out with his hands,' she whispered.

The man clenched his fist so hard that his knuckles turned white, but instead of saying anything, he gestured at a waiter for two more bottles of beer, and then placed his hand on top of hers. In any other situation, Ella would have thought that he was coming onto her, was encouraging a sob story so he could 'comfort' her, but the act felt so platonic, and he appeared so, well, not into her like that, that it felt okay.

'He sounds like a complete shit,' he said, and Ella nodded slowly.

'He was,' she agreed, and after a beat they both smiled at each other.

'I'm Danny,' the man said, and he combed his fingers through his reddish-brown hair.

'Ella,' she replied, and as she took another sip of her beer she felt happier than she had in a long time. 'It's really good to meet you.'

After that, Ella and Danny quickly became inseparable. They were caught in their own little bubble of boozy nights out, long hot days sunbathing on the beach, and evenings of wandering around trying different foods from street sellers. Danny was on holiday by himself too, and after a couple of days they decided he should move his stuff out of the plush resort hotel he'd been staying in, and into Ella's bungalow. He'd been drunkenly crashing there night after night anyway, and it made perfect sense.

'Are you sure you wouldn't prefer to move into my hotel?' Danny asked Ella, as she helped him lug his suitcase across the sandy paths to her bungalow. Ella shook her head. 'As much as I like hot showers and air-con, there's something a bit more authentic about this little bungalow on the beach, even if it is set up purely for tourists.'

'Yeah, who likes hot showers when you have all this?' Danny grinned, as he looked at the spartan room with a critical eye. They'd left it in an utter mess that morning, and the bright sunlight that streamed through the window didn't help.

Ella rolled her eyes. 'I *could* have moved into your comfortable, middle-class, middle-aged hotel, but this is way more fun,' she said. 'And besides, we're closer to the bars.'

'And to other people,' Danny remarked, as he watched two boys slowly approach their front door. He'd seen the boys checking them out as he and Ella had wheeled his cases through the resort, and he knew it was only a matter of time before they came over. 'Listen, Ella, I've not been entirely straight with you . . .' he began, but before he could finish his sentence, the bungalow door was pushed open.

'You're Danny Riding, aren't you?' one of the boys announced loudly. He was a typical Brit abroad – blistering red skin, a pot belly under a Kingston United shirt, and shorts down to his calves.

Ella had looked at the boys, and back at Danny, but she chose not to say anything.

'I knew it was you!' the other boy exclaimed, and he

nudged his friend. 'How about that? Danny Riding in the same resort as us. Brilliant goal against Spurs last season, mate,' he continued, oblivious to the confusion on Ella's face.

'Yeah, you really showed them who's boss,' the other boy said.

Danny smiled. 'Thanks lads,' he said, and Ella glanced at him. His whole demeanour had changed – he'd puffed up his chest and looked cocky. Arrogant. 'Shame we didn't do the same to Chelsea,' he continued. 'We'd have topped the table if we had.'

'You'll do it next season,' one of the boys said, and he couldn't hide his delight at meeting Danny Riding, super-striker for Kingston United. 'Don't s'pose we could get you to sign my shirt, could we mate?'

Danny grinned. 'It would be a pleasure.'

'So you're a famous football player?' Ella asked in astonishment as soon as the boys had left. 'Why didn't you tell me?'

Danny had looked uncomfortable. 'It's not easy being me, you know,' he said eventually. 'People don't want to be friends with me; they want to be associated with me, to be seen with me. And they don't care about who I am, not really. They can't see past the fact that I'm a footballer, that I'm famous.'

'But when I asked you what you did, you said you were a PE teacher!' Ella exclaimed.

Danny shot her a wry grin. 'I'm sorry,' he said, but he couldn't help laughing. 'I wasn't sure if you knew who I was, and I wanted to check . . .'

Ella had crossed her arms over her chest. 'But you lied to me!'

'For a good reason,' Danny had said calmly. 'If I told you I played for Kingston United you'd have been so dazzled or turned off that you wouldn't have opened up to me, and we wouldn't have had so much fun these last couple of days.'

'That's rubbish,' Ella protested hotly, but the more she thought about it, the more she realised Danny was right.

'I was going to tell you when I thought we were proper friends,' Danny had said, and without saying a word, Ella walked over to him, and gave him a massive hug.

'We are proper friends,' Ella confirmed. 'And even though you're a famous footballer – who I *have* heard of, by the way – I won't hold it against you. You can't help which job you fall into, after all.'

'That girl's totally checking you out,' Ella murmured into Danny's ear as they danced under the moonlight on the beach. Fires had been lit, music was being played loud, and Ella didn't think she'd ever had so much fun. The setting was definitely part of it – who wouldn't have fun at an impromptu beach party with travellers from all over the world? – but it was Danny who was making the evening so special. Danny who made her laugh, who made her feel good about herself. Danny, who made her feel like she could not only be completely herself, but the very best she could be.

Danny shrugged. 'I'm not interested,' he said, and Ella rolled her eyes.

'You haven't even looked at her.'

Danny gave the girl a cursory glance and turned back to Ella. 'Nope, still not interested,' he said, but before Ella could say anything, the girl wandered over. She was stunning. She had long chestnut hair, her knockout figure was clad in tiny denim shorts and a sequinned bikini top, and she had the face of a model.

'I'm Becca,' the girl announced, as she began to dance next to Danny. He smiled at her politely, but didn't say anything. Ella frowned at him.

'This is Danny, and I'm Ella,' she said, to make up for Danny's silence, and the girl laughed.

'I know who *he* is,' Becca said. 'Everyone knows Danny Riding.' She pouted suggestively, and Ella swallowed her laughter. As beautiful as the girl was, she couldn't be more obvious.

'You're a great dancer,' Becca said to Danny as she tried again. 'You must have amazing co-ordination from being a footballer player.'

Danny smiled briefly. 'Thanks,' he said as politely as he could, but Ella could see he felt uncomfortable. Becca, however, couldn't.

'Do you fancy getting a drink with me?' Becca asked, and Danny stopped dancing.

'I'm sorry, but I'm fine as I am,' he said in a stilted tone, and Becca put her hand to her mouth.

'Oh God, I'm mortified,' she exclaimed insincerely. 'This must be your girlfriend, right?'

Danny nodded. 'That's right,' he confirmed, and he took Ella's sweaty hand in his. 'Ella's my girlfriend.'

Becca smiled at her so insincerely that Ella raised her eyebrows. 'If you feel like changing your mind,' Becca whispered loudly to Danny, 'I'll be here all night.'

'I don't think I will,' Danny said, and he pulled Ella away from the party, and onto a more private part of the beach.

'You didn't have to do that,' Ella said, as they sat down

to watch the party from a distance. 'If you wanted to hook up with her, I'd have been fine by myself.'

Danny shook his head. 'When I said I wasn't interested, I meant it. Did you mind pretending to be my girlfriend?' he asked.

Ella laughed. 'Of course not,' she said. 'I'm happy to pretend to be your girlfriend any time you like if it makes your life easier.'

Danny stared at the sand for a while, and Ella wondered what was wrong.

'I've had lots of fake girlfriends in my time, but after a while they all got sick of pretending.'

'Fake girlfriends?' Ella asked. She couldn't be more confused. 'Why do you need fake girlfriends? To stop girls like that coming onto you?'

Danny nodded slowly.

'Well, I can see why,' Ella continued, in a teasing tone. 'It must be hell on earth to be good-looking and famous and to have hundreds of sexy girls after you.'

'It is,' Danny agreed, but Ella could still see there was something on his mind.

'Danny, what is it?' she asked cautiously, but before Danny could say anything, everything suddenly made sense. 'You're gay, aren't you?' she asked softly, and Danny moved his head so slightly that Ella only barely saw his nod.

'My manager, Aaron, says I should date girls because it's good for my image. It's impossible to be a gay footballer in the Premier League because, despite the FA's best efforts, there's still a hell of a lot of homophobia in the sport. But the girls I date can't find out I'm gay in case they sell their story, and I hate leading them on. I'm not that sort of person.'

Ella exhaled. An idea was beginning to form in her head, but she didn't know if it was ridiculous or genius.

'I could be your girlfriend—' she began, but Danny cut her off.

'No way,' he said. 'I wouldn't let you do that.'

Ella felt stung. 'Why not? What's wrong with me?'

Danny shook his head. 'There's nothing wrong with you. Aaron would *love* you because you're smart, pretty and normal, but I couldn't ask you to do that for me. You wouldn't be able to have a relationship with anyone else if you were with me.'

'You're not asking me to do anything, and besides, I don't want a proper relationship ever again. Seriously. It hurts too much. If you were my boyfriend you'd never hurt me. How could you? It's not like you could cheat on me.'

'But what if you met someone?' Danny asked, and Ella laughed.

'What if I didn't? Danny Riding, you're the most amazing man I've ever met, and to be honest I've never bonded with anyone the way I have with you. I know we've only known each other a short time but I feel like you're my soul mate. A platonic soul mate.'

Danny reached over and took Ella's hand.

'Being my girlfriend won't be easy,' Danny said slowly. 'You'll have to abide by Aaron's hundreds of rules, the press may want to know things about you, and you'll be in the spotlight.'

Ella thought about this for a moment. 'How did the other girls deal with it?' she asked, and Danny laughed.

'That was the bit they liked the most,' he said. 'They wanted to be famous by association, and because I felt like I was using them, I didn't really mind. They thought I was distant and unaffectionate, but in return they got to have their photos in the papers, and one of them even went on a reality TV show.'

'I'm not that kind of girl,' Ella began, but Danny interrupted her.

'Darling, if you were, you'd have insisted we move into my plush hotel rather than staying in your slummy beach bungalow,' he grinned.

'So will you let me help you?' Ella asked, and Danny nodded.

'Let's see where it takes us,' he said. 'I love hanging out with you and I feel like I can tell you anything, so it's practically a relationship anyway. Just one without sex.'

'Okay then, deal,' Ella said, and she shook Danny's hand up and down.

'You're amazing, you know that?' Danny said, and Ella laughed.

'Damn right I am,' she replied, and as Danny kissed her hand, she wondered if – however unconventional it was – she had found a happy ending.

'Do I look all right?' Ella whispered to Danny, as they entered the ballroom of The Dorchester. She was wearing a Versace gown in white silk-crepe, and with the barely there nude inserts and low back, she felt slightly naked. Her Givenchy beige leather sandals were ridiculously high, and her hands sweated against her Valentino eggshell tulle clutch. She looked sensational, but she didn't normally dress so revealingly. Aaron had insisted she look knockout, and she hated to let him – or Danny – down.

'Babes, you look sensational,' Danny murmured into her ear, as he led Ella through the room. All eyes were on them, and Ella felt a little wobbly. This was her first official event at Danny's side – they were there to help launch a new range of football boots by Putto, the manufacturer that sponsored Danny – and she felt out of her depth. She plastered on a smile, and quickly looked at her husband. Despite his broad grin and relaxed air, she knew he felt even more uncomfortable than she did. For some reason Danny just hadn't wanted to come tonight, and Aaron had practically had to force him into a tux and out of the house. Ella didn't know why.

'It's so great that you could both be here!' chirruped Bailey Brinton, the blonde American PR girl for Putto, the Italian makers of the best football boots in the world. 'We've got loads of photo sessions lined up, and a couple of journalists want to interview you too. Hope that's okay!' she said, and Ella knew it wasn't a question. Danny was paid to rhapsodise about just how great Putto was, and Ella was there to help. It was their job for the evening.

'It's good to be here,' Danny said stiffly, and Ella squeezed his hand. She didn't quite know what had got into him, and hadn't ever seen him moody like this. He was normally so cool, and never let anything faze him. Luckily Bailey didn't notice.

'We've got loads of press here, ranging from the nationals to the football magazines, and we've even got a bloggers' room. We have loads of editors from football and celebrity sites trying on the collection and taking photos of it. Tonight's going to have awesome coverage everywhere.'

Danny's grin froze, and then slid slowly into a frown. This time Bailey caught his expression, and she paused uncertainly.

'It's going to be brilliant,' Ella interjected as smoothly as possible, hoping to distract Bailey from the look on her husband's face. 'We're just so excited about the new collection. Danny's been telling me all about how the boots are made for support and power – although I have to admit most of what he said went over my head.'

'Yeah, I don't know much about the boots either. I used to work in music PR in the States, so this stuff is kinda new to me too. I know they have carbon fibre shanks and leather uppers – but don't ask me what that means,' she laughed.

Ella grinned at her. Maybe events like these weren't so bad. As they walked around the exquisite, pre-war ballroom, Ella kept catching the reflection of her and Danny in the black Spanish glass panels around the room. They looked perfect, every inch the glamorous power-couple at an exclusive launch party. The only downside was Danny's dour expression.

'What is *wrong* with you?' Ella asked quietly, after Danny had given monosyllabic answers to a brief interview with someone from the *Mirror*. 'We should be having an amazing time – you're the star tonight, after all – but you're really tense.'

'I just want to be at home,' Danny mumbled. 'There's an Inter Milan game I really wanted to watch.'

Ella stared at him for a moment. 'Danny,' she began, 'we both know that's not true. What is it?'

A flash of guilt swept over Danny's face, but just as he opened his mouth to answer, a man appeared in front of them. He was wearing a beautifully cut Hugo Boss suit, and was gorgeous, with penetrating blue eyes and dark blonde hair. Ella thought he looked a little bit like Daniel Craig mixed with Ewan McGregor, but there was something about him that made him seem slightly cruel, or a little bit hard.

Just as Ella was trying to work out what it was she noticed he was staring at her, and even though it was rude to check anyone out so openly, his eyes ran over every curve of Ella's body. He was undressing her with his eyes and imagining her naked, and Ella could feel his gaze prickling her skin. It instantly turned her on, and she flushed.

'Sorry to interrupt, but I absolutely had to introduce myself,' he said charmingly, and he lifted Ella's hand and kissed it lightly.

'No need to introduce yourself,' Danny said as cheerfully as he could. 'You're Johnny Cooper, aren't you?'

Johnny smiled. 'That's me. But I'm surprised you recognise me – I wouldn't think you'd watch daytime TV.'

Ella looked at her husband, and then to Johnny. Come to think of it, he *did* look familiar. As she was checking him out he caught her eye, and her face blazed again. She didn't normally react this way when she met men. What was wrong with her?

'I'm at the training ground a lot in the morning, but when I'm in I slump in front of the TV and watch *Cooper's Kingdom*.'

'I'm glad you do. I thought the only people who ever watched my show were housewives,' Johnny replied. 'And how about you, Ella Riding, do you ever watch *Cooper's Kingdom*?' he asked lightly.

Ella shook her head. She knew of the programme as quotes from the celebrity interviews Johnny did often appeared in magazines. But afternoon chat shows weren't really her thing.

'Oh, that's a shame. I was hoping you'd appear on it. I'd love to have you as a guest – really get to know you better.'

His ice-blue eyes bored into hers, and Ella began to feel

unsettled. His tone suggested innuendo, but only she had picked up on it. Danny was blithely unaware.

'That's a great idea,' Danny said enthusiastically, as he looked at his wife. 'Ella would be the perfect fit for your show, and she'd love to do it. She could show off about the work she's been doing at *Cerise* magazine.'

For some reason Ella – who was already awkward with what she now recognised as unwanted lust – felt irrational anger rising up inside her. How dare Danny offer her up to this man like she was a stupid little girl who could do tricks on a TV show? Danny wasn't in charge of what she did – or didn't do – *she* was.

'I think you'll have to speak to Aaron Kohle, our agent,' Ella said as evenly as she could. She knew her reaction was unfounded, but she didn't like this Johnny Cooper. She hated the way he looked at her as though she were a piece of meat, hardly helped by the way Danny was offering her like a sacrificial lamb. 'Aaron looks after all my media appearances, and he might not feel your show's right for us.'

Danny turned to Ella in surprise. 'Of course he would,' he remarked, and out of the corner of her eye she could see Johnny smirk. At that moment she hated both men. 'Aaron's been talking about getting you on TV, and this would be brilliant for you. It would be a chance to show you're not just a pretty face.'

Ella took a deep breath, and faced Johnny square on. It took all her strength not to show the instant hate she felt for him. 'Like I said, speak to Aaron Kohle, and we can discuss it,' she said. Hopefully Aaron would agree with her, and put Johnny – and Danny – off this idea. She didn't know why she'd had this almost wanton reaction to him, but she knew

Johnny made her feel uncomfortable. She wanted to get away from him, and fast.

'I'll do that,' Johnny said easily, and he reached for Ella's hand again. This time she moved it away before he could brush his lips against it. 'Lovely to meet you both.' He grinned, and both Danny and Ella watched him as he walked away.

'At least *something* good will come out of tonight,' Danny muttered, as he dropped his act and let his emotions slump again. 'That show would be really good for you.'

Ella didn't know what to say. Maybe it was his swagger, or the way he knew he was good-looking on top of being a talented TV presenter, but he'd caused an immediate reaction in her – one of lust and hate. He was arrogant, over-the-top charming, and clearly rated himself as a ladies' man.

Ella knew that going on his programme would be a very bad idea.

The rest of the night turned into a champagne-fuelled blur. What seemed like hundreds of people came up to them to make small talk, and as the evening went on Danny's bad mood started to disappear. Whatever had been bothering him was beginning to drift away, and Ella saw her husband again: the happy, carefree man she adored.

'Tonight's going totally well,' Bailey exclaimed as she bounced up to them, a glass of fizz in her hand. 'Everyone *loves* the new soccer boots, and my bosses are really happy with the night. We're going to get loads of exposure.'

Danny smiled at her. This time it was genuine.

'That's great,' he said, and he ran his hands through his hair. 'We've had a brilliant time, haven't we, Ella?'

Ella nodded, and her violet eyes shone. Once she'd got used to her dress and being the centre of attention she'd had the perfect evening. Not even meeting Johnny Cooper had dampened her spirits.

'There's just one more person I'd like you both to meet — he's been waiting all night to chat with you.'

'Bring him over,' Danny said easily, and he put his hand on the small of Ella's back. The night was nearly over, and it had been a triumph. But then again, of course it had. Everything Ella and Danny touched turned to gold.

'Danny, I'd like you to meet Sancho Tabora. He's a celebrity blogger who's a *massive* fan of yours.'

Sancho stood in front of the couple and stuck out his hand to Danny. His hair was a shade of light purple, he had four days' worth of stubble on his chin, and he was dressed in a silver suit. He stood out amongst the rest of the men in black tie, and Ella wondered how she'd not spotted him earlier.

'So good to *finally* meet you,' Sancho said icily, and he offered his hand to Danny. It hovered in the air for a second longer than was polite before Danny reluctantly took it. Ella took her eyes away from the colourful man standing with Bailey and glanced up at her husband. His face had gone pale, and he was shaking.

'What was that all about? And who was that Sancho man?' Ella asked Danny softly as they collapsed on the sofa in their drawing room. Danny had lit the fire, and the room, despite its size, was gorgeously cosy. In contrast Danny was cold and distant.

'I don't want to talk about it,' he said abruptly, and he stared into space, nursing a whisky.

Ella wasn't having any of it. 'We've got to talk about it,' she pressed. 'We're married, you're my best friend, and you're clearly upset about something. Darling, you're entitled to your privacy, but I want to help. Who is he, and why did you react like that when you were introduced to him?'

Danny put his head in his hands. He was close to tears.

'He's a bastard,' Danny said eventually, his voice full of emotion. 'He's a fucking bastard who's twisted and bitter and won't leave me alone.'

Ella inhaled sharply. 'What do you mean?'

'Everyone knows him as Sancho Tabora, the snarky blogger who's taken the world by storm and is the UK's answer to Perez Hilton, but I know him as Steven Turner, who was, until recently, the boyfriend of my first lover . . . and a man who keeps blackmailing me about being gay.'

'He's blackmailing you? Are you joking?!'

Danny shook his head. 'I wish I was. Apart from you, Aaron, Yves, and Mike – my first boyfriend – he's the only other person who knows I'm gay. And he loves having that power. Mike was my boyfriend after I left school, and when I joined the Kingston United youth squad I told him it was over. Our relationship had reached its natural end, and I didn't think it was fair to keep him in the closet along with my sexuality. I couldn't do that to him, so I ended it. He took it pretty badly, but he moved on. And then he started seeing Steven. Sancho. Mike told Steven about me, and he's been blackmailing me with it.'

Ella considered this for a moment. 'But babe, you've been in the main team for years – why's he only starting to threaten you now?'

Danny knocked back his whisky. 'It's not a new thing,'

he admitted. 'He's been blackmailing me ever since I got my first pay packet from the club. You know his website, SanchosWorld.com? Well, guess who gave him the money to start it up and employ staff. And guess who paid for that ridiculous suit he was wearing tonight.'

'But that's terrible! He has to be stopped! Oh Danny, you poor thing.' Ella was outraged. She couldn't believe this had been happening, and for so long. She hated the thought of Danny going through this all by himself.

'How do you suggest I stop him?' Danny asked wearily. 'I can't do anything about it. I can't trust the police not to go running to the newspapers, I can't get a court order to stop him for the same reasons, and even though Aaron's offered to manage Sancho in return for him calling it quits, he's refused. Nothing can be done. I just have to live with it.'

'Isn't blackmail illegal though?' Ella asked slowly, and Danny nodded. 'Surely the newspapers wouldn't run the story because of that.'

'It is illegal, but the only way to stop the press from reporting about blackmail cases is to get an order or a PCC request . . . and if I do that I need to out myself to the courts. Which I don't want to do.'

Ella considered this. 'But when footballers have affairs they take out super-injunctions to remain anonymous,' Ella said. 'Why couldn't you do something similar?'

'I thought about it,' Danny admitted, 'but I don't want to risk it. Aaron spoke to our lawyers and they said that we could take out a super-injunction, but because of how the press is right now with all the phone hacking stuff and police backhanders, it may not work. I mean, look at what happened to Ryan Giggs and that sorry mess he got himself into. The last thing I want is people gossiping about me when I'm trying to protect myself.'

Ella considered all of this with a heavy heart. 'Is that why you were so moody tonight? Because of Sancho?'

Danny nodded. 'I knew he was going to be there, and I couldn't stand the thought of coming face-to-face with him. I'd never met him, and I wanted it to stay that way. I knew he was going tonight – he emails me quite a lot, little threatening bits and pieces along with demands for cash – but I thought maybe he hadn't turned up. That maybe he was too ashamed of how he's behaved to attend.'

Ella leant back on the sofa and pulled her heels off. She didn't know what to say, or what to suggest. All she knew was that she could be there for Danny, and she could hold his hand while they tried to figure this out.

## *Chapter Six*

'I've had a phone call about you,' Aaron announced as he swept into the Ridings' eat-in kitchen. Ella was finishing her breakfast at the scrubbed pine table, but she was still in her dressing gown and hadn't even thought about brushing her hair or sweeping a touch of make-up on her face.

She briefly wondered if it had been such a good idea to give Aaron a key to their house, but then she remembered that he technically owned it. Danny was certainly rich enough to have bought it himself, but Aaron liked to have what he called 'gentle control' over his clients. It didn't worry Danny – Aaron wasn't about to throw them onto the streets, and if he did they had plenty of money to buy somewhere themselves – so it didn't bother Ella. She just would have preferred a bit more privacy.

'Oh yes?' Ella said, as she swallowed the last of her porridge. 'I hope it was a good one.' She didn't know why, but sometimes she felt like Aaron was her teacher or her father or something. Why did she always feel like he was about to tell her off?

'It was a great one,' Aaron said, as he helped himself to coffee and sat on the chair opposite her. 'Have you ever heard of *Cooper's Kingdom*? It's on Channel Four, normally in the daytime, but it's proving so popular they're moving it to prime time. Johnny Cooper hosts it and interviews celebrities. It's cult TV gone mainstream.'

Ella briefly closed her eyes. 'I have heard of it, yes,' she replied slowly. She knew what was coming.

'Well guess what, sweetheart, they want you to appear on it! Johnny Cooper has asked for you especially!'

Ella concentrated very hard on looking pensive yet delighted.

'But Aaron, it's daytime TV. I always thought you said I should know my own value, and I don't think daytime TV is really it, you know?'

Aaron took a long gulp of his coffee. 'But like I said babe, they're moving the show to primetime – Friday nights, nine o'clock. You don't get a better slot than that, and you'd be on the first evening airing. They're predicting eight million viewers. It doesn't get bigger than this.'

Ella bit her lip. 'I'm just not sure this programme is the right fit for my image. I mean, it's about celebrities. And I'm not one. Surely I'm not famous enough to be on his show?'

'You *are* a celebrity . . . and you'll be a lot more famous after you've been on this programme,' Aaron sighed, and Ella could tell he was losing patience with her. She was supposed to jump up and down and be excited about this opportunity. It was a great chance for her to get on TV and it would introduce her and the Riding brand to a new audience. She just wished Johnny Cooper didn't present the show – he made her skin crawl, and she had a bad feeling about him. He was dangerous. 'All you need to do,' Aaron continued, 'is sit on a chair, look pretty, and make clever small talk about your life. It's perfect for you; they're going to pay us ten grand for your appearance and I said you'd do it.'

Ella plastered on the biggest smile possible, and even though it was a cliché, she clapped her hands together in delight. 'Well, if you think it will be good for us, I can't wait to do it,' Ella said as enthusiastically as she could. 'It *is* a great opportunity; you're right.'

Inside her heart was sinking. She really didn't want to go on this programme, and she especially didn't want to see Johnny Cooper again. But being Danny Riding's wife was her job, and she was determined to do the best she could for her husband. It was only fair, when he provided her with the most perfect lifestyle imaginable.

'I've had another email,' Danny said casually, as they curled up in front of the TV that evening. His green eyes were focused on the second season of one of his favourite shows – *America's Hits* – but Ella knew he wasn't really watching it. How could he concentrate on anything when Sancho Tabora had ramped up his number of emails to Danny from one or two a month to several a day? It was relentless.

'What did this one say?' Ella asked lightly as if they were chatting about something that didn't really matter.

'He wants a hundred grand. Next week.' Danny still hadn't taken his eyes off Madison Miller, the presenter, who was introducing another contestant on *America's Hits*. 'I said it would be fine.'

Ella swallowed. She wasn't sure how much Danny got paid, although she knew it was an awful lot. But a hundred grand? This was the most money Sancho had ever demanded, and ever since the Putto launch at The Dorchester, he'd been asking for more and more, and pushing harder each time. Where would it end?

'Right,' she said, with difficulty. She knew how much Danny was hurting, and she also knew she was powerless to stop it. She decided to change the subject. 'So, guess what I'm doing next week?'

Danny remained silent for a moment, and Ella wondered if she'd said the wrong thing. Every time she tried to be sympathetic, or tried to find a solution to end the blackmailing, Danny got angry and frustrated with her. Changing the subject was a last resort.

'What are you doing next week?' Danny asked finally, and Ella breathed a quiet sigh of relief.

'Well, I'm popping into *Cerise* to do some more outfits – the theme's about being pretty without looking like I've been sexually objectified by a man – and I'm going to be a guest on *Cooper's Kingdom*, too. How cool is that?'

For a second, Danny's eyes lit up. 'That's awesome,' he enthused. 'I can't believe you're going to be on one of my favourite shows.'

Ella grinned. Okay, so she totally and absolutely hated the idea of being filmed while sucking up to Johnny Cooper, but it was worth it just to cheer up Danny.

'Want to come along? You could watch us filming if you like. I'm sure the production crew wouldn't mind.'

'When is it?' Danny asked with interest.

'Thursday afternoon. Are you free? I'd love it if you could come.' Ella didn't mention she wanted Danny there as protection from Johnny's mesmerising stare. She remembered how he looked at her, and how it made her feel. It was like she was turned on and repulsed at the same time. If

74

Danny came, he would be her shield. Her reminder of what she had, and why she didn't want lust ever again.

'Damn, I can't come – I offered to help at the Kingston United Training Academy on Thursday. We have a couple of schools visiting, and I said I'd help out.'

'Can't you cancel?' Ella asked in a small voice.

Danny considered it for a moment, and Ella held her breath. But then he shook his head.

'I can't,' he said eventually, and Ella could see his mood visibly changing again. That little spark of interest was drifting away. 'I can't let the kids down – they know I'm coming, and they'd be so disappointed.'

Ella was disappointed too, but she chose not to say anything. Why make Danny feel even worse than he already did? Damn Sancho Tabora. Damn him.

'So, welcome to my house, Ella Riding,' Johnny remarked with a flourish, as Ella turned up on the set in the outskirts of Kent. *Cooper's Kingdom* was made by an independent production company, Fairytale Productions, and was filmed in a studio made to resemble Johnny Cooper's living room. 'I'm so glad you could come.'

Ella eyed him. He sounded perfectly polite, but there was something in his voice that suggested innuendo, and something in his eyes that made her think he was mocking her. Perhaps he was. People who didn't know her tended to treat her like she was a footballer's wife stereotype: vacuous and only interested in clothes, make-up, and shopping.

'And I'm pleased to be here,' Ella said smoothly, as she looked around the set. She had to admit it was beautiful. The 'living room' was fitted out in velvety cappuccino and chocolate hues, and oak and apple-wood coffee tables were placed in front of comfortable brown leather sofas. A massive Jackson Pollock print hung on the ivory wall, and realistic daylight streamed through the windows, lighting up the room. It was exquisite.

'What do you think of my living room?' Johnny asked, as he flopped onto a sofa and looked around the set. 'It's an exact replica of the one in my Hampstead home – right down to the Conran side-tables. The production team blanched at the cost, but I had to have them. I have them in my home, after all.'

Ella shrugged slightly. 'It's okay,' she said. 'It's very nicely done, I can see that.' She was determined not to be charmed by this man, or to gush. But she had to be polite. It was hard.

Johnny didn't say anything for a moment, and Ella looked up at him. His clear blue eyes were searching her face, and it looked as though he was going to say something to her when a production assistant bounded over. The moment had gone.

'We're going to start filming the introduction and the segments of the show now, Mrs Riding,' the assistant said, as she clutched her clipboard to her chest nervously. She was young, maybe twenty-one or twenty-two, and was clearly in awe of both Johnny and her. Ella gave her a warm smile.

'Would you like me to disappear into the Green Room for a bit?' she asked kindly, and the assistant flushed.

'Well, you can go there if you like, or you can join the other guests just over there. Often people like to watch Mr Cooper introduce the show.'

Ella glanced over to where the three other guests were sitting. There was Clement Du Cussy, the well-known literary author and Booker prize-winner, Clinton Mogridge, the American sensation who'd won Wimbledon the previous year, and Mali Croswell, a gorgeous English actress who'd made it big in Hollywood. And even though she felt a tiny bit nervous about meeting people who were famous for being talented – rather than for marriage, as she was – she couldn't wait to be introduced to them.

Thank God she'd got changed though. She hadn't known what to wear, and had thought jeans and a pretty top would be okay, but Danny had warned her that everyone who appeared on *Cooper's Kingdom* practically wore black tie, so she'd slipped into her favourite new dress: an Oscar de la Renta gold ribbon and white tulle dress with gold Louboutin heels. Dressed like that, she felt like she was in league with everyone else.

Ella couldn't take her eyes off Johnny. He was saying his lines with a cheeky grin, and ignoring the autocue that was running in front of him. There was something so sexual about the way Johnny Cooper flirted into camera that she was drawn to him – to his rugged good looks, and his easy chatter about what was coming up on the show – and she despised herself for it. How had this happened? One moment she hated the man, hated how he'd eyed her up at The Dorchester like she was a piece of meat for the taking, and the next . . . well, she was as besotted as everyone else. He was just so hot.

But the moment Johnny finished saying his lines the spell was broken. He stopped filming, and as he ran his hands through his hair he shot a look over at Ella, as if checking she'd been watching his performance on set. Instantly she remembered how she despised how cocky he was, how much he seemed to rate himself, and it was as if the previous half hour had never happened. On screen Johnny Cooper was everything a TV presenter should be – likeable, knowledgeable, and a demon at thinking on his feet – but off air? He was just another man with a massive ego who probably needed to fuck as many girls as possible as affirmation of how attractive he was. It was an immediate turn-off for her. Well, it should have been, anyway.

'What did you think then, guys?' Johnny asked his four guests, who'd been sitting behind the cameras.

'Amazing,' breathed Mali Croswell. 'Absolutely amazing. I can't wait to be interviewed by you.' There was a slight pause as Johnny registered the suggestion in her tone, and then he broke into a huge grin.

'I can guarantee that being on set with me is even better than just watching,' he winked, and then he turned his attention to the author and tennis player, ignoring both her and the pouting, captivated actress.

Ella was indignant – she couldn't quite believe that Johnny Cooper had just flirted so openly with Mali, just like he had done with her earlier. She bit her lip and felt embarrassment wash over her. She was so *stupid*. All this time she thought he'd been behaving like he fancied her, like she was unique, but she'd been wrong. His little performance at the Putto launch? That was just Johnny Cooper being Johnny Cooper. He hadn't wanted her that night, or today. No wonder she and her silly, uncalled-for overreactions amused him. He flirted with anyone and everyone, and she was nobody special.

'I hope I get to sit next to him on the sofa during the show,' Mali whispered to her, as her famous big brown eyes shone in pleasure. 'He's so divine. And such a catch. My agent wasn't sure about me appearing on this show – and he has a point, I suppose, because I shouldn't be doing mainstream TV shows, only exclusive interviews and things like that – but I just couldn't resist! TV presenters are so sexy, aren't they, and they don't get sexier than Johnny Cooper.'

Ella smiled as sweetly as she could, and drank in Mali's gorgeousness. Her olive skin sparkled under the studio lights, and her long dark hair gleamed with health. She was young, stunning, and had recently taken Hollywood by storm, and by rights, Mali could have any man she wanted. Yet she was appearing on *Cooper's Kingdom* and very much had a thing for Johnny Cooper. Had Ella underestimated just how important, and how A-list Johnny was? She had a feeling she was about to find out.

Over the course of the show Ella started to feel ashamed at how she'd misjudged Johnny. Yes, he was gorgeous, and yes, he was charming, but as soon as she came on set and poured her champagne, Ella melted. Johnny was also clever, funny, and a brilliant interviewer. On camera he behaved impeccably, asking his guests questions about themselves and ensuring they were comfortable and could shine. How could they not? Johnny Cooper was a TV pro, who'd worked his way up the television ladder and was now hosting a cult programme of his own. They were lucky to be appearing on his show. Like Aaron had said, this was the hottest thing on TV at the moment, and it would boost her profile no end.

'So, Ella Riding, what's it like being a footballer's wife?' Johnny asked her, as he finished interviewing the tennis player. The cameras were trained on them, but Ella was so used to them now that she didn't feel nervous. It was her time to sparkle in the spotlight.

'As far as I'm concerned, it's amazing,' she said, as she sipped her champagne. The combination of alcohol and the studio lights had made her feel a little light-headed, but Ella was determined that it wasn't going to affect her performance. 'Danny's the perfect husband, and we just fit so well together. When we met I didn't realise he was a footballer, and I'd have married him regardless of his career. He could be a mechanic for all I care.'

Okay, so strictly that wasn't quite true; she probably wouldn't have married Danny if this wonderful lifestyle hadn't come with it, but nobody needed to know that. Theirs was a perfect partnership – it just so happened it was a good business relationship, too. Danny got a wife and could play it straight, and Ella got the fabulous happy ever after.

'A mechanic?' Johnny raised his eyebrows slightly, and Ella felt a tiny twinge of something in her stomach.

'Yes, a mechanic,' she repeated with a smile. 'I'm rubbish with cars.'

The tennis player laughed, and Mali stretched her body against the back of her chair. She was wearing a simple silk Chloe maxi-dress, but the thin fabric strained against her nipples, and suddenly all eyes were on her.

'Of course, being married to a talented footballer *does* have its advantages,' Ella continued, wanting to pull Johnny's eyes away from Mali's gorgeous body. 'I'm not going to pretend it doesn't. For example, I've got a great gig at *Cerise* magazine, and I'm sure that my surname helped with that. And I get to meet interesting people, and of course, appear on programmes like this.'

'So you got a job on a magazine because of your husband?' the author said. His face was a picture of distaste.

'No, not exactly. It certainly helped, but I wouldn't have been hired if I couldn't do the job. I'm a stylist and model, which is quite different from having one of those bimbo columns about shopping.'

'So you're not even a writer on this magazine?' Clement sneered. He didn't look convinced by Ella at all, and there was tension in the studio. Johnny just sat back and watched Ella carefully.

'Well, I write a little bit, but no, I put together high-fashion outfits based on themes. And then I model them.'

Mali and Clinton stared at her blankly, and the author rolled his eyes.

'Let me guess: you choose subject matters such as "what can I wear to get my boyfriend to propose to me?" and then you come up with a provocative outfit for girls to wear,' Clement knocked back his glass of champagne and challenged her with a glare.

'It's a bit like that, yes, but hopefully more intelligent,' Ella replied smoothly. 'My latest outfits are about dressing so a woman feels pretty, but not as though she's been sexually objectified by a man.'

'Says the footballer's wife in a designer dress that shows off her tits,' Clement muttered, and Johnny looked at his guests nervously. This was television dynamite, and Ella wondered if he was going to ask the director to stop filming for a second. She didn't want him to. She knew how to stand up for herself.

'Yes, says the footballer's wife,' Ella said calmly. 'But you shouldn't let the fact I'm married to a sportsman influence your opinion of me. You wouldn't do the same to Clinton's wife, would you?' she said, gesturing to the tennis player, who seemed to want to duck out of the crossfire.

The author looked like he was about to say something, but Ella wasn't about to give him the chance.

'Now, I'm not going to talk any more about my article or my work, because I don't think you'll give me a chance. You've stereotyped me and written me off without getting to know me, and I don't see why I should bother to change your mind. You think I'm a dumb clothes horse who only thinks about make-up and dresses, and if that makes you feel more secure about yourself, so be it.'

There was silence around the table for a moment, and Ella wondered if she'd gone too far. Every so often she got a bit too defensive about being married to a footballer, and probably said things she shouldn't have. She'd lost it once with Stacey before she'd married Danny, and if she'd done it this time – on a show with eight million viewers! – Aaron would not be impressed.

Johnny coughed quietly, and then smiled. His first evening TV show was going to be compulsory viewing. 'If thinking about dresses all the time makes you a clothes horse, well, I must be one too . . . Because I've been thinking about your dress all evening, Ella. It's been driving me wild.'

Ella grinned at him. The tension had broken, and Johnny Cooper had flirted with her again. She may not have wanted him to do it, and may have hated how sleazy he seemed when he stripped her naked with his eyes, but God, it felt good when he did.

There was a knock on the dressing room door, and Ella turned, pulling on a grey Donna Karan waterfall cardigan over her tight black tee. She'd taken off her dress, her shoes, and the heavy television make-up, and she felt happy and relaxed.

'I just wanted to say thanks for coming on the show,' Johnny remarked, and Ella smiled at him. He was a complete flirt, and she thought he was hot, but there was no danger there. Johnny flirted with everyone, and it was probably why he was so successful.

'Thanks for inviting me, I had a great time.'

'Even though Clement was a complete asshole to you?'

Ella laughed. 'Especially because Clement was a complete asshole. I got to stand up for myself on television, and hopefully prove to people that I'm more than Danny's piece of arm-candy.'

Johnny walked behind Ella and helped her with her cardigan, which had been falling off her shoulder.

'You're nobody's arm-candy,' he said softly, and as he touched Ella's back with his hands, she felt that twinge in her stomach again. This time she knew it would be harder to ignore. But she *had* to. She couldn't risk what she had with Danny for this.

She stepped away from Johnny and smiled as brightly as she could.

'Thank you,' she said. 'It means a lot to know you think that too.'

There was an awkward pause between them, and for a moment they just stared at each other. Johnny's gaze trailed over Ella's face and body and then, before she could stop him, he was kissing her. His soft lips brushed against hers, his hands trailed down the sides of her body and gently touched her breasts, and suddenly, she was pulled against him, and they were kissing furiously. Endlessly.

'I can't do this,' Ella gasped, as she forced herself away from Johnny. 'I'm married. I can't do this.'

Johnny simply shrugged. 'You don't love him,' he said,

almost casually. 'I know you don't love him, because you don't look at him like you look at me.'

Ella let out a little laugh of frustration. This was ridiculous. This was only the second time she'd met Johnny Cooper, and he thought he knew her? Thought that she didn't love Danny?

'And how do you think I look at you?' she asked. Her voice shocked her – it was higher than normal, and she sounded stressed.

'You look at me with a mixture of contempt and passion. Like you hate me, that you can't stand to be near me . . . but at the same time you can't bear to be without me.'

Johnny sounded so matter-of-fact, so blasé about it, that Ella felt a chill run through her body. Did he make a habit of this? Did he regularly go around seducing married women?

'That's not true at all,' Ella said finally, her voice trembling slightly. She knew she was lying, but she was determined not to give in to this man. She'd known from the moment she'd first seen him that he was trouble, and she was right.

Johnny smiled. 'Just you wait and see, princess,' he said knowingly. 'But if you don't fantasise about me when you're in bed with your husband, I'll definitely be surprised.'

Ella's mouth dropped open. This man was so smug and infuriating.

'If I'm thinking about you in bed, it will be with my husband, and we'll be laughing about you coming onto me and getting it so wrong,' she said finally.

Johnny raised his eyebrow again. He looked good when he did that, and he knew it.

'I'll see you soon,' he said, as he stood in the doorway to the dressing room. 'But next time, it won't be on a set in a studio. You'll be in my house, and in my bed. Just you wait and see.'

## Chapter Seven

'Aaron rang while you were sleeping,' Danny said conversationally as he walked into Ella's bedroom carrying a delicate silver tray. It was the second morning in a row that Ella hadn't wanted to get up, so it was also the second morning in a row that Danny had brought her breakfast in bed. She gazed at the tray listlessly. There were all her favourites – pain au chocolat, strawberries, freshly squeezed orange juice, and hazelnut-flavoured coffee. But she didn't want it. She didn't want any of it.

Ella forced herself to sit up against her eiderdown pillows. When she'd first seen her bedroom, she'd been seduced by how beautiful it was. A huge bed was swathed in gorgeously soft Egyptian cotton sheets, the walls were the palest pink, and creamy silk curtains fluttered against the windows. An antique French dressing table and mirror sat on one side of the room, and on the other was a beautifully carved Moroccan screen. When she'd seen some in Thailand she'd desperately wanted to ship one home, but her backpacking budget meant she couldn't afford it. Months later, Danny had remembered how much she'd loved them, and had bought her a screen more stunning than any she'd ever seen. Every time she looked at it she was reminded that her husband treated her like a princess.

Now though, in her gloom, her bedroom felt a little like an impersonal hotel room. She suddenly longed for her old bedroom, the one she'd had before she'd broken up with Fin and gone travelling. She wished she hadn't binned all her stuff before she went travelling – her Indian wall hangings, and her beat-up furniture from flea markets. It may have been cheap and cheerful, but it had been *hers*.

'Aaron's always phoning, and it feels like you're always announcing it like he's the bloody Messiah or something,' Ella said dully, as she rubbed sleep from her eyes. She knew she was being rude, but she just felt so down. She had done ever since she'd kissed Johnny Cooper. She'd managed to contain it, to keep it to herself, but when *Cooper's Kingdom* had aired that Friday she'd sunk even lower. Just seeing Johnny on screen, with her, was a reminder of how much she was attracted to him, and how alive she became in his presence. They sizzled. She could no longer lie to herself and pretend that she didn't want him. Because of course she did. She had done the moment she'd met him at the Putto launch.

Danny raised an eyebrow at his sullen wife, but he chose to ignore her tone. 'The ratings for *Cooper's Kingdom* are in, and the programme's a hit. It got twelve million viewers, and apparently that just doesn't happen any more, not even for *EastEnders*. Anyway, the producers phoned Aaron as soon as they found out and, well . . . we've got some amazing news for you. If this doesn't cheer you up nothing will.'

Ella wanted to wince at Danny's excited tone, but she caught herself just in time. Even though he was secretly with Yves, and they didn't have any sort of sexual or romantic relationship, she didn't really feel that she could tell Danny about her feelings for Johnny. She supposed that admitting that she wanted to be with another man would feel like a betrayal, and that if he knew about it, Danny would worry that their marriage was threatened – and that was the last thing she wanted.

Yet she wanted Johnny.

She wanted that passion.

Ella's whole body ached for Johnny, and during the long nights she curled up in lust, desperate for his touch, his kisses, his cock. But during the day she hated him. She wished she'd never met him and wished her body wasn't reacting so strongly to him, and ruining what was meant to be her happy ever after with Danny.

She had to stop thinking about him, and fast.

'So what's this amazing news?' Ella asked.

Danny sat on the edge of the bed and put the tray down as he struggled to contain his excitement. 'Well,' he began, 'like I said, the producers of the programme phoned Aaron to tell him about the ratings, but they also wanted to see if you'd be interested in presenting a new TV show for them!'

Ella sat up straight as adrenaline started pumping through her body. 'What?' she gasped. 'What did you say?'

Danny laughed. 'The producers of the show loved you so much that they want to make you a TV presenter, babe! How awesome is that?'

'Oh my God, oh my God!' Ella yelled, and she jumped out of bed and began pacing the room. Her bare feet brushed lightly against the sheepskin rugs dotted around the stripped hardwood floor, and suddenly she was in luxury again, not hell. Johnny Cooper and his kiss had been banished from her mind.

'You're kidding, aren't you? Wow . . . that's amazing.'

'The producers said, and I quote, that you are "a natural on screen", and that you "sparkle with a combination of your dynamite looks, conversational ability and gutsy opinions".' Danny looked at his wife with a satisfied smile. 'They want you, babe. It was like your appearance on *Cooper's Kingdom* was a screen test, and you won the audition!'

Ella sat back down on the bed and took a sip of orange juice to try and steady her nerves. Wow.

'I know you said that amazing things would happen to me once we got married, but I can't believe this is happening,' Ella whispered, and she flung her arms around her husband. 'This is so brilliant. What else did Aaron say?'

'Well, he said he had to run it past you to confirm, but that you'd adore the opportunity to present on TV . . . and that you'd love to work with those producers again. He also said to give his congratulations to you, and that he knew that appearing on that show was the right thing for your career . . . Oh, and that he's found someone named Nash Barnwell who he wants to manage you.'

Ella sighed in pleasure. She had the perfect husband, the perfect home, and now her career was going into orbit – and Aaron had hired a manager who was going to look after her! Exclusively!

'I should phone him to say thank you and set up a meeting with this Nash guy,' Ella murmured. 'Oh, and find out more about the show, too! Do you know what it's about?'

Danny thought for a moment, trying to remember what Aaron had said. 'I think it's current affairs led, but it's more pop-culture than politics. So things people are talking about now, like what celebrities are doing, new technology, what trends are appearing in major cities, fashion – that sort of stuff. It's a magazine format and involves interviewing people and talking to the audience too. They want you to focus on the fashion and music stuff, and your co-host will do the politics and news stuff.'

Ella blinked. 'A co-host! Does Aaron have any idea who it will be?'

Danny gave Ella a funny look, and popped a strawberry in his mouth. 'It's Johnny Cooper. Who else would it be?'

'I hear you're becoming *quite* the little celebrity,' Chastity sniffed, as the girls walked through the main foyer of Oatlands Park for the Kingston United vs Manchester City match. As usual, Chastity had completely overdressed and was wearing a bodycon Sass & Bide black and nude dress with Jimmy Choo peep-toe ankle boots. Ella had kept it low-key in black True Religion jeans and a cream Donna Karan knit.

'I'm not sure what you mean,' Ella replied lightly. They were being led past the roped-off areas, and the Kingston United fans were gawping and taking photos of them with their phones. Ella kept her voice measured, and a bright smile fixed on her face. Football fans – regardless of which team they supported – *loved* Danny Riding. He was the new great hope for the national squad, and was fast becoming a football legend, ranking up there with Rooney, Gerrard and Lampard. It was Ella's job to play the perfect footballer's wife whenever she was at Oatlands, so that was exactly what she was doing.

'Don't give me that,' Chastity hissed. 'I hear you're going to be presenting a new TV programme with Johnny Cooper. What did you do to get that? Give him a blow-job?'

Ella's smile froze. Of all the players' wives and girl-friends, Chastity was meant to be her 'best friend'. She wasn't exactly acting like it though.

'Let's talk when we're in the private box,' she murmured as quietly as she could. 'But in the meantime, would you please be quiet? We're surrounded by fans and officials and the last thing I want is you starting rumours that aren't even true.'

Chastity rolled her eyes. 'Whatever,' she said, and she waved and pouted at a couple of fans who were sitting near the box. Ella watched her with interest. Chastity may have been a shallow bitch sometimes, but she really did play the part of a stereotypical WAG brilliantly.

Ella didn't speak to Chastity until they'd both had a glass of champagne and the game was underway. As the teams jogged onto the pitch Ella scanned the faces of the players dressed in a kit of royal blue until she spotted Danny. He looked great – relaxed, but ready to win the game. She was so proud of him. But as much as she wanted to sit back and enjoy the match she had to deal with Chastity and her attitude. She turned to her.

'What is your problem, exactly?' Ella asked calmly, as she pushed her light brown fringe out of her eyes. 'Why are you being so nasty today?'

Chastity snapped her gum and glared. 'All I'm saying is that everyone knows that Daniella Davies was supposed to present this new show with Johnny, but he took one look at you on *Cooper's Kingdom* and demanded that poor Dani was chucked out and that you took her place. You! You have no presenting experience whatsoever. It's insulting to Dani, who just so happens to be one of my closest friends. We always hang out when we're out partying, anyway.'

Ella blinked. 'I didn't know Daniella Davies was lined up to present,' she said, and she wondered if there was any truth in what Chastity had just said. They were due to start filming the show soon, and she'd thought that the producers *had* left it quite late to ask her to be a presenter. But what did she know? She just assumed this was how things were done in TV land. Perhaps they were. 'Had she signed a contract or anything?'

Chastity kept her gaze on the pitch, her eyes trailing her husband as he dribbled the ball towards the goal. 'Of *course* she'd signed a contract. Well, I think so, anyway. She's very upset. They were going to give her five hundred grand to do that show, and they pulled out. Just like that. Or just because Johnny asked them to.' She looked up slyly at Ella.

'I saw you both on his little show. The attraction between you two was obvious. Have you shagged him?'

'Chastity! For fuck's sake keep it down. We're in public! And no, of course I didn't.'

'You should, you know. He probably has the hots for you. Even if you do dress like that.' Her eyes ran critically over Ella's outfit. Ella wasn't even wearing heels, just fur-lined Chloé boots.

'I'm married to Danny, and we're faithful to each other,' Ella said slowly. 'We don't cheat on each other. And I would never, ever, in a million years think about having sex with Johnny Cooper. I don't even like him very much,' she lied. She tried not to think about how he played centre-stage in all her fantasies recently, or how she wondered what he was doing or if he was thinking of her, too.

On the pitch Freddie had passed the ball to Danny, and Danny was running towards the goal faster than Ella had ever seen him do before. He then passed the ball back to

Freddie, who took aim . . . but missed. The ball shot over the goal, and the crowd booed in disappointment.

'Oh, I forgot, you and Danny are Mr and Mrs Perfect,' Chastity remarked moodily as Freddie kicked at the turf on the pitch in frustration. 'Whatever you touch turns to gold, blah, blah, blah. You're not Posh and Becks, you know. You never will be, regardless of all the little outfits you put together for that magazine, or however many sponsorship deals Danny gets.'

Ella rolled her eyes and concentrated on the match. Yves had just got the ball from a Manchester City player, and as he ran towards the penalty area he spotted Danny and passed it to him. Danny surged past several defenders, and then struck the ball powerfully towards goal. The goalkeeper barely had time to move before the ball flew past him and into the back of the net. Goal!

Ella jumped to her feet and cheered as Yves and Danny hugged each other to the sound of the fans chanting 'Royals! Royals! Royals!'

Maybe Chastity was right, Ella thought suddenly, as she clapped hard. Maybe they never would be David and Victoria Beckham, but if they kept on having this run of luck, things could only get even better.

'I've never worked for a footballer or his wife before,' Nash Barnwell said conversationally, as he and Ella sat in the garden drinking iced tea. It was a gloriously hot day, and the light breeze that tickled Ella's bare shoulders was scented with roses and jasmine.

'And I've never had my own manager,' she remarked as warmly as she could, but there was something about Nash Barnwell that put her on guard. He'd turned up at Castle

House in scruffy Levis and a striped Ted Baker shirt, and even though he was polite, friendly and professional, Ella felt a little uncomfortable, like she'd done something wrong but she didn't know what.

Nash smiled. 'I guessed. Let me tell you a bit more about myself. I started out in the music business, and for a while I ran the UK office of Slate Street, an American record label that recently went out of business.'

'Why did it go under?' Ella asked curiously. She didn't know much about the music industry, and hadn't heard of the label.

'Oh, it was nothing to do with me,' Nash said with a smile, although there was an edge to his voice. 'I'd left way before then. Apparently the American founder had a bit of a meltdown and got caught beating up one of his major acts. I'm not too clear on the details. After I left Slate Street I went freelance and managed a couple of UK music acts, and then I looked after several actors.' He named a couple of well-known and well-respected British movie stars. Ella was impressed.

'So what made you move into sport?'

Nash shrugged. 'I've always been a massive football fan – although I support Chelsea, rather than Kingston United – and it's where the money is. Footballers are seen as gods; they make an obscene amount of cash on the pitch, and pull in major sponsor deals off it. Sport stars are getting sexier and sexier, and I believe they're the future of celebrity in the country. So long as the footballers behave themselves, that is.'

'I have to agree with you on that. I had no idea how big the industry was before I met Danny,' Ella said.

'Well, why would you?' Nash said with a dismissive

wave of his hand. 'Aaron is looking to build on the success he's created with your husband, and eventually he'll take on more clients. Ultimately I'll be helping to manage those, but in the meantime I'm going to be looking after you.'

Ella took a long sip of her drink. There was acid in Nash's voice, and she didn't know why. Perhaps he felt it was demeaning to look after a footballer's wife. Or perhaps he was just an asshole.

'Aaron filled me in on your perfect love story,' Nash continued with a wry smile. 'You ran off to Thailand because your cupcake company went bust and your boyfriend dumped you, you met Danny on a beach, and you both decided you needed each other for a fairytale happy ending.'

Ella didn't like the tone of Nash's voice, but she nodded anyway. However you chose to word her story, those were the nuts and bolts of it. She just didn't like how Nash made it sound.

'And in case you were wondering, Aaron also told me the specifics about Danny's friendship with Yves Benoit,' he said in a stage whisper. 'I've signed what seems like hundreds of contracts and NDAs and your secret's safe with me. Believe me, I'm used to dealing with famous people and their private affairs.'

Ella shifted in her chair. She was wearing a Valentino lace dress in a rosy pink and even though she'd dressed coolly, and her feet were bare, she still felt uncomfortably hot. Nash didn't approve of her and her marriage – she got that – but she wasn't going to rise to his bait and defend herself. Aaron wanted Nash to manage her, and if they were going to get along, she had to play it safe.

'Are you married?' she asked Nash, as she wrapped her

hands around her icy glass in the hope it would help her cool down. It was disconcerting that the man in front of her knew her most intimate secrets, yet she barely knew anything about him. It didn't feel particularly balanced.

Nash shook his head. 'I was. I met a beautiful actress, married for *love*,' he said pointedly, 'and then six months after our wedding she announced she'd met someone else. I was devastated. We had a messy break-up, an even messier divorce, and I got hurt. So I swapped actors for the sport industry, moved to the other side of London, and set about rebuilding my life from scratch. I'm only just coming through it.' He took a sip of his iced tea thoughtfully, and there was a horrible, awkward silence as Ella struggled with what to say next.

'So,' Ella said as brightly as possible. 'What's going to happen next with you being my manager? How do you see this all working out?'

Nash sat back in his chair. His shirt stretched across his chest, and Ella suddenly realised how good-looking her new manager was. He had longish medium-brown hair that covered his ears and tapered down the back of his neck, arresting light-blue eyes, full lips, and cheeky freckles over his boxer's nose. He wasn't her type, but she could tell Nash Barnwell wasn't short of female fans.

'Well, I've been given your notes from Aaron, and my job is to boost your career. You're already doing really well at *Cerise* magazine, but I'm thinking further down the line. I can imagine that if everything goes well with your bits and pieces there, that in a couple of years you could launch your own fashion magazine. Kind of like how Oprah has her own mag in America.'

Ella gasped, but Nash wasn't paying attention to her and didn't notice her surprise.

'I think it's the natural next step. Rio Ferdinand has his own magazine, but I think you could launch one off the back of your personality and talent and really make a go of it. Of course, you wouldn't have to do too much work, as we'd employ a team to do it for you, but it would be a good brand extension for you. It would really cement you as someone powerful and inspirational.'

'I don't know what to say,' Ella murmured. To think that she could have her own magazine! It was mind-blowing!

'And you're about to start presenting *A Week in Wonderland* with Johnny Cooper, aren't you?' Nash continued briskly. 'I'm going to hold your hand through that, and make sure you — and the show — are as successful as can be. How's that going for you, by the way? Are you looking forward to the first live show?'

Ella tried desperately hard to put how she felt about Johnny Cooper out of her mind, and concentrated as much as she could on being professional. 'It's going well,' she said brightly. 'We've done a couple of run-throughs, and the first show's going out live next week. I feel sick just thinking about it, to be honest.'

'I'm not surprised. It's a big job, considering you don't have any presenting experience and have only been asked to do it because of who you're married to. I have a couple of methods to help you deal with live TV that I learnt from my previous clients, and I'll be there during the recordings if you need it.'

Ella was so grateful for any help that she failed to notice Nash's dig at her. 'Really? That would be so great. Danny can't come with me because he's so busy with training, so it would be good to have someone there for me.'

Nash eyed Ella thoughtfully. 'What about friends?' he asked her carefully. 'Do you have any friends who'd be interested in watching the recording and being there for you?'

Ella shook her head sadly. 'Aaron doesn't think I should really hang out with the partners of Kingston United players – although I see Chastity Taylor sometimes – and I've drifted away from my old friends. We don't have that much in common any more.' She thought of Stacey, and felt a deep pang of regret. She missed her step-sister so much, but it was impossible to try to see her like she used to. Their lives were so different.

'Well, don't you worry about that. I've been employed to look after you, and that's what I'm going to do.'

## Chapter Eight

It was ten minutes until show time, and Ella was convinced that she was either going to faint, be sick, or just die of fright. The studio lights beamed down onto the stage, audience members were buzzing with anticipation as they took their seats, and the production team rushed around making last-minute checks. Ella watched the action nervously, and she wondered if she could really go through with this – if she could really be a credible television presenter. Okay, so they'd rehearsed this show twice and it had gone smoothly, but she hadn't done it in front of an audience waiting for her to mess up. And it hadn't been broadcast. Live. In front of millions and millions of people. Oh God.

'Are you ready for this, Ella?' Nash's voice came through her earpiece, and Ella jumped in surprise. Nash and the production team were watching her every move on screen from the gallery, and even though she knew they'd have just seen her looking petrified, she took a deep breath and smiled.

'I'm good – a bit nervous, but really excited!' she gushed. What else could she say? The truth? That as much as she was honoured to have been asked to present the show, she felt totally out of her depth and so strongly attracted to Johnny Cooper that she desperately wanted to run away?

'Think of your nerves as a good thing,' Rachel West interjected. Rachel was one of those feisty, self-confident women who also happened to be one of the best producers in the country. She commanded absolute respect and Ella thought she was brilliant. 'Just remember everything we discussed in rehearsals, and channel that nervous energy into a knockout performance. Remember, if you get stuck just smile, press your finger to your earpiece, and we'll direct you from up here.'

Ella nodded. 'You guys have been great,' she said honestly, and she started to pace the set in the hope it would psych her up. She knew the audience was watching her as they got settled into their seats, and that as much as she wanted to, she couldn't have a pre-show meltdown. 'And Nash, thanks so much for being here. It means a lot to me.' Ella stood still for a moment and stared up at the gallery. Although she couldn't make out everyone's faces, she could see the outlines of people, and it was comforting to know Nash was up there. Okay, so he wasn't the friendliest of men, and there was something about the way he acted that made Ella feel like he disapproved of her in some way, but he was on her team. On her side. Having supportive people around her was a massive comfort, even if they were only doing it because they were on the Ridings' payroll.

'Just doing my job,' Nash said wryly, and Ella ignored the tone of his voice.

'Five minutes!' a voice called out, and suddenly the flurry of activity stepped up a notch. Ella started pacing again, and tried desperately hard not to think about what was about to happen. She concentrated instead on how her fierce Fendi heels were pinching her toes, and how – as much as she loved it – her stunning Marc Jacobs tank dress in antique violet and gold made her look chubby. It was true, TV *did* pile on the pounds, and even though she was slender, Ella's body wasn't built for the screen. She was too curvy, and had too much going on in the breasts and hip department to have the perfect TV presenter's body.

'You're so gorgeous when you're nervous,' a voice said from behind the cameras, and Johnny Cooper stepped out of the shadows. He was in a beautifully cut suit, but was heavily made up with standard TV foundation, and his dirty blonde hair was gelled into stiff peaks. During the last couple of rehearsals he'd just worn jeans and T-shirts, and he'd looked so sexy that Ella wondered if he could sense how attracted she was to him. Every time he'd caught her eye the memory of their kiss flashed into her mind, and her body became alert. Excited.

'Thanks, I think,' Ella blushed, and she continued pacing. It was hard enough dealing with Johnny when she was feeling okay – but today, right now, it was impossible. Her stomach was in knots, and she didn't need butterflies of lust added to the mix.

'Hey,' Johnny said so softly, that Ella paused and spun on her heel to look at him. 'It will be all right, you know. You're good at this. You can do this.'

Ella swallowed hard. 'What if I mess up?'

'You won't,' Johnny said reassuringly. 'We've done two rehearsals and you've sparkled on both of them. When the show starts the adrenaline will kick in and it will heighten your performance. You'll be funnier, sexier, and cleverer. It's a lot like being in love. Live TV brings out the very best in you.'

He gently placed his hand on her waist and gazed at her for a moment. For once he wasn't flirting, wasn't showing off, and for the first time it felt like he was being honest with her. She'd got so used to the Johnny Cooper who'd teased her with a kiss and flirted with her like it was a game that she'd never stopped to think who he was behind that mask. His blue eyes pierced her so powerfully that she felt like Johnny could see right inside her . . . And that he was really seeing her – Ella Aldridge, not Ella Riding, wife of a football player and pampered princess.

'You're Ella Riding, remember? You're married to one of the best strikers in the country, you're a stylist for *Cerise* magazine, and now you're a co-host of *A Week in Wonderland*. You're a star.'

Ella didn't know if she felt flattered that Johnny Cooper thought she was someone special, or disappointed that he didn't see the real her, the girl who was so much more than the glossy woman married to a footballer.

But she didn't have time to dwell on it.

In just a few moments they'd be live on Channel Four, and as the audience became quiet both Johnny and Ella gazed at the people in front of them. Almost everyone in the audience was smiling in anticipation, and some were even waving to them, as if they couldn't believe that Ella Riding and Johnny Cooper were in front of them.

'See how all these people can't wait for your big debut?' Johnny whispered. 'That's how everyone at home is behaving too. Everyone in the country *loves* you since you took on that wanker author on my show – they want this to work for you.'

Ella smiled – a real, broad smile – and ran her eyes across the rows of people watching her. She may not have had friends in the audience, but they felt like friends . . . except one. Ella froze as her eyes lingered on a figure sitting near the back. He was half shrouded by a shadow, but there was no mistaking his purple hair. Sancho Tabora was in the audience.

Three, two, one . . . Go!

'Hello and welcome to the first ever *A Week in Wonderland*. I'm Johnny Cooper, co-host of your adventures in our new programme . . .'

'. . . And I'm Ella Riding. As you probably know, this is the first time I've presented a show, and I have to say, I very nearly didn't do it.'

Johnny turned to look at Ella. 'Why's that then?'

'Well, my mother always told me not to talk to strangers, and here I am talking to eight million of them on a Friday night.'

The audience groaned, and Ella grinned.

'And my first on-air joke just failed miserably. Johnny, perhaps I'm not cut out to be a television presenter.'

'I wouldn't say that, Ella. I think you present yourself very well. Nice dress, by the way,' Johnny looked Ella up and down appreciatively, and the audience laughed and wolf-whistled. Ella had heard the joke several times in rehearsals, yet she still smiled as if it was fresh and funny. Of course, it wasn't funny. She desperately wanted Johnny to think she was sexy, but at the same time, she was petrified by his attraction to her.

'But enough about us,' Johnny continued, flirting with the camera that faced him square on. 'This show is all about *you*. We're about what you're currently talking about, what you're thinking, what you're feeling, and what you're wearing. Plus, of course, what you're eating.'

'That's right,' interjected Ella, with a coy grin. '*A Week in Wonderland* is about what's been going on in our lives over the past seven days – but we're not *Newsnight* . . . and Johnny definitely isn't Jeremy Paxman. We're about the frivolous and fun side of current affairs and trends.'

'But we're mainly about our lives. If you want to get in touch follow us on @Wonderland_Show on Twitter, and you're more than welcome to join our gorgeous studio audience too, if that floats your boat. So let's get cracking. In the news this week Gable Blackwood – the openly gay Hollywood actor – is running to be governor of Florida. There have been protests in the streets because of Gable's sexuality, and we want to know your thoughts on those marching—'

Johnny and Ella turned to a different camera, and then they were off.

An hour later it was all over, and Ella was brimming over in elation. They'd done it! They'd presented a full hour of current affairs discussion, based on breaking news, trends in music, fashion and food, and had introduced the hottest new band who'd played the show out. Ella couldn't believe it. It had gone without a hitch, and now she was on a major high.

'You were amazing!' Johnny crooned into Ella's ear, and he picked her up and spun her around on the stage. The audience was clapping hard, and the producers were saying their congratulations through their earpieces, but all Ella could hear and feel was the beating of Johnny's heart. Her breasts were pushed up against his chest, and the warmth of their bodies turned into an exquisite, electric heat. She kissed him briefly on the cheek, and could taste the saltiness of his skin.

'No, you were amazing.' Ella smiled, and she held

Johnny's gaze with her violet eyes. The chemistry between them was unmistakable, and Ella felt it force her back towards Johnny, and into his arms again.

But she had to pull back. She was married. She couldn't do this.

'I take it you're coming to the aftershow?' Johnny said, as he took Ella's hand into his and tugged her closer to him. 'You absolutely have to, you know. It wouldn't be a party without you.'

Ella swallowed hard. Nobody on the production team would be too offended if she said she had to go home, but Ella knew she had no choice. She had to go, if only for the photo opportunities.

'Of course she is,' a voice said, and Nash Barnwell was suddenly standing by her side. 'She's one of the stars of the show and she needs to be there.'

Ella smiled up at her manager. He had no idea, of course, that she was desperately attracted to Johnny. And she wanted it to stay that way.

'Is Danny coming too?' Ella asked Nash hopefully, and her heart sank when he shook his head.

'He's under Aaron's orders not to have too many late nights. He's got his underwear shoot with Armani the day after tomorrow, and even though make-up and Photoshop magic makes everything easier for everyone involved, Aaron still wants Danny fresh as a daisy.'

Johnny laughed and raised an eyebrow. 'Ella Riding, you never told me your husband was going to be an underwear model! What's he doing, one of those moody black and white shots where he looks all ripped?'

Ella nodded. 'He's the new face of their boxer shorts. He still can't quite believe it.'

Johnny looked impressed. 'And nor can I,' he said. 'To think that my co-presenter is married to the new face of Armani Underwear. Wow. They'll be asking you to pose in your knickers next – you know, how Victoria Beckham did with David?'

'Well, off the record, Armani *did* ask Ella to get involved, but we turned them down,' Nash confided to Johnny. It was no big deal if this piece of information got out. In fact, it would only enhance Ella's brand values if people knew she turned down Armani.

Johnny's face turned from impressed to incredulous. 'You're kidding, right? You turned Armani *down*?' He slowly looked Ella up and down, and drank in her curves. No matter how many classy outfits she wore, nothing could disguise the fact that her body was built for fucking, pure and simple.

Nash shrugged. 'It doesn't fit with what we want to achieve. And we certainly don't want Ella to be stripping off for money. No matter how much.'

Johnny couldn't tear his eyes away from Ella's body. 'That's a shame,' he said softly. 'Ella's got to be the number one most lusted-after woman in the country.'

Nash laughed as if he was one of the few who didn't think she was hot, and Ella prickled.

'And to think that we've achieved that without Ella having to get undressed,' he said wryly. 'Come on, let's go to the party.'

By the time Ella, Nash and Johnny got to Shoreditch House and had got the lift up to the Lounge the party was heaving. Every member of the production team was there, and various C-list celebs had crashed it. They knew, rightly, that the

*Wonderland* aftershow party was *the* event to be at that night, and everyone who thought they were anyone – even if they weren't – was there, posing for the photographers and knocking back the free champagne.

'It's not bad weather; I think you should set up court by the pool,' Nash directed, as they found the table he'd reserved especially for Ella. The turquoise swimming pool glittered under the dark orange sky, and it really was the perfect place for Ella to sit. From their table they could see everyone and catch all the action without being too involved.

Ella stretched out in her seat and surveyed the scene in front of her. All these people were here to celebrate the first broadcast of a show she'd just presented, so that made her – and Johnny – the stars of the evening. It was amazing. She was used to being stared at and treated like a princess when she was with Danny, but this, well . . . this was something else. This was all for her, and she was determined to enjoy every minute of it.

'Maybe we should go and sit inside,' Ella suggested to Nash, who'd ordered them a couple of Bellinis. 'It's buzzing in there, and I feel a little like I'm still on a stage out here.'

Nash looked at the Lounge thoughtfully. Everyone was raucously drunk, and people were shouting at each other, laughing, and dancing.

'No, I don't think so. It's better if you stay out here.'

Ella bit her lip. She loved the cool breeze fluttering against her hair, and the fact that she had the perfect view of the party . . . but she wanted to be *part* of that party. She didn't want to sit on the sidelines, and to have people come up to speak to her like she was receiving guests.

She stood up. 'Nash, I'm sorry, I know you think you

know what's best for me, but I hardly ever get to go out, and I'm not going to spend tonight watching everyone else have a good time.' Out of the corner of her eye she saw Johnny place his hand on the bare back of a model, and she felt a twinge of jealousy. She should be in there, with him.

Nash scowled. 'Fine. But I'm going to set some ground rules. The press is here, after all.'

Ella rolled her eyes. 'Look, I'm not going to make a fool of myself, or Danny, just by hanging out at my own aftershow. I'll have three drinks max, will charm the socks off everyone, and if I dance, I won't do it provocatively,' she said good-naturedly.

Nash paused for a moment, and then sighed. 'Do what you want, but don't get into any trouble. I can't afford to mess this job up.'

Ella stared up at him in shock. 'What does that mean? What sort of trouble do you think I would possibly get up to?'

'Nothing, nothing,' Nash said hastily. But it was too late, and he knew it. 'Okay, Aaron warned me that it's at events like these — when people feel a massive rush of release — that they get into trouble. You're overjoyed you've had a successful evening and you want to let your hair down and celebrate. I get that. But you have to remember you're *still* working. Just because everyone else is partying it doesn't mean you can let your inhibitions go. You're still Ella Riding, you know. And if you get too drunk or behave inappropriately it could ruin all our hard work so far.'

Ella bit her lip, hard. When she'd agreed to be Danny's wife she never realised that she'd practically be imprisoned. Yes, she had the perfect lifestyle and a beautiful home, but what was the point of it all if you couldn't have fun or be yourself? What was the point of all this success if you were lonely?

'Nash, I'm not going to do anything that embarrasses you or me. But I'm going to have fun tonight. I deserve it.'

And with that, she spun on her heel and rushed towards the group of people who were laughing wildly while knocking back tequila.

'Princess,' Johnny drawled, as he passed Ella a sticky-looking cocktail. 'You made it.'

'I made it?' Ella asked.

'Yes, you managed to escape the clutches of your power-hungry manager. I never thought you'd make it inside, and that you'd have to sit on your little throne by the pool all night.'

Ella put her hands on her hips and tried to look as indignant as possible. 'Well, my management team seems to think I'm somewhat special, and that I shouldn't have to mingle with people like you. You know, former children's TV presenters and out-of-work actresses. You're the very sort of people who should be *working* for me.'

Johnny stared at her for a second and then burst out laughing. 'That's why I like you, Ella Riding – because you have a personality. So many WAGs don't. Now, let me introduce you to Ansku Tiihonen. She's a very popular Finnish model who's on the verge of breaking the UK. Rumour has it she's just about to start modelling for a *very* well known retailer.'

'Johnny, you know you can't tell people about that!' the model giggled, and she playfully slapped Johnny across the chest. Ella stared at her. Her long honey-blonde hair reached her tiny waist, her blue eyes sparkled under thick black lashes, and she was all skinny limbs and big breasts. Ella hated her immediately.

'What?' Johnny laughed. 'I didn't say you were *definitely* about to start being the face of Topshop!' and he roared with laughter. 'I've not been on – or in – the high street for ages, you know,' he said provocatively, and ran his hands over Ansku's perfect figure. Ella felt sick with jealousy. She suddenly hated her curves, hated her choppy haircut, and wished she'd never left her seat by the side of the pool. She had to get away from Johnny, and fast.

'Nice to meet you, Ansku,' Ella said as politely as she could, and she started to walk away when Johnny grabbed her and yanked her back.

'Hey!' he slurred, his voice heavy with alcohol. 'Not so fast. Ansku really wants to chat to you.'

'Oh, I'm sure Ansku isn't interested in talking to your colleagues,' Ella began. 'Especially not me.'

'But I am!' Ansku said. 'I asked Johnny if he could introduce us. I watched you on *Wonderland* tonight, and I thought you were fabulous. I wanted to ask how you got into presenting.'

Ella stared blankly at the model in front of her. She was so gorgeous that she could probably walk into any career she chose. Forget TV presenting, she could be a Hollywood star if that's what she wanted.

'Well, the production team phoned my manager and asked me if I'd like to present the show,' she said slowly. 'They'd seen me as a guest on Johnny's programme, *Cooper's Kingdom*. I suppose they thought I was good on camera and that I could do it . . .' Ella trailed off. She knew she sounded slightly ridiculous. Whoever got invited to be a guest on one programme and then got a job offer as a TV presenter off the back of it? Nobody.

Ansku trailed one lock of golden hair around her finger, while keeping her other in the back pocket of Johnny's post-show jeans.

'And how did you get to be a guest on Johnny's show? Did your manager sort it out for you?' she asked curiously.

Ella stayed silent. She hated to admit it, but she knew she'd only been invited on *Cooper's Kingdom* because she was married to Danny Riding. She had her whole, wonderful life because of Danny, and not for any other reason.

'I invited her on,' Johnny interrupted smoothly, as he caught the expression on Ella's face. She looked pained, as if Ansku had asked the wrong question. 'I met Ella at a launch party and I absolutely had to have her on my programme. She wowed me.'

Johnny's simple explanation was enough for Ansku, who shot her a sunny smile and then changed the subject, while stroking Johnny's arm. Ella didn't think she could stand it for a moment longer. She *knew* that Johnny Cooper could have any woman he wanted, and he didn't need to show off in front of her to prove it. She excused herself as graciously as she could, and slinked back to the swimming pool, where Nash was checking his emails on his iPhone.

'Had enough of the fun people?' he asked her bluntly, as Ella sat down dejectedly.

She nodded, but the whole time her eyes were on Johnny. Ansku was draped all over him, and yet again Ella felt like a stupid little girl. She'd developed a major crush on someone who flirted with everyone and clearly loved playing the field. With models. Her eyes smarted with tears she refused to let fall.

'I think you've worked hard enough for one evening,' Nash said, as he put his phone down. 'I think it's time to call it a night.'

Ella couldn't think of anything she'd like more. 'I'd love that,' she replied gratefully, and she let Nash guide her inside so they could organise a car to take her back to Surrey.

But Johnny Cooper had other plans.

'Nash, man, I'd like you to meet Ansku,' he called out, and Nash and Ella turned to see Johnny and his model friend standing behind them. Ansku was smiling her happy, perfect model smile, and Ella felt her heart sink. She didn't have anything against Ansku, but she didn't want to be near her or Johnny. It was obvious they'd be going home together, and the thought of it physically hurt. She didn't think she'd *ever* been this jealous, and she was struggling to hide it.

'Hi, I'm Nash Barnwell,' Nash said politely, as he helped Ella into her simple Balmain leather jacket. 'And while it's great to meet you, Ansku, I'm afraid we're leaving.'

Ansku pouted. 'But I've been waiting to talk to you for like, for ever,' she said in her light Scandinavian accent. 'I wanted to come and meet you by the pool, but Johnny said you were working and I shouldn't interrupt.'

Nash glanced at Johnny, and then back at Ansku. She looked radiant in a black and white Just Cavalli mini dress, and Ella could tell Nash was struggling not to stare at her model-perfect body, her long hair, and her plump lips.

'Why did you want to meet me?' Nash asked with interest. He sounded friendly — friendlier than he'd ever been with her — and Ella could tell he couldn't quite get over how beautiful this model was. She was stunning.

'Because Johnny says you're Ella's manager, and that

you're the best manager in London. I've been looking to talk to someone about taking my career to the next level, and after I talked to Ella about how effortless her career trajectory was, I was hoping we could discuss you applying some of that magic to me.' She looked so eager, and so innocent, that Nash couldn't ignore her.

'I was going to chaperone Ella home,' Nash said, 'but I'd be happy to talk to you. Ella, you can get back to Castle House without me, can't you?'

'Of course I can,' Ella began, in her most dignified tone, but Nash didn't appear to hear her. It seemed that his baby-sitting duties were well and truly over.

'I'll see you to your car,' Johnny added smoothly. 'Just to make sure you get past the photographers, of course.'

He put his hand on Ella's back, and began to steer her away from Nash and Ansku. 'Do you fancy a nightcap?' he whispered in Ella's ear. His breath was hot on her neck, and just that tiny sensation by itself was enough to make her weak at the knees. 'I'd really like to talk to you.'

She knew she shouldn't, but Ella couldn't help herself. Couldn't keep hiding it. She was very quickly becoming addicted to Johnny Cooper.

*Chapter Nine*

Johnny took Ella's hand, and he led her through the beautiful rooftop gardens until they reached the balcony overlooking the city. The windows in the skyscrapers glittered like lemon quartz and citrine, and the glowing London sky burned amber. It was another beautiful night in the city, but Ella barely noticed it. Electricity was in the air, and Johnny's hand was enveloping hers. It was all she could think about.

She was on fire.

'I'll see you to your car soon, I promise, but I have to talk to you,' Johnny began, and Ella was surprised to hear him sound so nervous. Johnny was normally so cocky, so sure of himself.

'What's this about?' she asked in a low voice as she gazed up at him. But Johnny didn't say anything. He simply stared at her.

'We both know what this is about,' he said eventually, and he squeezed Ella's hand. 'It's been bubbling over from the very first moment I met you, and I can't stand it any more. I can't keep pretending.'

Ella held her breath. She'd fantasised about this moment every time she lay in bed feeling frustrated and desperate for his touch, but now it was here — now Johnny Cooper had told her he wanted her as much as she wanted him — she didn't know what to say. She just knew she couldn't let down Danny. She couldn't betray her marriage, and the promises she'd made to him on her wedding day.

'I don't know what you're talking about,' Ella murmured. 'I think you've got the wrong idea about me. I don't feel anything at all for you. Not like that.'

Johnny squeezed her hand tighter. 'I *know* you like me,' he pressed. 'You've liked me from the moment you met me. I know you have. I could see it in your gorgeous violet eyes.'

Ella pulled her hand away. 'You didn't see anything in my eyes, because I don't like you,' she protested, but she knew she didn't sound very convincing. She never had been a very good liar. 'I'm married, and I love my husband.'

'But does he do it for you? Do you dream of being with him every minute of every day? Do you get home and rip his clothes off, just so you can press your soft body against his? Do you lick his skin, do you ache for him, and do you melt when he gazes into your eyes?'

Ella refused to look at him. 'Shut up, Johnny,' she whispered, but Johnny continued.

'Does he stroke you so gently that your whole body lights up in fire? Does he kiss you deeply, or fuck you roughly? And does he make you come harder and longer than you ever have? Because Ella, if he doesn't do all of those things to you — *for* you — he's not the one for you. I am. I want to do all those things to you. And more. So, so much more.'

Johnny's voice was husky with lust, and despite herself,

Ella felt more turned on than she ever had in her life. She was desperate for Johnny. She wanted him. Now.

'He's my husband,' she said, as if those three words could banish her feelings for Johnny.

'But he doesn't love you the right way. He doesn't love you like I could. And I could, you know. I think you're amazing.' Ella heard Johnny's voice crack, and she finally looked up at him. There were tears in his eyes. 'I've never felt this way, and I know you're married, and I know you're not available, but Ella, God. I think we could be so right together. We could be amazing. *Please.*'

Ella felt her hands shake. She wanted Johnny so much, but what would Danny say if he found out? What would Aaron do?

She couldn't do this. She couldn't.

'I'm sorry, but I really can't give you what you want,' Ella said. It was time to get out of there, and fast. 'I'm a married woman, and you and I work together. It just isn't going to happen.'

Ella turned her back on Johnny and began to walk away as fast as her wobbly legs would allow. She'd only managed a few steps when Johnny grabbed her, spun her towards him, and pulled her into a dark corner where she prayed they wouldn't be seen.

'It *is* going to happen, and you know it,' Johnny snarled, and before Ella could react, he kissed her, pushing his lips hard onto hers. His hands trailed down the side of her body, and as they gently touched the sides of her breasts, Ella felt her body wind tighter and tighter in lust.

'I've got a room here,' Johnny whispered, as he ran his hands through Ella's hair, over her bottom, on the side of her face. She no longer cared about Danny, or her marriage, or if anyone could see them. She was lost in Johnny's touch. She was intoxicated.

'Then let's go to it,' Ella murmured, and her violet eyes dilated as they met Johnny's blue ones. They stared at each other for a minute as their hearts raced.

There was no going back.

Ella opened her eyes and briefly wondered where she was. The light in the room was different from the soft, dappled light that streamed through her bedroom windows at Castle House, and she could hear traffic: police cars screeching, lorries growling and car horns honking.

'Morning, beautiful,' Johnny said in a low voice, and Ella turned to him. God, she thought. She had done it. She'd slept with Johnny Cooper. Flashbacks of the night before – of Johnny licking the beads of sweat from her neck as he moved gently inside her, of how she'd arched her back in that exquisite near-pain of orgasm – raced through her mind, and she groaned softly. Ending up in bed with Johnny was obviously a mistake. But wow. What a mistake. She'd never felt like that. Ever.

'I've got to go home,' Ella began, but Johnny cut her off.

'There's no need,' he said with a smile. 'I phoned Nash earlier and he's going to square it with Danny. You've got the day off.'

Ella sat bolt upright. 'You *told* him? You told Nash we slept together?'

Johnny laughed. 'Of course not. I explained that you'd had a bit too much to drink last night, so I got you a room here. And then I said that after you woke up I was planning on taking you for a slap-up breakfast, and that we were going to spend the rest of the day together working out the next show.'

Ella blinked. 'And Nash believed you?'

Johnny curled his lips into a smile, and he slowly moved his warm hand up her thigh. 'Ella Riding, I can be *very* persuasive when I want to be. Haven't you noticed?'

Ella blushed as Johnny's hand rested at the top of her thigh, and she felt her body heating up again.

'But why would we talk about the next *Wonderland* when it's our day off? It doesn't make sense.'

Johnny shrugged, and for the first time Ella noticed just how fit he was. His naked torso was ripped – his pecs and abs were clearly defined, and dark blonde hair trailed from the top of his chest all the way down. He pulled the starched white sheet away from his body, and Ella's eyes feasted on the rest of him: his strong thighs, and his rock-hard cock.

'Who cares about sense when we have each other to play with,' he whispered, and he pulled Ella towards him.

For the first time in a long while Ella didn't give a damn about doing the right thing. She luxuriated in Johnny's body, and gave in to him.

How could she not when he felt so fucking good?

'So what are we doing for the rest of the day?' Ella asked Johnny coyly as they sat in the back of a cab with their sunglasses on. Ella was still in the antique violet and gold Marc Jacobs dress she'd worn during the previous night's show, and despite having a long, hot shower, she was convinced she still reeked of sex and alcohol.

'Well, since you're not really dressed for anything apart from presenting the best new show on the box,' Johnny said in a low voice, 'I thought we could go back to my place and hang out. I've organised a picnic lunch in the garden, and then I thought we could continue where we left off this morning.' His arm, which had been draped casually around the back of Ella's shoulders, dropped down slightly, and his hand began stroking the top of her breast. It turned her on instantly.

'Sounds good to me,' Ella said in a tiny voice, and she realised just how much she'd missed sex. Missed this. Hugs from Danny were one thing, but there was nothing like being wanted so badly by a man. Nothing like hot, melting desire.

God, she'd needed this.

'Then let's get you home, Miss Aldridge,' Johnny whispered, and he kissed her cheek gently.

Ella shut her eyes with pleasure.

Johnny's house was beautiful – it was one of those places where you relaxed and felt instantly at home. The heavy sage green front door of the Victorian townhouse opened into a long hall, and the stripped wooden floor was dotted with richly coloured rugs, expensive antique side-tables, and carefully chosen oil paintings.

Every room Ella walked into surprised her again and again. The living room – which she knew as it had been replicated on *Cooper's Kingdom* – was incredible, and the set on the TV show hadn't done it justice. The brown leather sofas and Jackson Pollock print were exactly the same as the ones on set, but what the programme failed to emulate was the vibe of the room, the atmosphere. The soul.

'I love it in here,' Ella said to Johnny with a smile, as she walked around the room looking at photos of Johnny's family and friends, sniffing the scented candles, and taking in the open fireplace, the sunlight streaming through the windows, and the gentle sound of a clock ticking.

'I do too,' Johnny replied, as he stood behind her and wrapped his arms around her waist. 'It's my favourite room in the house, apart from my bedroom. Want to check it out?'

Johnny led Ella up the stairs, and pulled her into his bedroom. There was a huge bed swathed in deep burgundy silk and purple corduroy cushions, a gold candelabra with black candles on the bronze mantelpiece, and unlike the rest of the house, the room was gloomy. Ella turned to Johnny in surprise.

'Black-out blinds,' he said, as if he'd anticipated Ella's question. She guessed he'd answered it many times before. 'Because of this . . .'

Johnny took a tiny remote from the bedside table, and suddenly the room lit up. There were tiny fairy-lights embedded into the floor and ceiling, and soft reds and oranges beamed down the walls from hidden places in the cornicing. The colours slowly started to change to turquoises and brilliant blues, and Ella gasped. It was like being in a designer hotel.

Johnny pressed another button on his remote, and suddenly a huge glass screen slowly fell from the ceiling. Ella stared at it for a moment as she tried to work out what it was, and quickly realised it was a wall of water, with cascading droplets sliding through the thin glass.

'It's for when I can't sleep,' Johnny admitted with a shrug. 'It helps me to relax. And when I want to watch TV, well . . .' he pressed another button, and instantly the water stopped, and the glass turned into an HD TV. It started playing *A Week in Wonderland*.

Ella's mouth fell open.

'I've never seen anything like that!' she exclaimed, and Johnny pressed pause. The screen showed Ella and Johnny smiling at each other as they discussed Gable Blackwood running to be governor of Florida, and Ella took her eyes away from the screen and focused on the man in front of her. He was so different from how she thought he'd be. His house was a proper home – there was nothing laddish about it – and even though he had enough gadgets in his place to rival the technology in Castle House, he wasn't bragging when he showed them to her. He just enjoyed them, and he wanted Ella to, too. He was becoming more and more likeable, and Ella could feel her addiction to him worsening with every minute that passed.

'Are you hungry?' Johnny asked her softly, and Ella shook her head. Her body was overflowing with luscious adrenaline, and she didn't feel like she could ever eat again.

'That's a shame,' he continued. 'Because I'm starving. You're going to have to work up an appetite.' Johnny pushed Ella onto the bed, held her arms above her head, and slowly unzipped her dress with his teeth so he could gaze at her naked body as he fucked her.

Ella thought she was in paradise.


'So tell me more about your childhood,' Ella asked, as she smeared a piece of Brie onto an oat biscuit and popped it into her mouth. After Johnny had ravished her – and as corny as that sounded, there really were no other words for what he'd been doing to her for the last couple of hours – he'd scooped her up, washed her gently in a luxurious bubble bath, and then dressed her in one of his shirts and some boxer shorts. They'd then gone into the garden, and sat on a soft blanket that had been laid with plates of cheese, fruit, and cold meats by Johnny's housekeeper.

Ella suddenly found she was starving.

'Oh, you know, it's the usual stuff. My parents are great – they live around the corner – and I grew up in Hampstead. I went to a boarding school, and I've never really lived anywhere else. Why would you when you live in the best city in the world?'

'But what about university?' Ella asked. He fascinated her. On screen Johnny Cooper came across as cocky and in love with himself, but in private, he was turning out to be more complex than she expected. She'd fallen for the confident and sexy man, but the person she was talking to now was quite different. He was sweet and lovely and seemed a much nicer person than she could ever have imagined. He was the best bits of Fin, and the funny bits of Danny, all rolled into one gorgeous package. Ella didn't know how she'd failed to realise this before.

'I didn't go,' Johnny said. 'All my mates did, and my parents wanted me to, but it wasn't for me. My mother's worked in theatre all her life, and I thought I wanted to be an actor for years. It was only when I narrated a school play that I realised I didn't want to be known for being lots of different characters. I wanted to be on a stage, and I wanted to be *me*.'

'So that's how you got into TV presenting?'

'That's how I got into it. I started at MTV doing work experience, and then I got to be an assistant, and then, when they did open auditions I got to be a newsreader. I only presented for sixty seconds every hour, but as soon as I started out I realised I'd found my calling. From there it was a step up to children's TV, and then bits and pieces until I got to present that morning TV show, and then onto *Cooper's Kingdom*. Which, as you know, has moved from day-time to prime-time.'

'And now you present *Wonderland* with me.'

'And now I present *Wonderland* with you,' Johnny said, his eyes shining. 'But tell me about you. How did you end up with such an amazing life?'

Ella filled Johnny in on what she'd done from the age of five until the week before, skimming over how much Fin had hurt her – why think about him right now when she was so blissfully happy? – and cutting out most of her relationship with Danny. Normally she'd tell the 'truth', in that they'd met on a beach, had an instant connection, and had fallen in love. But she didn't want to talk about Danny, and she didn't want to lie to Johnny. There was no need for him to know he was gay, or for her to reveal the truth about their marriage. It was none of his business.

'So you're as ambitious as me,' Johnny concluded, after Ella had finished filling him in.

Ella looked at him. 'I suppose when I started up Sweet Dreams you could have called me ambitious, but I'm not any more. When the business went under I lost my drive,' she said.

'Oh, I don't mean ambitious in the conventional sense,' Johnny remarked. 'What I mean is, you've been given this platform in the public eye, and rather than waste it, you're using it. You're working as a stylist on that magazine . . .'

'*Cerise*.'

'And now you're a TV presenter. It's like your marriage has given you the confidence to really push yourself to be a brand. And you're getting great results.'

'Well yes, I suppose,' Ella concluded, after she'd considered it for a moment.

'And that's what I like about you,' Johnny said with a smile. 'You don't know just how amazing you are.'

Ella grinned and lay back on the blanket. The clouds were racing through the blue sky, and she felt relaxed and content. If she could forget about the fact that she was married, and that she should be at home, she really could believe that life was perfect.

'I wish I could stay,' she said sadly, as she pulled out her mobile to see if she had any messages. There were several, all from Danny, asking where she was. 'I wish I didn't have to go home.'

'You don't have to go home, you know,' Johnny said in a matter-of-fact voice. 'You could stay.'

Ella shook her head and tried not to get upset. She'd spent the last twenty-four hours in the company of this man, and had never known anything like it. She'd started off not really liking him and now she'd practically fallen in love with him. She'd had great sex before, but she'd never experienced anything like the pleasures Johnny had shown her. The thought of going back to Castle House, and not being able to just *be* with Johnny was almost too much to bear.

'You could stay here for ever, you know. We could get dressed, find you some beautiful clothes to wear, go out for dinner, get some drinks, go dancing, and stumble home in the early morning.'

Ella smiled. 'I'd love to do that, but my husband is wondering where I am. I need to go home.'

Johnny ignored her. 'And then I'd take you to my bed, have my wicked way with your delicious body, and we'd talk late into the night. The next morning we'd be exhausted, but I'd make love to you, and then we'd go off to our amazing jobs on *Wonderland*. We could help each other with our lines, screw in our dressing rooms before the programme goes out, and we'd never have to leave each other's sides again. We'd be best friends and lovers. We'd be soul mates.'

Soul mates. Best friends. Since she'd met Danny, she'd thought of him as her best friend. Okay, so he had a lover, and you never knew, he might not mind her taking one too, but having sex behind Danny's back was one thing. And talking about being best friends and soul mates was another.

It was like she'd suddenly come out of a magic spell.

'I have to go back,' Ella said crisply. 'I'm married, and I shouldn't be here. Danny must be starting to worry.'

'So reply to his texts, or give him a ring,' Johnny said casually, as he sliced up a white peach. 'Say you're with friends, and you're not going to be home for a couple of days. What will he care, anyway? Isn't he in training for that big match coming up next weekend?'

'I can't. Danny and I are always honest with each other. I shouldn't be doing this to him—'

'But you already *are*,' Johnny stressed. 'You've already done it. You're *doing* it. You're sitting in my garden glowing from what we've been doing all day.'

'And I shouldn't be here.' Ella lowered her eyes and felt a tug of pain from inside her body. She'd always said she'd never have an affair, but right now she was in the middle of one. Her perfect world had been turned upside down and for the first time in ages, she felt like she wasn't in control. That she was at risk of losing her happy ever after.

'Ella, I want you to stay. I've never felt this way about anyone before. I can't let you go.'

Ella felt tears running down her face. Being in bed with Fin – and all her boyfriends before him – had always been good, but she'd never experienced anything like this before. It wasn't just sex. It was animalistic, and something she couldn't restrain. Every inch of her body – inside and out – wanted Johnny's, and no matter what her brain was telling her, it was like her nerve endings couldn't ignore him. She hadn't realised it until Johnny had been inside her, but she wasn't complete without him. It was like he was her missing piece.

'I'm falling in love with you.' Johnny's declaration crashed through Ella's thoughts at exactly the same moment she realised what she'd been experiencing wasn't just passion.

It was love.

And for the first time since Fin had broken her heart, she wasn't scared of it. Suddenly being in love seemed like the easiest, and the best thing in the world.

Or it would have been, if only she wasn't married to someone else.

Ella bit her lip, and pulled her violet eyes away from Johnny's mesmerising blue ones. 'But I'm married,' she said, 'and I can't hurt Danny.'

Johnny reached out and placed his hand on Ella's wrist. 'Forget about Danny. If you leave, you'll hurt *me*.'

Ella was torn, and all she could think to do was to run back home, to her beautiful bedroom in the turret of Castle House, and to have time and space to think.

'I have to leave you right now,' she whispered. 'But it doesn't mean I want to, or I'm not going to see you again like this. I have to think things over.' She caught sight of Johnny's pained expression, and she knew that if she didn't leave now, she never would.

She quickly found her crumpled Marc Jacobs dress in Johnny's bedroom, washed her face of her tears, and then hailed a cab that would take her to the safety of Surrey and her home.

*Chapter Ten*

'Babes, is that you?' Danny called out, as Ella shut the front door to Castle House, dropped her Mulberry Bayswater bag on the floor of the hall, and pulled off her heels. She padded through the house and expected to feel relief that she was at home, but for once the expensive décor and the luxury of the mansion didn't do it for her. Castle House was like a hotel – it was beautiful, but also impersonal. Eventually Ella found her husband slumped in front of the TV watching a recording of the Kingston United vs Manchester City match. As Ella walked in Danny paused the game and looked her up and down with a raised eyebrow.

'Late night?' he asked with a wry smile, and Ella grinned and sat down next to him. She knew her dress was grubby, and that she didn't look as polished as she usually did, but Danny had seen her a lot worse. He'd met her in her scruffy post-Fin clothes, after all.

'Yeah, really late night. Sorry I didn't phone, I had a few too many at the aftershow, and I lost track of time.'

'It's cool. Nash let me know you were safe. But who cares about that . . . I saw the show! Oh my God, you were *amazing*. No wonder you're glowing!'

'Really? You thought I did okay?'

'You were fantastic,' Danny said, and he reached over to Ella to give her a tight hug. 'I was so proud of you. Yves thinks you're a natural.'

Ella's face froze in a smile, and she felt her heart sink in guilt. She'd allowed herself to get caught up in Danny's enthusiasm, and for a moment she'd forgotten reality and believed that she and Danny really were husband and wife, in every sense. But of course they weren't, and they never would be. They were just friends.

'I'm glad you liked it,' Ella replied. 'It was such a shame you couldn't come to the recording. Maybe you can come to the next one?' Ella asked hopefully. If Danny was there, there was a chance Johnny wouldn't try to continue what they'd just started. If that was what she wanted. She just didn't know any more.

Danny sighed. 'It's not that I don't want to come, but . . .' He trailed off, and Ella looked at him closely. His smile seemed fixed, and she could see tension and tiredness in his face.

'My inbox is bulging with emails, and none of them good.'

'Emails?' Ella was confused for a moment, and then she remembered. Sancho Tabora. The blackmail. 'What does the latest one say?'

'The bastard wants five hundred thousand pounds – by next week.'

Ella gasped. 'How much?'

'I know. I don't have that kind of money in my current account, so I'm going to have to pull some strings with the bank so I can get to my savings. But it's not going to be easy.'

Ella sank back into the sofa and stared at Danny. She'd

promised him she'd think of a way to stop the relentless and expensive blackmailing, but she'd been so caught up in her own life, and with her growing feelings for Johnny, that she'd pretty much forgotten what was going on. If Danny didn't pay up there was every chance that Sancho *would* tell the world he was gay. And then it would be game over – for his football career, for their marriage, for everything.

'I thought he'd leave me alone for a bit after I paid the hundred thousand he asked for last time. But he's being relentless, and he's ramping it up. He wants half a million pounds by the end of next week, and who knows what he'll ask for next. One million? Ten? He knows that if I have it I *have* to give it to him. And that if I don't have it, I'll somehow be able to get it.' He buried his head in his hands.

'Maybe it's time to go to the police,' Ella whispered. 'You've kept all the emails he's ever sent you, and they're concrete evidence that he's been blackmailing you for years. He could go to prison, and you'd be left in peace.'

Danny ran his hands through his hair and looked up at Ella. He looked utterly defeated. 'But we've been through this. One whiff of *why* Sancho's blackmailing me, and my secret's out. There are no openly gay footballers in the Premier League, and as far as the players and fans are concerned, it needs to stay that way. It's not accepted. My career would be over and I don't want that. I want to go to the next World Cup. I want to be an England legend.'

'There *must* be a way, there has to be.'

'There isn't. The lawyers are stumped, and even though Aaron's made Sancho countless offers to make him famous in his own right, he isn't playing ball. Why should he when I appear to be a bottomless pit of money?'

Ella put her head on Danny's shoulder. She really didn't know what to say, or what the solution could be.

'What if you challenged Sancho?' she suggested, as she thought out loud. 'What if you told him you *aren't* gay? He can't blackmail you over something that's not true.'

'But I am gay, and he knows I am. My ex-boyfriend told him.'

Ella thought for a moment. 'What if Mike told him he'd lied? Maybe he could say he made it up to impress Sancho, or something like that.'

'We tried that too,' Danny said. 'We tracked him down, asked him to help, and after a fair bit of persuasion Mike agreed to give it a go. Sancho didn't believe it for a second . . .'

Danny trailed off as he looked at Ella properly. Her messy light-brown bob gleamed, her cheeks were flushed, and her violet eyes were shining, despite the slightest hint of dark circles under them. She was picture perfect. She was beautiful.

'You're amazing, you know,' he said eventually, as Ella noticed his eyes trailing over her face. 'I know that a lot of people think you're lovely . . . but not many people realise how smart and loyal you are.'

'I'm not smart,' Ella laughed, as she brushed the compliment away. 'If I was smart I never would have been with Fin, Sweet Dreams would be taking over the cupcake world, and we'd be able to find a way to stop Sancho from blackmailing you.'

'You *are* clever,' Danny smiled. 'Okay, so you might not have managed to get your company off the ground in the middle of a recession, but you have the best instincts of anyone I know. You mustn't beat yourself up about this

Sancho thing; if the lawyers and Aaron can't find a solution there probably isn't one.'

Ella smiled weakly. She'd become used to people telling her she was beautiful, but somehow it meant more when someone said she was clever. She supposed it was because she didn't really believe it herself.

'And I know that our relationship isn't a conventional one, and I know we'll never be lovers or anything like that, but Ella, I love you,' Danny continued, oblivious to how the smile on Ella's face was turning into a frown as the guilt of being with Johnny set in. 'I love you as much as I've ever loved anyone.'

For a brief, awkward moment, Ella didn't know what to do or say. But she came to her senses, and reached for Danny's hand.

'I love you too,' Ella said honestly, and she held his gaze. Danny was one of the best people she knew, and he was her friend. And no matter what, Ella was loyal to her friends and never lied to them.

'But there's something I need to tell you,' she said, as her heart began to race. She took a deep breath, and decided to come clean about what she'd really been doing during the last twenty-four hours.

'It's about Johnny Cooper and me. We're . . . we're having an affair.'

'So . . .' Danny asked with a glint in his eye. 'What does the fabulous Johnny Cooper look like naked?' He reached into a bowl of popcorn on his lap and chucked a couple of kernels over to Ella. She opened her mouth and tried to catch them . . . and missed.

'I'm not telling you that!' Ella exclaimed, as she found the popcorn on the sofa and threw it into her mouth. She'd changed into a fairly loose top and jogging bottoms, and for once she and Danny were having a night in: no managers, nobody to entertain, just them.

It was the perfect antidote to the crazy twenty-four hours she'd just experienced.

'But he's so hot!' Danny enthused, and Ella rolled her eyes.

'Just watch the film!' Ella suggested. 'You're the one that wanted to watch it, and you've barely looked at the TV since we put it on.' But Danny ignored Ella being bossy — he wanted the gossip.

'Look, you can't tell me you're having an affair with Johnny Cooper, and then run off to your bedroom without telling me anything.'

'I didn't run off.'

'You *did* run off, Ella Lucinda Riding.'

'Well, it was only to get changed. And to give you some space so you could get used to the idea.'

Danny chuckled. 'What's there to get used to? My wife's having an affair with a hot TV presenter. It's so cool. Besides, I had a feeling something was going on.'

Ella's eyes widened. 'What?'

'Oh come on, just because I'm gay it doesn't mean I don't notice when there's sexual chemistry. It was so obvious you liked each other at that Putto launch,' Danny continued. 'I knew it was only a matter of time before you got together.'

Ella pulled a face and ate some more popcorn so she had time to think.

'So why didn't you say anything to me?' she asked.

'What would I say?' Danny said patiently. 'That I predicted you and Johnny Cooper were going to have an affair? If I said it out loud there was no way you'd go on *Cooper's Kingdom*, and then you never would have got the presenting gig on *Wonderland*. Aren't you glad I didn't say anything?'

'I suppose so,' Ella said. And then she voiced the question she'd been dreading having to ask. 'Are you sure you don't mind?'

Danny put down the bowl of popcorn and paused the film. He sighed.

'Honestly? I do, a bit. But it's only because I don't want to see you get hurt.'

'How would I get hurt?'

'Babes, you're married to me. You're my wife. If you start a secret relationship with someone you know it can't go anywhere,' he said gently.

'I know that,' Ella said, and she unconsciously stuck her chin out defiantly.

'Do you really?' Danny asked searchingly. 'I don't think you've really thought this through. What happens if you fall in love with Johnny? You couldn't marry him, or live with him. And you couldn't have children with him. Your whole relationship would have to be played out behind closed doors, and you couldn't tell anyone – not even your closest friends or family – about it. Could you live with that?'

Ella heard the words, but she brushed them aside. She couldn't think so far in the future. She'd only slept with Johnny once, and she wasn't willing to think about just how much she liked him.

'The only reason I asked you to marry me was because you said you never wanted another relationship again,' Danny said as softly as he could. 'I know how much Fin hurt you, and I really believed that you didn't want to get involved with another man romantically again.'

'And I don't!' Ella exclaimed, but the moment Danny's green eyes caught hers she realised it wasn't true. It had been true at the time, but she'd been so full of hurt and despair that she couldn't imagine ever being in another relationship again. This whole Johnny Cooper thing had crept up on her, and now she was in an impossible situation. She wanted to be with Johnny so much that her whole body ached, but it wasn't possible. Not unless she left Danny . . . and there was no way she could do that to him. Danny needed her.

'Look,' Danny said, 'I haven't got a problem with you having an affair with Johnny. He's delicious, and it's obvious how much he likes you. But you have to think about what you're getting yourself into, and consider what Johnny could do to you. To us.'

'I *have*—'

'I don't think you have. What if he falls in love with you, and decides he wants to be with you all the time? Could you live with yourself knowing you've hurt him like that? And what would you do if your affair got found out? Your reputation would be ruined, and all the hard work we've done so far to have the "perfect marriage" would be for nothing.'

'You sound like you don't want me to do this,' Ella said sadly.

'Babes, I would never stop you being happy, and if Johnny makes you happy I'm all for it. I know you'd never do anything to intentionally harm our lives, and what we have, but you need to be so careful. You need to consider everything about this relationship with Johnny, and he needs to know the score – that you'll never leave me.'

Danny's words echoed in Ella's mind. She'd made a promise to always be Danny's wife, and that they'd be together through the good times and the bad. Up until now she'd never even considered walking away from the marriage – why would she? She was living her perfect happy ever after – but the moment Danny said those words, Ella wondered if she ever could. If she could ever have a life where she and Johnny could live out a blissfully happy ending.

'How serious is it with Johnny?' Danny asked, interrupting Ella's fantasy. She landed with a thud.

'It's not,' she said slowly, as her heart sank. 'We only got together last night. As far as he's concerned it could just be a one-night stand.'

As Ella said the words out loud pain ripped through her body, but she knew – just knew – that this wasn't a one-night thing for Johnny. He'd said they were soul mates. He said he was falling in love with her. And she believed him.

'Well, that's okay then,' Danny said, satisfied. 'As long as it's just sex, and it's discreet, then it should be okay. We'll have to run it past Aaron and Nash, of course—'

'What!' Ella yelped. 'I'm not running my sex life past Aaron. Or Nash!'

Danny sighed. 'Ella,' he said seriously, 'you have to. It's damage limitation in case something goes wrong. Aaron and Nash need to know what you're up to. It's important. They control all aspects of our lives, and they can help you—'

'I don't want Aaron or Nash to control every bit of my life!' Ella cried out. She felt protective of her new relationship, defensive of having to admit what she was up to, and she was suddenly close to tears. 'What I have with Johnny is nothing to do with you, or with Aaron, and I'm going to keep it that way!'

'But you can't,' Danny said simply. 'When we got married you agreed that you'd have no secrets from any of us. You can't *not* tell Aaron.'

Ella stood up. Popcorn fell onto the floor and she trod it into the carpet. She didn't care.

'I'm not telling anyone about Johnny, and neither are you,' she said furiously. Her eyes were blazing in anger. 'Johnny's part of my *private* life, and I intend for him to stay that way. I've given up all control to be your wife – God, I can't even choose my own outfits – but I'm not giving up control of my relationship with Johnny. Never.'

Ella stormed out of the living room and ran up the stairs to her bedroom, where she threw herself onto her bed and burst into tears.

Johnny tipped the room-service waiter, closed the penthouse door behind him, and then picked Ella up and swung her around the hotel room. 'God, I'm so pleased you agreed to an early dinner before we go to the studio,' he said huskily. 'I don't think I'd have managed to do a run-through and then a whole show without needing to fuck you in the middle of it. It would have been unbearable.'

They were in a suite at the Sanderson Hotel in central London, and to ensure their privacy they'd arrived separately, with large sunglasses masking their faces. While Johnny dealt with room service, Ella had wandered around the room, marvelling at how the entire eighth floor of the hotel had been made into a gigantic suite. There were two bedrooms, both with silver-leaf sleigh beds, the bathroom had a gorgeous steel floor-standing bath, and sheer curtains were draped against glowing glass walls that acted as room dividers.

'I ordered bits and pieces we could share from the restaurant downstairs,' Johnny remarked as he led her into the dining room, and then he grinned as he watched Ella's eyes widen as she lifted the lids off the gleaming silver serving domes. There were noodles with poached lobster, crispy soft-shell crab, papaya and pork belly salad, roasted duck, rib-eye steak skewers . . .

'I don't think I can eat all of this,' Ella said faintly as she took in all the food. It was a Malaysian banquet.

'You don't have to eat any of it,' Johnny smiled, and he raised his eyebrow. Ella immediately felt lust rise up inside her, and she swallowed hard.

'We should eat before we go on air,' she whispered, but Johnny acted like he hadn't heard her. He scooped her up, placed her gently on the bed, and began to undress her as slowly and as carefully as he could.

'We'll eat when I'm ready,' Johnny grumbled, and Ella gave into him. Of course she did. Why else would she have come to the hotel if it wasn't to be close to Johnny again?

An hour later Ella couldn't get enough food. She stood by the table as she devoured the crispy crab, and ripped pieces of steak coated in chilli and sesame from skewers.

'I thought you said you wouldn't be able to eat,' Johnny laughed, and Ella blushed.

'I worked up an appetite,' she admitted as they sat down to their cold dinner. She thought of the picnic they'd had at his house several days earlier, and how spending time in bed with him made her hungry. 'You seem to do that to me.'

'And what else do I do to you?' Johnny asked.

Ella swallowed. 'You make me feel like I've come alive,' she said honestly. 'Like my body is on fire.'

Johnny leant back in his chair. 'You're falling for me,' he said matter-of-factly. 'You try to hide it, but when we're in bed it's obvious.'

'I've never hidden anything with you,' Ella grinned, but she didn't acknowledge what Johnny had just said, didn't confirm how much she liked him. The truth was that she'd been falling for Johnny Cooper from the moment she'd met him. And they both knew it.

'Even though it's cold, this food is amazing,' Ella said, her eyes dancing as she changed the subject.

'Well, make sure you eat enough so you have lots of energy for tonight. I'm really looking forward to doing the show with you later,' Johnny said conversationally, as he picked up a piece of lobster expertly with his chopsticks.

'Me too. It's such a coup that Gable Blackwood's actually agreed to appear tonight by satellite link. Although I agree with the producers – he should only be on for five minutes. It's last week's news.'

'Absolutely,' Johnny said. 'But that's not what I was going on about. I meant I can't wait to stand on live TV while smelling of you. I can't wait for us to be together on camera, and for us to share that same post-coital glow.'

Ella felt her face flushing again. She'd never come so hard, or so fast, as she had just done with Johnny.

'Nobody will be able to tell we've just had sex,' she laughed. 'Or if they can, they won't think we've just done it with each other.'

Johnny raised his eyebrows. 'You read all the pieces in the paper last week about the "obvious chemistry" between us on screen,' he began. 'Maybe people will put two and two together and think we're an item. I almost hope they do.'

Ella put her fork down. 'Johnny, we can't let anybody find out about this. I'm married.'

'Yes, but you don't love him.'

'It's not like that,' she said, and she paused for a moment. 'I love Danny, but our relationship's never been particularly . . . sexual. But he *is* my husband, and I'd never want to hurt him.'

Johnny leant forward. 'So what are you saying?' he asked. He no longer looked relaxed. 'That if it came to it you'd choose Danny over me?'

Ella shut her eyes. She didn't want a fight. Not now. Not with Johnny.

'This is still very new,' she began as diplomatically as she could. 'If we were doing the dating thing we'd only be on our second date this afternoon. But I can't deny my feelings for you. I'm mad about you. I can't stop thinking about you. I think I'm obsessed!' she laughed, and luckily Johnny laughed too.

'I think I am too,' he murmured, and Ella's heart soared. 'I just wish you weren't married.'

Ella sighed. 'I know what you mean,' she said. 'But let's just see how this goes. We need to be sensible about it – the last thing either of us wants is to get found out. It would destroy my marriage, and our reputations.'

'You're right,' Johnny said, as his eyes flashed with something she couldn't quite work out. 'The last thing we want is for this to end up in the press.'

*Chapter Eleven*

Ella took a sip of her champagne, watched the lush French countryside whizz by, and tried as hard as she could to get the wide grin on her face under control.

She didn't normally get excited about seeing fields – especially ones that looked exactly like the patchwork of green and brown that surrounded Castle House – but this time she couldn't help it. Every time she looked out of the train window and caught sight of the farms and tiny towns, a jolt of electricity rushed through her. They were in France! She and Johnny had two carefree days of being anonymous ahead of them . . . and in one of the most romantic cities in the world. Okay, so they had to play it cool right now because they were in a public place and could be caught out, but every time Ella looked at Johnny she felt herself get a little bit more turned on. She couldn't wait to get to the hotel so she could be alone with him.

'Have you been to Paris before?' Johnny asked Ella as he watched her gazing out of the window. The setting sun streamed through the glass of the Eurostar train, and as it caught her face her eyes sparkled and her light brown hair shone like spun gold.

'Only once, with Fin,' Ella replied, as she remembered

the 'romantic weekend' her ex-boyfriend had taken her on. They'd flown to Charles de Gaulle airport from London, and by the time they'd found a cab and endured a two-hour drive to the hotel, they'd both become irritable. The hotel, which had looked so good on the internet, was dirty, tired, and on the outskirts of the city, and the only place they'd managed to find dinner that night was a twenty-four-hour supermarket. They'd spent their first night in Paris eating crisps and dry pieces of sausage in their hotel room, and the only programmes they could find on the TV were in French.

The weekend had got worse. While Ella was looking at a map on the Metro a homeless man had rubbed his filthy hands over her ass, and none of the shops that she'd wanted to go to were open. Wine was expensive, waiters pretended not to understand Fin's French, and the whole thing had been a disaster. They'd not even managed to have sex.

'It wasn't the best weekend away I've ever had,' Ella admitted, and as she thought of Fin she unintentionally compared him with Johnny. They were completely different.

'So you haven't experienced the pleasures of Paris properly? Good. I want to be the one to show you my favourite city in the world.'

At Paris Nord station they got into a chauffeur-driven car, and as they settled into the leather seats Ella expected Johnny to wrap his arms around her, or to rest his hand on her bare thigh. Instead he looked out of the tinted window and kept his face expressionless. Ella felt her heart sink – she'd expected Johnny to at least kiss her as soon as they had some privacy – but she told herself not to read too much into it. After ten long agonising minutes of being ignored, Johnny turned to her, and his ice-blue eyes pierced hers.

'You want me, don't you,' he stated simply, and the corners of his mouth turned up in a small, cruel grin. Johnny let his eyes roam across her body, and Ella felt his gaze on her skin, as if it was penetrating the simple cotton Aubin & Wills dress she was wearing. She squirmed, and Johnny laughed out loud. 'Ella, you're so obvious.' His tone almost sounded like he pitied her.

Without saying a word Johnny raised the partition between them and the driver, and then he pulled Ella onto his lap so she was facing him. There was a delicious moment of nothingness, and when Ella could stand it no longer she scrabbled at Johnny. Her hands ran across his hard, muscular body, but when she leaned in to kiss him Johnny restrained her two hands with his one, and tilted her head back with the other.

'Easy now,' he said softly, and Ella moaned in desperation. Johnny took his hand away from Ella's chin, and then, with a spiteful smile, he slipped it in between her legs. She was wearing a tiny thong, and as she felt Johnny's finger lightly rub the silk and chiffon she could barely contain herself. But just as Ella thought she was going to lose it, Johnny pulled his hand away, and gently placed her back on the seat next to him.

Without saying another word he lowered the partition, and resumed looking out of the window as they drove along the Champs-Élysées.

By the time they'd got out of the car and through the large glass doors of the George V hotel, Ella could no longer hide her desire. She was lost in an exhilarating mix of desperate longing for Johnny and sweet frustration. She needed him. Now.

'We should go to our room straight away,' Ella murmured in Johnny's ear. 'What if someone spots us here? It's probably the most well-known hotel in Paris.'

Johnny glanced at her, but took his time walking around the art deco foyer. Every so often he stopped and marvelled at the crystal chandelier, or gazed at the huge flower arrangement dominating the room. '*Wonderland* isn't broadcast in France,' he said eventually, but he barely looked at her. 'Nobody here knows us; our secret's perfectly safe.'

Ella wasn't convinced, but she was so desperate for Johnny's touch that she didn't really care, and when they were whisked up to the Empire Suite, Ella pushed Johnny onto the huge bed of dark wood and smashed her body against his.

'What's the rush?' Johnny asked in mock surprise, and Ella practically growled at him. 'Is something the matter?'

Tiny beads of sweat had appeared on Ella's body, and she whipped her dress off in one easy movement. Apart from her silk thong she was completely naked, and she stared at Johnny with such need, such hunger, that he couldn't look away.

Ella's hands trembled as she unzipped Johnny's fly. He was harder than she'd ever seen him before, and without giving him another chance to tease and taunt her she pushed her body against his.

As soon as Johnny entered her she came instantly, and then, after a long, lavish hour of sex, she came again.

Afterwards Ella lay on her side, and watched him as he dozed. His dirty blonde hair was messy from where she'd pulled at it, and she could see the beginnings of a love bite on his neck, and on his chest. Johnny shifted slightly in his sleep, and before she knew what was happening, he had flung his arm over her, and pulled her closer to him.

Ella nestled her face against the dark blonde hair on his chest, and as she breathed in the scent of him, she realised she no longer just wanted Johnny. She needed him, and she'd always need this.

When Ella woke up the next morning she found herself alone in the huge, luxurious bed. For a moment panic engulfed her and she wondered if Johnny had left her – what was it about him that made her feel so insecure? – but she could smell coffee from the living room, and realised that Johnny had ordered breakfast.

'I wasn't sure what you'd like, so I ordered practically everything,' Johnny said by way of a greeting, as Ella slunk around the varnished wooden table and gave him a kiss. The door to the terrace was open, and a place at the table had been set so she could see the Eiffel Tower. It was incredible.

'We have waffles, crepes, French toast, cereal, fruit, croissants, pain au chocolat . . .' Johnny continued, as he watched Ella staring at the Eiffel Tower. She'd slipped on a dressing gown, but it couldn't hide the spectacular curves of her body.

'There's so much,' Ella said, as she gazed at all the food. 'We'll never be able to eat it all.'

Johnny put down his paper and laughed. 'I know how hungry you get after you've been in bed with me though, and it's been hours since we last ate – especially as we missed dinner.'

Ella sat down and took a bite from a warm, buttery

croissant. It was heavenly. 'God, this is amazing,' she mumbled. She finished it off in minutes, and then reached for another one. 'Will you still love me when I put on a few pounds?' she joked.

Johnny smiled. 'I think you're incapable of putting on weight.'

Ella beamed. 'And that is exactly why I like you. You say all the right things.'

'It's almost like I'm your gay boyfriend,' Johnny joked, and even though she was careful not to react, or to change her expression, Ella felt her blood run to ice. Johnny didn't suspect that Danny was gay, did he?

'Well, if you're not into women I'm afraid our affair is going to have to come to an end. I'm only with you for the way you use your body,' Ella teased back, hoping her voice sounded light and carefree. 'Well, that and all the food you ply me with.'

'There's a reason for all this food, you know. You need lots of energy for the rest of the day.'

Ella laughed. 'You're insatiable. Do you want to go back to bed already?'

Johnny smiled. 'It's tempting . . . but I want to show you Paris first. Eat quickly, and then go and get ready. My favourite parts of the city are waiting to meet you.'

Ella chewed her second croissant and smiled to herself. She had a generous breakfast, a gorgeous man, and a day wandering around a beautiful city. Things really couldn't get any better.

They started the day off at the Musée des Arts Forains.

'This is one of my favourite museums in the whole of Paris,' Johnny explained, as they entered the iron-framed warehouse. 'Of course, the Louvre is the most spectacular, but I think this is one of the most interesting – and fun – museums in the world.'

'What sort of museum is it?' Ella asked. Her French wasn't great, and she'd never heard of it before.

'It's a collection of old fairground rides and attractions,' Johnny explained. His blue eyes were shining, and Ella didn't think she'd ever seen him so excited. He was like a little boy. 'Some of them are even from the nineteenth century.'

As they wandered around Ella could see why Johnny thought the museum was so special, and as she watched him enjoy himself she fell a little bit more in love with him. He danced in the Salon de la Musique as a sculpture chimed and flashed in time with a 1934 Mortier organ, and in the Salon de Venise, Johnny whooped with joy as they took a ride on a gondola carousel.

The whole place had a vintage carnival atmosphere, but after an hour or so Ella began to feel uneasy. The lights dazzled, grotesque funfair faces appeared out of nowhere, and her senses were on overload. It was fantastical, seedy, overtly sexual and fast-paced. She needed to get out. She needed fresh air and reality.

'Can we go?' Ella whispered to Johnny as he examined a chipped statue of a scantily clad dancing woman. 'It's very hot in here.'

'Of course we can,' Johnny said, and he pulled Ella close to him. His smile was warm, but his ice-blue eyes were unreadable.

'I mean, I don't mind staying a bit longer if you want to see more,' Ella said hastily. 'It's just a bit much for me.'

'Don't be silly. I know the collection inside out. Let's move on.' He squeezed Ella's hand, and she squeezed it hard in relief. It felt so . . . dangerous in there, and she much preferred the idea of strolling around the beautiful neo-classical stone buildings, and along the Seine.

'If you'd like some fresh air, how about a trip to the Arc de Triomphe? Have you seen it up close before?' Johnny asked. 'It's like an island in a sea of roads and traffic, but it's absolutely beautiful. I think it's lovelier than Marble Arch.'

They hopped in a cab and made their way to the Arc de Triomphe, and when they got there, Ella could see what he meant. She hadn't realized that it was so ornate.

'The four main sculptures are *Le Départ de 1792*, *Le Triomphe de 1810*, *La Résistance de 1814*, and *La Paix de 1815*,' Johnny explained in an impeccable French accent, and he looked at Ella expectantly. She didn't understand a word of what he'd just said, so she just nodded enthusiastically.

'And my favourite sculpture on the Arc is *La Bataille d'Aboukir* . . . Do you know about it?' he asked, as he led Ella to the south façade to see it. Again, Johnny was incredibly passionate about showing Ella something he loved, and even though things about war bored her, she asked him to tell the story.

'The battle was part of the French invasion of Egypt in 1798,' Johnny began, and Ella did her best to look attentive. Everyone thought Johnny was a bit of a lad, and only interested in women, TV, and more women . . . but this side of Johnny – the intelligent, well-read side – was what she adored.

'The French attacked the Turkish army – who were helping the British liberate Egypt from French rule – and they broke through the first defensive line really quickly. The second line proved to be much harder, but after withdrawing and rethinking what they were doing, the French were victorious.'

'So what is it you like about the sculpture? The art? Or the story behind it?'

'Oh, the story behind it,' Johnny mused. 'It's all about getting what you want. At first it looks easy, and you think you're onto a winner, but then completing the deal may be harder than you anticipate. It's something that I think about a lot when I'm trying to achieve something. It's about not counting your chickens.'

Ella thought for a moment. 'I can see why you like it,' she eventually said. 'You can apply that idea to a lot of things.'

Johnny nodded, and then smirked. 'You have no idea. Anyway, do you want to go to the top of the Arc to take in the views, or would you prefer to go shopping?'

Ella felt her spirits rise. 'Shopping!' she exclaimed, and Johnny laughed. 'I thought as much. Think of it as my reward for you being so good this morning and letting me see two of my favourite places in the city.'

'Of *course* I "let" you go to your favourite bits of Paris,' Ella said indignantly.

Johnny kissed the top of Ella's head. 'I know, but I can tell you weren't as into them as I was. Let's go.'

The rest of the day was spent in a beautiful blur. Ella tried on gorgeous clothes in Chanel and Dior on the Champs Élysées, and then they went to the Marais where they popped into vintage shops and looked at 1950s watches, 1960s sunglasses, and 1970s knee-high boots. Johnny spent an age browsing a jazz record shop, and they both fell in love with a store that sold reissues of furniture and canvases and photos by independent artists.

'I wish I could buy some of this stuff,' Ella whispered, as they stared at some black and white photos of Paris from the 1940s.

'Why don't you?' Johnny asked her. Ella shrugged. She could buy whatever she wanted – she knew that – but she'd never hang any prints of Paris in Castle House. As beautiful as they were they'd always remind her of Johnny, and the life she wanted with him but couldn't have.

'I could buy you a couple?' Ella suggested. 'These would look gorgeous in your bedroom.' She gestured at two prints of a naked woman smoking a cigarette. The photos were taken in the 1960s, and were classically and beautifully French.

'I'm not interested in having anyone naked in my bedroom apart from you,' Johnny said easily. 'But if you like them I'd love to buy them. It can be a reminder of our magical weekend together.'

Ella beamed.

'And maybe,' Johnny continued, 'they'll be on *our* bedroom wall one day. And you and I will be in our huge bed in our huge house, and we'll look at these photos and remember when our love was illicit. When we desperately wanted a future together but couldn't have it.' His voice was still light, but a darkness had fallen over Johnny's face.

'Maybe,' Ella said uncertainly, but the thought of having a future where she and Johnny lived together happily ever after both petrified and delighted her all at once. She wanted it so much, but she was afraid she could never have it.

'Let me buy them,' Johnny said. 'And we'll take one each. I can tell you wouldn't be comfortable putting yours up in your house, but perhaps one day your photo will be reunited with mine. I hope so, anyway.'

Ella didn't know what to say, so she squeezed Johnny's hand and hoped that was enough.


'You're where?' Nash exclaimed. He sounded cross. 'In Paris? God, Ella, why?'

Ella winced at the sound of Nash's voice at the end of the phone. She and Johnny had been swooning over the crème brûlée in Les Deux Magots when her phone had started to ring incessantly. Eventually Ella had glanced at it, and when she saw Nash was trying to speak to her she excused herself.

'The production team suggested Johnny and I come to Paris to do some research for *Wonderland*,' Ella began, the lie catching in her throat. 'So we decided to do it. And I needed a break.'

Nash was silent for a moment. 'Isn't that what researchers are for?' he asked evenly. 'To do the research?'

'Well, yes, but when the opportunity came up I knew I wanted to do it. We're finding out lots about the city; it's amazing.'

'Ella,' Nash began slowly, 'when I couldn't get in touch with you I spoke to Danny, and he was very vague about where you are and what you're doing. Is there something you're not telling me?'

Ella felt her heart beating so fast she thought she might faint. She sat down on a bench and rather than thinking about what she was about to say next, she let her eyes wander across the people walking past. It was a cliché, but Ella couldn't take her eyes off the impeccably dressed women with their tiny dogs, and the handsome, flamboyant men that draped their arms around them. People who lived in Paris really were beautiful.

'I'm having an affair with Johnny Cooper,' Ella admitted, her voice small. 'Danny knows all about it. He was covering for me.'

There was a long pause. 'How long has this been going on?' Nash spat. His voice was spikier than she'd ever heard it.

'Not long,' Ella said. 'But long enough for me to know I'm in over my head. I tried so hard not to get involved, but I couldn't help it. Johnny swept me off my feet.'

'So it's serious?' Nash barked, and Ella cowered. She'd always known that Nash wasn't keen on her, and this confirmed it.

'I think so. But I don't know what to do.'

'The first thing we need to do is talk to Aaron,' Nash said as he furiously went into damage-limitation mode. 'He'll have experience in this sort of thing, and—'

'No!' Ella exclaimed, as she interrupted Nash's train of thought. 'You can't tell Aaron. He'll go ballistic.'

'You do know you're putting me in a difficult position by asking me not to tell my boss about this,' Nash said angrily. 'Tell me what you have against Aaron being told, because if he finds out from someone else he'll be furious.'

Ella paused and watched a couple walk past. They were holding hands and were obviously crazily in love. They reminded her of what she and Johnny were like when they were together.

'I know this might be hard to understand, but Johnny is something exclusive to me. He's a part of my life that isn't controlled by the Riding machine. He represents something personal. Something private. When I'm with him I'm not

"Ella Riding, wife of Danny and slick media personality". I'm just Ella Aldridge. I'm just me. If Aaron knew about this, well . . . He'd try to control it. That's if he even allowed it. And you know what? That's a risk I'm not prepared to take. I don't want anything to ruin what I have with him.'

'And when you say "him" I take it you mean Johnny?' Nash asked wryly.

Ella flushed.

'I hate to be the one to rain on your parade,' Nash spat, 'but what about Danny? Aren't you concerned about ruining what you have with your husband?'

'That's not going to happen,' Ella said with such steely resolve that Nash stared at the phone in surprise. 'I'd never do anything that would ruin my marriage.'

'If the press even gets a tiny sniff of this your marriage will be in trouble. People will question your motives for marrying Danny and label you a gold-digger; they'll wonder why you're fucking around, and journalists will start to dig. They might even uncover Danny's relationship with Yves and that will effectively ruin both men's careers. Is this affair really worth it?'

'Yes,' Ella whispered. 'It really is.'

She knew she was being selfish – and that by marrying Danny she'd agreed to conditions that she was effectively breaking – but she couldn't help herself. She couldn't help the fact she'd fallen hard for someone who wasn't her husband.

'I'm going to talk to Danny about this, right now,' Nash said threateningly, but Ella couldn't say anything. She was too choked up. 'Danny might be okay with you waltzing off to Paris with your lover, but I'm not. He deserves better than that from you.'

'Who was that on the phone earlier?' Johnny asked Ella later that evening as they were lying in bed. Ella had been so exhausted from walking around Paris all day that she'd begged Johnny for some time out, and true to his word, Johnny hadn't even tried to have sex with her. Instead he'd scooped her up in his arms, and let her doze on his chest.

'When?' Ella asked sleepily. She didn't think life could get much better than this. She wanted to stay in Johnny's arms for ever.

'When we were in Les Deux Magots,' Johnny said gently, and Ella sat bolt upright. She'd almost forgotten that she'd told Nash about her affair.

'It was Nash,' Ella replied quietly, and she shifted slightly and sunk back into the softest pillow she'd ever rested on. 'He wanted to know where I was. And who was with me.'

Johnny raised an eyebrow. 'So what did you tell him?'

'I told him about us,' Ella said simply. 'I had to.'

Johnny pulled Ella towards him and kissed her on top of her head. 'And what did he say?'

'What could he say? He's never really liked me, and I think I've made him hate me even more. He's concerned that if news of our relationship gets out that I'll ruin my marriage to Danny for ever, and it will reflect badly on him.'

Johnny held Ella tightly. 'But it can't be a great marriage if you're here with me,' he said. 'Isn't it already ruined?'

Ella shut her eyes. How could she explain her relationship with Danny without giving away his secrets?

'What I have with Danny is special,' she began slowly. 'We have a great marriage, but we don't have sex that much.'

'So, what, if you had more sex with your husband I'd be out of the picture?' Johnny asked. His voice was tense.

'No!' Ella exclaimed. 'What I mean is I don't feel that way about him. I love him, but it's like the sort of love you have for a brother. There's no passion, no extremes. There's no spark. Not like what I have with you. I've never had anything like this with anyone.'

'Not even with Fin?' Johnny asked quietly, and Ella struggled to contain her surprise at how insecure he was being.

'Not even with Fin,' she confirmed.

'So leave him,' Johnny said simply. 'You don't have the feelings for Danny that you have for me, so you should leave him. Be with me. Let's make a home and put our 1960s naked girl photos on our bedroom wall.'

'I can't,' Ella replied, and it physically hurt to get the words out. 'I promised Danny a marriage, and I can't leave him.'

Johnny leapt out of bed. 'You're not making sense,' he said angrily, and for the first time Ella could see a flash of frustration in his blue eyes that wasn't sexual. 'You don't love him. Not like you love me.'

Silence hung in the air, and Ella drew her knees up to her chest under the expensive sheets of the bed.

'I *do* love you,' she admitted. 'I love you more than I've ever loved anyone. But I can't leave my husband. Not yet.'

Johnny looked torn. 'So what am I meant to do?'

'Wait for me?' Ella asked in a small voice. 'Danny isn't my happy ever after – you are. I'm just not in a position to be there yet.'

Johnny sighed and sat down on the bed again. He put his

arms around Ella and kissed the tears that had begun to run down her face.

'I'll wait for you for ever, princess. Of course I will. You're everything to me, my whole world, and hopefully my future, too.' Johnny's ice-blue eyes began to well up in tears, and Ella clung to him. 'I'm so in love with you,' he said huskily. 'You're incredible. You're the one.'

'You're the one too,' Ella said honestly. Not only did she believe it, but she felt it, too. She felt it with her whole body. Johnny was her soul mate.

'I've had the most perfect weekend with you,' Johnny whispered. 'I want you to remember this weekend for ever. And know that if you left Danny for me, our life would be as amazing as this all the time.'

Ella choked back her tears. This really had been the best weekend of her life.

So long as she had Johnny in her life, everything would be perfect. He was her Prince Charming. Her all.

*Chapter Twelve*

The mid-morning sun was streaming through the window of the Empire Suite at the Georges V. Ella and Johnny had woken up and had long and luxurious sex, and after a decadent bubble bath and a lazy breakfast, they decided to hit the streets of Paris again.

'What shall we do today?' Ella asked Johnny as she gazed in the mirror and applied a touch of mascara. She didn't bother with any other make-up – why would she? She was glowing.

'Whatever you want, sweetheart,' Johnny replied absently. He'd been standing on the balcony taking in the view, but he didn't seem very relaxed.

'Perhaps another museum?' Ella suggested. 'Or a gallery?'

Johnny shrugged – he was fidgeting, and he appeared distracted. Ella walked over to him, wrapped her slender arms around his broad back, and rested her head on his shoulder. As soon as she began to kiss his neck she felt his muscles relax.

'Is something the matter?' Ella asked.

Johnny turned to face her and grinned. It was that sexy, wolfish smile that got her every time.

'I'm just sad today's our last day of being together like

this,' he admitted. Despite his smile his cold blue eyes were downcast, and Ella knew he was struggling with reality: they were together now, but soon they'd have to go back home. She'd return to Castle House and her perfect, footballer's-wife life, and he'd go back to Hampstead to rattle around by himself. She could see why he felt wretched.

'But I don't want to ruin it by being miserable,' Johnny continued. 'Everything's perfect – and today's going to be great, even better than yesterday.'

Ella smiled tenderly at him. 'So shall we go?'

Johnny looked Ella up and down appraisingly. She was wearing a black lace Stella McCartney dress that clung to every curve, and bow-embellished Miu Miu flats. She looked gorgeous.

'Let's go.'

Johnny took her hand, and they strolled into the lift laughing and talking quietly to each other. As the lift glided from the eighth floor downwards they started to kiss, and they were so lost in each other that they barely noticed when the doors to the lift opened up in the foyer. Ella laughed and tried not to blush as a couple of American tourists caught them in action, and she practically skipped along the polished marble floor as they crossed the foyer. When they reached the doorman he greeted them with a warm smile, and Ella didn't think life could be more complete than what she was experiencing right here, and right now.

Johnny took Ella's hand again, and he was just telling her how much he'd love to fuck her in the serene Jardin des Tuileries, when—

Flash! Flash! Flash!

For a moment Ella didn't know what was going on, and

her first thought was that lightning was crashing down on them. But then she heard her name being called, and as she squinted through the lights, she saw them: paparazzi, half hidden behind the carefully pruned bushes that divided Avenue George V in two.

'Ella! Ella, over here!'

'Johnny! How long have you been poking your co-star?'

'Ella! Does Danny know you're cheating on him?'

'Ella! Don't footballers do it for you any more?'

'Ella! Ella! Ella!'

They both froze in the lights, and then Johnny sprang into action. He dropped Ella's hand, spun her around and pushed her back into the hotel.

'Oh my God,' Ella whispered, as they rushed back to the lift and to the safety of their suite. 'How do they know?'

'Know?' Johnny said. He looked as shocked as she was.

'Know that we're having an *affair*,' Ella practically yelled.

Johnny sat on the edge of the bed and ran his hands through his hair.

'We were holding hands,' Johnny said simply. 'If we weren't having an affair I doubt we'd be doing that.'

Ella slumped on the floor and burst into tears.

'Oh my God,' she cried again. 'This is so awful. I knew we shouldn't have stayed here; I knew it was too open, too obvious . . .'

Johnny kneeled in front of her.

'Shh, Princess. Shh. It will be okay. It might not be okay for a day or two, but it will be okay.'

Ella shook her head. 'It's never going to be okay. Everyone's going to know I've been cheating on Danny. My reputation is ruined.'

Johnny stroked her hair quietly until her tears ran out.

'I promised him,' Ella moaned. 'I promised Danny I wouldn't get caught out, but I have. I've fucking ruined everything.'

Ella began sobbing in earnest, and there were no words that could rescue her from her desolation. No words that could comfort her. Johnny sat with her for half an hour, and then, when she'd calmed down, he lifted her up, put her in the bed, and kissed her all over her body.


'This is so fucking bad, you have no fucking idea!' Aaron roared the next day, as Ella and Danny sat very still, and very upright in their seats in the drawing room of Castle House. 'You stupid fucking whore!'

'Aaron, seriously, I'm as angry as you, but there's no need for language like that.'

'Oh no, posh boy?' Aaron spat at Nash. 'You fucking tell me what language is appropriate when *your* client goes and messes up the biggest football brand in the UK at the moment. Do you have any shitting idea how much money I stand to lose because of this?'

Aaron paced the room, not caring if pieces of furniture got in his way or felt the wrath of his kicks. What use were Hepplewhite cabinets or a Chippendale chairs when your clients couldn't even keep their knickers on? That's if they even *wore* knickers. Aaron wasn't sure Ella did.

'There's no proof that Ella's having an affair,' Nash said calmly, and Ella looked at him in surprise. Was he on her side? 'All the newspapers have are photos of Ella and Johnny holding hands. It could be seen as a friendly thing. Or we could say that Ella hurt her foot and Johnny was helping her. There are a million ways we can spin this.'

'Don't give me that,' Aaron yelled. 'They're having an affair and the sexual tension in that photo is bloody obvious. What were you even *doing* in Paris?' He spun and turned on Ella. His black hair stuck to his sweaty forehead, and he looked like a thug. She tried not to shrink in her seat, but it was hard not to.

'Having sex,' Ella said as honestly as she could. But as soon as it left her mouth she knew it was the wrong thing to say. It had sounded glib. Like she didn't care.

'Having sex?' Aaron screamed. 'We didn't give you this lifestyle, these designer clothes, these jobs, so you can have fucking sex with a two-bit TV presenter. You're here for one reason only – to be the best footballer's wife you can be. And now you're nothing. *Nothing*. And you could take down Danny with this. Is that what you want? You stupid little cow.'

'I'm sure it will all be okay,' Danny piped in, but Aaron turned on him too.

'Oh what do you know? All you know about is playing football. You know fuck all. You're useless, the lot of you.'

'Aaron,' Nash said firmly. 'I really think you should calm down and think about the situation. Yes, it looks bad, but there's no proof about what Ella's been getting up to, and we can sort this out. We can sue.'

'How can we sue if the papers are right?' Aaron bellowed. 'She's been fucking him! She just bloody admitted it!'

'Can you please stop talking about me like I'm a hooker,' Ella said, her voice wobbly. 'I know I've messed up, but like Nash said, there has to be a way out of this.'

Aaron eyed Ella for a moment. Even though this was the darkest moment of his career, and he hated Ella with a passion that he hadn't known existed, he was still struck by how lovely she was. She was dressed in a simple cream Fendi dress, and despite her face being pale and her hair hanging limply, Ella exuded glamour and natural beauty.

'A way out of this? Says who?' Aaron remarked, as he narrowed his eyes. 'Says Little Miss Slut, here?'

'Really, that's enough!' Nash said, and he stood up. 'Aaron, you're obviously upset, but insulting Ella is not going to help. I suggest you go outside and get a breather, and we'll talk about this when you're calm.'

'Are you telling me what to do?' Aaron said in a low voice, as he squared up to Nash. Nash was big and burly, but he was nothing compared to Aaron, who'd grown up in the boxing rings of the East End of London.

'I am,' Nash replied calmly, and there was a moment's pause as both men eyed each other. Ella held her breath, and then Aaron backed down.

'I'm not fucking happy about this,' Aaron muttered, and he stormed out of the drawing room and slammed the door behind him.

Ella, Nash and Danny all breathed a sigh of relief.

'Oh shit,' Ella said, as she massaged her temples and shut her eyes. She slumped back on the Chippendale chair and dug her bare feet into the Oriental rug. 'I've really messed up, haven't I?'

'Well, yes, you have,' Nash said, his eyes flashing with restrained anger.

'What are our options?' Danny asked calmly, and Ella looked at him properly for the first time since she'd arrived back from Paris. He looked pale and drawn, and Ella felt a pang of regret. She'd hurt him.

'First of all, we can issue a statement saying that Ella

and Johnny are just friends, and that they were in Paris for research purposes,' Nash began. 'Although I'm not sure how that will wash with the press. They're not likely to believe it.'

'So what else can we do?'

'We can get an injunction out, which will effectively stop the papers and magazines from writing about the affair, but if we do that it's almost like admitting guilt. And it won't stop the rumours on the web.'

Ella rubbed at her eyes. She was trying very hard not to cry and to stay strong, but she still couldn't quite believe this was happening. She couldn't believe that this was the consequence of her falling in love.

'We can admit the affair, of course,' Nash continued. 'We can say Johnny seduced Ella, and that it was a one-off moment of weakness on her part. Make him out to be the bad guy—'

'No!' Ella yelled. 'We can't do that. This isn't just his fault.'

'Or we can do nothing. We can say nothing, you can put on a united front, and it can be business as usual. It's worked for footballers in the past when they've been caught in difficult situations, and it could work again.'

'I don't know what's for the best,' Danny mumbled. 'Everyone thinks Ella's cheated on me. What if they start digging into our relationship? What if they discover the truth? That's the last thing I want.'

'If we put out an injunction, journalists will definitely start examining you both a lot more closely. They'll want to know what it is you're hiding.'

'So we won't do that,' Danny said. 'And I don't think we should admit the affair either. It reflects badly on me. Like I'm not a real man. Like I can't keep my wife happy.'

'Agreed,' Nash said. 'So I suggest that we put out a statement saying that Ella and Johnny are just friends, and that they were in Paris for work purposes. We sit tight, say nothing else, and in a couple of weeks you should both go out to a very public event and put on a show of unity.'

'That won't be hard,' Ella said, as she took Danny's hand and kissed it. She felt terrible for the pain she was causing him.

'Then that's what we'll do,' Danny said. His jaw was set, and his face was grim. Ella could hardly stand to look at him. Instead, she turned to Nash.

'Thank you for restraining Aaron,' she said quietly. 'I really appreciated it.'

Nash glared at her, and there was a pause, as if he was trying to work out what to say. 'I wasn't doing it for you. I was doing it for Danny.'

'IS ELLA RIDING JOHNNY? EXPLOSIVE NEW PICS!' splashed the *Daily World*, as they ran a photo of Ella and Johnny's first kiss on the rooftop of Shoreditch House.

'HAS JOHNNY COME LATELY, ELLA?' screamed the *Sun*, as their photo showed Ella and Johnny leaving the roof to go to Johnny's room.

'WILL RIDINGS SPLIT OVER KISS PHOTOS?' asked the *Daily Mail*, as they led on a photo of Ella and Johnny leaving the members' club the next morning. They were clutching at each other and kissing desperately, and there was no doubting what had happened the night before.

Each newspaper carried five or six crystal-clear photographs of Ella and Johnny kissing on the roof of Shoreditch House at the *Wonderland* aftershow party. In the photos the sexual tension between Ella and Johnny was obvious, and nothing the Ridings could say or do could hide what had happened that night. This wasn't a friendly peck on the cheek between two celebrating colleagues. This was lust, pure and simple.

It made the sober statement released the previous day — one that claimed that an affair between Ella and Johnny was nonsense — laughable. They'd been busted, and there was nothing they could do about it.

'The paparazzi are still by the gate,' Danny said wearily as he walked into Ella's bedroom. It was midday, but she was still wrapped up in her cotton sheets, and her cream silk curtains were still closed. Despite the room feeling stuffy and hot, it didn't even cross Danny's mind to draw them or open the window to let in fresh air. Ella was in exile.

'I'm sorry,' Ella said in a tiny voice. She looked pale, and there were heavy black shadows under her eyes. 'I didn't mean for any of this to happen. You know I didn't.'

Danny didn't know what to say. His first instinct was to hug her, to tell her that everything would be okay — but he couldn't. She'd fucked up in a massive way, and there was no getting away from it.

'I have to go to the training ground,' he said stiffly. 'If you leave the house, make sure you get some protection against the paparazzi. There's about twenty of them out there, and they're desperate for some shots.'

'I'm not going anywhere,' Ella said sadly. And it was true, she wasn't. Aaron had overridden Nash's authority and banned her from leaving the house until the fuss died down. For the first time ever Aaron's rules didn't seem suffocating. She had no desire to get out of bed, and the thought of seeing anyone but Johnny filled her with dread.

Johnny.

Just thinking his name made her ache for him, but Aaron had taken her mobile, unplugged all the landlines in Castle House, and even taken her laptop. There was no way to get in touch with him.

'It's for your own good,' he'd said gruffly the day before at one of their twice-daily crisis management meetings. 'It's just for a week or so, until all this dies down. You never know, your phone or email may have been hacked by a red-top – which would explain how they found out you were screwing around – and the last thing we need is fuel being added to this fucking fire.'

Ella hadn't the strength to argue with him.

'But what about work?' she'd asked. Nash and Aaron had looked at each other uncomfortably.

'Ella, the producers of *A Week in Wonderland* have decided that it's best you don't return to the show,' Nash said evenly.

Ella's mouth had dropped open. 'What?' she'd whispered. 'Why?'

'Because you've *been screwing around*!' Aaron had roared, as he lost his patience. 'No TV show wants to be associated with you. Your reputation's gone to the dogs, and the programme makers think you're a bad influence and people will deliberately turn over if they see your stupid little face. They've drafted in Daniella Davies – she's going to be co-presenting with Johnny.'

Tears had slid down Ella's face. It didn't seem fair that Johnny could keep his job, yet she'd been quickly sacked. 'What about *Cerise*?' she'd asked. She hadn't really wanted to know the answer, but she'd hit rock bottom, and she'd thought that she might as well get the inevitable over with.

'The editor, Lucy, sent me an email saying that they don't need your services at the moment, but when they do they'll be in touch,' Nash had said as delicately as he could.

Ella had just nodded sadly, and walked slowly up to her bedroom and shut the door. Her pale-pink bedroom was impersonal, but for once she didn't mind that. It was as empty as her life was, and it seemed appropriate for the state she was in.

Hours later Nash visited. Despite knowing that he hated her, Ella couldn't help but acknowledge how good-looking he was, and how in control he appeared. His longish medium-brown hair had been cut slightly, but his full lips and blue eyes were exactly the same. She wondered briefly what had happened with him and Ansku Tiihonen, the model Johnny had introduced him to at the *Wonderland* aftershow party, and decided it was none of her business.

'We're up shit creek,' Nash announced as he sat on the edge of Ella's bed. He looked uncomfortable to be there. 'SanchosWorld.com has hundreds of photos of you and Johnny together, and Sancho's been selling them to the nationals and making a packet. Like, millions of pounds. I've heard from my contacts on the papers that he's going to leak a collection every other day for the next couple of weeks.'

'But how?' Ella asked. She didn't understand it. 'How did he get those photos in the first place?'

'I don't know,' Nash said as he shook his head. 'He has photos of you in Johnny's garden, leaving Johnny's house, and lots of you in Paris. He must have known about your affair right from the start.'

An image of Sancho in the audience of the first

*Wonderland* flashed into Ella's mind, and she groaned. He must have picked up on the sexual tension between her and Johnny from that and got a photographer to trail her. How could she have been so stupid to assume he wasn't up to something?

'He's been blackmailing Danny, you know,' Ella said, and Nash nodded.

'I know. Aaron filled me in when I took the job. And now it looks as though he's found another way to cash in on you and your husband. He's a vindictive little man, isn't he?'

Ella wanted to pull her soft cotton sheets up over her head and to disappear for ever. This was such a mess, and it was all her fault.

'We can try and take out an injunction against Sancho, but I don't think that will do any good,' Nash continued. 'This is unstoppable, and all we can do now is accept that it's happening, and try to ride it out.'

'So there's really nothing we can do?' Ella asked. She felt weak and defeated.

'I don't think so,' Nash said. 'Although . . .'

'What?'

'*We* may be out of ideas, but I was wondering if Johnny had any thoughts about it. I know the press is making him out to be innocent in all of this by suggesting you're a money-grabbing temptress, but he can't be pleased about the unwanted press attention.'

'Johnny will be hating it,' Ella said confidently. Johnny was all about his image, and while he loved having a reputation as a ladies' man, he wouldn't have appreciated being called a home-wrecker, or a pawn in 'Ella's fame-hungry game', as one paper was calling it.

'Exactly. I don't know him very well,' Nash continued, 'but it's worth asking him, isn't it?'

Ella nodded. 'But I can't get in touch with him. Aaron's confiscated my phone and told me I'm not allowed to contact him for a week or so. At least until this dies down, anyway.'

Nash stared at Ella for a moment, and then he slowly pulled his phone out of his Diesel jeans. 'If Aaron knew I was doing this he'd kill me, but what the hell. Give him a ring, see what he thinks. It can't hurt and it could help.'

'What if he hates me?' she mumbled, as she scrolled through Nash's iPhone for Johnny's mobile number. 'What if he thinks this is all my fault?'

Nash gave Ella a long, lingering stare. 'If he thinks that then he's not worth it,' he said eventually. 'I'll give you some privacy,' he said, and he walked towards the bedroom door.

'Thank you,' Ella whispered, and Nash stared at her for a moment.

'I'm just doing my job,' he said expressionlessly, and then he left the room.

As soon as Ella heard the sound of Johnny's voice at the end of the phone she started to shake uncontrollably. He affected her so much . . . and she missed him so much, too. But what if Johnny didn't feel the same way? What if Johnny didn't give her a chance and hung up on her? She wouldn't blame him. Johnny hadn't asked for such intense and negative press coverage, and he had to be hurting as much as she was.

'Johnny . . . it's not Nash, it's me,' she said quietly, as she struggled to find her strength. 'It's Ella.'

There was a long pause, in which Ella's heart jumped into her throat, but as soon as she heard Johnny laugh in delight she knew it was going to be okay. She knew phoning him had been the right thing to do. Of *course* he wouldn't hang up on her. He *loved* her.

'Princess,' Johnny said warmly. 'How are you?'

Ella paused. She hadn't got out of bed for the last couple of days, hadn't washed, and had barely eaten. She wasn't doing too good. 'I'm okay,' she began. 'I'm finding it a bit tough, but I'm hanging on in there.'

'Good, good!' Johnny remarked breezily. 'Can you believe all this coverage? This is the biggest story of the year. I can't get my head around it!'

Ella blinked. Johnny sounded . . . happy. But he couldn't be happy about what was going on. Could he?

'I'm so sorry,' Ella began. 'We think we know who's behind all the photos that keep appearing, and it sounds like there's more to come. I think they even managed to get shots of us in your garden.'

Johnny was silent for a moment. 'Well, it's not the best thing to happen to our careers, but there's no harm done, is there,' he said. 'It's not like it wasn't going to come out eventually.'

Ella was stunned. 'Your career may be okay, but I've been sacked from *Wonderland* and *Cerise*. My reputation is in tatters, and Danny's desperately unhappy.'

'Yes, I'm sorry about that,' Johnny said. 'But you need to think about the positives. This way you can leave that sham of a marriage.' He sounded upbeat and buoyant. He sounded the complete opposite of how Ella felt. She didn't understand it.

'I can't leave Danny now,' Ella croaked. 'There's no way I could do that to him.'

'Why not?' Johnny asked easily. 'You told me you don't love him like you should – why stay with him?'

Ella shook her head. 'Because he's my *husband*,' she stressed. She knew it sounded lame, but what else could she say? That she'd promised to stay with him for ever so the public would never find out their new favourite striker since Rooney was gay?

'Well, it's your call,' Johnny said. 'Now, is there anything else? It's just I'm on set and Dani and I need to run through our lines.'

Ella concentrated very hard on ignoring the pain that was rippling through her body. Johnny didn't mean to sound so abrupt, so dismissive of what she was going through. He was busy, and even though he wasn't saying anything, he was clearly pissed off about the press coverage and that was why he was being so . . . weird.

'Nash and I were wondering if you had any thoughts on how we could stop this. How we could spin the story of our affair, or if we could find a way to prevent more photos coming out.'

Johnny paused for a moment, lost in thought. 'No, not really, but you've kind of put me on the spot there. Let me have a think about it, and I'll call you, okay?'

'Okay,' Ella said. 'Aaron's going to get me a new mobile, because he's worried about my voicemail being tapped, so as soon as I have the new number I'll give you a ring. Is that all right?'

'Darling, that's more than all right,' Johnny laughed. 'Bugger, I'd better go. I'll speak to you soon, okay?' he said, and without waiting for a response, he hung up.

It was only after Ella gave Nash his phone back that she realised that the one thing she really needed Johnny to say – that he loved her, and that he'd be there for her – hadn't been said.

*Chapter Thirteen*

Danny was like a caged tiger. Despite living in a home with a cinema, a swimming pool, a games room and a gym, Kingston United's most famous football player was prowling around Castle House doing nothing at all. Except, perhaps, getting more and more wound up. When it all got too much and his resentment reached fever pitch he took his frustration and boredom out on his wife.

'I *still* can't see Yves you know, and it's all your fault,' he said angrily to Ella as they stared at the TV. The final of *America's Hits* was on, but neither of them was enjoying it. They were both too miserable.

Ella bit her lip. 'I'm sorry,' she replied, but she knew voicing her regret wouldn't make Danny feel any better. She'd apologised so many times in the last couple of days that her words had lost their meaning. 'If there's anything I can do—'

'I think you've done enough,' Danny said curtly, and he sighed. 'It's not the end of the world, but shit, it feels like it.'

Ella felt tears spring to her eyes. She didn't think she'd ever cried so much, and she was sick of it: sick of being so wet, so weak. She'd always thought she was strong – she *was* strong, for fuck's sake – but the impact of the photographs Sancho had sold to the press had nearly destroyed her.

Nobody in the country liked Ella Riding any more. She'd started her career in the public eye as a glamorous rising star who was married to one of the most talented footballers in the UK, and now everyone thought badly of her. They thought she was a tramp. A gold-digger. And a cheap wannabe who'd only been after Danny for his fame and fortune.

There were debates on the TV and the radio about whether Danny should leave Ella, and her infidelity had created a storm in the press. Normally it was the footballers who played away. It was never the wives.

'It will get better,' Ella said softly, as she sniffed back the tears. She hoped her words would be of some comfort to her husband, even though they weren't for her. How could they be? Everyone hated her, Danny despised her, and Johnny wasn't taking her calls. Things couldn't get much worse. 'The storm will pass, everything will be back to normal, and then the public will like me again,' she continued. '*You* might like me again.'

'Shit, Ella, do you ever think of anyone but yourself?' Danny said so forcefully that Ella was momentarily stunned. 'To be honest, I don't really care about the public liking you right now. Not only has Aaron banned Yves and I from seeing each other outside of training and matches, we're still not allowed to phone each other. You're not the only person hurting here.'

He ran his hands through his red-brown hair and point-edly stared at the TV. He'd had enough of this, and he just wanted to relax and forget about what was happening. Ella was making it so very difficult though.

'Has Sancho been in touch?' Ella asked in a small voice.

She hadn't wanted to ask, but she knew she had to. It was Sancho who seemed to be behind this mess, and Danny had a direct line to him.

'Will you give it a rest?' Danny snapped. 'I don't want to talk about this any more. Not tonight. Not ever.'

'But—'

'But what? Why do we need to go through this in detail? I've already told you Sancho sent an email thanking us for all the photo opportunities you provided him, and that since he's made millions from the snaps he sold he's decided to leave me alone for a bit.'

Ella looked down at the floor. 'I was just wondering if he'd kept his promise,' she said dejectedly.

'He has,' Danny replied curtly. 'Although it's only been a couple of days and it's too soon to tell. Now if you don't mind I've been looking forward to this final, and I'd appreciate it if you just kept quiet.'

Danny trained his brilliant green eyes on Madison Miller, who looked beautiful in a J. Crew black silk-organza bandeau dress and Burberry heels. Ella envied the dress, but she coveted Madison's career even more. Watching her on *America's Hits* sharply reminded Ella of the buzz of presenting a live TV show, and how it had been taken away from her. Her depression sunk in even deeper. She could have been the next Madison Miller.

But now she was nothing. Her attempt to try something different – to be a TV presenter rather than an entrepreneur – had failed as well, and now she was back where she'd started. She was nobody. Or worse, she was a famous nobody with a bad reputation.

Ella shut her eyes and tried to stay calm, but she couldn't get the image of Sancho sitting in the audience of

*Wonderland* out of her head. Okay, so she shouldn't have had an affair, and shouldn't have allowed herself to fall so deeply for Johnny, but she never would have done it – never would have gone on his show or agreed to present *Wonderland* with him – if she'd known it was going to end up like this. Of course she wouldn't have.

The more Ella thought about it, the angrier she got. It was fair to say that she'd despised Sancho for blackmailing Danny, but since he'd sold the photos of her and Johnny her hatred for him had reached a new level. Danny had always said Sancho was hell bent on getting as much money out of him as possible, but despite all the hundreds of thousands of pounds her husband had given him, Sancho had still gone and done this. He'd seen an opportunity – Ella falling in love – and he'd made the most of her weakness.

Ella pulled her knees up to her chest and ignored the theme music of *America's Hits* as the show went to a commercial break. She was lost in thought. After Fin had cheated on her she thought she'd never be able to fall in love again . . . but she had. And Sancho had no right to make her ashamed of her feelings for Johnny, and he had no right to use them to his own advantage. Whatever happened, Ella wasn't going to be embarrassed of what she'd done. In fact, she was going to feel the reverse, and be proud that she'd opened up to a man again.

The fact that she'd not spoken to Johnny in days, and that he wasn't answering her calls, was neither here nor there.

By taking something so private and special to her and turning it into something that was meant to humiliate her, Sancho had made it personal.

She would never be able to forgive him. One day, Ella thought, she was going to get even.

## ELL OF A RIDE: ELLA CHEATED ON EX FOR DANNY

Exclusive by MATTHEW PARKER, News Editor, *Daily World*

**KINGSTON UNITED** fan Fin Perrault told last night of his anguish when he discovered his fiancée, Ella, had cheated on him with Royals striker Danny Riding.

In revelations that shatter Ella Riding's image even further, Fin told how Ella:

- **BEGGED** to move in with him, but refused to help with the rent;
- **CHATTED** up other men in front of him;
- **CHEATED** on Fin with Danny Riding, whom she met on a holiday in Thailand where she said she was 'going to find herself'.

Fin said: 'Ella is red-hot in bed, but I never thought she'd cheat on me. When I proposed she seemed over the moon, but she soon set her sights on other men. I feel like a fool. I was really taken in by her – she's not as innocent as she makes out.'

### DRINKING

The first time Ella cheated on Fin was with one of his friends, who asked to remain anonymous.

Car mechanic Fin said: 'My mate told me one night that Ella had come on to him, and that she'd said we'd split up. My friend had sex with her, but he was horrified when he found out she'd lied and that we were still together.'

Fin, who lives in London, admitted he was ready to stick the boot in then and there, but Ella begged him to give her a second chance.

'Ella's a gorgeous girl with a great body, and she's hard to resist. She promised she'd never cheat on me again, and I believed her. Then a few weeks later she said she wanted to go on holiday to "find herself". I agreed she could go and even gave her cash for the flights because she didn't have any money. Despite all her millions, she still hasn't paid me back.'

## TROUBLE IN PARADISE

Ella was on a beach in Thailand when she spotted Kingston United star Danny Riding.

'She told me that as soon as she saw Danny she knew he was "the one" and she made her move,' Fin said. 'She knew who he was because he used to be one of my favourite footballers, and she knew he was loaded.'

Sources close to the Ridings reveal how Ella:

- **PRETENDED** how she didn't know who the Kingston United striker was;
- **SEDUCED** Danny Riding by teasing him in skimpy bikinis;
- **MADE LOVE** to him the night they met.

Fin says: 'I've kept my silence all this time, because who wants to admit their bird has left them for a footballer? But now it's time for the whole world to see that Ella is nothing but a user and a gold-digger. I hope Johnny Cooper knows what he's letting himself into.'

**JOHNNY COOPER**'s pal has admitted that Johnny is shocked by the latest revelations about his former co-star and lover. The friend says: 'Johnny really thought he was going to spend the rest of his life with Ella, but now he doesn't know what's going on, or what he's going to do.'

Ella stared at the photos of Fin in the *Daily World* in shock. She couldn't believe he'd gone to a paper and sold them a load of lies . . . and that they'd published them. Just when she thought it couldn't get any worse it did, and she was half furious, half sickened. If she could, she'd jump on a plane and escape somewhere, assume a secret identity, and . . . and . . . she didn't know what. Try and find a way to get back at Sancho and clear her name, or something. She couldn't think straight.

'We could probably sue over this article,' Nash said quietly as he wrapped his large hands around his steaming cup of coffee. 'Clearly none of this is true – and I'm sure we could prove it.'

Ella took a deep breath and tried not to look at the paper again. The photos of Fin doing his best puppy-dog expression were almost too much to bear.

'But we couldn't, could we?' she said, as silent tears ran down her cheeks. 'The only people who could confirm that the reason I went to Thailand was because Fin dumped *me* are all his mates, and he's probably bought their silence. It's hopeless.'

'But you didn't cheat on Fin, did you?'

'Of course not,' Ella sobbed. 'Obviously I didn't cheat on him with Danny, but I never cheated when we were together, either. I loved him, was practically obsessed with him. And I never would have done that to him.'

Ella and Nash stared at each other for a moment, and then Nash stood up, walked around the scrubbed kitchen table, and held Ella in his arms. Ella was so shocked that her tears instantly dried up. Why was Nash suddenly being so nice to her?

'This is hard now, but this is the worst it's going to get,' he murmured quietly, as he wrapped his firm body around Ella's frail one. 'I promise you nothing else bad will happen. It just isn't possible.'

Ella couldn't quite believe that Nash was there for her. He smelt peppery and sweet, of cedar wood and grapefruit, and because it felt like a lifetime ago that someone had touched her and had offered her physical comfort, she allowed herself to sink into Nash's arms.

'But do you think Johnny is really having second thoughts about me?' she asked in a small voice. 'I don't think I could stand it if he wasn't interested in me any more.'

Nash pulled away and stared intently at the *Daily World* again, as he flicked through the four pages the paper had dedicated to Fin's revelations.

'You said he's not returning your calls,' Nash began as professionally as he could, as if he hadn't just been holding her against his chest. 'So I suppose you don't really know how he's feeling. If it was me I'd be feeling quite cut up about this stuff in the paper about you cheating on Fin—'

'It's not true though!' Ella interrupted angrily.

'But Johnny doesn't know that, does he?' Nash replied calmly.

Ella frowned. She couldn't believe that Johnny would think she was a gold-digger, or worse, a girl who made a habit of sleeping around behind people's backs. 'He *knows* me though,' she said. 'He knows I'd never do anything like that.'

Nash raised his eyebrows. 'Ella,' he began delicately.

'Technically you *have* been doing something like that. In everyone's eyes you've been having an affair.'

Ella stared at the plate of biscuits in front of her and pushed it away. She knew she wasn't eating properly, but she didn't care. 'But Johnny said he loves me,' she said softly. 'He knew I wasn't comfortable having an "affair", and he loves me. I know he does.'

'Then he'll phone,' Nash said simply. 'If he loves you as much as he told you he did, he'll get in touch.'

Ella hoped with all her heart that he was right, but she didn't want to think about it any more. She couldn't. It hurt too much.

'Nash . . .' Ella began slowly, 'why are you being so nice to me today? I always thought you hated me.'

Nash sighed and looked away. 'I never hated you. I just . . .' His voice trailed off.

'What?' Ella asked curiously.

'I suppose I didn't respect you. When Aaron told me about your sham marriage to Danny I assumed you were a gold-digger, and were just out for what you could get.'

Ella's mouth dropped open. 'It was never about the money! Or the lifestyle!'

Nash had the decency to look a little bit sheepish. 'I know that now,' he concluded, 'but what was I supposed to think? Why would anyone as lovely and as gorgeous as you decide to enter into a loveless, sexless marriage if not for fame and fortune?'

Ella thought about this. 'So what made you realise that's not who I am? Not what I'm about?' she asked.

'After the phone call I made to you in Paris I had a long chat with Danny. He told me about how close you two were

— that you're best friends — and that you married him to help him.'

'I could have told you that, if you'd just asked.'

Nash nodded. 'I know. I shouldn't have jumped to conclusions. I admit I'm a bit bitter about marriage ever since my wife left me, but despite that, I believe that marriage isn't something to be taken lightly, to be entered into for any reason apart from love.'

'I agree with you, and Danny and I *do* love each other,' Ella said softly. 'It just wasn't the romantic, traditional sort. After Fin, I genuinely believed I'd never fall for another man again. Johnny Cooper was never part of my plans, and I never, ever thought I'd have an affair — even one approved by my gay husband.'

'I know that now. I'm not proud of how I behaved towards you, and I'm sorry. I've not really been there for you, and I want to be. I tried to be professional but you were clearly aware of my personal feelings towards you, and I apologise.'

Nash looked so stiff, and so uncomfortable, that Ella wondered if she should give him a hug like he'd just given to her. Instead she reached out and awkwardly patted his hand.

A week passed, and Johnny hadn't phoned. The damning newspaper articles castigating Ella had died down, Danny was given permission to see Yves in private, and the Ridings' life was starting to get back to normal. Even Aaron's bad mood had eased up.

'Give it another week and it will be time for you and Danny to hit the town,' he said as he towered over Ella. She was fully dressed in a daisy-print Anna Sui mini dress, but she was laying on her bed, not caring what Aaron thought of her or if the linen of her dress creased.

'Oh yeah?' she asked listlessly. 'That will be a load of fun.' Jesus, she thought, she had to snap out of this.

'Yeah,' Aaron replied curtly. 'There's a benefit dinner for some charity or something next week, and you're going. There's a red carpet, photographers, the works. It's a great opportunity for you and Danny to show the world how in love you both are.'

'But we're not in love, are we?' Ella remarked facetiously. She knew she was being difficult, but she couldn't seem to help herself.

'According to the contract you signed, and the vows you made at your wedding, you definitely are.' Aaron's eyes ran over Ella's body. Her face was pale, her normally slender body was doughy, and her skin was dry and spotty. She really did look like shit.

'You've got a week to sort yourself out,' Aaron snapped. Who did this girl think she was, anyway? Victoria Beckham? 'And believe me, girlie, if you don't get your act together I have ways to make you snap back into shape.'

Ella sat up. 'Are you threatening me?' she asked slowly. She knew she should care about being spoken to like this, but for some reason she didn't. She just felt numb.

Aaron moved his face so close to hers that she could see the broken blood vessels around his nose.

'Yes I fucking am . . . and if you don't do what I say, I'll do a lot worse,' he hissed.

Ella blinked, and then laughed. 'Oh, whatever,' she said, and she flopped back down on the bed. For the first time since she'd known him she was not scared of Aaron Kohle, no longer intimidated by his power. She had bigger things to think about, and as soon as Aaron slammed her bedroom door in disgust, Ella picked up her new iPhone. She'd phoned Johnny twice today, and each time she'd left two pleading messages on his voicemail. She didn't know how many times she had to apologise for the press attention, and tell him she wasn't a love-cheat, but she'd do it as many times as it took. Life as Danny Riding's wife was only bearable if she had Johnny.

She couldn't do this without him.

But just as Ella began to dial Johnny's number, there was a knock on her bedroom door. Danny.

'Aaron's really pissed off with you,' he said awkwardly, as he lay down on the bed next to her. It was the first time that they'd ever shared a bed together, and Ella was surprised at how uncomfortable she felt. It was as if Danny was encroaching on her personal space, which was ridiculous. Despite everything, they were friends. Perhaps their friendship had been rocked recently, but they were in this together. They were partners.

'I know,' Ella sighed. 'He's annoyed because he thinks I'm not kowtowing to him any more. But I'll still do everything he asks me to do. Don't worry.'

Danny was silent for a moment, and Ella turned on her side to face him. God, he was sexy. His green eyes sparkled as they caught the light from the window, and he had the faintest shadow of stubble on his strong jaw. For the briefest moment Ella wished that Danny wasn't gay – that he really *could* be her happy ever after – but she knew it was impossible. And that for as long as she lived this life and pretended to be his wife, she'd never find that happy ending.

'It's not you being rude that's bothering him,' Danny eventually said, and Ella's violet eyes widened in surprise.

'No?'

'No. He's worried about you. He thinks you've lost your spark . . . your drive. He doesn't think . . .' Danny's voice trailed off, and Ella sat up.

'He doesn't think what?'

Danny sat up too, and he took Ella's hand in his. He hadn't wanted to hold her hand in a long time, but as soon as her hand was enveloped in his, Ella felt warm love rush through her. It wasn't sexual love, nor was it passionate, but it was love all the same. She'd missed him.

'He doesn't think you want to do this any more. He doesn't think you want to be my wife.'

Ella bit her lip. She'd had a feeling this conversation was coming, but she hadn't expected it to be so soon.

'I don't know what to say,' she began awkwardly. 'Part of me *loves* being your wife. I love spending time with you, love our life, and am so proud of you. It's amazing to be part of your world, and I'm so grateful for the opportunity and for everything you've given me. I know I've messed up, and that you probably don't think I appreciate sharing your life with you, but . . .' Ella's voice disappeared, and she looked down at her sheets.

'But?' Danny pressed gently.

'But I don't know if I can do this any more,' Ella said honestly.

Danny let go of her hand, and as Ella sneaked a look at him she saw he looked deflated. Defeated. She'd never seen him like that.

'Is it because of Johnny Cooper?' he asked quietly. 'I know he can give you passion and excitement, but Ella, you always said that you didn't *want* that. That you didn't trust it, and that you know it doesn't last.'

'But you think it lasts!' Ella exclaimed. 'It's exactly what you and Yves have, and you're not scared of it.'

'That's true,' Danny said slowly. 'But I thought you were different from me. From everyone.'

'I thought I was too,' Ella agreed, and she cast her mind back to how she'd declared that she was never going to have a relationship again. After Fin had broken her heart she'd told herself she was never going to allow herself to fall in love, or to feel that thunderous passion that swept you up completely.

But she had.

And if she could get through this – if she could stand Johnny not returning her calls, or potentially never speaking to her again – she could get through it again. If there had to be a 'next time', if Johnny really didn't want to be with her, she knew that she could risk falling in love again. Because she knew how empty her life felt without that burning infatuation and excitement, and she didn't want a life without it.

A life with Danny meant she couldn't have it, and she knew what she had to do.

'I'm sorry,' Ella said, and as she said it her eyes filled with tears. When she'd married Danny she'd intended to stay with him for ever, and to be his perfect wife, but she couldn't do it any more. 'It's over.'

Danny squeezed Ella's hand tightly, and to her surprise, his eyes filled with tears too.

'I knew it was too good to be true,' he said simply. 'And I don't blame you for your decision. But you know, you don't have to leave. We can work something out, sort out a deal with Johnny so you can be with him too, so you can still see him . . .'

'It wouldn't work,' Ella said sadly. 'I don't want my happy ever after to be part time, and I don't want to see my Prince Charming only when Aaron Kohle says it's okay. I want all-consuming happiness, and to have that I can't be with you any more.'

Danny nodded. 'But what if Johnny doesn't want to be with you any more?' he asked as Ella winced. 'You could stay. You have the perfect life, the perfect house, the perfect clothes . . .'

'And no job, no friends, and a bad reputation that's going to take a while to get over,' Ella finished for him.

'Is it really that bad?' Danny asked softly, and Ella nodded.

'I have to leave and I have to start my life again,' she stated, but as she said it she wondered if it was really possible. Could a fallen wife of a footballer ever make it alone in the big bad world?

'I love you, and I really wanted this to work for *you*,' Ella said. 'But it's time to think about myself, and start my life again.'

'I don't want you to,' Danny whispered. 'Let us try to make you happy.'

Ella shook her head and felt her resolve harden. Whatever happened next, she had to do this. It was time to make it on her own.

## Chapter Fourteen

The papers had been beside themselves when they'd found out that Ella and Danny had separated, and the story splashed on every front page over and over again. It was the story of the year, the biggest scoop ever, and everyone was talking about it. As soon as he could Aaron had spun a tale to his contacts about how Danny had finally kicked her out, and when it made the front page of the *Sun* he taunted her by waving it in her face.

'Danny's kicked you out,' he sneered, as he flung the paper at her. It hit her on the chest, but Ella didn't react, or pick the paper up. She wasn't about to give Aaron the satisfaction.

'You know what that means, don't you?' Aaron continued, as he paced the floor. 'It means you actually *have* to leave now. I own Castle House, and I don't want you in my property any more.'

'Hang on, that's not fair,' Danny interjected, but Aaron wasn't having any of it.

'It's more than fair,' Aaron snapped. '*She* ended your marriage, and according to this paper, you've booted her out. So she needs to go.'

'God, it doesn't have to be so brutal,' Danny said, but Ella interrupted him calmly.

'Danny, it's fine,' she said. 'Aaron's right – it *is* time for me to leave.'

'But you don't have to go immediately,' Danny said firmly. 'Take a couple of days, pack up your clothes and your jewellery, and choose which furniture you want—'

'She's not getting her hands on anything,' Aaron yelled. 'She can walk out of here in a bin bag as far as I'm concerned. We own all of this stuff, and Little Miss Shag-Around isn't having any of it.'

Danny eyed Aaron with a look of distaste. It was the first time Ella had ever seen him look angry with his manager. It impressed her.

'Don't be so stupid,' Danny said. 'If she leaves the house with nothing the papers will find out about it, and I'll end up looking callous. Is that what you want?'

Aaron's expression shifted slightly. 'You're right, Danny-boy. Didn't think of that.' He turned to Ella. 'You can have your clothes and some of your jewellery – the cheap stuff – but you're not having my furniture.'

'That's fine with me,' Ella said as civilly as she could. 'Thank you.'

'Yes, you should be thanking me. You're walking away with thousands of pounds' worth of shit,' Aaron spat. 'And you don't deserve it.'

Ella shrugged, and picked up the newspaper as if to say their conversation was over. It was only when Aaron's back was turned that Danny gave her a friendly wink, and Ella smiled back. He was a decent person, and despite everything, he continued to be on her side. It meant the world to her.

Although Ella felt that the latest front page about her and Danny splitting up was another grey cloud hanging over her, she hoped the silver lining would be a phone call from Johnny. As Ella packed her belongings in the calm of her bedroom in Castle House she kept one eye on her mobile, but despite willing it to ring, it never did. At least, not with a call from Johnny.

'So you've split,' Stacey said as a greeting after Ella answered the phone. She'd wavered for a minute before taking the call – it had been months since she'd spoken to her step-sister, and she wasn't sure if she had the emotional strength to deal with their uncomfortable relationship right now – but Ella knew she had to. However you looked at it, Stacey was a friend. She was family. And even though they'd not spoken for months, Stacey was reaching out to her.

'It's been horrible, Stace,' Ella whispered. 'I didn't mean to, but I fell so hard for Johnny and I've ruined my marriage. Danny's disappointed with me; Johnny won't take my calls; and my life as I know it is over. I need to move out of Castle House, and soon.'

She heard Stacey sigh down the end of the phone, and Ella knew instinctively that even if she wanted to, she couldn't ask to stay with her. She'd neglected their relationship, and they'd barely spoken after she'd married Danny. How could she ask Stacey for anything after the way she'd behaved?

'So what are you going to do? Move in with Mum and Phil?' Phil was Ella's father, who'd married Stacey's mother Margaret a few years after Ella's own mother had passed away.

'I can't,' Ella began. 'Wherever I go there will be people trying to get interviews or photos. They'd trample all over Margaret's flowerbeds and she'd kill me.' Ella was only half-joking, but the truth was she didn't feel like she *could* go back home. Ever since her father had married Margaret all those years ago they'd been distant, and she couldn't remember the last time she'd properly spent any time with them. It had been years.

There had been an awkward silence at the end of the phone, and then Stacey had sighed again. 'You could always stay with me and Jay,' she'd said eventually. 'The sofa's quite comfortable, although I'm not sure there's enough room for all your stuff.' Her voice trailed off, and Ella knew she couldn't accept the offer.

'It's okay,' she'd said softly. 'Nash has offered me his spare room until I work out what I'm going to do.'

'Nash?' Stacey asked in surprise. 'Who's he?'

Ella briefly shut her eyes. There was so much Stacey didn't know, and so much Ella had to fill her in on. But right now she didn't have the energy.

'Aaron Kohle employed him to be my manager, and even though I thought he hated me, he's really come through for me. I wasn't sure about taking up his offer, but I don't think it's a good idea to live alone right now. Not until everything's calmed down.'

Ella didn't mention that she was petrified about being alone late at night, and that she was worried about not having security and protection from the paparazzi and angry Kingston United fans that thought she was the devil incarnate. But apart from taking Nash up on his offer, what could she do? Despite the money Danny had generously given her – for him it was a month's salary, but for her it was a fortune – she didn't want to squander it on big burly bodyguards who could walk down the street with her. And, she thought, she'd look ridiculous – like she thought she was someone special.

It hadn't crossed her mind that Nash would offer her a room in his flat, but when he'd sat her down and said he wanted to help to make up for his previous behaviour, she found herself giving in to his offer. She'd thought that Nash would be angry with her too – after all, if she'd stayed with Danny he would never have been fired – but he was adamant about looking after her, saying that even though he wasn't on the payroll it didn't mean he wasn't concerned.

As Ella thought about how surprising Nash continued to be, she packed her clothes and realised she'd have to sell them – they'd have no place in her new, more simple life. The gorgeous silk Alberta Ferretti dress, the pleated Miu Miu skirt, and the Marc Jacobs bow-top would all have to go, she thought sadly, folding them as carefully as she could. There was no getting away from it: she might not be in urgent need of money *yet*, but she didn't know how quickly she could get a job, and she knew that as beautiful as the clothes were, she wouldn't feel comfortable wearing them again.

It was time to stop playing the part of the footballer's wife, and go back to being herself again. Ella Aldridge had been happy in Topshop and H&M, and she couldn't wait to start wearing that stuff again. In fact, it would be kind of liberating.

'It's not a very big flat, and my spare room is tiny, but hopefully it will help until you work out what you want to do next,' Nash said, as he put Ella's bags down in the hallway and turned to her. Her whole body – and demeanour – looked slumped and exhausted, and Nash eyed her thoughtfully.

'It will be okay, you know,' he murmured, as Ella tried not to cry. She knew she was being slightly pathetic, but suddenly her whole world had changed, and for the first time in ages, she didn't know where she was going or what she'd do next.

'I know,' she sniffed, and she pulled her eyes away from the floor and looked at her new bedroom. Nash wasn't kidding, it was minuscule – smaller than the walk-in wardrobe she'd had in Castle House – but there was something about it that felt homely and secure. Ella realised she was the luckiest girl in the world, even if her love life was in tatters.

Ella still phoned Johnny every day, and every day Johnny refused to take her call, and he often switched his mobile off after the first couple of rings. Ella didn't understand it. She'd seen him on *Wonderland* flirting with Daniella Davies, but the pain of watching him live on screen was too much for her, and she flicked the TV off, prompting a raised eyebrow from Nash.

It was over. She got that. She just didn't understand why.

Later that night Ella couldn't sleep for obsessing over Johnny and Daniella. Was Johnny flirting with her replacement like he had with her? After each show did they go to bed together? Did he make love to Daniella like he used to with her? Ella couldn't stand it. She'd never been the jealous type, despite what Fin had said about her, but right now she couldn't get the image of Johnny and Daniella together out of her mind.

Ella knew she was tormenting herself, and that there was no proof that they were sleeping together, but she couldn't help herself. Her mind went into overdrive as she remembered how Johnny used to make her feel in bed — and she imagined him doing the same things to Daniella: kissing her, stroking her, licking her . . . Ella tossed and turned and grew more agitated, and as she pictured Johnny making Daniella arch her back in orgasm just as she'd once done, she let out a small cry of anguish.

'Hey, are you okay?' Nash said, as he appeared in the doorway to Ella's bedroom. He was naked apart from some fairly tight boxer shorts, but Ella barely noticed his state of undress through her tears.

'I'm fine,' she sniffed, but she knew she couldn't fool Nash. It was impossible.

He walked the few short steps to Ella's single bed, and then awkwardly sat on the edge of it.

'You've had a rough time,' he said stiltedly, as if he felt uncomfortable at the intimate, domestic situation he found himself in. 'It's okay to be upset.'

Ella nodded and as she held his gaze more tears began to fall. Nash looked at her for a moment, and without another word he pulled her into his arms as she wept. As Ella buried her head against Nash's bare chest, she remembered how she used to lay on Johnny, and a fresh wave of pain coursed through her body. She'd never be with Johnny again. It was almost too much to bear.

'Shh, it's okay,' Nash whispered, as he gently stroked Ella's hair. Despite just wearing a vest top and some shorts, her body was warm and her hair was sticky with sweat, but Nash didn't seem to mind. 'Just let it all out, and you'll feel a bit better,' he said, and even though it was late and he needed to get some sleep, he held her until her salty tears stopped falling on his chest.

'You must think I'm stupid,' Ella croaked, as she wiped the last of her tears away.

'I don't think you're stupid at all,' Nash replied. 'You've had your heart broken,' and instead of releasing her, he pulled her even tighter to his body so Ella could feel his toothpaste-scented breath against her neck, and the closeness of his bare skin against hers.

'I think you're perfect, you know,' Nash murmured. 'And Johnny is an idiot. If you were mine I'd never let you go.'

'Really?' Ella said, and she felt Nash nod.

'Really.'

Ella moved her body closer to Nash's, and quietly draped her thigh across his. Their naked legs entwined, and Ella could feel the heat from Nash's body blending with hers. Outside everything was quiet and still, and as Nash moved his hand from her head and began to stroke Ella's upper arm, a sweet sensation of lust rippled through her body.

Ella swallowed hard, and wondered if Nash was feeling the same way and thinking the same thing . . . but of course, he wasn't. Nash was being kind to her out of guilt for his previous behaviour towards her, and he was just comforting her like he'd comfort anyone else. And as for her? Ella was self-aware enough to understand she was on the rebound, and the last thing she wanted was to ruin her friendship with Nash over a misunderstanding of his kindness.

She slowly moved her body away from his, and gently pecked Nash on the cheek.

'Thanks for being there,' she said softly. 'I'm feeling better now.'

Nash held Ella's gaze for the longest moment, and without saying another word he crept back into his bedroom. Exhausted from crying, Ella quickly fell asleep.

As the days went on Ella and Nash began to merge into each other's lives. There was something so easy and comfortable about living with Nash that Ella felt like she'd been in his flat in Hoxton for ever, when in reality it had only been a couple of weeks. They'd wake up, eat breakfast together, and then they'd both begin their job hunt. Nash would pound the streets meeting former colleagues, and Ella would stay in the flat to browse various websites, even though she knew it was futile. After making a couple of calls to recruitment consultants it became crystal clear that she wasn't going to be able to get a job until she became less famous, and despite feeling like she was nobody special, it seemed that other people didn't agree with her. Her wedding had been on the cover of *Hello!* for God's sake, and she'd briefly been presenting the hottest new show on TV. Of *course* she couldn't work in an office or pub. It was ridiculous.

But what could she do? The obvious solution was to work for herself again, and preferably from home – or a hired desk or office – but she didn't have any experience in anything solid apart from baking cupcakes, and she wasn't going to do that again. Obviously she could use a computer and she wasn't shy, but what did she know? She knew about fashion, but probably no more than fashion bloggers and people who read *Vogue* every month. She had a good understanding of the football industry, but only from an outsider's point of view. She'd never cut a sponsorship deal or had to handle any of that. And she didn't really have any contacts.

Her perfect job was out there. She knew it. She just had to work out what it was, and how she could make money out of it.

She had to.

'I've hit the jackpot! Nash exclaimed, as he walked into the flat late one evening. Ella was on the sofa in jogging bottoms and a vest, and even though she knew she looked rough, it didn't matter. Nash didn't care what she looked like, and it was kind of liberating – like they were an old married couple that could be completely themselves with each other.

Ella pulled herself into a sitting position and grinned. 'Oh yeah? Did you win the lottery?'

Nash shook his head and laughed. 'Even better. I had supper with Ansku in The Book Club, and she helped me come up with a plan.'

Ella swallowed hard. 'Ansku?'

'Yes, you know, Ansku Tiihonen. We met her at the *Wonderland* after-party.'

'The model?'

Nash nodded, and Ella bit her lip.

'I didn't know you kept in touch with her,' Ella said lightly. She didn't know why the thought of Nash seeing Ansku had instantly bothered her. It was probably because she was a pal of Johnny's, but – if she was honest – it was also because she was a little bit jealous, too. Even though she didn't fancy him, there was no denying that Nash was hot, and that girls loved him.

'We see each other now and again,' Nash said easily. 'She's good fun. You'd like her.'

Ella remembered Ansku's honey-blonde long hair, tiny waist, and big breasts, and didn't think she would.

'I'm pleased she's helped you,' she said. 'What did you come up with?'

Nash beamed. 'I'm going to set up a model agency with her,' he said delightedly. 'Ansku's not happy with her agent, and she knows loads of dissatisfied models who are looking for a new way of being represented. We're going to create an agency that they *want* to join.'

Ella was impressed. 'Do you think it will be easier than being a sports agent?'

Nash shrugged. 'I suppose so,' he said thoughtfully. 'I thought working in sport was the answer to my prayers, but Ansku knows the business like the back of her hand, and since I have experience managing actors anyway, we think it could be perfect. We'll start with models, and then when the time's right we'll diversify.'

'It sounds like you've got it all worked out,' Ella said, and Nash noted the wistful tone in her voice.

'And what about you?' he asked. 'Have you had any ideas about what you're going to do next?' Nash asked.

Ella shrugged. 'I don't know,' she said matter-of-factly, although every time she thought about it a chill ran through her body. Not knowing how or when she was going to get an income petrified her. 'Nobody seems to want to employ me.'

Nash nodded thoughtfully. 'If you could do anything, what would it be?'

'Well, my dream career would be being a stylist again. Do you remember that shoot I did for *Cerise*? I loved it, and they said were going to give me more work . . . but then the Johnny thing happened. And Aaron said they didn't want me any more.' Ella suddenly looked downcast, but she pulled herself together and forced a smile.

'What about friends?' Nash asked. 'I never would have considered getting into the model business if it wasn't for Ansku. Do you know anyone who could help you get a job?'

Ella bit her lip and tried not to feel embarrassed. 'I don't really *have* any friends. I mean, I have Stacey, my stepsister, but whenever I phone her she's a bit bitchy, and I don't blame her.'

'What do you mean?'

'Well, I suppose when Danny whisked me off my feet I neglected her. I felt so awkward about having this amazing life, and Stacey was a bit jealous, so it was easier not to talk.' Ella sat in silence for a moment. 'She's got engaged though, which is brilliant news. And I'm invited to the wedding. Although they haven't set a date yet.'

As she heard herself talking, Ella didn't think she'd ever sounded more pathetic. She didn't want to say she'd hit rock bottom – she had somewhere to live, she had money, and she was healthy – but her days were lonely and sad when Nash was out. Losing Johnny was even worse than Fin cheating on her and then dumping her. She just wished she could speak to him. Just wished she could regain a tiny bit of her former happiness to fuel her.

'I'm always going to be here for you, Ella,' Nash said soothingly, and Ella smiled.

'I know,' she said. 'But you have your own life and a business to start.'

'Maybe you could help us, or we could represent you at

the very least – help you find work that way,' Nash suggested, but Ella gave him a wry smile.

'I'm Ella Aldridge now, and so long as I don't marry another footballer or get involved in a scandalous affair involving a TV presenter, I'm nobody.'

Nash smiled. 'At least you've come to terms with it,' he said. 'I don't think Chastity's going to feel the same way.'

Ella looked at Nash curiously. 'What do you mean?' she asked, and Nash looked surprised.

'Haven't you seen the *Daily World* today?'

Ella shook her head. 'I don't read the papers any more. I can't stand them.'

Nash rummaged in his bag and threw a copy of the *Daily World* over to her. As Ella saw the headline her eyes widened, and she read the front page and the double-page spread with her mouth open.

Poor Chastity.

## TAYLOR MADE! FREDDIE'S GOT TEEN KNOCKED UP

Exclusive by MATTHEW PARKER, News Editor, *Daily World*

**KINGSTON UNITED** was rocked again last night as the football giants discovered Freddie Taylor has been having an affair with Claire Broome, 17, and that she's four months **PREGNANT**.

We can exclusively reveal that Freddie Taylor:

- **FLIRTED** with the waitress in front of his **WIFE**;
- **SEDUCED** the 17-year-old with flowers and intimate dinner dates;
- **DUMPED** Claire when he found out she was **PREGNANT**, and tried to make her get rid of the baby.

The *Daily World* has discovered how Freddie met sexy Claire when she was working as a waitress in a local café. Sources say the pair met earlier this year when Freddie and his wife, Chastity, visited the café in Kingston for a romantic lunch.

One insider said: 'They have definitely been meeting up for a while. It has been a badly kept secret in the football world, but Freddie has finally been exposed for the love-rat he is.'

A source close to Claire, who lives less than six miles from the Taylors, said: 'Claire fell in love with Freddie the moment she met him – she was dazzled by his good looks and charm. Freddie convinced Claire he was planning on leaving Chastity, and it was only a matter of time until he romanced her into bed.'

## SHAME

Last night humiliated Freddie was confessing his disgrace to wife Chastity. Freddie now expects Chastity to throw him out of their £4 million mansion in Surrey.

Freddie told a pal yesterday: 'I've messed up. Chastity might not forgive me and on top of that I'm going to be a dad.'

Ella put the paper down and sighed heavily.

'Chastity will be in bits. I should phone her,' she remarked to Nash, as her eyes ran over the photo of Claire Broome. She didn't look like the sort of girl who normally slept with footballers – the type who wore too much fake tan, over-the-top fake eyelashes, and dressed like a hooker in the nightclubs that were home to her hunting ground. This girl looked . . . well, nice. Normal; like a victim, rather than a predator. Ella didn't know if that would hurt Chastity even more – knowing that Freddie had probably pursued her, rather than the other way round.

'She's probably changed her number,' Nash said, as he scrolled through his phone looking for the number of Freddie's agent. 'But if you give me a minute I can see if I can get it for you.'

Ella smiled faintly. It was all a bit déjà vu – her having to console Chastity over Freddie's philandering ways – but this time it was even more serious. The papers had got hold of it, and Chastity's humiliation had been amplified in the glare of the trashy media spotlight. Chastity needed a friend, and Ella could be there for her. After all, even though she'd been the 'cheat' she'd kind of just gone through it all herself. She knew how horrible it was to have your private life twisted and put on the front page of a newspaper.

'I'd like that,' Ella said, and after a few minutes Nash scribbled a mobile number on a scrap of paper and handed it to her.

Now all Ella had to do was ring her. She took a deep breath and punched the number into her phone.

*Chapter Fifteen*

'And this is where you can sleep,' Ella said softly, as she gestured towards the large squishy sofa in Nash's living room. Chastity stared at it for a moment with dull eyes, and then sank into it without a word. God, Ella thought. She really was in a bad way. The Chastity she knew would have thrown a tantrum about not getting a bedroom of her own at the very least. But she supposed this was what happened when the man you loved got someone else pregnant.

'Can I get you anything?' she asked, as she eyed Chastity carefully. She was still tanned, still picture-perfect, but she'd lost her energy, her drive.

Chastity shook her head. 'Thanks, but I'm fine.'

This was the first thing she'd said since she'd got there. Her driver had driven for hours, twisting and turning through the Surrey lanes to get rid of the paparazzi, and after circling the city a few times they'd eventually pulled up outside Nash's flat. Chastity could have stayed in her mansion, could have checked into a luxury hotel, but she wanted to be with friends, and Nash had offered his sofa to her for a few days, joking that before long his flat would be overrun with heartbroken WAGs.

Ella hovered nervously, and then decided to pour them

some orange juice anyway. She turned away from the kitchen counter in the open-plan reception room and noticed Chastity was crying silently. She walked towards her and hugged her as best she could.

'I know it hurts,' she whispered as she felt Chastity's body shake in her arms. 'But it will get better, I promise. You will start to feel better.'

Chastity pulled away from her friend and sat up. 'What do you know about pain?' she said angrily. It was like Ella had sparked a tiny flame inside her. 'All you know is about causing pain. You did exactly the same thing to poor Danny.'

Ella bit her lip; to everyone apart from the few who were in Danny's inner circle it was the truth. Superficially she *had* cheated on Danny. But she didn't want Chastity to think badly of her. Not if they were going to be friends. Proper friends.

'It wasn't quite like what the papers reported—' Ella began, but Chastity cut her off.

'What, so you weren't sleeping with Johnny Cooper?'

'I was,' Ella said quietly. 'But it was more than that. I fell in love with him.'

Chastity shrugged. 'It doesn't excuse it. Danny loved you and he gave you the world – and that was how you repaid him.'

Ella struggled to find the right words. She couldn't tell Chastity that Danny was gay, but she wanted her to know the truth.

'That's not strictly true,' she began carefully. 'Yes, he loved me, and I loved him . . . but in a platonic way. Our relationship was more of a good friendship than a romantic affair.'

Chastity laughed. 'Don't give me that – he bought you a Ferrari. Men don't do that unless they're in a red-hot relationship.'

Ella picked at her baggy Levis.

'Trust me on this; it wasn't that sort of relationship. We never even had sex.'

Chastity's eyes widened. 'What?'

'We didn't have that sort of relationship.'

'Hang on a minute. I'm struggling with this. So you never had sex ever? Not even on your honeymoon?'

Ella shook her head.

'I don't understand.' Chastity looked perplexed, but she was no longer angry with Ella, or thinking about Freddie.

Ella shrugged. 'We just got on really well, and we decided to get married. We were the best of friends, and it just seemed less . . . complicated than having a "normal" relationship. It worked for us.'

Chastity trained her wide blue eyes on Ella. 'So you basically had an open relationship?'

'Yes, something like that. Danny knew all about Johnny and he didn't mind.'

'And you didn't mind him sleeping with other women?' Chastity asked incredulously. She couldn't understand it. Ella had married one of the hottest men in football, and had actively chosen not to sleep with him. It was crazy.

'That was the deal. I agreed to it before we got married.'

Chastity slumped back onto the sofa. 'I've never heard anything like it. But then again, why not? It's probably an arrangement Freddie would like. I could be the trophy wife in the mansion, and he could sleep with as many wannabe WAGs as he wanted.'

She paused for a moment, and then let out a little bitter laugh.

'What am I saying?' she continued. 'That's exactly the arrangement we have. Or had. And even though he keeps saying he'll change, he never does. Do you think if he got help – like, counselling or something – it would work? That he'd stop cheating on me?'

Her voice was so hopeful that Ella felt bad about telling her friend the truth.

'I don't know,' she said. 'I don't think so. If he loved you, really loved you, he wouldn't cheat on you.'

'But he says he loves me,' Chastity muttered exhaustedly. 'He says he just can't help himself. That it doesn't mean anything.'

Ella sighed again and rested her head on Chastity's shoulder.

'Isn't that what they all say?'

'Freddie really means it, though. He thinks he has a sex addiction or something. It really isn't his fault.'

'Chastity, this isn't about him sleeping around any more. He got a girl – a seventeen-year-old girl – pregnant. And he's going to be a father.'

'He could probably just pay her off,' Chastity said to herself. It was as if she couldn't even hear Ella. 'Give her a million quid and tell her to move abroad with the baby.'

'Chastity!' Ella practically yelled, and Chastity blinked.

'But he says he wants to be part of the baby's life,' she continued. 'That if this girl is going to keep it, he wants to know it. Help raise it. That sort of thing.'

'And how do you feel about that?' Ella asked.

'How do you think I feel about it? It's like he couldn't give a flying fuck about me. He promised never to hurt me.

He promised to respect me. But he's going to have a baby with someone else.' Tears began to slide down her beautiful face again, and Ella reached for her hand.

'You don't have to put up with this, you know,' she said softly. 'You can leave him. Properly.'

'But I love him,' Chastity sobbed.

'But, babe, I don't think he loves you.'

'I can make him love me; I know I can.'

'You can't,' Ella said as soothingly as she could, although she knew her words were cutting deep into Chastity's heart. 'And you can do so much better. You can be with a man who loves you so much he treats you like a princess.'

'I don't know if that man exists,' Chastity mumbled.

'He does,' Ella replied. But she wasn't thinking of Johnny as she said it. She was thinking of Nash.


'So what do you think of this one?' Ella said as her Pied a Terre boots – taken from Castle House because she loved them too much and couldn't bear to leave them behind – clicked across the gleaming parquet floor. The three-bedroom apartment was beautiful, with exposed brickwork, beautiful Victorian-style cornicing, and marble fireplaces in every room. The apartment block was on top of a hill in leafy Crystal Palace, and the floor-to-ceiling windows took in a panorama of the whole of the city, from Big Ben to Canary Wharf. Flats didn't get more luxurious than this.

'It's not exactly central London, is it?' Chastity replied as sullenly as she could. 'It's practically Zone Ninety. We may as well be back in Surrey.'

'We can't afford central London. And as lovely as this flat is, we can barely afford it.'

'We can afford whatever we want,' Chastity said flippantly. 'Freddie said he'll pay for wherever I want to live. And I want to live in Central London. Like Chelsea . . . or maybe Mayfair. How much are apartments in Mayfair?'

Ella glanced quickly at the estate agent, whose eyes were as round as saucers. She knew he'd be going straight to the papers with this.

'Can you give us a moment, please?' Ella asked, and the estate agent did a funny little bow and ducked out of the flat.

'Are all estate agents as weird as him?' Chastity asked as she watched him shut the front door behind him. 'He smells funny too. Like onions.'

'Some are, but that's not the point. You have to be careful about what you say in front of strangers. You know they'll phone the newspapers as soon as they can and quote you.'

Chastity shrugged and walked towards the window to stare at Canary Wharf in the distance. 'So what? What does it matter? My life's over anyway.'

'No it's not,' Ella said. 'It's the start of a new chapter, that's all.'

'It's so easy for you to say,' Chastity said tonelessly. 'You're not me. You haven't been hurt.'

Ella laughed incredulously. '*I* haven't been hurt? Johnny Cooper loved me and dumped me, and the papers all think I'm a gold-digging bitch who used the great Danny Riding.'

Chastity blinked. 'But that was ages ago, and it was all your own fault anyway.'

Ella struggled not to snap. Despite softening since the exposé about Freddie came out, bits of the selfish, self-centred Chastity Taylor still appeared.

'Chastity, it was only two months ago, and I still can't get a job and I still don't know what I'm going to do. And you know what? It hurts. Johnny doesn't want to know me, and it hurts me every single minute of every day. I don't feel like I'm ever going to get over it, but you know what? Life moves on, and you have to go with it. You have to.'

'I'm not getting a job,' Chastity said sullenly. 'I don't see why I should. If I can't be with Freddie then I'm going to divorce him and milk him for all I can.'

Ella sighed. 'But what will you do with yourself?'

'Go shopping, go to the gym, get a new famous boy-friend who will make Freddie jealous?' Chastity shrugged. She hadn't really thought about it.

'I think you'll be bored,' Ella said, and Chastity laughed.

'I don't see why. I didn't work when I was with Freddie and I was perfectly happy.'

Ella knew the estate agent was lingering by the front door, and that now wasn't the time for a proper heart-to-heart with her friend, but she couldn't let what Chastity had just said pass.

'I don't think you *were* happy,' she said bluntly, and Chastity's eyes widened. 'You were so caught up in looking perfect and behaving perfectly that you lost yourself. You forgot how to have fun, how to let your guard down.'

'That's not true,' Chastity said defensively.

'Babe, it is true, because I watched you do it. And I think that working will help you find yourself again. And give you a reason to get up in the morning.'

Chastity sighed heavily. 'You're not going to let this go, are you?'

Ella shook her head.

'I can't get a job though,' Chastity said.

'I know. Nor can I. Which is why I'm thinking of

starting a company, just like Nash is. And maybe we can use that third bedroom as an office; it's big enough for two desks, you see . . .' Ella's voice trailed off, and she watched Chastity carefully, hopefully looking for signs that her friend would agree to helping her set up a business. It was a big ask – but Ella really did believe Chastity needed a purpose in her life that wasn't based around shopping and looking good.

'So getting this flat and using the third bedroom as an office will help me get on with my life?' Chastity asked. Her voice was flat, and she wasn't overjoyed by the idea. But she could see Ella had a point. 'Fine. Let's get it then. Let's get this Crystal Palace flat and move out of Nash's place and let's just get on with it. We'll take it. I won't bother with a mortgage since it's so cheap – I'll just pay cash.'

'But it's seven hundred and fifty thousand pounds!' Ella said incredulously.

'And it's the least Freddie Taylor can do.'

'So now what?' Chastity asked as she wiped tiny beads of sweat from her forehead. They'd spent the last few days moving all their belongings into the Crystal Palace pent-house, and after lots of hard work and late nights, the place was coming together. Even though she thought of the flat as Chastity's – as there was no way Ella could contribute to the purchase price without blowing all her savings – Chastity had generously put her name on the deeds too. Ella had tried to talk her out of it, but Chastity was having none of it. 'If your name's not on the certificate it won't really be your home too – and I want it to be,' she'd said as they sat in the solicitor's office. And Ella, touched beyond belief, found that as much as she tried to say no, Chastity wouldn't let her. The flat was theirs. It was their new beginning.

'Now we relax,' Ella said with a grin. She had a smudge of dirt on her cheek, but she looked great – the best she had in a long time. She was lean, sparkling, and radiated energy. In comparison Chastity still looked drawn and depressed, but Ella knew it would take time. Chastity had truly loved Freddie, and the fact that he had got a teenage girl pregnant was almost too much for her to bear. It took every ounce of strength for her to get up in the morning, and if she didn't keep busy she dissolved into a puddle of salty tears.

'You know, I'm not sure about this colour scheme,' Chastity remarked, as she flopped into a purple velvet chair. They'd repainted the room a bright white, and then had bought statement pieces to show the space off – a fuchsia sofa, a turquoise coffee table, and a red leather rocking chair – so the room was like one big pop-art canvas. Ella loved it, and didn't think anyone could be depressed when they walked into their home.

'But it's perfect!' Ella exclaimed. 'It's exactly what we wanted.'

'I know, but . . . but it's not very sophisticated, is it? It's not very classy.'

Ella frowned. 'It's incredibly classy. It's just different from what we're both used to. Just because we don't have antique chairs from the sixteenth century, or Ming vases, it doesn't mean we're not sophisticated.'

'I just don't know if Freddie would like it, though.'

Ella tried not to roll her eyes. 'Chastity, do you like it?'

A smile began to form on Chastity's mouth. 'I love it. It's fresh and girlie without being over-the-top.'

'And what do you think Freddie would think of it?'

'That's it's girlie and over-the-top.'

'And do you care?'

Chastity paused, so Ella pressed the point.

'Do you care what Freddie Taylor – who got a seventeen-year-old pregnant – thinks about how you decorate your new flat?'

Chastity laughed. 'I couldn't care less,' she said gleefully, and Ella smiled. Perhaps Chastity was getting over her cheating, philandering husband. Just a little bit.

'But really, what do we do now?' Chastity asked Ella as they sat at their frosted orange dining table and ate take-out Chinese. It was the first official meal in their new home, so they'd matched the greasy meal with vintage Perrier Jouët champagne to celebrate.

'What do you mean?' Ella replied through a mouthful of duck and noodles. She'd been wondering what Nash was up to that evening. She missed him being around all the time.

'Well, we have the flat, and you've set up the spare room as an office . . . but what do we do? What's our business going to be?'

Ella swallowed her food and thought for a moment. 'I don't know,' she said slowly. 'But I do know that between the two of us we'll think of something. We have to. I used to run a cupcake company that went under, but I have to admit I picked up some business skills, despite it being a complete disaster. Have you ever worked?'

Chastity raised her eyebrows. 'Before I met Freddie I was PA to an editorial director at a major publishing house, and I was going to business school in the evenings.'

Ella dropped her chopsticks. 'What?'

Chastity laughed and flicked her long blonde hair over

her shoulder. 'What? Do you think I'm stupid because I look like this and because I married a footballer?'

Ella was speechless for a second. 'No . . . but I had no idea. Jesus. Business school?'

Chastity shrugged. 'I loved being a PA, but I wanted to work myself into a position where I had a PA of my own. I wanted to be in charge.'

'Of what?' Ella asked curiously. She couldn't quite believe that Chastity Taylor, who had long blonde extensions, wore thick false eyelashes every day, made sure she had a spray tan once a week, and was regularly in the magazines for wearing crazy tight outfits to the supermarket, had been to business school.

'I don't know,' Chastity mused. 'I always wanted my own magazine, but I was more interested in the financial side of it than the editorial. You know, how to make sure it made money even though a lot of magazines aren't. It's kind of what my boss did, but I'm not sure he was very good at it. I was dying for a chance to look at the figures properly.'

'But you're loaded,' Ella said excitedly. 'If you wanted to you could easily launch a magazine.'

Chastity shook her head. 'I'm not loaded. Far from it, really – mainly because I signed a pre-nup and because, well, I suppose I'm too proud to ask Freddie for any more money. He offered to buy me a flat, and I accepted because I had to leave our home, but that's as much as I want to ask for. If he offered it I'd take it. But I can't ask.'

'Suppose we could get the money though,' Ella pressed. 'Would you want to? Could you be any good at it?'

'I think if I really put my mind to it and focused I might be okay at it – I learnt so much when I was a PA, you have no idea – but I can't concentrate at the moment. I can't concentrate on anything. I just miss Freddie so much, and it's like the pain's engulfing me. I can't do anything with my brain.'

'Maybe we could start a magazine in a couple of months,' Ella mused, but Chastity cut her off.

'I don't want to run a magazine,' she said. 'I don't think now's the right time to launch one, and if we did it, it would have to be right. We'd need investors and a board, and it would never just be ours. We need to do something else.'

Ella nodded, and picked up her chopsticks again. For a second she'd had a tiny flash of inspiration about what they should do, but it had gone.

'I think it's time these extensions got cut out,' Chastity said as she stared at herself in the mirror. She was dressed in tight ripped jeans and a crop top that showed off her enviably flat stomach, but her feet were bare, and she was hardly wearing any make-up.

'Really?' Ella asked. 'I thought you loved your hair.'

'Oh, let's be honest, I look like a drag queen,' Chastity remarked drily. 'And I only got them done to keep Freddie. Not that it worked.'

'So you're going for a new haircut?'

'I think I'm going for a whole new look,' Chastity said thoughtfully, and she stared at her friend. Since she'd moved out of Nash's flat Ella had burst out of her slump, and she'd started taking care of her appearance again. She was in a simple outfit of a loose cream T-shirt, a grey fluffy cardigan, tight khaki trousers, and towering suede ankle boots and she managed to look cool, fashionable and classy all at the same time. The reflection that faced Chastity was none of that. She looked tired, cheap and like she was trying too hard.

'Can you help me?'

Ella stood up and stared at her friend objectively. She was so used to how Chastity looked that she couldn't quite imagine her with a different image. Unless . . . a vision of Chastity in a classic black dress with fierce heels and glossy hair popped into her head, and suddenly Ella felt excited.

'I'd love to,' she said honestly. 'It can be your first stop in your search for your happy ever after.'

'And it could be the start of you seeing if you've still got that styling talent that magazine thought you had,' Chastity said knowingly, and Ella raised an eyebrow. Every so often Chastity would say something so perceptive that Ella couldn't quite believe that the girl in front of her was the same one who'd chewed gum as her chief bridesmaid.

It was time to give Chastity a look that showed off her true personality.

To begin the day Ella took her to a smart but discreet salon in Kensington, and after three hours her long blonde extensions had been swapped for a shiny, swinging, shoulder-length cut that flipped up at the ends. Chastity's hair looked like it belonged on a catwalk model – it was still long and a gorgeous buttery blonde, but it was edgy. It made you look at it, and – almost disturbingly – want to touch it.

After the trip to the salon they went shopping. Out went the revealing designer outfits and in came the classics; cashmere cardigans, silk-mix T-shirts, beautifully cut jeans from J Brand, wide-legged trousers from Joseph, and skirts from Pringle and Burberry. There was nothing too revealing, nothing too sexy, and at first Chastity wasn't sure about what Ella was picking out for her.

'I feel a bit frumpy,' she complained as she stared at herself in a grey silk column dress from Chloe. 'You can't see my cleavage *or* my legs, and I know that you can show one or the other without looking tarty.'

Ella smiled, even though the clothes she held were beginning to make her arms ache. 'That's true, but you're showing your face – and that's stunning enough on its own without you needing to show off anything else.'

Chastity was mollified. 'Well, if you think I can pull it off,' she said, and she accepted all of Ella's other recommendations without a word, and Ella was genuinely pleased. She knew it was too soon after the 'affair scandal' for her to consider being a stylist – be it a personal shopper or someone who put together outfits and looks on magazines – but if Chastity trusted her maybe she really did have a talent. Or maybe what she was really good at was reinvention: helping women to find themselves again. As she watched Chastity try on endless outfits, she thought about it more and more, and she wondered if there was a way she could do styling anonymously. Ella Riding couldn't get away with a job like that – the press would deride her and she'd have no clients – but she could do it anonymously, or under a different name.

It was something to think about when she had the chance . . . and when Chastity wasn't demanding a pair of trousers in a slightly smaller – and therefore tighter – size.

When they got back to their flat at ten that night they were exhausted, but happy. Chastity stood in front of her full-length mirror again, but this time she couldn't stop smiling.

Ella thought she looked like a different person, like she was brand new. Clean.

'Freddie would hate this look, you know,' Chastity said as she stared at herself. 'But you know what? I don't really care any more. I spent such a long time moulding myself into the type of woman he wanted me to be, but even doing that didn't stop him from cheating. So now I'm just me. A shiny, expensive-looking me who's thankful that Freddie forgot about this credit card he gave me.'

Ella grinned. It was the first time that Chastity had mentioned Freddie's name without being angry or with her eyes filling with tears, but more importantly, she was right. Why change yourself for a man? If they didn't adore you for who you were and what you really looked like, they weren't worth it.

She just had to keep telling herself that, and stop wondering if Johnny would ever get in touch.

'And, well, I want to say something to you,' Chastity said. 'I've been meaning to say it for ages, but I was embarrassed to bring it up.'

Ella frowned. 'What are you talking about?'

'I wanted to say sorry for being such a bitch to you. When you were with Danny I was so jealous of you. You had everything – the perfect fairytale – and I hated you for it. Freddie was fucking around and I was miserable, and even though I took it out on everyone around me, I mainly took it out on you.'

'Chastity, it's okay you know—' Ella began, but Chastity cut her off.

'It's not okay. I was really bitchy towards you, and you never did anything to deserve it. And ever since you phoned me and told me to come to Nash's flat I've been amazed at

217

how generous and gracious you've been towards me. I don't deserve it.'

'Of course you do.'

'God, Ella, you're just so nice to me!' Chastity exclaimed.

Ella grinned. 'It's because I like you. Yeah, you said some pretty horrible things to me – but it's all forgotten. It's easy to forget about it if it means we're friends.'

Chastity smiled. 'I'll make it up to you one day, I promise,' she said. 'I'll do something amazing for you like you have for me. Because I don't know how I'd have dealt with the Freddie stuff without you.'

Ella gave her a hug. 'It's been my pleasure,' she said.

## Chapter Sixteen

Ella and Chastity stared at the blank pages on their laptop screens and felt depressed. For the last couple of weeks they'd both sat in their office from ten a.m. until six p.m. trying to work out what sort of business to start, and it wasn't going well.

Each day their plans ranged from fantasy – moving to Buenos Aires and importing clothes from UK designers – to the desperate – dog walking in South London – but nothing came close to being something they really could do. Everything was a daydream, nothing was reality, and the whole idea of starting a business was disheartening.

'So between us we have magazine experience, a bit of business experience, a failed cupcake company and a stint at styling for *Cerise*,' Ella said eventually, breaking the tense mood in the room. 'I'm sure there's something in there that we can work with.'

'What about a magazine that's heavy on styling advice?' Chastity suggested.

'It could work. But you said you don't want to run a magazine,' Ella replied, and Chastity sank a little lower in her chair.

'Oh yeah,' she said, and she chewed on a nail. 'Well, you

used to run a cupcake company, so how about something to do with catering? We could do a roast dinner home delivery service on Sundays for people with awful hangovers.'

Ella considered it. 'We'd need lots of money, a kitchen we could rent, catering staff, health and safety certification, a delivery operation . . .' Her voice trailed off.

'Okay, so not dial-a-roast-dinner,' Chastity said as brightly as she could, and Ella rubbed her eyes, thankful she'd not bothered with make-up that day. She was tired, and trying to come up with a business concept was harder than she'd thought it would be. Everywhere you looked there were entrepreneurs popping up with great ideas, but she couldn't think of a single viable one. It was frustrating beyond belief.

'Maybe we're looking at this all wrong,' Ella said. 'We're thinking about what we've done, and using that to guide us. Maybe we should think about what we can *do*.'

'I don't think I understand.'

'We're thinking of magazines and catering because we have some sort of experience in them,' Ella continued, 'but we don't have enough of the *right* experience to do something credible or successful. So maybe we should broaden our horizons – think about different sectors and jobs that we *could* potentially do, even if we haven't before.'

Chastity bit her lip. 'I don't know,' she said. 'Isn't it better to do something we've already done – something we know we're good at?'

Ella sighed. 'I don't know,' she said. 'All I know is that the only thing we're really good at is being married to footballers . . . well, we were before both our marriages went down the drain, anyway.'

'Ha. We could do a book called *How to be a WAG*,'

quipped Chastity. 'Only nobody would buy it because we were clearly awful at it.'

'We're awful at coming up with ideas, too,' Ella said glumly.

'Probably because we've been stuck in this room for what feels like for ever, and there's just the two of us. Maybe we need someone who can look at us objectively and help us.'

'Like a therapist?' Ella asked.

'Aren't they really expensive? No, just someone who knows us – someone who could say what our strengths are and bounce ideas around with us.'

Ella thought about how little they'd achieved since they'd started 'working', and how her bank account was starting to look a bit scary considering just how lavishly they'd furnished the flat. Chastity was right. But who could they trust to help them? Who did Ella trust over everyone else? A slow smile spread across her face as an image of a man popped into her head.

'I think I know just the person.'

'Wow,' Nash said, as he took his coat off and walked around the girls' apartment. His eyes ran over the boutique-style furniture, and then trailed across to the huge windows with panoramic views of the city in the distance. 'This is incredible. Obviously I was offended when you told me you were buying a place together – I really thought walking around my flat in just my boxers would tempt you to stay – but this flat is something else. It's even sexier than me.'

'Not quite a mansion though, is it?' Chastity sniffed dramatically, before breaking into a smile to show she was joking. 'But at least it's all ours.'

'And we decorated it all by ourselves,' Ella said proudly,

trying to get the image of Nash in just his boxers out of her mind. Under his flannel shirts and jeans he was as buff as Danny, and seeing him wander around his flat half-naked had been pretty disturbing. It was like finding your brother attractive or something.

'Maybe you should think about a career in interior design?' Nash suggested, as he sat on the fuchsia sofa. In comparison to the pink velvet behind him, Nash looked even more rugged, and Ella caught Chastity giving him a quick once over. Her heart raced with jealousy – Chastity wouldn't try and seduce Nash, would she? She told herself to stop being so silly. Of course she wouldn't. And so what if she did? It wouldn't affect her friendship with him.

'We thought about it,' Ella said, trying to concentrate, 'but it wouldn't work. In the public's mind we're two failed WAGs. I had an affair, and people think Chastity's a vacuous shopaholic. We're not exactly going to get people begging to work with us.'

'Perhaps the first thing you should do is start reinventing yourself – at least in the eyes of the press. You both look so different from how you did when you were still in your marriages. If the papers ran some decent pieces about you with some gorgeous photos it could change public opinion quite quickly.'

'That *could* work,' Chastity commented, but Ella picked up something in her voice that made her think she was sceptical of the idea.

'It's tried and tested,' Nash continued. 'Ansku and I have been setting up our model agency, and we took on a girl who had the worst reputation in fashion; she used to turn up late, drank and took drugs on shoots, slapped a photographer, stole clothes. The works. But she's turned her life around, and we were willing to give her a chance. The first part of getting her work was convincing the industry that she'd cleaned up her act. After enough PR it worked, and jobs are flying in.'

'How's it going with Ansku?' Ella asked lightly. She wasn't sure why she felt so jealous. It was probably because Ansku was stunning in a way she'd never be.

'It's going well.' Nash grinned. 'People think models are dumb, but when she's not playing up to that image in public she's totally smart and very business-orientated.'

'It sounds like you've got it all sorted,' Chastity said. 'But I'm not sure I want to go down the route of winning the press over before we can start a business.'

Ella looked at her in surprise. 'Really? It seems like such a good idea.'

'Really,' she replied. 'I'm sick of being in the papers and being talked about, and the last couple of weeks have been a breath of fresh air: no paps, no column inches, nothing. I don't want to have my whole life dependent on whether editors decide to like me or not.'

Once again, Ella was surprised at Chastity's perceptive remark. It was like her makeover had liberated her, and the intelligent side of her personality – the side that she'd repressed for Freddie because he liked his wife to be dim – was blooming.

'If you're not going to try to get the press's approval your business will have to be as low-key as possible,' Nash said, and Ella agreed.

'We're cool with that, but it's working out what to do that's tricky.'

'How about helping people improve their lives?' Nash suggested. 'It's almost like you're both completely different people since I last saw you. It's like you've done a home makeover show . . . but on yourselves.'

Ella's heart began to race, only this time it wasn't because she'd caught Chastity checking out Nash's broad shoulders and muscular arms under his checked shirt – it was because of what he'd said.

'I like it,' Chastity said slowly. 'But how could we do it anonymously if we're doing the job? We could employ someone and tell them what to do, but it wouldn't really be honest. Or fun.'

'We could do a website,' Ella said almost dreamily. Nash's idea had thrown her into a weird daze, and she felt a bit like she was sleepwalking. Her brain was running on autopilot, putting everything into place, and all she could think about was formulating this idea. 'We could use your magazine experience and do a website.'

'What, so people could contact us through it?' Chastity looked unconvinced.

'No, we could do a website with tips on how to have the best life possible, how to be the best you can be without needing a man to help you, and if we could make money from it—'

'We could sell advertising space. And maybe syndicate content,' Chastity said quickly. She saw where Ella was going with this and she liked it. She liked it a lot.

'And we could run it anonymously,' Ella continued, 'or say a footballer's wife is behind it to get a bit of PR, and we could do a weekly email with the best bits . . .'

'And sell sponsorship on the huge database numbers we'd build,' Chastity finished.

The girls stared at each other excitedly. This was it. This was what they could do. It would be hard – they'd need help building and designing the site, and they'd have to work out where they'd get content from – but this was definitely, one hundred per cent it.

'It sounds incredible.' Nash grinned, and he caught Ella's eye. 'It would basically be a site that shows women they don't need a handsome prince to whisk them off their feet to a happy ending. That they can do it all by themselves.'

'That's it!' Ella exclaimed, with a beam. 'We can call it "Your Happy Ever After – How to Get the Fairytale Life Without a Prince".'

Nash sat back in the sofa and stretched his legs. 'See? I knew you didn't need me to help and you were just using it as an excuse to see me again,' he said with a smirk, and as he held Ella's gaze she felt a rush of hot, sexual happiness wash over her. Scalded and embarrassed by her thoughts she pulled her eyes away from him and beamed at Chastity instead.

They were going to make YourHappyEverAfter.com a success, and they couldn't wait to get started.

'What do you think about pink for the background of the site?' Ella asked Chastity, as she trawled through the internet, taking in different colour schemes. 'Would it be cool to reclaim pink as a powerful, can-do colour, or would it just look patronising?'

'I think you're over-thinking this,' Chastity said. 'Light pink is cool. And it means we don't have to tell people the site's for women. It will be obvious.'

'That's true,' Ella said, and she made a note of it. There was so much to do, and so many things to think about that if she didn't write everything down she was convinced she'd forget something important. 'And what do you think about the strap line? Is "How to Get the Fairytale Life Without a Prince" anti-men?' She looked worried.

'It's *fine*,' Chastity stressed. 'Maybe you should take a break.' They'd been working fourteen-hour days for a couple of weeks, and it seemed like they were nowhere near to getting the site up and running. Who knew launching a website would be so much work?

Ella sighed. 'You're right. I'm driving myself mad . . . but this is so much fun.'

'It is. Look, why don't we just crash in front of the TV tonight and try not to think about anything at all – and especially *not* think about YourHappyEverAfter.com?'

'Deal,' Ella said. 'And we can order something in. A pizza.' She couldn't stop grinning. The structure of the website was starting to take shape, and Chastity had spent days on the business plan, researching all the different areas that could bring in revenue. According to some statistic she'd dug up, a third of people were unhappy with themselves and their lives, and this spurred Ella on even more. Why not create something that could help people be happier? It seemed like the obvious thing to do – and if they could make a career of it, even better.

'I'm loving life right now,' Ella said, as both girls flopped on the sofa. Chastity picked up the remote and fiddled with it.

'Me too,' she said with a smile. 'It's a good distraction from Freddie, and all that pain. It's still there – it really doesn't feel like I'm ever going to get over him – but it's definitely helping me not think about it.'

She pointed the remote to the plasma TV they'd had mounted in the wall, and suddenly the screen was filled with the face of a gorgeous man. His dirty blonde hair was artfully messy, his ice-blue eyes penetrated through the screen, and his perfect, sexy, cruel little smile gave both girls such a jolt that Chastity dropped the remote. It fell onto the parquet floor with a crash.

It was Johnny Cooper.

Ella couldn't drag her eyes away from the screen, and as she drank in his image she let out a little moan of anguish. Seeing Johnny's face again was like a stab wound to the heart, and she doubled over in emotional pain. She couldn't bear to see his face again, but she couldn't pull herself away from his image. God, she loved him. She loved him so much.

'Shit,' Chastity exclaimed, breaking into Ella's trance, and she rushed to pick up the remote, to change the channel. To do anything that would help.

'Leave it on,' Ella said firmly, although her voice was wobbling. Johnny Cooper was her addiction, and even though she barely spoke about him – and pretended she didn't even think of him – she did. She thought about him all the time. Ached for him.

'I can change the channel,' Chastity said softly, but Ella shook her head. She knew the best thing to do was flip over, put on something like *Come Dine With Me* and forget that Johnny Cooper's beautiful face had just beamed into their living room, but she didn't want to seem weak. Johnny Cooper was her past, wasn't he? He shouldn't impact on her present.

'It's fine,' she said, but both she and Chastity knew it wasn't. How could it be?

'He's looking well,' Chastity remarked conversationally to fill the silence. Ella glanced over at her and saw her friend looked a bit awkward.

'He is,' she agreed, and it was true. She didn't think she'd ever seen Johnny look so exquisite. His hair was slightly longer, and his face was lightly tanned and relaxed, as if he'd just been on tropical holiday. She'd read that *A Week in Wonderland* was getting record ratings every week, and she'd also seen something about how Johnny was planning on breaking America. There was absolutely no reason why he wouldn't be as successful over there as he was here. He was hot, charming, and a natural presenter. He was perfect.

God, she missed him. She missed the smell of him, missed wrapping her arms around his body, and missed resting her head on his shoulders as she breathed in his intoxicating scent. An image of how he'd made love to her in Paris — how his huge thighs had gripped her body, and how he'd pushed her deep into the bed as he'd kissed her — flashed through her mind.

Fuck. Why had he dumped her? They'd been perfect together.

Luckily Chastity broke into her thoughts before they consumed her totally.

'I've been thinking about Johnny Cooper recently,' she said, as Ella swallowed hard and tried not to cry. Seeing his face on the screen had done something to her. It was like she'd been put on rewind and was back in her bedroom in Castle House, desperately waiting for Johnny to phone her. No words could describe that urgency she felt when it came to Johnny, or the passion they'd created between each other.

'Oh?' Ella just about managed to say.

'Yes. I didn't want to bring it up, but the more I think about what Johnny did to you, the more it bugs me.'

'It bugs me too,' Ella joked weakly.

'I just can't understand why . . .' Chastity trailed off

when she caught sight of Ella's stricken face. 'Oh. It doesn't matter.'

'It does matter. What were you going to say?' As much as it hurt to talk about Johnny, it almost seemed more unbearable not to.

Chastity stared at Ella for a moment, and then took a deep breath. 'I've just been wondering why he dropped you. You told me that he loved you, and that he wanted you to leave Danny – but when you *did* he wanted nothing more to do with you. I just don't get it.'

Ella shrugged. 'The only reason I can think of is that all the negative press about me put him off. That he didn't want to tarnish his reputation by being with me properly.'

'But that's the point. His reputation was already stained because he was exposed as your lover. Wouldn't the best thing for him have been to make your relationship official? So he didn't look so heartless? So it looked like your affair meant something?'

'It *did* mean something,' Ella said defensively.

'And you got dropped from *Wonderland*, but he didn't. His career has rocketed, and it's probably because he had an affair with you, not in spite of it.'

'That's just how it is, I suppose,' Ella said finally. 'It's never the men's fault when it comes to affairs, is it? People always blame the woman.'

Ella watched Chastity staring at Johnny on the screen for a while, and wondered what her friend was getting at.

'Would you mind if I did a bit of digging on Johnny? Maybe try to find out exactly why he never phoned you when you left Danny?'

Part of her didn't want Chastity to. She didn't think she could bear it if she found out Johnny had been seeing someone else, that she'd been one of many playthings. But another part of her – the stronger part perhaps, the part that was energised by creating YourHappyEverAfter.com – was desperate to find out what had happened.

'Okay,' Ella eventually said in a small voice. 'Do some digging. I'm not sure you'll find anything though.'

She shifted her eyes away from the screen and onto her friend. She didn't think she'd ever seen a more determined expression on Chastity's face.

The weeks rushed by. Ella found a team of freelance developers and designers who could work on YourHappy-EverAfter.com, and she and Chastity spent hours arguing about what the content of the site should be and who should be in charge of it.

'*You* should write it,' Chastity said.

'But what do I know?' Ella said. 'I only know about me – and a bit about you – and that's not enough to inspire people to be happy, to help create their perfect life.'

'You know more than you think you do,' Chastity muttered. 'I just think you're being down on yourself, and Nash does too.'

'What do you mean by "Nash does too"?' Ella asked. As lovely as Chastity was to her now, she could still be incredibly blunt.

'It's just that Nash and I were talking and he thinks you're still not over Johnny and that it's knocked your confidence a bit.'

Ella laughed. 'That is ridiculous.'

Chastity held her gaze. 'Is it? If it is why don't you write the content for the site?'

'Because I don't think it's sensible,' she said firmly.

'What if I got ill? What if a bus hit me? Then we wouldn't have any content.'

Chastity rolled her eyes. 'Then you build up an archive of stuff that can be published when you're not around. Like when you go on holiday and stuff.'

Ella shook her head. 'Look, I know you and Nash think you know what's best for me all the time, but I've actually come up with a solution for this,' she said smugly. Her eyes were shining. 'I've been doing loads of research on the internet, and the more I think about it, the more I think it will work.'

'What is it?' Chastity asked. Ella looked ridiculously pleased with herself.

'Well, I was on YouTube, and I saw a video of a girl showing how to pluck eyebrows perfectly, and I really liked it. I mean, nobody ever taught me how to pluck my eyebrows, and I thought it was really interesting.'

Chastity stared at Ella's flawlessly arched eyebrows incredulously. 'You're going mad,' she said eventually. 'Johnny Cooper has made you go bonkers.'

'And then I saw another video by a girl who was telling the camera about how she'd been dumped, and how dancing lessons helped her gain her confidence back,' Ella said, ignoring Chastity.

'I don't understand.'

'I realised that we don't need to tell anyone how to have their happy ever after because the internet's already full of helpful, amazing advice. There's just nowhere where it's all accumulated. And that's what YourHappyEverAfter.com will be.'

Chastity's expression slowly changed into a huge smile.

'So we select bits and pieces by other people and post them on the site?'

'Yes! From how to create the perfect business plan to how to deal with grief to how to buy a flat by yourself . . . I really think it will work. There's amazing, useful advice from women all over the world on the web, but it's not in one place. We can become that place! We can be a destination for girls who want to improve their lives. To feel more fulfilled. To have their happy ever after by self-improving and learning and—'

'And becoming the woman they've always wanted to be,' Chastity finished.

The girls stared at each other.

'Obviously we always credit everyone, and we always link back to the sites the information came from,' Ella continued, as she put her business head back on. 'But I don't see there will be a problem with it. If anything people will hopefully want to be featured on the site as it will give them more exposure.'

'Ella Riding, since when did you become so smart?' Chastity asked.

Ella shrugged. 'It's amazing what you can achieve when you have to,' she said, and she turned back to her screen again.

She didn't say what they were both thinking: that it was amazing what you could achieve when you were desperately trying to get over the love of your life.

# Chapter Seventeen

'So this is where you're living now,' Stacey remarked emotionlessly, as she walked around the Crystal Palace flat. She looked great – she was glowing, her hair was longer than Ella had ever seen it, and she was wearing the latest Diesel jeans and a cool blazer from Zara – but her expression was carefully blank, as if she was struggling to contain all her feelings about seeing Ella again. 'It's very nice.'

'Thank you. We spent a lot of time trying to get it just right,' Ella said, as Stacey wandered over to the wall-mounted plasma TV.

'And a lot of dosh too, by the looks of it. I thought you said you were poor? And that you were living with your old manager?'

'I was,' Ella said awkwardly as she thought about Nash, 'but when Chastity left Freddie we decided to get a place together.' She hated that she felt so defensive whenever she spoke to Stacey, but she couldn't help it. Compared to the money she'd had at her disposal when she was with Danny she *was* poor, but she knew that compared to most people – including Stacey – she was rolling in it. For now, anyway. She might still be desperately unhappy, but to others she was still 'living the dream'.

'Oh yeah, and how is Chastity?' Stacey asked. Ella noted an undercurrent of bitterness in her voice.

'She's okay. Taking one day at a time, and trying to concentrate on the website we're going to launch. She's not had it easy, you know, Stace.'

Stacey sat down on the purple velvet chair and shrugged. 'It sounds to me like she's had it easy. Everyone knows if you marry a footballer that he'll cheat on you, and to make up for it you have access to all his cash. I don't know why she was so surprised.'

Ella bit her lip. A few years ago she'd have said exactly the same thing about Chastity and Freddie, but things were different now. The people they were talking about weren't just faces in a trashy magazine. Chastity was her friend.

'Not all footballers cheat,' she said softly, 'and Chastity never thought Freddie would do that to her.'

'Bet she'll be getting a big payout from the divorce though, which will make the whole thing easier to handle,' Stacey remarked, and Ella sighed. Chastity had gone out for the afternoon, ostensibly to talk to a web developer, but really she'd disappeared to give Ella some space for Stacey's visit. She was coming back in time for the supper Stacey had offered to make, and Ella really wanted her friends to get on. It was important to her.

'Look, I know you think you don't like Chastity, but you need to give her a chance. She's not like the girl you've read about in the magazines.'

Stacey's eyes narrowed and she let out a little laugh. '*I* need to give *her* a chance? Are you kidding me? Why should I?'

Ella's mouth dropped open. 'I don't understand,' she managed to say eventually. 'What's upsetting you so much?'

Stacey crossed her arms. 'I don't see why I should be friends with her. You practically dumped me – me, your *family* – as soon as you got with Danny, and Chastity was my replacement. I wasn't even a bridesmaid at your wedding; *she* was.'

Ella sat down on the sofa and rubbed her eyes. She'd known she'd have to sort it out with Stacey eventually, but she'd kind of hoped that Stacey would forgive and forget without saying a word. Obviously it wasn't going to be that easy.

'I messed up,' Ella said softly. 'I know I should have demanded that you were my bridesmaid, and I definitely should have included you more in my life with Danny.'

'Yeah, you should have.'

'I just . . . I just didn't feel like I could have said anything. I know it's not an excuse, but Aaron – Danny's manager – didn't let me do anything for myself. I couldn't even choose my own clothes.'

Stacey shrugged again. 'You chose that life though,' she said simply. 'Which meant choosing a life where you treated me – and everyone else who'd been there for you before Danny – like shit.'

Ella looked down at the floor. She hadn't realised it was possible to feel worse, but she did. She felt terrible.

'I'm sorry,' she said. 'I wish I could go back in time and change my behaviour. You have no idea.' Ella wasn't just thinking about how quickly she'd ditched Stacey because hanging out with her was 'uncomfortable' – she was thinking about how she'd agreed to marry Danny because she was scared of love, how she'd had an affair that could have ruined Danny's career, and how, ultimately, she'd been incredibly self-centred. No wonder Nash hadn't liked her.

Just because she'd been unhappy it didn't mean it was okay to be so selfish.

Ella heard Stacey sigh, but when she didn't say anything she forced herself to drag her eyes from the floor and to her step-sister. To her surprise Stacey was smiling.

'You know, I wasn't sure I'd be able to forgive you so easily, but I do,' Stacey said simply, and Ella couldn't quite believe it.

'You're letting me off that easy?' she asked in astonishment. 'You didn't forgive Kelly Black for *six years* after she ripped the head off your favourite Barbie.'

Stacey grinned. 'Yeah, well, Kelly Black wasn't aunt to my first child, was she?' she said slowly, and it took a moment for Ella to understand what her best friend was saying.

'You're pregnant?' she gasped, and Stacey nodded.

'And I can't imagine having a baby and not having you in my life. You made a mistake – obviously – but life's too short to hold silly grudges. I want you to be my best friend, and I want you to be family to my baby. So what do you say?'

Ella was so choked up that she couldn't say anything at all.

'I can't believe you're five months pregnant!' Chastity exclaimed as they sat down for supper in their dining room. 'You're not even showing and you're still tiny!'

Stacey grinned. 'Give me another month or two and I'll be well on my way. Mum says she didn't start to show until her seventh month and then she suddenly got enormous.'

Ella eyed Stacey's belly. There was the slightest swell to it, a tiny bit of roundness that hadn't ever been there before.

Quite unexpectedly she felt a pang of longing. She'd assumed that she'd end up having a family with Johnny, and they'd even gone as far as imagining what their baby would look like. That was never going to happen now, and it hurt.

'God, this beef is amazing,' Ella exclaimed in an attempt to change the conversation. 'Stace, thank you so much for cooking for us; this is such a treat.'

'Yeah, especially as we rarely cook for ourselves,' Chastity agreed. 'Well, I make beans on toast, and Ella's not bad at baking cupcakes, obviously, but that's as far as our repertoire goes. It's so good to have a home-cooked meal.'

'What did you used to do before you lived together? Did you eat out every night?' Stacey asked Chastity curiously, and Ella smiled to herself. She could tell that Stacey was ever so slightly in awe of Chastity Taylor, despite any resentful feelings she'd had. And who could blame her? Since Chastity had left Freddie she was an even bigger household name, and was being speculated about even more than Victoria Beckham and Coleen Rooney combined.

Chastity shrugged. 'Our live-in chef made us whatever we wanted,' she said casually. 'He wasn't too bad – he did a stint at some Gordon Ramsey restaurant in America – but he had a bit of an attitude problem.'

Stacey's eyes widened. 'What do you mean?'

'Well, he refused to tell me the calorie count of our meals, despite me making that a condition of his employment,' Chastity said with a frown as she stabbed at her beef. 'And once he cooked some fish in a butter sauce, when I specifically told him I was doing a dairy-free diet before a red-carpet event.'

'That's terrible,' Stacey said, and Ella shot a quick

warning look at her. She could hear the laughter in her step-sister's voice.

'It really was — it was the end of the world,' Chastity sighed, and then she smirked. 'Of course, I *was* a complete shallow, spoilt bitch back then.'

Ella grinned. 'You really were,' she agreed, and Stacey laughed.

'I can't believe you two have both packed in your foot-baller's wife lives completely so you can start your own business,' she said. 'If I had an ex with loads of money I'd damn well make sure he paid up.'

Chastity smiled, but her eyes looked sad. 'I used to think that too, but if I'm going to get over Freddie I need him out of my life completely, and being financially dependent on him wouldn't help.'

Ella nodded. 'And that's one of the reasons we're setting up the site — so that we can help other women take control of their lives and their happiness, even if it's just in a small way.'

'I think it's a great idea,' Stacey said. 'It seems like it's a good distraction, too. But, Ella, what else are you doing apart from working yourself to the ground? Are you going out? Having fun? Are there any men on the horizon?'

Ella was momentarily stunned. The thought that she might have turned into a workaholic hadn't even occurred to her, and she looked at Chastity, who — thankfully — looked as taken aback as she felt.

'I watch TV sometimes,' Ella began slowly, 'but no, I've not been out since Danny and I split up. I suppose I've been so busy concentrating on the website that it hadn't even crossed my mind. Working is really helping me get over Johnny.'

'And besides,' Chastity said, 'Ella's so busy being friends with Nash that she doesn't have room for any other man in her life.'

Ella shot Chastity a look, but Chastity shrugged innocently and ignored her.

'And I'm really busy looking into Johnny Cooper's life when I'm not working,' Chastity continued, oblivious to Ella's glare. 'It's more time consuming than I thought it would be.'

Stacey raised an eyebrow. 'What do you mean?' she asked, and Ella rolled her eyes as Chastity explained that she thought there was something odd about Johnny.

'Have you discovered anything?' Stacey asked, and Chastity paused.

'I found some pictures of Johnny, from way before you knew him, from when he was a children's TV presenter. I was looking at a news and picture agency site – mainly for YourHappyEverAfter.com but also because I wanted to see old photos of me because I really *am* that egotistical – and I came across loads of pictures of Johnny.'

Ella bit her lip. 'Go on,' she said.

'Well, he's with *so* many different women in these pictures! Most of them span about a couple of years, and in every one he has a different woman. He was definitely a player before he got properly famous.'

'But that doesn't mean anything,' Ella said, 'and I know what he's like. Even though he's gorgeous he's also quite insecure, and he flirts with girls to make himself feel better. It's like he only feels happy when he's being adored by women.'

'But so many women?' Chastity pressed. 'I've spent a bit of time looking at the photos, and I've managed to identify a few of the women in the pictures. They all work in TV, and they all could have potentially helped him in his career.'

Ella felt a wave of anger rush through her, and she struggled to contain it. She was really starting to feel like Johnny Cooper was in her past, and she wasn't sure she wanted Chastity bringing him up all the time. 'So what?' she said. 'People tend to date people they meet through work – it's nothing new.'

'Chastity might have a point though,' Stacey said. 'Johnny could be one of those men who only sleep with people to get ahead.'

'And you think that's why he slept with me?' Ella asked. She knew she looked upset now, but she couldn't pretend she wasn't. 'That's a load of bollocks. There's no way he'd have done that.'

'Will you come and look at the photos though?' Chastity asked softly. 'Come and see if you recognise any of the women Johnny was photographed with.'

Ella shook her head in disgust. 'If it means we can put a stop to this train of thought of yours I'll do anything,' and she stood up. 'Come on then, show me these photos.'

The girls walked into the office, and Chastity made Ella sit down before handing her a stack of printouts. She started to sift through them, and with every photo she looked at she felt more ridiculous. What was she doing? She didn't recognise any of the girls with Johnny, and she didn't see the point of doing this. She needed to move on, not stare at endless photos of Johnny looking happy with other women.

'Anything?' Chastity asked softly, as Ella shook her head. She turned over photo after photo, and was about to give up on the whole thing when something made her freeze. It couldn't be, could it? She stared at the photo more closely, and instead of looking at the woman to the left of Johnny she concentrated on the man on his right. His arm was casually looped around Johnny's broad shoulders, and it looked like he and Johnny were the best of friends.

'What is it?' Stacey asked. 'Do you recognise someone?'

Ella felt her body turn to ice. 'I do.'

'But I don't understand why you're so upset,' Chastity said, after she'd poured Ella a brandy. The girls had retreated into the tranquillity of their living room, and as they made themselves comfortable Ella tried to calm down.

'It's hard to explain,' she began, as she struggled to work out what the photos meant. It must have been a coincidence that they'd been photographed together. There was no way they knew each other, or that they were as close as the series of photos suggested. And even if they had met once, it didn't mean anything. It couldn't.

Stacey cleared her throat. 'Why don't you start at the beginning,' she suggested, 'and tell us who the person with Johnny is?'

Ella glanced at the photos again and felt sick.

'He's called Sancho Tabora, and he runs—'

'He runs SanchosWorld.com,' Chastity said. 'I've heard of him. He wrote some really bitchy blog posts about some of my outfits last year.'

'Yes. That's him.'

'So how do you think he and Johnny know each other?'

Ella bit her lip. 'I don't know,' she admitted. 'They probably met at some showbiz party or something. It's just . . .' Her voice trailed off. She'd promised Danny and Aaron she'd never reveal the truth about his sexuality to anyone, so how could she explain that Sancho had been blackmailing Danny?

'It's just what?' Stacey asked softly.

'It's just that I hate Sancho Tabora, and I'm freaked out by the idea that he and Johnny could be friends.'

Ella watched Stacey and Chastity give each other concerned looks, and she knew she wasn't making any sense.

'What's your beef with this Sancho guy?' Stacey pressed, and Ella buried her head in her hands. She really didn't feel like she could share Danny's secret, but she *could* tell them about how Sancho had ruined her life.

'I spotted Sancho in the audience of the first *Wonderland* that Johnny and I filmed, and after that I think he got a photographer to trail us and take photos of us in lots of compromising positions. After he got the snaps of us in Paris he began selling all the photos to the papers for a fortune. If he hadn't cottoned on to the sexual tension between Johnny and me, we'd never have been caught out.'

'But what if Johnny and Sancho are friends, and Johnny told him about your relationship?' Chastity suggested. 'What if he didn't guess and he knew about your affair because Johnny spilled the beans?'

Ella's mouth dropped open. 'Johnny never would have done that to me!' she exclaimed. 'I know you find it difficult to believe, but Johnny really loved me, and he never would have hurt me like that.'

'He hurt you by not getting in touch after your affair was exposed,' Chastity muttered, and then she sighed.

'Look, maybe Ella's right, and Sancho just guessed about the affair,' Stacey suggested. 'He probably knows what Johnny's like – Ella, don't give me that look, you said yourself that Johnny's a flirt – and he took an educated guess after seeing you both together.'

Chastity shrugged. 'Maybe. Or maybe there's more to it than that. God, I wish you'd let me hire a private detective so we can just be done with it,' she said.

'I'm not having a private detective follow Johnny!' Ella shrieked. 'And I'm getting really uncomfortable with all this talk. Chastity, I know you're trying to help, but honestly, I'm nearly over Johnny and I'm wondering if this is going to make me feel worse.'

Chastity wasn't about to give up. 'Babe,' she began gently, 'I just have a feeling something's not quite right here – and I know you feel it too.'

Ella began to speak – to say she felt nothing of the sort – but Chastity wouldn't let her.

'We're starting to find stuff out now, and I think the only way you're going to have complete closure and be able to move on is if you know why Johnny ditched you.'

Stacey agreed. 'Chastity's right,' she said. 'You're always going to wonder why Johnny never phoned you back. I know you're practically over him and that you want to move on, but you're always going to wonder what happened.'

Ella frowned and thought for a moment. Her friends *did* have a point, and she supposed that once they'd done their digging and come up with nothing, it would all be over for good. 'I don't want to hire a private detective,' she said finally. 'They cost fifty grand or something, and it just feels really underhand.'

Chastity smiled. 'We can find out about Johnny and Sancho's friendship in other ways,' she said, and she grinned at Stacey, who immediately knew what she was getting at.

'Yeah,' she said. 'What if someone we knew befriended

Johnny – say at a nightclub or something when he's a bit drunk – and got to know him better?'

Ella shook her head. 'Who do we know who can do that for us?' she asked.

'How about me?' Stacey suggested, and as Ella looked up at her, she saw her step-sister's eyes had taken on the same expression as Chastity's – they were gleaming with determination.

Ella tried not to laugh. Both of them were so set on doing this for her, and saying no to either of them didn't seem to be an option.

## Chapter Eighteen

'So we're ready to go?' Chastity asked excitedly, as she shifted from one foot to the other. She was dressed in thick black tights, Topshop khaki shorts, a Vanessa Bruno wrap cardigan, and her skin and hair were sparkling. Chastity had never looked lovelier, but Ella didn't notice just how beautiful her friend was. All her attention was trained on YourHappyEverAfter.com.

With one tiny click of the mouse the site would be up and running, and their launch – a quiet go-live where they checked the site didn't have any technical problems – would begin. It was scary and exhilarating all at once.

For the last month the girls had worked every hour they could, and they only stopped to grab something to eat or to hang out with Nash when he came over. When Ella couldn't sleep – often because she was wired from spending too much time in front of her computer – she worked even more. Work, and the website, had become her obsession. It was the first time since Sweet Dreams had gone under that she'd created something tangible out of her thoughts and imagination, and seeing the site come together was addictive. She wondered why she'd let the failure of her cupcake business put her off trying to achieve things. Working was invigorating – it felt so much more honest than when she was married to Danny and her main career was being a wife – and it was also a distraction. A distraction from how she'd let Danny down, a distraction from how Johnny had treated her, and . . . well, it was a distraction from Nash and the feelings she refused to admit she had about him.

'We're ready,' Ella said with a small smile. She checked the content on the site was immaculate, ensured the analytics in the backend had been put in properly and was ready to register their traffic, and then turned to look at Chastity. 'Shall we?' she said with a deep breath.

Chastity bit her lip and then did a little jump. 'Let's do it!' she grinned, as she hovered behind Ella's chair, and Ella clicked the mouse.

YourHappyEverAfter.com was live, and their new business had begun. The pale pink site, written by 'Crystal in her Palace', a 'former WAG who wants to make the world a better place' was out there, and Ella and Chastity couldn't contain their excitement. They'd reached a milestone, and not only had they created a site that they were proud of, they'd also transformed along the way. They were no longer heartbroken and listless, but energised and excited about the future.

Who needed to be married to a footballer when you could create a career all for yourself?

'So it's finally live!' Nash announced as he walked into the girls' living room with a bottle of champagne. He couldn't stop smiling at them, and Ella basked in his presence. Ever since they'd lived together, there was something about him being around that made her feel relaxed. Safe.

'I checked YourHappyEverAfter.com out at home, and

the site looks impressive,' Nash continued. He was in his usual London-rugged uniform of jeans, shirt and trainers, and Ella couldn't pull her eyes away from his body, his face. Was he aware of the effect he had on women . . . on her? She wasn't sure.

'Thanks,' Ella replied, and she swallowed hard. It was too soon to be thinking about getting involved with another man – not when she was probably still on the rebound from Johnny – and it was definitely not cool to be thinking about Nash this way. He was a friend, not a potential lover. It was ridiculous.

'Now it's live we can finally get our lives back. Or try to get them into some sort of order,' Chastity added, as Nash popped the cork on the champagne bottle and poured them each a glass.

'Ah, that's where you're wrong,' Ella replied, as she took her champagne flute from Nash and took a sip. She didn't look him in the eye while she was having these thoughts about him. She just couldn't. 'This is where it starts to get tough: we now have a website to run and make successful.'

'I'm sure you'll manage it,' Nash said easily. 'If anyone can do it I know you can.'

Ella tried not to blush. 'How are things going with the model agency?' she asked, deflecting the conversation away from her. The rush of launching the site, and the adrenaline that came with it, was having a strange effect on her.

'It's going well,' Nash said as he sat down in his usual spot on the sofa. 'We need some capital if we want to expand, so I'm talking to some investors about potential funding.'

'It sounds extremely serious,' Chastity said with a frown, and Nash ran his hands through his hair.

'It's not too bad. Ansku and I have different opinions on

the various ways we could grow the company, and we need to work out which way to take it before we get serious with investors.'

'What's it like working with Ansku?' Chastity asked curiously. 'Ella and I get on great, despite having our differences in the beginning, but how's it working out with Ansku? Do you get on?'

Nash considered this for a moment and then smirked. 'It can be difficult. We get on really well out of work – she's good fun and I enjoy her company – but we're still finding our way working together. She can be quite fiery.'

Ella concentrated hard on keeping her face composed. She didn't begrudge Nash a relationship, albeit one with a stunning and intelligent model, but she didn't want to know about it. Nash was *hers*: her former manager, her friend. She knew it was crazy, but she hated the thought of sharing him with anyone.

'Well, here's to your agency becoming a success,' Ella said, halting the conversation about Ansku and raising her champagne flute in the air. She made sure her tone was light, and tried to ignore the heavy feeling in her heart.

'And here's to YourHappyEverAfter,' Nash replied, and Ella forced a smile. Her happy ever after? If her fairytale ending was going to involve a man she doubted it would happen for a very long time. Best just to enjoy the website and concentrate on making it a success instead.

'So, I met him! I met Johnny!' Stacey called as she bustled into the girls' flat. She dumped her shopping bags on the parquet floor, ripped her coat and scarf off, and rushed over to the sofa.

Ella blinked. She'd known, obviously, that Stacey was

planning on going to all the spots that Johnny liked to hang out at – the clichéd Boujis, Chinawhite, Embassy and the Roof Gardens were his favourites – and after borrowing a designer outfit from Chastity and spending a fortune on soft drinks in these places, Stacey had eventually tracked him down.

'How was he?' Ella asked wryly. She couldn't quite believe that her step-sister had managed to have a conversation with Johnny.

'He's very charming, isn't he?' Stacey remarked, as she wrapped her hands around a mug of hot chocolate that Chastity had passed to her. 'Quite a smooth talker.'

'So what happened?' Chastity asked, and Stacey's eyes grew bigger as she remembered the previous night.

'Well, I was at the Roof Gardens doing a circuit of the place like I normally do, and I spotted him sitting in a corner with a—' She broke off, and quickly looked at Ella.

'It's okay, you can say he was with a girl,' Ella said calmly.

'Um, yeah, so I spotted him with a set of twins. They were blonde and just the type of girl that goes after anyone on TV. You know, tight dresses, super-high heels, and loads of make-up. Anyway, I had a couple of drinks at the bar and got chatting to other people, but I kept on catching his eye – as if I was flirting with him, but also playing it cool.'

Ella couldn't help but grin. 'I remember you doing that the night we met Jay for the first time,' she said.

'Exactly. And it worked a treat then, didn't it? So after an hour or two of this, I noticed Johnny slipping behind one of those gauze panels, and I decided to follow him. He cornered me by a loveseat, so we sat down and he drank a bottle of champagne.'

'What did you drink?' Ella asked. While Stacey was pregnant she obviously wasn't going to touch alcohol.

'I told him I'm a recovering addict and I don't go near alcohol and drugs, and he very kindly got me some sparkling water,' Stacey said. 'He was extremely courteous when he found out.'

'God, it sounds like it was easy to get talking and that he was a complete gentleman,' Chastity said incredulously, and Stacey nodded.

'I think it helped that I was in the most amazing dress in the world.'

'What were you wearing?' Ella asked curiously. Ordinarily she'd have chosen an outfit for Stacey to wear, but she'd left it to Chastity to decide – mainly because it felt odd finding an outfit that could help her step-sister seduce Johnny.

'I was wearing a metallic, electric-blue silk mini dress by Versace!' Stacey exclaimed in delight. 'It was on the runway a few seasons ago, and Chastity had never even worn it. It has patent leather plating on it, and it looks kind of like a tiny dress made of armour. It's seriously amazing, and it totally made me stand out against the pinks and reds of the Roof Gardens bar.'

'Wow,' Ella breathed. 'I remember that dress from the shows. It's incredible.'

'It really is. I had no trouble at all getting any man's attention – least of all Johnny's.'

'So what happened next?' Ella asked.

'We chatted for ages. I did the required thing of fake pretending I didn't know who Johnny was, and he asked me all about myself. Like I said, he was very charming, and very attentive. His eyes never left my face. Or my tits.'

'And did you say what we planned? That you're just a party girl who's still looking for the right career to come along?' Chastity asked. Before Stacey had begun her assignment they'd spent hours painstakingly trying to work out what Stacey should say to Johnny when she eventually met him. They'd decided she should keep her name – if Johnny found out she wasn't called Stacey he'd stop trusting her in a second – but they agreed she definitely wouldn't be engaged, pregnant, or working as a personal trainer in a gym. She'd be carefree, single, and the sort of girl who didn't have any money, but never seemed to go without.

'Totally,' Stacey said, 'and he believed every word I said. Being a bit of a vacuous party girl meant I fitted in perfectly.'

'Then what happened?' Ella wondered. Had Johnny made a pass at her?

'Then Johnny gave me his card, told me he'd be in Chinawhite tonight, and that he'd love to see me there. Which is why I'm in London again, and which is why I'm back here to raid Chastity's wardrobe. I couldn't wear the Versace number again, could I?'

'Absolutely not,' Ella said. If Stacey was going to wow Johnny she needed to look a million dollars. And luckily for her step-sister, Ella knew a thing or two about putting together a knockout outfit. It may have felt weird helping Stacey to seduce Johnny, but Ella knew that if she didn't get closure eventually she'd always wonder what she'd done wrong.

'Show us what you've got then, Chastity,' Ella said as enthusiastically as she could.

As Stacey walked into the Temple Bar at Chinawhite, she felt everyone's eyes on her – men were openly drooling, and women were shooting filthy looks in her direction. The Julien Macdonald lingerie-inspired silk-chiffon dress was sensational, there was no doubt about it, but Stacey had never looked or felt so naked. The top of the dress was effectively a flimsy black lace bra, and the blush and lace skirt swept across the top of her toned thighs. She was gorgeous, sexy, and just the right side of slutty. There was no way Johnny would be able to ignore her.

'You made it,' Stacey heard Johnny murmur in her ear, as she reached the bar. He'd already placed a possessive hand on her lower back, and she turned and air-kissed him like Chastity had taught her to – without making contact and with an expression of slight disdain. He stank of booze, and had clearly been drinking for hours.

'I made it,' Stacey replied. She watched Johnny's gaze greedily trail across her body, and she tried not to shiver in distaste. Okay, so Johnny was good looking, but he was so sleazy. She couldn't believe that Ella had fallen for him. Her step-sister had really lost the plot on this guy.

Johnny led Stacey through the dark room lit in reds and oranges to a discreet corner tucked away at the back. They sat close together on the velvet banquette, and without Johnny saying a word a bottle of champagne and an alcohol-free cocktail appeared on the carved wooden table closest to them. Stacey couldn't fault the service, even if her company made her skin crawl.

'Here's to us,' Johnny said, slurring slightly, and Stacey smiled sweetly. She had a feeling tonight was the night that he was going to spill the beans.

'To us,' she echoed, and as Johnny began talking – *at* her, rather than with her – she tried not to let her eyes glaze over. Johnny was on a high from presenting the edition of

*Wonderland* that had gone out earlier, and he was telling her an anecdote about how his co-presenter – Ella's replacement – had fluffed most of her lines that night.

'I've seen the show,' Stacey interjected, 'and you and Daniella have great chemistry.'

Johnny raised an eyebrow. 'I thought you said you didn't recognise me when we met last night.'

Stacey paused, and then shot Johnny her cheekiest, flirtiest smile. 'I didn't recognise you,' she said slowly, 'because you're so much better looking in the flesh.'

Johnny chuckled. 'That's true, of course,' he said. 'And yes, Daniella and I *do* have great chemistry on screen . . . which is marvellous when you consider she's so bloody dumb and I can't stand her.'

Stacey leaned in. 'Really? You don't like her? But everyone's talking about whether you two are having a secret relationship,' she improvised.

Johnny leant back against the crushed velvet of the banquette, and puffed out his chest. 'Oh yeah? God it's so tiresome to have people obsessed with my sex life,' he said proudly, and then, as the thought occurred to him, he winked. 'Or is it just you who's wondering if I'm shagging Daniella?'

'I'm so busted,' Stacey breathed, doing her best impression of an airhead. 'But what can I say? I think you're really cool.'

Johnny nodded, as if he'd expected this. 'I think you're cool too,' he said. 'But I don't sleep with my co-stars. I've learnt my lesson, trust me.'

Stacey feigned innocence. 'I don't know what you mean,' she remarked, and Johnny laughed.

'It turns me on when girls play dumb, so keep doing it,

sweetheart. We both know what I'm talking about. Or who I'm talking about, I should say.'

'Ella Riding?' Stacey asked, and Johnny nodded, before gulping back some champagne.

'That's right, Ella Riding.'

Stacey chewed on her lip. She'd been wondering how to bring up Ella without it looking too obvious, but Johnny had just done it for her. She had to tread softly though. She didn't want to put him off.

'Do you want to talk about it?' she asked carefully, and Johnny shrugged easily.

'Not much to talk about. She was hot and I couldn't resist her.' He knocked back another glass of champagne. 'It wasn't the proudest moment of my life, I must admit. Having an affair is exhilarating and madly passionate, but having it splashed across the front pages kind of puts a dampener on things.'

'Danny and Ella split up after that, didn't they?' Stacey said. Her heart was racing, and despite her drink her mouth was dry. She desperately wanted Johnny to explain why he didn't continue his relationship with her step-sister, but she knew there was no way she could ask him about it directly.

'So I heard,' Johnny said easily, and his eyes drunkenly travelled from Stacey's heavily made-up face down to her cleavage. Stacey knew her tits were pregnant-impressive, but now was not the time for them to distract Johnny from their conversation. It was time to play hardball.

'You looked so happy in those paparazzi pictures,' Stacey said casually. 'If you're not involved with Daniella, well, maybe you and Ella could try again. Legitimately this time.'

Johnny swayed slightly in his seat, and didn't answer

Stacey for the longest time. She held her breath and wondered if she'd blown it.

'You really fucking want me, don't you?' Johnny eventually slurred, as his eyes focused on Stacey's tits again. 'You think you're being subtle, yet you couldn't be more obvious if you tried.'

Damn. Stacey managed to keep her expression neutral, but inside she was furious. She'd been so close to finding out why Johnny had broken her step-sister's heart, but Johnny's ego and libido had thwarted her.

'Any girl would want you,' Stacey purred smoothly, frantically trying to work out how to get the conversation back on track.

Johnny brushed the compliment aside. 'Tell me something I don't know. But you know what, princess? I don't sleep with people I meet in nightclubs. I'm not saying *you'd* do it, but there are so many girls out there looking to sleep with celebrities so they can do a kiss and tell in the papers.'

Stacey's eyes widened. 'I'd never do that!' she exclaimed, and it was one of the first honest things she'd said to Johnny. 'I'm not that kind of girl.'

Johnny didn't speak for a moment as he assessed Stacey. His eyes drank in her pretty face, her gym-honed body, and her slutty dress, and he leaned in closely to her.

'That's a shame,' he murmured, his breath sour with alcohol. 'Because I thought you *were* that kind of girl.'

'And then he told me that if I ever needed money I should give him a ring,' Stacey concluded, as she filled Ella and Chastity in on the previous night.

Ella frowned. 'I don't understand,' she said. 'Was he suggesting that he'd pay you to sleep with him?' Confusion

255

was etched all over her face. She knew in her heart that Johnny didn't use prostitutes, and because of that, what he'd said to Stacey didn't make sense.

'I don't think so. Maybe he likes me and knows of a job I could do. Like being a hostess in one of those clubs.' Stacey didn't sound convinced, but she couldn't work out what Johnny had meant either.

'Maybe Johnny buys expensive gifts for the women he sleeps with,' Chastity suggested, but Ella shook her head.

'Johnny's flash, but not like that. He just wouldn't do that.'

Chastity sighed. 'Well, there's only one way to find out, and that's to ring him in a couple of days.'

'Not tomorrow?' Stacey asked, and Chastity shook her head.

'No. It will look too keen, and the last thing you want to do is come across as desperate. Let's sit on it until the middle of next week and see what happens next.'

'Sounds good to me,' Stacey said, as she rubbed her eyes. She'd got back to the girls' flat at six that morning, and was utterly exhausted. 'Hopefully I'll be able to convince him to spill the beans, and then you'll have some closure, Ella.'

Ella nodded and wondered if they were really doing the right thing. The more they delved into Johnny's life, the more uncomfortable she felt. Stacey had described Johnny as a completely different man from the one she'd fallen in love with, and the more Stacey talked about him the more a little voice in her head asked if she'd really ever known Johnny at all.

Who was Johnny Cooper, really? As much as she knew it would hurt, Ella knew she absolutely had to find out.

## Chapter Nineteen

## WHO'S BEHIND CRYSTAL'S TIPS?

Exclusive by MATTHEW PARKER, News Editor, *Daily World*

NEW WEBSITE YourHappyEverAfter.com has got the whole country buzzing as people ask which former WAG is behind it.

We can reveal that YourHappyEverAfter.com, which provides advice to women on how to have a happy life without a MAN, is run by a WAG who wants to 'make the world a better place'.

The website, which has been live for several weeks, has taken the UK by storm, and is one of the fastest growing websites in the country. Some of the anti-men tips include:

- **HOW** to find a good divorce lawyer;
- **WHAT** to do if you catch your fella in bed with another woman;
- **THE** best way to get over a bad relationship; and
- **HOW** to live a happy life without a husband.

Internet expert Milo Yiannopoulos said: 'It's not often a new website gets so much traffic, but YourHappyEver-After.com is an instant hit because of the advice written by real women.'

**ANONYMOUS**

The website is run by 'Crystal in her Palace', who says she used to be married to a Premier League footballer.

A spokesperson for Ladbrokes said: 'We're taking bets on who's behind the website. Carlotta Saunders, the short-haired ex-wife of Arsenal player Claude Saunders is current favourite at 6/1, and Ella Riding, who famously romped with Johnny Cooper, is at 100/1.'

The man-hating website, which also offers advice on how to find the perfect pair of jeans and how to write a business plan, is so pro-women that it's prompting rumours that whoever's behind it is GAY.

A source close to the website said: 'The woman who's running YourHappyEverAfter.com doesn't want her identity to be disclosed, as she fears it will overshadow the good work she's trying to do.'

*We think it's more a case of her wanting to stay in the closet. But we've looked in our crystal ball and predict we'll find out who this man-hating WAG is very soon.*

Ella flung the newspaper against the wall of their small office, watched it crash against the parquet floor, and then stared at Chastity in disgust. Her morning had been going beautifully until Nash had phoned to warn them about the piece in the *Daily World*, and as soon as she'd got the paper from the newsagent and read the article she'd been furious. Livid. Who did that journalist – Mark Parker or whatever he was called – think he was?

'The *Daily World* says we're gay because we're helping women find their happy ending without a man,' she said incredulously, as she shook her head. 'I can't believe it. I always knew the *Daily World* was sexist and that they make stuff up, but this is out of order. It's so offensive.'

Chastity shrugged casually as if the piece didn't bother her. 'What did you expect from them? That they'd run a gushing feature about how great it is that women can actually stand on their own two feet?'

'No, but I didn't expect them to say it's a website run by a man-hater. It never even crossed my mind that that's how it would be perceived.' Ella folded her arms across her chest and looked cross.

'The website doesn't come across like that; they've just angled their article to make it sound like it does. And besides, they're the only newspaper saying that. All the others think the site's great, especially the *Daily Mail* and *Stylist*.'

Ella frowned and picked up the copy of the *Stylist* to read the piece again. As her eyes ran over the glowing article she felt her anger subside. The *Stylist* article was even better than the one that had appeared in *The Times* the day before. It was the perfect bit of PR.

'God, the papers really love this "run by a former WAG" angle, don't they?' Ella said eventually.

'It's because they think all WAGs are dumb bimbos who couldn't work a computer if they tried.' Chastity grinned, as she flicked her waterfall of blonde hair from one side of her face to the other. 'When in reality, we're not stupid. That's just how we're portrayed by the press.'

Ella shot her friend a look.

'And, erm, we sometimes pretend that we're clueless so our husbands don't feel threatened.' Chastity's grin turned into a sheepish smile, and Ella couldn't help but smile back.

'I just can't get over the fact that everyone's so surprised that a former WAG could actually do something with her life – and that it would be successful.'

'Just how successful has the site been this week anyway?' Chastity asked, and Ella didn't even need to look at her computer to know the answer.

'We've had over four hundred thousand visits, and each visitor's looked at about six articles,' she replied proudly.

'Is that good, do you think?' Chastity asked, but both girls knew the answer. It was amazing.

'It's so good that both Diet Coke and Rimmel both want to advertise with us,' Ella said smugly, and then she named the amount of money both deals would make them. It was a figure so big that Chastity's mouth dropped open in shock.

'Wow,' she said. 'Just, wow.'

'I know. And this is just the beginning,' Ella said, as her violet eyes shone in excitement. But as she looked at Chastity she could see she was deep in thought.

'Now we've got the website up and running, I kind of think it's time Stacey made that call, don't you?' Chastity said as nonchalantly as she could. 'I mean, if Stacey doesn't ring him soon, it's likely that Johnny will have forgotten all about her.'

Ella sighed. In the excitement of launching the site and getting press for it, she'd almost forgotten all about Johnny. It was like the natural high that came from working – and becoming successful off the back of it – was a balm for the pain that Johnny had caused. But she also knew Chastity had a point. She still needed closure from her relationship with Johnny, and the only way to get it was if Stacey got back in touch with him.

'I'll get her to make the call,' Ella said as she realised that despite the website, it was back to reality. Well, nearly.

'Oh my God,' she cried, as her eyes glanced at the newest email to appear in her – well, Crystal's – inbox. 'The person who does the commercial partnerships for Wonderbra has got in touch and she says they want to sponsor our newsletter. Chastity, we haven't even *launched* our newsletter yet.'

Things were getting better and better, and regardless of what Stacey did – or didn't – find out about Johnny Cooper, Ella knew that wasn't going to change. It just couldn't.

'I'm so proud of you,' Nash exclaimed as he and Ella sat at a table in a quiet restaurant in Soho. They were in the basement of a tall, skinny Victorian building, and the only lighting came from flickering burgundy candles that were dotted about on heavy oak tables. It was dim and atmospheric enough for Ella to go unnoticed, and as she leant against the exposed brickwork she realised that for the first time in ages she felt relaxed and carefree. The website was a success, she was no longer in mourning for the relationship that she and Johnny never had, and Danny had even been in touch to wish her well. Everything was perfect.

'So how much money did you say your website was making again?' Nash continued as he raised an eyebrow.

Ella laughed and tried not to think about how hot Nash looked in a simple white shirt and jeans. He was her friend – *just* her friend – and that was all there was to it. She had to get over this ridiculously inappropriate crush once and for all.

'I didn't, but it's enough for both Chastity and I to draw a salary and to pay for a member of staff when we need one.'

Nash shook his head. 'I can't believe how much you've achieved in such a short time.'

'Never underestimate two women scorned by famous men.' Ella grinned, and Nash smiled back at her.

'I'll bear that in mind,' he replied as he gazed at her, and he realised he'd never seen Ella look happier or healthier. She was simply dressed in a cream silk T-shirt, black Top-shop skinny jeans and an olive-green blazer, but despite the lack of designer labels she'd never looked better. She was radiant.

'And as well as getting the website off the ground, Chastity has been playing detective. If you think I've been working hard it's nothing compared to what she's been doing.'

'What do you mean?'

'Well,' Ella said, as she lowered her voice. 'Chastity thinks that I'll only be well and truly over Johnny if I have closure.'

'Closure?' Nash echoed.

'Yeah. Even though I'm practically over him now she thinks I won't really be completely happy until I understand why Johnny never got back in touch . . . so she's been doing a bit of digging and has put together a plan.'

Nash shook his head. 'Chastity came up with this?' he asked incredulously. 'Chastity Taylor who only ever thinks of herself?'

Ella burst out laughing. 'She's changed. And she wants to help me.'

'So what's the plan?'

Ella looked carefully around the room to check nobody was listening in on their conversation, and lowered her voice even further.

'My step-sister got all glammed up, met Johnny in a club, and has got to know him. She got to know him so well that he gave her his phone number,' Ella said triumphantly. There was a pause as she took a bite of bread.

'And?' Nash prompted.

'And Johnny said that if Stacey ever needed money that she should give him a ring. That he could help her out. So Stacey phoned him, and she's meeting Johnny to talk "business" next week.'

Nash took a swig of his red wine. 'Do you think this is safe?' he asked. 'Because it doesn't really sound it.'

Ella's violet eyes widened. 'Of course it's safe!' she exclaimed. 'We're talking about Johnny Cooper here, not some random guy she's met off the street. As much as I can't understand why Johnny chose to break my heart, I do know that he's not dangerous.'

'But what sort of business do you think he has in mind for your step-sister? Because from where I'm sitting it sounds like prostitution . . . what will she do if he wants to sleep with her?'

Ella rolled her eyes. 'Johnny's not *into* prostitutes,' she said. 'Trust me. He can't bear the idea of paying for something he thinks should be delivered to him on a plate.'

Nash held Ella's gaze for a moment, and Ella could see his eyes were full of concern for her.

'Really, it will be okay. Besides, you don't need to worry about me any more, remember? You're not on my payroll.' She'd forgotten how Nash took it upon himself to look after her all the time, and as much as she liked it she knew he had to stop. Especially if she was going to shake off the crazy crush she had on him. 'Now, tell me the latest news about the agency, and how's Ansku doing?'

'It's going really well. We're almost definitely going to

get the funding we need to expand, and our list gets bigger every day – we've got some really great girls on the books.'

Ella grinned. 'It must be hell having to work with hot young things every day.'

'Oh, it's torture,' Nash laughed. 'But someone has to do it, and I don't mind. It's quite interesting, when you come down to it.'

'What do you mean?'

'Well, say a client wants a girl with long brown hair who looks "edgy". We'll send along a selection of girls who we think fit the bill, but the tiniest thing can make or break a girl's chance of getting the job,' Nash said.

Ella frowned. 'Like what?'

'A particular fashion label was after a size-eight girl who could model a trench coat perfectly. They wanted a brunette who could pull the look off, but also gave off a continental vibe. So we sent a very successful French model along, but they rejected her because they didn't like the shape of her nostrils.'

Ella's mouth dropped open.

'I'm not kidding. The poor girl lost a seventy-thousand-pound job because the client wanted her nostrils to be rounder.'

'God. Think what that would do to your self-esteem,' Ella remarked.

'I know. It's brutal. Luckily Ansku's been there and knows what it's like, so she can pep the girls up when things get tricky.'

'And how is your relationship with Ansku?' Ella asked, although she didn't really want to know the answer. She still felt strange thinking about her, and couldn't work out why she felt irrationally jealous every time Nash mentioned her name.

Nash shrugged. 'Things are going well. I never could have set the agency up or got it off the ground without her – as much as she likes to argue, she's also the perfect business partner.'

'And how's everything else with her?'

Nash looked puzzled. 'In what sense?'

'In the romantic sense of course!' Ella said lightly.

'Um . . . there is no romantic sense. Ansku and I don't have that sort of relationship. We never have done. God, could you imagine trying to work with someone you were having a relationship with? It's almost as ridiculous as the thought of you and I getting together.'

Ella swallowed hard and refused to look Nash in the eye. 'But that night at Shoreditch House . . . didn't you and Ansku go home together?'

Nash shook his head slowly. 'No. Why would you think that we did?'

Ella thought hard and tried to remember that fateful night. 'Because you so obviously fancied her,' she said at last. 'And she clearly liked you.'

Nash burst out laughing. 'Ansku wanted to pick my brains about her career – and what she could do outside of modelling – and I didn't fancy her in the slightest.'

'But how could you not?' Ella pressed. 'She's stunning.'

Nash gave Ella a wry smile. 'Ansku *is* beautiful, but Ella, she's not my type. She never has been, and she never will be.'

Ella tried not to smile, but she felt her heart leap with pure, unequivocal joy. Okay, so Nash had also said that the idea of the pair of them getting together was ridiculous . . . but he wasn't right *all* the time, was he? As Nash continued to talk about some of his more demanding clients, Ella wondered what Nash would be like as a boyfriend, and then quickly nipped the thought in the bud. Nash *was* always right, and he was right about this. Getting together with him would be stupid and it would definitely ruin their friendship.

Wouldn't it?

'Good evening, darling! I wondered when I'd see your pretty face again,' Johnny leered, as Stacey walked into the nondescript hotel room Johnny had given her directions to. They were in Euston, but they could have been anywhere in London, or anywhere in the world. The room was sparsely furnished with an MDF desk and TV unit, and the bed was covered in a yellow and blue striped blanket that looked as though it would be itchy to touch. The curtains were a murky green, the lampshades were cream and crooked, and the overall vibe of the place was one of a hotel that no longer bothered to try. It reminded her of a resort she and Jay had stayed in on a package holiday to Egypt.

'They do rooms here by the hour,' Johnny continued, as he patted the edge of the bed and gestured for Stacey to join him. 'But trust me, I never need that long.'

Stacey forced a smile and gingerly sat down on the corner of the bed. 'I'm sure you don't,' she replied lightly. 'But I'm jealous of the lucky girl who gets a full hour of your expertise.'

Johnny laughed and loosened his tie, and Stacey stared at him. Okay, so he was good looking and she supposed he could be charming, but she still couldn't work out what Ella had seen in him. There was something so . . . seedy about him. Thank God he'd dumped her, she thought. If Ella and Johnny had ended up together, who knew what would have happened.

'So, you're interested in making a bit of money, are you?' Johnny said, as he swiftly moved the conversation onto business. It seemed as if the thought of Stacey trying to seduce him made him nervous. 'Well, you've come to the right place.'

Stacey nodded. 'But I still don't understand what sort of work you're talking about. You'll have to excuse me for being dim – it happens sometimes.'

Johnny raised an eyebrow. 'I'm sure you're much smarter than you look. Now, what I'm talking about involves the utmost discretion, but if you think you can handle it there's a lot of fun to be had, and *loads* of cash.'

Stacey wanted to ask if whatever Johnny was talking about was legal, but she thought better of it.

'I'm perfectly discreet,' she eventually said, in a breathy voice. 'Many of my married male friends would say so, anyway.'

'Good, good, that's what I like to hear. So, you have affairs?' Johnny asked directly, and Stacey worked hard to hold his gaze. Lying didn't come naturally to her at the best of times.

'I wouldn't say they're affairs,' she remarked after a pause. 'I'd say they're friendships that mean I don't have to get a job.'

Johnny nodded, and he eyed Stacey up carefully. She'd borrowed another one of the dresses Chastity used to wear in her former life as a WAG, and she supposed that the very short, tight, low-cut Lanvin dress suited her 'ultimate party girl' character perfectly. Her make-up was heavy but immaculate, and Chastity had made sure Stacey's auburn hair was glossy and neat. If Stacey was to pull this off, she had to get her character down as faultlessly as possible, and that meant looking like she really was one of those girls who hung out on the international party scene.

'What would you say if I told you this job is quite similar to what you do now for fun . . . but just a little more high profile?'

A slow smile spread across Stacey's face, only this time it was real. He believed her! 'I'd say that sounds incredibly interesting,' she said. 'And I'd love to know more.'

Johnny stared at Stacey for what felt like for ever, and when he didn't say anything she began to feel nervous. Had she said something wrong? Or acted in a way that meant he didn't trust her? But eventually he nodded and stood up.

'Then we need to get going. My business partner is only in the office for an hour or so tonight, and we're going to have to hurry.'

As the taxi drove through bits of London Stacey had never seen before, she began to feel slightly nervous. Meeting in a hotel room – where Ella and Chastity knew she was – was one thing, but getting in a car with Johnny Cooper and driving through the city to an unknown destination was another. She slipped her hand in the Fendi handbag Chastity had lent her, and wondered if she should press record on the MP3 recorder she'd bought specifically for tonight.

'I don't think I recognise where we are,' Stacey said lightly as she hit the record button on the tiny machine in her bag. It had so much memory that it would record for hours. 'Are we still in north London?'

Johnny shook his head distractedly as he fiddled with his phone. He'd been sending text messages ever since they'd got in the car, and she supposed he was telling his business partner they were on their way.

'We're heading west,' he mumbled. 'The office is near Alperton.'

'Is that in London?' Stacey asked, and Johnny paused and looked up at her.

'It is, but I'm guessing it's a part you've never been to before.'

'Most of my friends live in Mayfair and Chelsea,' Stacey said smoothly, as the taxi moved slowly in the late evening traffic. 'I don't know west London that well.'

'Well, now's your chance to find out a bit more,' Johnny replied, and he went back to his phone, concentrating on the messages he was sending and receiving .

By the time the car pulled up outside a deserted industrial estate, Stacey had begun to feel a bit sick. She knew that Ella had said she could trust Johnny not to hurt her or do anything stupid, but she'd also thought Johnny was the love of her life and look how that turned out. As she got out of the car and stared up at the offices, she instantly felt full of regret. If something happened to her neither Ella nor Chastity would know where she was. Come to think of it, even she wasn't sure of where she was herself. 'Near Alperton' was pretty fucking vague.

Johnny put her hand on the small of Stacey's back, and began to lead her through the industrial estate, which was lit only by sparse orange lights.

'This is an interesting place to have an office,' she said lightly, as she concentrated hard on walking in her Miu Miu heels so she wouldn't have to think about what might happen next.

'It's not my first choice of location, but it's out of the way and discreet,' Johnny said in a neutral voice. 'It's perfect for remaining private.'

'Private?' Stacey asked nervously, but it was as if Johnny couldn't hear her. Or he was pretending not to, anyway.

'Not long now,' he finally said, and he gestured up to the only office that still had lights on. 'It's just up here.'

Johnny pulled open a heavy iron door, and as they began to walk up the concrete steps Stacey felt her legs wobble. She loved Ella a hell of a lot, but what had she been thinking when she agreed to this? She was pregnant, for fuck's sake. If anything happened to her or the baby Jay would be beside himself.

But it was too late now. There was no way out.

'Here we are,' Johnny said, as they reached a wooden office door, and as he pulled it open Stacey was astonished to see five or six twenty-something kids practically plugged into computers. They were all typing furiously, and they barely noticed her or Johnny walk in.

'What is this place?' Stacey asked. 'And why are the staff here so late?'

'I own a website,' Johnny said simply, and as he guided Stacey across the cheap blue carpet of the open-plan room, she strained to see what the boys were typing on their screen . . . but she couldn't quite work out what they were doing, or what they were writing.

'Well, when I say I own it, that's not strictly true. I'm more like an investor. Anyway, I'd like you to meet my business partner, who's the real star of the show.'

Johnny stopped outside an office, pushed at a door with a flourish, and there, sitting behind a desk, was the person Stacey had come to meet.

Her mouth dropped open.

It was Sancho Tabora.

## Chapter Twenty

'So this is the girl,' Sancho drawled as he looked up from the notes on his stainless steel desk and stared at Stacey's perfect, gym-honed body and flaming red hair. 'Bit short, isn't she?' he commented to Johnny, as if Stacey wasn't in the room.

'She's not *that* short,' Johnny said defensively, before surreptitiously checking out Stacey's heels. Her Miu Miu shoe-boots added at least four inches to her height, but he wasn't going to let that put Sancho off. 'Not if she wears skyscrapers, anyway.'

Sancho continued to eyeball Stacey until she began to feel deeply uncomfortable. Thank God she'd pressed record on the MP3 player in the cab. She didn't want to forget a single word that was said in this room. That's if she managed to get out of it.

'I'm Stacey,' she said, after mustering up all the courage she could. She could hear her voice wobble, and she told herself to sort it out. This was her one chance to help Ella find out why Johnny had dumped her, and she couldn't afford to mess it up. 'It's really great to meet you – I'm a big fan of your site.'

'Oh, so you recognise me, do you?' Sancho barked with

a short little laugh, and Stacey wasn't sure what to say. How could she not? His purple hair was inimitable, and even though he wasn't in one of the crazy silver suits that he normally wore to high-profile events, there was no mistaking him.

'Well, yes. I love celebrity gossip, and I always check out SanchosWorld.com.' She shifted nervously from one foot to the other before remembering she was meant to be acting confident. It was harder than she thought it would be.

'The boys outside will be pleased to hear it,' Sancho said sarcastically as Johnny gestured that Stacey should take a seat. 'They like nothing better than to hear that people like their work . . . especially since they're always moaning that they don't get a byline.'

'So the team out there write your site for you?' Stacey asked in surprise, and as Sancho laughed again she flinched. She'd always assumed SanchosWorld.com was a one-man band, rather than a proper operation with an editorial team behind it.

'She's quick, isn't she Johnny?'

'We're not thinking about employing her to be clever,' Johnny said wearily, and he leant back in his chair.

There was silence.

'If you don't mind me asking, why *am* I here?' Stacey asked. 'Johnny said that there was an opportunity for me, and I'd love to be involved in anything you do.'

Stacey knew she sounded like she was at a job interview, but she was still genuinely stunned to be sitting in an office shared by Johnny Cooper and Sancho Tabora, and she couldn't quite pull off the casual party-girl routine.

'So you'd like to be involved, would you?' Sancho said

thoughtfully. 'I suppose you could fit the bill, but we'd want to know how far you'd go to make money.'

'I'd do anything,' Stacey began, but Sancho shook his head.

'If you say it you've really got to *mean* it.'

'She means it,' Johnny interrupted. 'We've been through this already. She's practically doing it already.'

Stacey looked from Johnny and then to Sancho, and wondered what she'd got into. Were they pimps? Ella had joked that Nash had jumped to the conclusion that Johnny wanted her for prostitution, but Ella had been adamant that it wouldn't be the case. Had her step-sister got it badly wrong? She'd never forgive herself if she had.

'I know what you're thinking,' Sancho said slowly, as if he were reading Stacey's mind. 'And I'm not in the market of hiring out girls for sex. What we do is a bit more sophisticated than that.'

Stacey tried not to let out a huge sigh of relief.

'But before we tell you what we do, we have to be confident that we can trust you. We're both high profile, and we wouldn't want to risk our careers because of you.'

'You can trust me,' Stacey said, her voice the clearest it had been since she'd walked into Sancho's office.

'We'd need proof,' Sancho mused. 'How could we work out if she's trustworthy, Johnny boy?'

Johnny rolled his eyes, and something told Stacey they'd been through this routine many times before.

'She's not a cop,' Johnny said. 'And I'm pretty sure we can trust her.'

Sancho shrugged. 'She needs to prove it.' He turned back to Stacey. 'What are you willing to do to prove that you're not going to screw us over?'

'I'd do anything,' Stacey said. Her mouth had suddenly turned dry, and she wasn't sure she liked where the conversation was going.

'Like I said, I'm not into using girls as prostitutes, but there's definitely an element of that to what we do. Would you be willing to have sex with Johnny boy here on camera?'

Stacey blanched. If she said no she'd be sent packing, but if she said yes . . .

'There's no need for that,' Johnny remarked casually, breaking into the tense silence. 'She's fucked me already. She's good.'

It took all of Stacey's willpower not to look surprised. Why was Johnny covering for her?

'Is this true?' Sancho snapped, and Stacey nodded.

'We did it in the hotel room before we came here,' she whispered, and Sancho sighed.

'Was she good?'

Johnny nodded. 'Perfect.'

'She passes the test then,' he said, and he spun on his chair so he could tap a few words into his keyboard. 'Our business is using girls like you to create sensational stories. If you get my gist.'

Stacey sat very still. 'I'm not sure I do,' she admitted, and Sancho sighed again. He looked annoyed.

'What Sancho means is that we keep our ears to the ground, and if we think someone will take the bait, we expose them.'

Stacey stared at Johnny. She was still none the wiser.

'For fuck's sake,' Sancho muttered, and he turned his computer screen towards Stacey. 'See this story here?' he said, as he gestured at the *Sun* website. He'd pulled up an article about how a famous actor had been caught cheating on his wife with a buxom blonde. 'We created it.' He tapped at his keyboard again, and then another website appeared. 'And this one here, on the *Daily World*, we created that one too. Everyone thought Richard Hepburn was faithful to his wife of a million years, but we knew differently. All we had to do was put a pretty girl in front of him and he was ours for the taking.'

'You honeytrap famous people?' Stacey asked, and Johnny nodded.

'We've been doing it for years. Sancho hears about celebrities who can't keep their dicks in their pants, and then we send along a girl to get photographed with them. We then sell the photos to the newspapers and make a packet. It's big business, obviously.'

Stacey wasn't aware that she'd been holding her breath until she let it out. 'So that's how SanchosWorld.com gets all the exclusives,' she said eventually. 'That's how you manage to beat the papers to the biggest stories.'

'You're not as stupid as I thought you were,' Sancho mused. 'So what do you say? Fancy being part of it? We know of a particular actor who likes the red-head look you've got going on, and we reckon he'll fall for your ample charms without much effort.'

'Would I need to sleep with him?' Stacey asked.

'Would that be a problem?'

'No . . . I was just wondering exactly what the job description was.' Stacey was trying desperately hard to keep her cool, but her mind was whirring.

'Here's the deal. You hook him, you show him a good time in front of our secret photographers, and then you do whatever the hell you want with him in private. We'll pay you ten thousand pounds for your time. It's a one-off gig, because once your photo's been in the papers we can't use you again.'

'It sounds fantastic,' Stacey murmured. 'Will I be identified in the photos?' she asked, and Sancho shook his head. 'You'll be the mystery girl, and we'll never identify you. If one of your mates happens to go running to the papers though, it isn't our problem.'

'Then I'll do it,' Stacey said. 'Of course I'll do it.'

Sancho gave her a huge grin. 'Darling, once Johnny chose you, you never really had a choice.'

Stacey smiled sweetly, safe in the knowledge her MP3 recorder had picked up everything.

Ella could hear Stacey and Chastity talking to each other excitedly, but she couldn't quite make out what they were saying. It was as if she'd fallen underwater, and everything was hazy. She could make out their voices, but she couldn't define the words, couldn't grasp what was going on. Ella knew her heart was racing, and that a thin film of sweat had suddenly coated her body, but she didn't know how to stop the fear and panic that had engulfed her. She felt trapped in ice-cold terror.

'Ella, are you okay?' Chastity's voice sliced through the fog that overwhelmed her, but it was all she could do to shake her head slightly.

'I think she's in shock,' Ella heard Stacey say, but it sounded as though her voice was coming from far away.

'I was set up,' Ella murmured. Her voice was thin and frail, and she wasn't even sure her words had even left her mouth. She tried again. 'Sancho and Johnny set me up.'

Chastity and Stacey looked at each other. Their

discovery about what Johnny Cooper and Sancho Tabora had been up to could wait.

'She's been asleep for a couple of hours,' Ella heard Chastity whisper as she felt a warm palm on her forehead. 'She had a bit of a shock.'

'I'm not surprised,' a male voice said, and Ella knew instantly it was Nash. She opened her eyes.

'Hey, Sleeping Beauty,' Nash said softly. He was crouching by the sofa, so close to her that Ella felt as though she was drowning in his brown eyes. How had she never noticed how gorgeous they were before?

'Hey,' she mumbled, and sat up. Her head was pounding, and it wasn't until she looked around the room and saw the concern on her friends' faces that she remembered. Johnny and Sancho. Shit. She could feel tears well up in her eyes, and she angrily brushed them aside.

'I really thought Johnny loved me,' Ella said eventually. Her voice was hollow, and matter-of-fact.

'We all thought he did,' Nash said softly. 'He took us all in . . . and you're not the only one he's done this to.'

Ella looked down at the gleaming parquet floor of her living room.

'But I am, aren't I?' she said. 'Sancho and Johnny have always got girls to trap men who have affairs, but what Johnny did to me was in a completely different league. He knew that my marriage to Danny was a sham, and he exploited it. He got me on his TV show, he convinced his producers to make me a presenter with him, and then he seduced me. They could have used someone anonymous – like a male model or something – but Johnny must have actively decided he wanted this job for himself. Because he knew it would give him an even bigger profile. He used me, and he made money from me.'

The realisation of what Johnny had done to her washed over her again, and she began to feel sick.

'Here, drink this,' Nash said, as he held out a glass of water. Ella took it gratefully.

'Sancho was always looking to make as much money from Danny as possible, and he found a way to do it. It was through me.'

Chastity looked confused. 'I don't understand,' she said finally. 'What's Danny got to do with this?'

Ella buried her head in her hands. She'd kept Danny's secret from her friends for so long that it had become second nature to her. Now though, both Chastity and Stacey deserved to know the truth.

'Danny's gay,' she said simply, as she locked eyes with Nash who gave her a supportive smile. 'Sancho knows, and he's been blackmailing him about it for years. I suppose honey-trapping me with Johnny was just another way for him to make money out of the situation.'

The living room was full of silence as Chastity and Stacey tried to take in this new piece of information.

'Danny Riding's *gay*?' Chastity repeated. Her big blue eyes were wide and she looked stunned. 'When did you find out?'

Ella sighed. 'I've always known. When we met on that beach in Thailand I genuinely had no idea who he was. I thought he was hot, but I wasn't looking for a relationship, and we quickly became friends. When he told me he was gay I was pleased – it meant there would be none of that "is he being friends with me because he fancies me" stuff – and when he told me he played for Kingston United I was blown away.'

'I knew there was something a bit odd about your relationship,' Stacey mused. 'You were *so* in love with Fin, and before you went off to Thailand you promised yourself that you'd never get involved with another man again. And then the next thing I heard was that you and Danny were engaged. It's not like you to jump from man to man.'

Ella gave Stacey a wry smile and tried hard not to look at Nash. It was true, she wasn't the sort of girl who went from relationship to relationship, but it didn't mean she didn't think about Nash that way sometimes. That she didn't wonder if Nash could be something more than just a friend. Ella pulled her knees up to her chin so she could rest her head on them. 'It just seemed like the perfect thing to do. Danny could never come out, I never wanted to fall in love again, and we just got on so well that at the time it made sense to get married.'

'But where does Sancho come into it?' Chastity asked. 'How does he know Danny's gay?'

Ella explained how Danny's ex-boyfriend had got involved with Sancho when he was still called Steven Turner, and how Sancho had started blackmailing Danny as soon as he could.

'But why would Danny just give him money?' Chastity said shrilly. 'Surely Aaron would have put a stop to it.'

'Aaron tried to stop it,' Nash interjected smoothly. 'He did everything he could to stop Sancho, but nothing worked. After the exposé on Johnny and Ella appeared in the papers Sancho stopped blackmailing Danny for a while, but I've heard he's ramping it up again.'

'He's got to be stopped,' Ella said wearily. 'This whole situation has got to finish, now.'

'We *can* stop it,' Stacey exclaimed. 'We can take the recording of my meeting with Johnny and Sancho to the police, and we can tell them what they've been up to.'

Nash shook his head. 'I don't think that will work,' he said. 'I don't think talking about doing something is proof enough.'

'Then I'll go through with the job, and we'll get proof that way,' Stacey said. Her eyes were alive with determination.

'But you're pregnant,' Ella said. 'What if you get hurt?'

'The only people who'll get hurt will be Sancho and Johnny,' she said with as much resolve as she could muster. 'Mark my words.'


'Are you really okay?' Nash asked Ella as she lay on her bed later that night. Stacey had gone home, Chastity was catching up on her YourHappyEverAfter.com work, and Nash had refused to leave Ella's side. He'd gone to the shops and come back laden with soup and bread, and after making sure she'd eaten a decent amount of food he'd carried her into her bedroom and placed her gently on her bed. Ella couldn't remember the last time she'd been so lovingly looked after – in fact, she wasn't sure she'd ever had a boyfriend who cared for her so sweetly – and despite the horror of finding out Johnny had been using her throughout their whole relationship, she felt safe and secure.

'My headache's gone and I'm feeling a lot better,' Ella said with a smile, and she stretched slightly under her cream blankets. Her bedroom at Castle House had been perfect, but this room was really hers. It had duck-egg blue walls, distressed French style white furniture, and lots of fluffy sheepskin rugs everywhere. It was warm, inviting, and it felt like home. 'It's good of you to be here.'

'When Chastity phoned the office to say you'd collapsed I rushed straight over. Of course I did. We're friends, aren't we?'

'We are.' Ella nodded, and touched Nash's arm. 'You're like my fairy godmother or something. It always seems like you're rescuing me or coming to my aid.'

'In that case I'm your knight in shining armour.'

Or my Prince Charming, Ella thought, but she didn't say it out loud. She didn't dare.

'I don't mind if you want to go home, you know,' she said, changing the subject. 'You've been here for hours.'

Nash grinned. 'Are you trying to get rid of me?'

Ella shook her head. 'Absolutely not. But if you have something you need to do in the office or at home I'll understand . . .' Her voice trailed off as she caught Nash's gaze.

'I have nothing to do apart from be here with you,' he said, and he lay down next to her. It reminded Ella of the time they'd snuggled up together in bed in Nash's flat, and she wondered if Nash was thinking of it too. That had been the first time she'd realised just how much she liked him. That she wanted him.

'God, you must have a really boring life then,' she said lightly.

'Must do,' Nash agreed, and they lay in Ella's bed in silence for a while, listening to their breathing as it began to mimic each other's until they were perfectly in sync.

'You've had a hell of a day again, Ella,' Nash said eventually. 'If I found out I'd been given a new career and then seduced just to create a sensationalist news story I don't think I'd be as calm as you.'

Ella let out a short little laugh. 'I'm not calm inside,' she said. 'But I don't see the point in throwing things around. Besides, I wanted to find out why Johnny broke up with me and now I know why he did – he didn't need me any more. His job was done.'

Nash let his gaze trail across Ella's face. Despite what she'd found out her violet eyes still had innocence in them, and she was still able to smile.

'Aaron always said he never asked questions if he wasn't sure he'd like the answer, and he was right. I knew that Chastity's digging would unearth something horrible – but I had no idea it would end up being something like this.'

'What did you think she and Stacey would find out?'

Ella thought for a moment. 'I suppose I assumed that Johnny had been stringing me along and that he'd met someone else. That was what Fin did to me, and it seemed obvious that Johnny would do the same thing.'

Nash eyed Ella thoughtfully. 'Not all men are assholes, you know,' he said eventually. 'And not every man will cheat on you or fuck you around.'

Ella bit her lip. 'It doesn't feel like it sometimes.'

Nash pulled Ella close to him, and she shut her eyes and breathed in his scent. He smelled of washing powder and of something peppery. She loved it.

'Trust me, some of us are good guys.'

For some reason Ella felt like she was going to cry in despair, so she concentrated hard on the matter at hand, rather than matters of the heart.

'It's really good of you to put us in touch with a

photographer,' she said briskly. 'Do you really think he'll be up for the challenge?'

Nash shifted slightly away from her and Ella could feel his body tense.

'Oh, absolutely,' he said smoothly. 'Adam Russell used to take photos of wild animals in Africa, and the fashion shoots he's currently doing are boring him to tears.'

'And he knows what he's got to do?'

'Ella, he knows what he's got to do. Don't worry about a thing – we're going to nail these creeps once and for all, and then you can have your happy ever after. Dot com.'

Ella laughed, and she prayed that Nash was right. She also refused to listen to the voice in her head that said you never really had a happy ending without a man.

## Chapter Twenty-One

Stacey stood in the lobby of the May Fair Hotel and waited anxiously for the signal. She'd told Jay that she was spending the night at Ella's flat again, and when he'd believed her she'd felt wracked with guilt. She hated lying to her fiancé, but if Jay had known the truth there was no way he'd allow her to go through with it. Not that she was sure what 'it' was, or how it would end.

She spotted a flurry of activity in the dark bar, and Stacey knew that Elliot Thomas – the former soap star who'd recently won *I'm a Celebrity, Get Me Out Of Here!* – had left his suite at the top of the hotel and made his grand entrance. Elliot's star had been on the wane since he'd left *Jubilee Crescent* – the soap that had made him – but ever since he'd shown off his tanned, buff body in the jungle, teenage girls and housewives across the country had fallen in love with him all over again.

They loved him almost as much as his wife did.

'Time to move in for the kill,' a passing man murmured to Stacey, and she took a deep breath. It was show time. She teetered on her heels and walked from the lobby into the bar and scanned the room. Elliot Thomas was lounging on one of the deep velvet sofas, and he already had drinks lined up on the copper-coloured table in front of him. Plenty of party girls in various states of undress surrounded him, and Elliot looked as though he didn't have a care in the world.

If Johnny and Sancho had their way he soon would do, she thought darkly.

Stacey ordered a glass of tonic water at the bar and shifted her position slightly so she could see if Elliot had noticed her. As predicted, Stacey was the only redhead in the room, and she'd already caught the actor's attention. Elliot was openly staring at her, drinking in the curves of her body that were tightly covered by a burgundy Jean Paul Gaultier dress. Ella had chosen it from Chastity's over-flowing wardrobe because it matched Stacey's hair perfectly.

'God, men are stupid,' Stacey muttered to herself, and she turned back to watch the barman create a complicated-looking cocktail. She could feel Elliot's eyes on her, and she knew the best way to entice him was to play hard-to-get. Being obvious wasn't her style, and besides, she didn't want to come across as desperate.

'I couldn't help but notice your fabulous dress,' a voice murmured in her ear ten minutes later, and Stacey shivered in revulsion. She plastered on a sexy smile and turned around.

'I'm only sorry my fabulous dress didn't notice you,' she purred effortlessly, although inside she felt sad. When he'd been in the jungle Elliot Thomas had rhapsodised about how much he loved his wife, and how he couldn't have gone through his post-*Jubilee Crescent* blues without her support. Now though, it was like she didn't even exist.

'Well, allow me to introduce myself to it,' Elliot said with a smarmy smile. 'Or does your dress recognise me already?'

Stacey laughed out loud. 'My dress *definitely* recognises you, Mr Thomas. How could it not?'

Elliot smiled his perfect, made-for-TV smile, and Stacey grinned back at him. She used to love watching Elliot on TV and there was no denying he was sexy, even if he was a complete arsehole.

'Can I buy you a drink?' Elliot asked hopefully, and Stacey shook her head.

'I've got one already, thanks,' and she turned back to the bar.

'But you deserve so much better,' Elliot said, and Stacey glanced at him from over her shoulder.

'What do you mean?' she said.

'You deserve a drink from me.'

Stacey paused for a moment. 'But why should you buy *me* a drink when there's several other beautiful girls in this bar?' she asked.

Elliot shot her his megawatt smile again and shrugged. Stacey had always thought he was good-looking – how could she not? – but in that moment she saw his mass-market appeal. He was gorgeous . . . and if this had been any other situation she'd have been excited to be talking to him. She would even have asked for his autograph.

'Why *shouldn't* I buy you a drink?' he replied. 'There's enough of me to go around . . . and besides, don't you want to tell your friends that Elliot Thomas chatted you up?'

If only he knew, Stacey thought.

'You're right,' she said out loud, and Elliot moved his hands through his floppy blonde hair.

'I always am. It's why I'm a star . . . or so everyone tells me.'

'So what brings you to London?' Stacey asked as Elliot ordered a bottle of champagne. It was vintage and expensive, and Stacey wished she could have a sip. She needed the Dutch courage.

'My PR set up loads of interviews with newspapers and magazines. It's such a drag coming down here from Manchester, but people want to know all about me,' Elliot said with a weariness that Stacey could tell was false.

'Wow,' she said. 'That's amazing.'

'Yeah,' Elliot sighed. 'But it's so tiring being fawned over all the time. One journalist even made a pass at me. But she wasn't my type.'

'And what's your type?' Stacey asked lightly.

'I'm looking at her.'

Stacey smiled at Elliot, and as he led her over to a private corner of the bar, she felt a tiny jolt of excitement. He was hooked.

Stacey stared down at the intoxicated TV actor who was dribbling in her lap and sighed.

For the last three hours she'd listened to Elliot tell his life story, and time had passed incredibly slowly. She didn't think it was possible for anyone to believe his or her own hype, but Elliot Thomas had proved her wrong. He'd just been explaining how he was thinking of going to Hollywood to become a world-famous star when the copious amount of alcohol he'd drunk kicked in. Suddenly he turned from a standard-issue egotist into someone narcissistic and needy.

'You're amazing,' Elliot mumbled into Stacey's lap, and she reached out to stroke his hair. When they'd realised that Elliot only had eyes for Stacey, the majority of girls in the bar had left in a huff, and only the hardcore drinkers remained. The night was definitely reaching its end.

'No, you're amazing,' Stacey said in a breathy voice. 'I don't think I've ever met anyone as inspirational as you. You have no idea.'

'No, *you* have no idea,' Elliot slurred. 'You're really, *really* amazing. The most amazingist.'

Stacey laughed. 'And you haven't even seen what I can *really* do,' she said flirtatiously, and Elliot sat up. He swayed ever so slightly, and Stacey put her arm around him to keep him still. He didn't even notice.

'Oh yeah?' he said. He could barely focus on her, and Stacey realised that if she'd really planned to seduce him, he wouldn't be able to perform. He could hardly keep his eyes open.

'Yeah,' she whispered in his ear. 'And as well as being amazing, I can't fucking keep my hands off you.'

'I can't keep my hands off *you*!' Elliot exclaimed. 'It's a sign!'

'It really is,' Stacey murmured. 'I have a room here . . .'

'I have a suite here!' Elliot said. 'It's a sign!'

Stacey counted to ten. He was one of *those* drunks, then. 'It *is* a sign,' she repeated. 'But Elliot, we should go to my room.'

'Why?' he asked petulantly.

Stacey thought hard. 'So I can slip into something a little more comfortable,' she said eventually. 'And I have a present for you, too.'

'I like presents!' Elliot announced, and it took all of Stacey's strength not to roll her eyes. 'And I like you. You seem to understand me. Not many people do . . .' His voice trailed off, and Stacey realized that she was seeing the real Elliot Thomas – the insecure, unsure actor who was boosted by other people's interest and didn't feel like he was anyone when he wasn't the centre of attention.

'You don't feel like anyone understands you?' she asked softly, and Elliot shook his head.

'The only person who really understands me is my wife,' Elliot mumbled. 'But since I came out of the jungle she doesn't seem to even like me very much. She doesn't want to come to London with me, she doesn't want to leave her job to come to America with me.' His blue eyes focused for a second and his gaze held hers. 'I love her, but I'm lonely. I'm so lonely.'

Stacey led Elliot from the bar towards the lift and as she propped the actor up she noticed some of Johnny and Sancho's men watching her carefully. She could see the small cameras with long lenses they held in their hands, but if she hadn't known to look for them, she'd never have noticed them at all. Stacey knew they were taking their photos, but there was no noise, no camera flashes – nothing.

'But *you* seem to understand me,' Elliot slurred as they walked towards the lift. 'I could probably fall in love with you and *you* could be my wife!' He dropped to his knees and clasped his arms around her legs. 'Will you marry me?'

Stacey left Elliot on the floor for a few seconds – it was one of those picture-perfect moments Sancho had encouraged her to get – and then tried to lift Elliot up, but he was too heavy. 'I'll do anything you like if you'll accompany me to my room, darling,' she said as tenderly as she could. She hated the idea of Elliot's drunken body crashing into her pregnant body and she wanted him to stop hanging off her.

'I'll try,' he whimpered, and after several attempts he managed to stand. 'Let's go up to your room,' Elliot declared, and as Stacey caught a brief nod from one of the photographers, she grimaced. Mission accomplished.

'So these are the shots I managed to get of Sancho and Johnny's photographers,' Adam Russell explained as he lay out a selection of glossy, full-colour prints on Ella and Chastity's orange dining table. Everyone was there – Ella, Chastity, Stacey and Nash – and as they gazed at the photos they all agreed each was perfect. Adam had managed to get the photographers in every shot, and you could clearly see them pointing their cameras at Stacey and Elliot. The paparazzi had been papped, and they'd been so caught up in their work that they hadn't even noticed.

'These are brilliant,' Chastity said in awe. 'You captured the moment perfectly.'

Adam Russell fixed his dark brown eyes on Chastity for a moment longer than necessary and then smiled back. 'Well, you guys told me what I had to do, and I did it. That's my job.'

'And Stacey, you look great,' Ella added. She still couldn't quite get her head around the circumstances – that her step-sister was in a *situation* with Elliot Thomas. And that she was wearing Jean Paul Gaultier. In the May Fair Hotel. The whole thing just felt completely surreal if she thought about it too much.

'Thanks.' Stacey yawned. 'I have to say, when the night was over I didn't feel too great. I was exhausted from having to talk to Elliot all night. He's one of those men who loves the sound of his own voice . . . but underneath it all he's just really insecure and wants to be looked after.'

'But what happened when you made it up to your room?' Ella asked curiously.

'God, nothing happened – and nothing would have. I'm engaged, remember?'

Ella grinned. 'And pregnant. But thank God for your attractive pregnancy breasts, huh?'

'Hey! He fell for my personality, I'll have you know.'

'Erm, wasn't it your hair he was into?' Chastity interjected, and Stacey rolled her eyes.

'Anyway, as soon as he danced over to the bed – that's right, he *danced* – he fell onto it. He mumbled something about how he's never cheated on his wife before – and I believed him, he was really awkward with me – but before I could say we didn't have to do anything he was out cold. I changed out of that beautiful dress into my jeans, paid for the room, told the staff to keep an eye on him because he was so wasted, and got a cab back here. He probably woke up wondering why his suite had shrunk into a normal room.'

Chastity laughed slightly louder than necessary, and Ella noticed her eyes were still on Adam Russell, who was gazing back at her. He seemed mesmerised.

'I almost feel sorry for him,' Nash said, before bringing the conversation back to business. 'But now that you have these photos what are you going to do with them? Whatever you decide to do, you have to do it soon – before Sancho puts his story about Elliot Thomas having an affair on his site. And Stacey needs to fill her boyfriend in on everything too – just in case he gets the wrong end of the stick.'

Everyone turned to look at Ella, who bit her lip. 'Nash, what do you suggest?' she said. She knew they had great ammunition – when you put the photos with the recording Stacey had made there was no denying what Johnny and

Sancho were up to – but she wasn't sure what they could do with it.

Nash thought for a moment. 'You could confront Sancho and Johnny and tell them that you know about their kiss-and-tell scam,' he said. 'But I'm not sure what good that will do you in the long run. It probably wouldn't stop them from doing it again to someone else, and to be honest, they probably wouldn't even care that you know.'

'Why wouldn't they care?' Ella said quietly. She felt like the wind had been taken out of her. Okay, so she'd only gone into this wanting to know why Johnny hadn't ever returned her calls, but now she knew what they were up to, she wanted to do the right thing.

Nash sighed, and Ella noticed he looked tired. He'd been putting every hour he could into his new business, and on top of that he never failed to be there for her when she needed it. At that moment Ella resolved to look after Nash as much as he'd looked after her. 'Because they don't care what you think of them,' he said reluctantly. 'They think you're a stupid WAG who could never hurt them.'

Ella thought about how Sancho had blackmailed Danny for years, and how Johnny had made her fall in love again, only to toss her aside once he'd got what he was after. In a twisted way she was grateful to him – she'd been adamant that she was never going to give her heart to anyone, and Johnny had broken down those walls – but she mostly hated Johnny, and despised both of them. Sancho had milked Danny for all he could, and then to make even more money they'd played with her emotions and ruined her life.

And they didn't even care.

'I'm going to phone the *Sunday Times*,' Ella announced calmly, as she pictured the journalist who had done that

292

profile of her. It felt like it was a lifetime ago, but it was time for everyone to know who Ella Aldridge really was, and just what she was capable of.

'I'm going to tell them exactly what Johnny and Sancho did to me, and I'm going to expose their little money-making scheme so they can never do it to anyone else ever again.'

'Are you sure you want to do this?' Chastity asked, as she put her hand over Ella's fist. 'There's probably another way – we just have to put our heads together.'

Ella smiled. 'Sancho and Johnny think it's okay to ruin people's lives by setting them up and taking photos of them, so I think it's only fair that we do the same to them,' she said in determination. 'We've played them at their own game, and now we're going to win.'


When the news broke it was everywhere.

The *Sunday Times* ran eight pages about the scam, and suddenly Johnny Cooper was thrust back into the spotlight. This time, he wasn't being applauded for managing to have an affair with Ella Riding; he was being derided, and in a matter of minutes he'd gone from the golden boy of television to public enemy number one.

Before Ella did her interview with the paper she was nervous. She'd spent such a long time avoiding the press that willingly going to them and putting herself in the limelight felt like the antithesis of everything she'd worked for. But with Nash's support she went to the *Sunday Times* and told them everything she knew. At first they were sceptical – Ella Riding was a wannabe, wasn't she? And wasn't she just trying to get even with a man who'd loved and dumped her? – but when she produced Stacey's tapes and the photos

Adam had taken, the journalists began to believe her. With a bit of digging the paper had uncovered the true story, and when they told Ella what they'd uncovered she was left stunned. She'd been a pawn in a dirty game, only this pawn had turned around and fought the kings.

It turned out that Johnny and Sancho weren't just friends, they were also cousins, and their relationship had been cemented when they were both sent to the same boarding school by parents who'd never had much time for them.

Sancho – or Steven, as he'd been known then – had spent years desperately trying to be a showbiz journalist, but he was essentially lazy, and couldn't be bothered to put the work in. He'd thought access to celebrities – and the parties they attended – should be his fundamental right, and after time and persistence he got to know the right people and began to mix in showbiz circles, telling everyone he was a blogger who would eventually rival Perez Hilton.

According to the newspapers, it was Johnny who suggested they start their kiss-and-tell scam. Sancho was always bragging about celebrities he knew to be playing away, and Johnny – who at this time was still trying to make it as a TV presenter – realized this could be his way to riches. They started off small at first, using glamour models who wanted to be famous, but as time went on they started to make millions from the photographs they sold. By this time Johnny was famous in his own right, and was bringing in a healthy income from his TV work, but Sancho, who'd obviously known Danny was gay for years, saw Ella as the ultimate celebrity to scam. Johnny volunteered to do the job himself. It had to be done right, and Johnny wouldn't trust anyone else to do it.

But he also fancied getting to know Ella Riding a hell of a lot better. Who wouldn't?

As people opened up their morning papers and switched on their computers all anyone could talk about was what Johnny and Sancho had been up to. It was the scoop of the year as it had it all – celebrities, sex, money and power – and it was a story that refused to go away. Suddenly Ella was repainted as the victim, an innocent girl who'd been seduced for money and hadn't stood a chance against Johnny and Sancho, and her face began to appear in trashy celeb magazines again – this time in a positive light.

Meanwhile Fairytale Productions announced that Johnny was suspended from *A Week in Wonderland* while they did an internal investigation over the claims, and after police raided the SanchosWorld.com office – investigating allegations of prostitution with intent to defame those in the public eye – the website shut down.

A week after the story broke, Johnny and Sancho went underground. Nobody knew where they were, and Ella was glad. She wanted both men out of her life for ever, and she hoped that they remained out of sight for good.

'We brought them down,' Chastity laughed gleefully, as she and Ella reread all the cuttings they'd acquired about Johnny and Sancho. 'Not only did we find out why Johnny never phoned you back, we also found out something a lot darker, and we've stopped them from hurting anyone else ever again.'

Ella smiled. 'We did it,' she said, but she knew deep down she wasn't as elated as she should be. Even though she was over Johnny, it still hurt knowing that he'd used her so callously. And what made it worse was that he was such a good actor, and that he was so believable. Or was it that she had so wanted to believe that Johnny was her Prince Charming that she'd fallen for him blindly? Had there been warning signs? Could she have spotted what Johnny had been up to? She didn't know.

All she knew was that she'd fallen in love with someone who'd made his fortune doing the same thing to countless others . . . but unlike the others she'd stopped him from ever doing it again. If that wasn't revenge, she didn't know what was. The thought brightened her mood.

'Here's to us.' Ella grinned, and this time her smile reached her eyes. 'Here's to two former WAGs showing everyone what they're made of – and that we're not the dumb bimbos people like to think we are.'

She and Chastity raised their cans of Diet Coke to each other, and each took a long gulp.

'But now that we've taken down Johnny and our website's running smoothly what do we do next?' Chastity asked. 'We can't stop here. How about going public with the website and telling everyone we're behind it? That's the next logical step to take, isn't it?'

'We could go public,' Ella said, 'but I like having a part of my life that's completely anonymous and isn't linked to me in any way. I know that doesn't make sense really, but do you know what I mean?'

Chastity nodded. 'Totally,' she said. 'It's like the website is successful because of the work we've done, rather than because it belongs to Chastity Taylor and Ella Riding, former footballers' wives.'

'Exactly. But I also like the idea of building upon that success,' Ella continued, 'and to do that we probably would have to admit that we're behind it.'

'We've got a lot to think about,' Chastity mused, and Ella nodded.

'We do, but right now all we need to do is sit back and celebrate. After all, we've not only become businesswomen, but we've also taken on the bad guys and won.'

'To us,' Chastity announced again. 'To celebrating our Happy Ever After, and to deciding what we're going to do next.'

Ella grinned. 'To us,' she echoed. 'And even though I don't know what comes next, I do know that whatever we decide to do it will be bloody good. It has to be.'

# Chapter Twenty-Two

'So how do you feel now everything's out in the open and Johnny and Sancho have been exposed?' Nash asked Ella as they drank champagne in her living room. She'd invited Nash over on the pretext of him sharing a celebratory, home-cooked meal with her and Chastity, but at the last minute Chastity had gone out for a few 'quiet drinks' with Adam, and the two of them were trying to roast a joint of beef together. Ella knew it was hopeless – she didn't know why she was unable to cook any food except cupcakes – but they'd managed to put it in the oven at the right temperature, and now all they had to do was wait.

'Something doesn't feel right,' Ella admitted as she fiddled with her champagne flute. 'Chastity and I were celebrating the other day and looking at all the press coverage, and even though I'm pleased we uncovered Johnny, it doesn't feel like the ending I was looking for. It's not that it's an anticlimax, it just feels like we've missed something . . . that a piece of the puzzle is still missing.'

Nash raised his eyebrows. 'But we covered all the bases,' he said. 'And what we didn't know the paper found out. It's all there, in black and white, and millions of people have been reading about it.'

'I know,' Ella said. 'But the story doesn't feel over. Not yet. It just doesn't feel like I've got my happy ending.'

Nash mused on this for a while. 'Maybe what you're looking for is an apology,' he suggested. 'Maybe exposing Johnny feels good, but what you need is for him to explain why he did what he did to you.'

'Maybe. But I know why he did it. He knew Danny and I weren't in a sexual relationship, and he knew that I'd be his for the taking. He also assumed – correctly – that he'd be able to raise his own profile by getting "caught" having an affair with me. Even if he apologised it wouldn't make a difference. He wasn't sorry when he was doing it, and he'd only be sorry now because he's been caught out.'

Ella rested her head on one of her hands and gazed at Nash. 'I just thought that once all this was out in the open I'd feel different. I mean, I should feel different, shouldn't I? People now know that Johnny seduced me – and that I wasn't the evil harlot who cheated on Danny for no reason – and as well as that I have my own successful business. So why aren't I happier?'

Nash gazed into Ella's violet eyes, but just as it looked as though he was about to speak he changed his mind.

Ella felt a tiny tug at her heart. Before her mother passed away she used to read stories to Ella where the happy ending involved a girl getting whisked off her feet by a handsome prince. Okay, so real life wasn't like that, but after everything she'd been through, didn't she deserve a decent man?

Didn't she deserve someone like Nash?

The tug of longing grew even stronger, and Ella wished she could say something to him. But she couldn't. How could she? Nash was one of the most important people in her life, and if she misjudged him and ruined their friendship her happy ending wouldn't even be moderately cheerful. Just as she was trying to work out what to say the smoke detector in the flat started to screech loudly, and they both jumped to their feet and raced to the kitchen.

'I think it's done,' Ella remarked, as she pulled the battery out of the smoke detector and then eyed the smoking tray she'd taken out of the oven.

'It's definitely done,' Nash agreed, as they both stared at the meat. It looked like a big lump of charcoal. It was ruined.

'I have a pizza in the fridge,' Ella grinned. 'Do you think it will go with the champagne?'

'Darling, anything goes with champagne. But please put it in the oven soon; I'm starving. How long does it take?'

'Um, about fifteen minutes,' Ella said, as she flipped the pizza box over and read the instructions. 'Don't you miss those days of being at Castle House when gourmet suppers appeared out of thin air?'

'Yeah, how *did* you manage to eat so well when you lived there? And how can you be so appalling at cooking now?'

Ella smiled. 'I ordered all our meals from a personal chef,' she admitted. 'I don't think Danny even knew. Or if he did, he never said anything.'

Nash raised his eyebrow. 'So why didn't you order in tonight?' he asked. 'Am I not worth impressing?'

'You're definitely worth impressing, Barnwell. But I thought I'd keep it real and try to do it myself. Only, I don't seem to be very good at it. Plus getting meals from a personal chef is bloody expensive.'

Nash shook his head slowly. 'You're helping to improve the lives of thousands of women with your successful website, and you've just brought down Johnny Cooper and Sancho Tabora, but you can't cook. You're amazing.'

'And that's why you love me,' Ella joked lightly, as she bent over and slid the pizza in the oven. But as soon as she said it she regretted it. The light-hearted atmosphere had turned into something else, something unidentifiable, and she wished she could take her words back.

Nash stared at Ella's back, and then he came up behind her. He circled her with his arms and pulled her so she was leaning close against him. He gently kissed the top of her head, and Ella was just about to spin on her heel to place her lips on his when he stepped away. She turned around and looked at him.

'That's why I love having you in my life,' Nash said simply, and then he gave Ella such a dazzling smile that she couldn't help but grin back.

'Don't lie,' she said as calmly as she could, as if kissing him was the furthest thing from her mind. 'You only like having me around because you know you'll never eat well and you'll eventually lose weight.' She prodded a finger into Nash's rock-hard stomach and turned back to the pizza before he could see the lust in her eyes. If Nash was ever going to kiss her, that had been the moment.

And he hadn't.

Perhaps they were best suited to being friends, after all.

'What's that noise?' Nash muttered, as Ella sat bolt upright in bed. Her head was pounding, her skin was clammy and her mouth was dry. She reached for her glass of water and took a big gulp. It made her feel like she was about to be sick and she knew, without a doubt, that she had the hangover from hell.

'It's the intercom,' she managed to say, as she took in the scene of her bedroom. The air was stuffy, and even though she was normally pretty neat, the room looked like a bomb site. Designer clothes were strewn across the floor – Ella vaguely remembered Nash asking her to give him a fashion show of some of Chastity's more ridiculous, pre-divorce outfits – and there were several empty champagne bottles lying on their sides. Nash was on top of her bed, fully dressed in jeans and a shirt. He looked as rough as she felt, and Ella felt a wave of disappointment run through her. He'd slept over, but he hadn't even kissed her.

Ella pulled herself out of bed, grimaced as her hangover headache pounded through her body, and slowly walked towards the front door. Chastity hadn't come home last night, and Ella half expected to see her face peering up at her through the video intercom. When she glanced at the screen properly, her heart gave a little leap. It wasn't Chastity; it was Danny.

Ella smiled to herself and pressed the button to let him up to the flat.

'God you look like shit,' Danny announced as he walked in and looked around. 'Are you ill?'

Ella bit her lip and shook her head. 'Nash came over for supper and we had a bit too much to drink,' she said, as Nash walked out of her bedroom and joined them in the hall.

Danny glanced at him and back to Ella. 'Am I interrupting something?' he asked suspiciously, as his eyes twinkled.

'God no!' Ella exclaimed. 'It's nothing like that! Nash just crashed here because he was too drunk to get home . . . I think.' To be honest, she couldn't really remember getting to bed, or when Nash had decided to stay the night. She had a fleeting memory of her resting her head on his chest in the middle of the night, and of him draping his arm over her body, but just as she tried to remember it properly the memory vanished.

'Yeah, you're definitely *not* interrupting anything, apart from my beauty sleep.' Nash winked, and Ella shot a look at him. He was running his hands through his light brown hair and even though he had dark circles under his bloodshot eyes, he looked amused at the thought that anything would ever have happened with him and Ella. She felt disappointed again, but was determined not to show it.

'You know Nash is like my big brother . . . just like you're like my younger one,' she said as pointedly as she could. 'Anyway, forget about that – it's so good to see you!' Ella held her arms out and Danny enveloped her in a huge bear hug. She realised at that moment just how much she'd missed him.

'Why has it taken you so long to come and see me?'

'Why has it taken you so long to issue an invitation?' Danny replied, and then he rolled his eyes. 'To be honest Aaron told me I was never allowed to see you again, and I thought he was right – at least until the dust settled. But then you found out all that stuff about Johnny and Sancho and I figured Aaron couldn't be angry with you any more, so sod it. Here I am. Do I get a tour of your amazing pent-house apartment? I still can't believe you live with Chastity, you know. Is she still a bitch?'

Ella washed her face and brushed her teeth, and then led Danny around her flat. Okay, she was still dressed in a pink T-shirt and bright orange cotton knickers, but it didn't really matter. Danny knew her inside out and it very obviously didn't make a difference if Nash saw her bottom or not. He wasn't into her like that. She got it.

'Wow, it's the very opposite of Castle House, isn't it?' Danny remarked as he stood in her living room. He looked at the incredible panoramic view of the rest of London and then sat on the fuchsia sofa with a sigh.

'Yep,' Ella replied happily, as she sat down beside him. Nash was busying himself making toast in the kitchen, and Ella hoped he'd manage to do it without burning it like she probably would have. 'We wanted to make it feel like "ours" rather than that of a couple of footballers' wives. We think we did a pretty good job.'

'But how did you afford it?' Danny asked. 'Did Freddie pay for it?'

Ella nodded. 'And we're working now, too.'

Danny's mouth dropped open. 'You're working? God, so much has changed. What are you doing?'

'We launched a website,' Ella said smugly. '*And* it's making money. We're even thinking about getting an office and some staff.'

Danny shook his head. 'I'm impressed,' he said, and he took Ella's hand and squeezed it tightly. 'Actually, I'm more than impressed. I'm proud of you, too.'

Ella beamed, and in that moment she felt her hangover start to ease off a bit. All she needed was a can of Coke and perhaps a bacon sandwich and she was sure she'd be right as rain.

'Um, I burnt the toast,' Nash said quietly as he stuck his head around the living-room door, and Ella tried not to laugh. 'I'm desperate for a bacon sandwich and some

Coke . . . do you guys want some too? I'll pop down the café to pick some up.'

Ella's silent laughter vanished and she stared at Nash for a second. It was almost like he was reading her mind deliberately to wind her up, but that was impossible, wasn't it? 'Yes please,' she said, and they both looked at Danny, who shook his head.

'Aaron has me on this macrobiotic diet and I'm only allowed brown rice and beans. A bacon sandwich would definitely be "yin".'

Ella tried not to look gobsmacked but she couldn't hide the smile that played on her lips. 'What? You're kidding me, right?'

'Aaron thinks it will help with my performance on the pitch,' Danny said defensively, 'and I'm willing to do what it takes. I haven't scored a goal in four games now and I don't want to get benched.'

'Kingston United would never bench you!' Ella laughed as Nash went out to get their breakfast.

Danny shook his head. 'They would, you know,' he said. 'They're all about results and at the moment we're fourth in the table. If I play badly in my next game I'm done for.'

'But Danny, eating rice isn't going to help you get a goal. You know that. You need to work out what the real problem is and solve that.'

Danny was quiet for the longest time, and after a while he walked over to the floor-to-ceiling window so he could gaze at the city. It was beautiful.

'Your exposé on Johnny and Sancho was really some-thing,' he said in a soft voice. 'I was stunned when I read it.'

'I know,' Ella said, as she scrambled to her feet to join him. She could see condensation from Danny's breath on the window, and she suddenly realised the flat was cold. She rubbed her bare arms with her hands. 'It seemed they targeted me all along – that's why I was invited on *Cooper's Kingdom*, and that's why I was given the presenting slot on *A Week in Wonderland*. Johnny wanted me in easy reach so he could seduce me.'

Danny sighed. 'We should have seen through him, but your star was rising so fast that being asked to be a TV presenter didn't seem so ridiculous.'

'Even though I had no experience in it?' Ella asked quietly.

'We made a mistake,' Danny said, as he looked at her guiltily. 'Aaron made a mistake.'

Ella frowned. 'You mustn't think this was all your fault,' she said. 'Nobody could have known what Johnny and Sancho were up to.'

'But we should have,' Danny stressed. 'We knew Sancho wasn't about to stop blackmailing me, and we should have run proper checks on Johnny.'

'But even if we had we never would have linked Johnny to Sancho. And besides, it's over now. They can't hurt us any more.'

Danny turned to look to Ella, and she was surprised to see there were tears in his eyes.

'That's where you're wrong.'

'So explain this to me again to see if I can make sense of it,' Nash said as he massaged his temples. He clearly had a killer hangover, but his concentration was focussed solely on Danny, and Ella loved him for it.

'The last time I heard from Sancho was when he emailed

to thank me for the millions he'd made out of the photos of Johnny and Ella together,' Danny said.

'And now . . . ?' Nash asked.

'Now Sancho's been in touch again and he's furious. He's livid that Ella cottoned onto his honeytrap scam and he wants revenge.'

'But how can he have revenge?' Ella asked, as she looked worriedly at Danny and Nash. She was with two men who made her feel safe, but even their presence didn't make her feel better about the situation.

Danny buried his head in his hands. 'His email said that it's not about the money any more; that it's about him having retribution . . . and that he's going to tell the papers I'm gay.'

Ella's mouth dropped open. 'But he can't do that!' she yelped. 'What Chastity and I did has nothing to do with you!'

'Sancho doesn't see it that way,' Danny said wearily. 'He sees you as an extension of me – which is why he was so keen to get Johnny to seduce you – and now you've hurt him he wants to hurt me back.'

'Oh for fuck's sake,' Ella groaned. 'I knew this wasn't over. I *knew* it.'

'So what do I do?' Danny asked, and as Ella knew the handsome, famous footballer was scared.

Nash moved over to sit next to Danny and put his arm around him. 'We'll work it out,' he said as comfortingly as he could. Ella caught his eye and they gazed at each other for a moment. They had to find a solution for this. And fast.

'Aaron says we should throw money at the problem – offer Sancho a million pounds, maybe two, but I know it's not going to have any effect,' Danny continued. His voice was dull, but it didn't need any expression to convey how distressed he was. His face said it all. 'It's not about the money for Sancho any more, not really.'

'But what is it about?' Ella asked.

'It's about Sancho feeling exposed, and his website being taken down,' Nash replied, as Danny nodded in agreement. 'You effectively ruined his career, and now he wants to do the same thing to Danny.'

'But he can't do that! He just can't!'

'He can,' Danny said.

'Well, if he wants to ruin someone's career he can ruin mine. He can go to the papers and make up lies about me or, I don't know, say *I'm* gay.' Ella knew she was clutching at straws, but she desperately didn't want Danny to be revealed as gay in the papers. It would destroy him.

'You're gay?' a voice said from the doorway, and all three of them turned to see Chastity. 'Well, I'm definitely not. I just had the most *amazing* night with Adam.'

Ella stared at her friend for a moment, and then Chastity realised that they weren't alone.

'Oh, hi Danny, how are you?' she said breezily as she threw her keys onto the table and flopped onto a chair with obvious post-coital exhaustion.

Danny glanced up at her, and Chastity looked shocked when she saw his eyes were filled with tears.

'I'm fine, thanks,' he said. 'I mean, I'm a gay footballer, and Sancho Tabora is about to out me in the press to ruin my career, but apart from that things couldn't be better. How are you?'

*Chapter Twenty-Three*

## DANNY RIDING: I'M GAY AND NOT ASHAMED

Exclusive by MATTHEW PARKER, News Editor, *Daily World*

**KINGSTON UNITED** striker Danny Riding opened his heart last night to reveal he is gay. The football star said in an exclusive interview: 'I'm proud of who I am, and I think it's important for people to know the truth.'

Danny, who was recently married to ex-TV babe Ella Riding, admitted that since he's played for Kingston United he's felt isolated because he fancies men.

'I never wanted to deceive my fans, but the football world can be a harsh place if you're gay. I found it hard to tell people about my sexuality, and I felt isolated because of it. With Ella's support and friendship I now feel ready to show the world who I really am.'

Danny, who is currently single, said that he had reservations about opening his heart.

'Someone recently tried to blackmail me about my sexuality, and even though I managed to prevent this from happening it flicked a switch in me. I don't want to live my life looking over my shoulder when I've done nothing wrong, and it's because of this that I have decided to tell my fans the truth: I'm gay.'

## ELL OF A GIRL

Danny admitted that loyal Ella didn't know Danny was gay when they got married, but has been his rock since he admitted his sexuality to himself.

'Ella has been brilliant,' Danny revealed. 'We were best friends when we married and despite my sexuality that hasn't changed. She understands that I want to stop deceiving people and be myself, and it was with her encouragement that I've taken this step.'

## ROYAL TREATMENT

When asked about how his fellow Royals teammates had taken the news, Danny said: 'They've been great. Kingston United is one of the best clubs in the world, and it has some of the best players, who are also good friends. Many of them have said they're not surprised about my sexuality, and they've closed ranks with me. I feel very lucky.

'Justin Fashanu was the first footballer to come out, and he had such a negative experience that it nearly put me off telling the truth. But times have changed. Gareth Thomas, the Welsh rugby legend, has talked about how much happier he is now that he's out and proud, and I'd like to be a role model like he is.'

Danny said that he hopes his revelations will prompt more athletes to admit their true sexuality to the public.

'If I can do it I hope that other footballers will feel that they can come out. It's 2012 and it's time for us to show there's nothing wrong with being true to yourself. The fans will accept you for who you are.'

'I'm so proud of you,' Ella sobbed, after she managed to get through the scrum of paparazzi outside Castle House and into Danny's arms. 'I can't believe you came out!'

Danny shrugged, but he couldn't hide his huge grin.

'I decided enough was enough,' he admitted. 'And after I sat down with Aaron and told him what I was going to do I felt a massive rush of freedom. Once Aaron knew my mind was made up he was fantastic – he got the coach and the Kingston United PRs over, and we planned the best way for me to do it. Seeing the front page of the *Daily World* was the most amazing feeling – I'm free. I feel totally and utterly free.'

Ella laughed in delight. 'And what's the reaction been like?' she asked.

'It's been incredible,' Danny said, and he showed her the hundreds of bouquets of flowers that he'd been sent from well-wishers. 'Nobody's said a bad word about me, and even though Aaron's sure there will be a backlash – and a few choice chants from the terraces when we play West Ham at the weekend – I'm ready for it. I'm just not prepared to lie any more.'

Ella wiped the tears that were running down her face. 'Well, I think you're unbelievably brave, and I'm behind you one hundred per cent.'

'I know you are,' Danny said, and he squeezed Ella closer to him. 'I never would have even considered doing it if you weren't.'

'And what does Yves say?' Ella asked.

'He's happy for me,' Danny said. 'He's not ready to come out himself, but I think that given time he will do. I'm sure he will. I don't think we could ever admit to being a couple – that might be a step too far for the Kingston

United fans – but that doesn't matter. I can be myself now, and guess what?'

'What?'

'A gay charity has been in touch and they want me to be their ambassador! It's amazing; I'll be able to help teenagers who aren't sure about their sexuality, or are too scared to come out.'

'That is amazing,' Ella said. She was delighted for Danny – of course she was – but she was also slightly nervous for him. When the rush of exhilaration had gone Danny would find that his place in the football world had changed, and she wasn't sure what that place would be yet. She hoped it would be okay.

'And the BBC has asked me if I'd like to start appearing on *Match of the Day* on the weekends we don't play – you know, so I can comment on games and players' form and things like that!'

'Really?' Ella said. Her mouth dropped open.

'Yeah. Aaron was a bit worried about the public reaction, and he got in touch with his TV contacts to see if there were any presenting roles available should I decide to retire from the game.'

'Retire?' Ella asked. 'Would you do that? I thought you really wanted to play in the next World Cup!'

'Oh I do, I really do, but if the fans decide they can't cope with having me as a player then I'll have to accept that . . . and being a football presenter is the next best thing.'

'But, Danny,' Ella began slowly. 'You always said that football is your life, and that if you couldn't play you don't know what you'd do. I mean, the whole reason we got married was to boost your profile and to act as a cover for your sexuality, so that you could play and get great sponsorship deals.'

Danny shrugged. 'I thought playing football was the be all and end all, but you know what? I was wrong. Being true to who I am is more important, and I'd rather be myself and happy than a miserable, closeted footballer.'

Ella shook her head in disbelief. 'Do you mean that?' she asked, and Danny nodded.

'I want the fans to accept me – of course I do – but I'm a realist. Once all the fuss has died down the fans might decide they can't cope with seeing an openly gay footballer on the pitch, and if that's the case I don't want to have to listen to homophobic chants and boos every time I get a touch of the ball.'

'And if that happens you'll pursue a presenting job?'

Danny smiled. 'If that happens I'll happily hang up my boots and try my best to make homosexuality more acceptable in football however I can.'

Ella gazed at her former husband – at his gorgeous, piercing green eyes, his reddish-brown hair, and his sensual full lips – and she smiled again.

He really was one of the most incredible people she'd ever met, and she knew, without a doubt, that Danny Riding would be okay whatever happened.

'It really is all over now,' Chastity said a few months later as they sat in a mint-green hospital waiting room. 'Danny's out and happy, I'm thinking about moving in with Adam, and I can't believe we've finally got a real office for YourHappyEverAfter.com! With staff!'

Ella grinned. 'I know,' she said happily as she stretched her Lucky Brand denim-clad legs in front of her. 'And how amazing was that email we got from Fairytale Productions this morning?'

Chastity shook her head, checked there were no nurses prowling the waiting room, and then pulled her iPhone out of her bag so she could look at the email again. 'It's just, I don't know, extraordinary. I can't quite believe that a TV production company wants to turn YourHappyEverAfter.com into a TV show, and that Channel Four is really into the idea,' she said, as she reread the email for the hundredth time that day.

'But it makes sense, when you think about it,' Ella explained. 'The site's all about helping women improve their lives without the aid of men – and there's nothing like that on TV.'

'And how do you feel about their idea of us presenting it?' Chastity asked. 'It means admitting to the general public that we're behind the site.'

Ella bit her lip. 'You know what? I think I'm cool with it. No, I'm more than cool with it – it really excites me. Not only will we be consultants on the programme but we'll also be its public face. It sounds brilliant.'

'I bet you never thought you'd be on TV again,' Chastity remarked, and Ella shook her head.

'I really thought Johnny Cooper had ruined that for me, but despite only presenting *A Week in Wonderland* briefly it gave me the opportunity to show I can do it. It's just a dream come true, isn't it?'

'It really is,' Chastity said. 'And it's definitely a happy ending. Hey, did you ever find out what happened to Johnny?'

Ella shook her head. 'The last I heard he was thinking about reinventing himself as an actor – well, he is good at it,

I suppose — but I don't know if that rumour's true or not. Only time will tell, I suppose.'

'I hope he disappears off the planet,' Chastity mumbled, but Ella was more pragmatic about him.

'I don't really mind what he does, so long as he stays away from me.' Ella took a sip of her vending machine coffee and grimaced. 'I know Johnny's a complete bastard, but he kind of did Danny and I a favour by making me fall in love with him. If I hadn't left my marriage Danny probably never would have come out . . . so there's that to be grateful for.'

Ella also thought about how Johnny had opened her eyes to love again, and how she was no longer scared of falling for someone or being in a relationship. He may have been out to ruin her life, but Ella had managed to find some good from it, and for that she was thankful.

Just then a figure appeared in front of them. It was Jay, and he was crying tears of joy.

'It's a girl!' he announced, and despite herself, Ella welled up too.

'Oh my God,' she managed to say through her sobs. 'That's amazing. Can we see them?'

Jay nodded, and he led Ella and Chastity towards the room where Stacey was holding her brand new daughter. She looked absolutely exhausted, but Ella had never seen her so happy.

'I did it,' Stacey said simply, as they all stared at the tiny baby, whose face was scrunched up under her tuft of golden-red hair.

'She's beautiful,' Chastity whispered, and Ella nodded in agreement. She found she could barely speak.

'Ella, it goes without saying that we'd like you to be her

godmother, but . . .' Stacey trailed off and looked at Jay, who grinned back at her.

'We wanted you to be the first to know that we're going to name her after you, too.'

Ella could barely contain herself. 'Really?' she said unbelievingly. 'You're going to name your baby after me?'

Stacey nodded and began to rock the tiny baby in her arms as it began to stir. 'We're not going to call her Ella exactly – we thought that would be too confusing – but we thought Gabriella, or Gaby for short, would be the perfect dedication to you. If you're okay with it?'

'I'm more than okay with it,' Ella said. She was practically speechless. 'I'm honoured.'

'Well, you shouldn't be,' Stacey said bossily. 'You're not only the best step-sister and best friend I could have, you're also one of the most inspirational women I've ever known. Most people would have cracked under the year you had, but you didn't just get through it, you conquered it.'

She reached over for Ella and put her spare hand into hers, and Ella squeezed it back in response. They all gazed at Gaby, who was snuffling into Stacey's chest, and each of them felt that her birth represented new beginnings for all of them.

It was one of the best days of Ella's life.

## Chapter Twenty-Four

Ella surveyed the empty flat and felt a bit sad. Chastity had finally moved all her things into the small house in Chelsea she was renting with Adam, and without her junk – her designer shoes littering the living room, her make-up on every counter, and her bits and pieces everywhere – the flat felt a bit lonely. Ella felt lonely. She'd told Chastity that she was delighted for her and Adam; and it was true, she was. Even though she'd see her every day in their little office in Soho, she'd still miss her. Ella hadn't realised just how much she'd come to rely on Chastity's company. It was definitely the end of an era.

'What do you think you'll do now?' Chastity had said the night before as they'd packed her things into boxes. 'Will you stay here? We could always rent it out if you wanted to move somewhere else.'

Ella had shrugged. 'I'd like to stay here for the time being, but maybe I'll get a flatmate. I don't know. I need to see what it's like to live alone.' She'd never lived alone before and she had to admit that a part of her was looking forward to seeing what it was like.

'You could always ask Nash to move in,' Chastity said innocently, but there was a flash of knowing in her eyes.

'He's round here often enough and I bet he'd like to live rent-free for a bit.'

Ella had shaken her head. She'd not seen much of Nash recently; she'd been so busy setting up their new office, and having meetings with Fairytale Productions about the TV show. But she knew it wasn't a good idea. Not when she had feelings for him. It would be unbearable, especially if he brought dates home.

'Nah,' Ella had said as off-handedly as she could. 'He wouldn't want to anyway. I think he's happy where he is.'

Chastity had smiled. 'Well, it was just an idea,' she'd said, and she'd let the matter drop. Ella knew her feelings for Nash were obvious to her friend, but to her credit Chastity had never brought it up.

But that was yesterday, and today Ella was sitting on her sofa in complete silence, wondering if living alone was the right thing to do. She was just trying to reorganise the room a bit, to make it feel a bit less empty, when her intercom rang. Ella glanced at the video screen and her heart soared. It was Nash.

'I've got some news,' Nash said, as he took his coat off and walked into the living room. Ella trailed behind him, wondering how it was possible she could fancy this man so much, and how he clearly had no idea. 'I think you need to sit down.'

Ella did as she was told, and as she gazed into Nash's brown eyes, she knew instantly that what Nash said next wasn't going to be pleasant.

'I've just got off the phone to Aaron,' Nash began, and he reached for Ella's hands. She felt herself crumble under his touch. 'And I'm afraid, well . . .' His voice trailed off, and Ella felt fear run through her body.

'Oh God,' Ella gasped, and her eyes instantly filled with tears. If anything had happened to Danny she didn't know how she could bear it. Nash seemed to read her mind, and he pulled her closer to him.

'Aaron says that the police got in touch with him and it looks like Sancho's gone.'

Ella sat bolt upright. 'What?' she exclaimed. 'What do you mean?'

'It sounds as if Sancho knew he wouldn't be able to cope in jail, and, well, it looks like he's run off abroad some-where.'

Ella let out a little moan of relief – it wasn't Danny; it was nothing to do with Danny, thank God – but Nash mis-interpreted it and pressed her body against his warm chest. Ella could feel his muscles under the cotton of his plaid shirt, and as much as she didn't want to, she pulled herself away.

'I thought you were going to tell me something terrible had happened to Danny!' she admonished. 'I thought . . . I thought . . .' An image of Justin Fashanu flashed through her mind, and she felt dizzy and sick with relief.

Nash's eyes widened. 'No!' he said furiously. 'Danny's fine! Well, he's not fine – he's in shock about Sancho – but nothing's happened to him. He's okay.'

Ella took a few deep breaths and steadied herself. 'So Sancho's gone for good?' she asked, and Nash nodded in confirmation.

'It seems he got a fake passport.'

'Did he leave a note?' she asked, and Nash paused.

'He did. He left one for Danny. Apparently he apolo-gised in it.'

Ella nodded. She wasn't sure what she was feeling right now, whether pleased, sad, or just confused – but she knew she didn't feel herself. She pulled her legs up to her chest and hugged them tight.

'Poor Johnny,' she said quietly, and Nash stared at her.

'Johnny?' he asked, and Ella blinked.

'As much as I hate Johnny it was always a source of comfort that he still had Sancho,' she tried to explain. 'I mean, Johnny lost everything – and he deserved to, don't get me wrong – but I always wondered if he'd be okay, and if he had people looking out for him. I hoped that Sancho would have been there for him, but now he won't be.'

Nash stared out of the penthouse window at the view of London. It was a bright, crisp day, and he could see for miles.

'You're not ever going to be over Johnny, are you?' he muttered, and it sounded more like a statement than a question.

'I've been over him for months,' Ella said slowly, and when Nash didn't react, she pulled at his arm. 'Nash, seriously, I'm over him.'

Nash shook his head. 'Sometimes I thought you were – especially when you seemed so happy – but other times you'd have a far-away look in your eyes, and I knew you were thinking of him. Of Johnny fucking Cooper.' Nash sounded almost angry, and suddenly it all made sense.

'I wasn't thinking of Johnny—' Ella began, but Nash didn't seem to want to hear it. He seemed disappointed. Hugely, bitterly disappointed.

'I'm going to go,' he announced, and he stood up and got his coat. 'I wasn't sure how you'd react to this news – I don't know how to react to it myself – but I can see that you don't need me here. You don't need me here at all.'

Ella wanted to cry. 'I do need you here,' she began, but Nash just let out a little laugh.

'You don't need me, or want me; you just want a security blanket,' he said gruffly, and before Ella could say anything more, or protest, he'd walked out of her front door and into the streets of Crystal Palace.

Ella could have screamed with frustration.

'You've got to help me,' Ella said the next day as she and Chastity sat in their office. They'd had a meeting with their editorial director – whom they'd poached from *Cerise* magazine – about the content for the next week and they had a couple of hours before they had to interview for an SEO manager.

Chastity looked up from her screen and into Ella's worried violet eyes.

'What do you mean?' she asked, and Ella bit her lip. How could she explain it? She opted for the simplest explanation.

'I'm in love with Nash,' she said eventually, and when Chastity didn't react she added, 'and I have been for months.'

Chastity smiled. 'I know,' she said. 'I thought it was kind of obvious.'

Ella narrowed her eyes. 'You knew? I thought you did, but why didn't you say anything?'

'Because it was none of my business. And besides, I knew that you'd talk to me about it when you were ready.'

Ella rested her chin in her hand. 'The problem is Nash thinks I'm still in love with Johnny Cooper. And no matter what I say he doesn't seem to believe me.'

'You're not, are you?'

Ella laughed. 'No!' she exclaimed. 'Not even a little bit. But how can I get Nash to listen to me? How can I make him understand?'

Chastity considered this for a moment. 'I suppose you

can only make him listen if he's willing to,' she said slowly, 'and I think he's a bit like you too – in that he's scared of getting hurt.'

'I'd never hurt him,' Ella said quietly. 'I love him.'

'Then that's what you've got to convince him of,' Chastity said sensibly. 'Don't talk to him about how you're not in love with Johnny any more – talk to him about how much you love him, and how you want to spend the rest of your life with him.'

Ella nodded. 'Do you think it will work?' she asked, and Chastity shrugged.

'It has to, wouldn't you say?'

Ella finished lighting the candles she'd scattered all over the living room, and then turned the lights down low. Each tea light was in a pink or purple glass pot, and the effect against the stark white walls was dazzling. It looked so beautiful. She could smell the joint of beef slowly roasting in the oven – she was determined not to burn this one – and she'd made sure the champagne was cold. Everything had to be perfect.

Nash buzzed the intercom, and it took all of Ella's strength not to remember how he'd been with her the last time he was here. It had only been a week ago that he'd come to break the news of Sancho's escape, but it felt like it had only been yesterday. She'd been so busy, and so preoccupied with planning this night to perfection, that the week had flown by. But now it was here she was petrified. This was it: her one moment to convince Nash of her feelings for him, and to show him she was ready to give him her heart.

She hoped he was ready to receive it.

'Something smells uncharacteristically good,' Nash said

as he walked into the hallway. Ella wanted to jump on him there and then, but she knew it wouldn't do any good. She had to tread carefully.

'I'm trying to cook us some beef again,' she said lightly. 'To make up for how things were left last week.'

Nash nodded, and produced a bottle of wine. 'I wanted to say sorry too. It was a bit of a weird moment, wasn't it?' he said.

Ella led Nash into the kitchen, and she settled him on a stool at the breakfast bar while she struggled with the wine bottle's cork. The champagne was for when they celebrated. If they celebrated.

'It's okay,' Ella said. 'These things happen. And I don't blame you for thinking that I was still in love with Johnny. I can see why you thought that.' Okay, so that was a bit of a lie – she had no idea why Nash would have even considered that to still be the case – but she wanted to smooth things over.

'It's just that for the longest time you seemed obsessed with him,' Nash started to explain, and Ella felt her heart sink. She didn't want to talk about Johnny Cooper any more; she wanted to talk about them. 'When he left you it was like you turned into a crazy person. You must have checked your phone a hundred times a day to see if he'd called, and when he didn't you'd phone him all the time. I've never seen anything like it.'

Ella swallowed hard. 'What I had with Johnny wasn't real,' she said slowly. 'I didn't really know him, not properly, and he captivated me – he said and did all the right things, and I thought that was enough.'

'Enough?'

'Enough to prove that it was okay to have a relationship

323

with someone again. Enough to prove that not all men were like Fin.'

Nash sighed. 'You've been through a lot, I know, and I can understand that you're not completely over everything that happened to you.'

Ella felt panic rise up in her. This was it. This was the moment that she had to prove to Nash once and for all that she was over Johnny. 'But I am,' she said seriously. 'It took a lot of determination and sleepless nights, but through setting up the website and finding out what Johnny really was up to, I am over him. For the longest time I didn't think I'd ever be over him, but what I learnt along the way is that even though he ripped my heart out, he never really had it. He held it in his hands and he toyed with it, but my heart was never his.'

Nash took a sip of wine. 'That's some speech,' he said eventually, and Ella rushed to correct him.

'It's not a speech,' she explained, 'it's the truth. And I am most definitely over Johnny Cooper.'

Nash stared at Ella for what seemed like the longest time, and she felt a tiny ball of hope begin to uncurl inside her.

'If you really believe that you're over Johnny – and all that mess – then I couldn't be happier for you,' he began to say, but just then his phone began to ring. He looked at it, and then smiled to himself. 'It's Ansku,' he said apologetically, 'and I've really got to take this. Hang on.'

Nash excused himself into the hallway, and as Ella waited for him in the kitchen she could hear him talking. He sounded so light, so happy . . . and it made Ella realise that it had been some time since Nash had been like that with her. She couldn't remember the last time she'd heard Nash laugh – properly laugh – or when he'd last seemed relaxed around her, and she suddenly felt very tired. What was she doing? Nash wasn't in love with her. He wasn't even vaguely into her. To him she was just a former client who'd had a rough time, and because he was a nice guy he'd been there for her.

It was heartbreaking.

'Sorry about that,' Nash said, as he walked into the kitchen, and when Ella saw the light in his eyes she felt her insides shatter into thousands of pieces. Without meaning to she began to sob, and once she'd started she couldn't stop.

'Has – has something happened?' Nash asked in alarm, and Ella shook her head. She could barely speak.

'I just realised something I should have known a long time ago,' she said, but she didn't elaborate further.

Nash sat back down again and stared at her. Ella knew she was coming across as crazy – and perhaps she was – but she really didn't feel like she could help it. She struggled to pull herself together.

'How's Ansku?' she asked politely, as she tried to change the subject, or, at the very least, remove the spotlight from her.

Nash frowned for a moment, and then replied. 'She's fine,' he said. 'We've had some good news. We've been trying to open an agency in New York, and our lawyers just closed the deal. We're going to have an office in Manhattan!'

Ella forced the biggest grin on her face that she could and tried to look pleased. 'Nash! That's so exciting! New York!'

Nash smiled. It was a perfect, easy smile. 'I know!' he exclaimed. 'We're over the moon! We'll have to go out there to set it up of course, but we've been planning it for ages and we can't wait to get started. I was a bit worried about expanding so soon, but like Ansku says, when the timing's right, it's right!'

Ella struggled with all her might to keep her smile on her face. 'She's right about that,' she said. 'It's all about timing.'

'Exactly. And, well, it will do me good to get out of the country for a while.' Nash suddenly looked sober, and Ella felt pained. She knew what he meant. He wanted to get away from her – to cut those ties.

'Well, it sounds like you've got a lot on!' she said with forced joviality. 'So don't feel like you have to stay for supper. I mean, it's only beef and it will probably be disgusting, and you must have lots to talk about with Ansku.'

'I still have time to celebrate with you,' Nash said softly, but Ella knew he didn't mean it. How could he?

'Really, it's okay,' Ella said as firmly as she could. 'You should get going.'

Nash wordlessly left the kitchen and put his coat on. As he buttoned it up he stood in the doorway to the kitchen and watched Ella carefully. She wished he wouldn't. It was taking every single bit of strength she had not to fall apart.

'Well, if you're sure,' he said, and he started to move towards the front door. Ella heard his footsteps on the polished parquet floor and a tear slid down her face.

'Oh,' Nash said suddenly, and he appeared in the doorway again. 'I've just remembered, I left my scarf in your living room last time I was here, I'll just grab it . . .' and before Ella could stop him Nash was standing in the dim living room, taking in the scene that Ella had painstakingly created.

On the floor in front of him the pink and purple tea light holders lit up a perfect heart, and in the middle of it sat the bottle of champagne in a silver bucket. The softest music was playing – Keane, his favourite – and the living room looked so romantic, and so like something out of a fairytale that Nash was momentarily stunned.

But then he turned to Ella.

'Did you do this for me?' Nash asked quietly, and Ella was torn. She was so embarrassed that she wanted to deny all knowledge of it, but she knew it would be futile. She nodded, took a deep breath, and decided to tell the truth.

'Nash, I love you,' she said gently, as if each word was breaking her heart. 'I've been in love with you for months, and at times it's been unbearable. When you accused me of still thinking of Johnny last week I could have laughed. I don't think about Johnny any more; all I think about is you. You're the best man I've ever met, and the sexiest too, and there have been times, so many times, when I've wanted to jump into your arms and tell you just how much you mean to me. But I was scared to. I was scared to lose your friendship, and the thought of that would have killed me.'

Nash opened his mouth to speak but Ella was resolute. She had to say it all now or she never would.

'I know that you don't think of me like that. There have been so many times when you could have kissed me, or told me how you felt, but you didn't, and I know you don't fancy me. I don't really think you like me any more. And now you're moving to New York with Ansku, and I don't blame you. You've spent so much time with me, healing me, and you deserve some time to yourself. I just wish I'd known that before I did all of this –' she gestured to the display of love she'd created in her living room – 'and made a fool of myself. I'm sorry.'

Ella was sobbing now, hard, and when Nash didn't come over to her she felt even worse. She'd embarrassed him and put him on the spot when he clearly didn't feel the same way about her, and she knew she'd lost him for good. Ella forced herself to look up at Nash one final time, and was stunned to see he was half smiling and half crying too. Their eyes met, and suddenly he was in front of her, and he was kissing her, and Ella could feel his warm lips on hers and their tears combining in salty lakes on their cheeks.

'I love you too,' Nash said. 'I love you so much.'

Ella cried even harder. 'Do you mean it?' she said, and Nash nodded ferociously.

'I've loved you from the moment I met you in Castle House,' he said, 'when we sat in the garden and you were playing the role of Danny Riding's wife so perfectly. When you started seeing Johnny I thought it would kill me, and then when you broke up and you were devastated I didn't know how I'd cope. I never thought for one second you had feelings for me – I just assumed I was like a big brother to you. That I was just a friend.'

Ella laughed. 'You're the love of my life, Nash Barnwell,' she said. 'You always have been. I just didn't see it.'

Nash scooped Ella up and carried her into the living room so they were standing in the middle of the flickering tea light heart. The scented candles made the room smell slightly of roses, and Ella felt like she was in paradise.

'Well, you can see it now,' Nash said, 'and I do too. So how about it, Ella Aldridge? Will you let me be your boyfriend so we can have our happy ending?'

Ella was overcome with joy.

'Yes,' she said happily. 'Let's do it – let's live happily ever after,' and as Nash began to kiss her again Ella realised she wasn't scared of being hurt or of having her heart broken again. Nash wasn't just the kindest, sexiest, funniest man she'd ever met.

He was also her best friend – her Prince Charming.